REDEMPTION

Other books by Denise Grover Swank:

Rose Gardner Mysteries
(Rom com southern mysteries)
TWENTY-EIGHT AND A HALF WISHES
TWENTY-NINE AND A HALF REASONS
THIRTY AND A HALF EXCUSES (May 2013)

The Chosen Series
(Paranormal thriller/romance/urban fantasy)
CHOSEN
HUNTED
SACRIFICE
REDEMPTION

The Chosen Shorts Series
(prequel short stories)
EMERGENCE (The Chosen Short #1) Emma's story
MIDDLE GROUND (The Chosen Short #2) Will's story
HOMECOMING (The Chosen Short #3) Reader's Choice

On the Otherside Series
(Young adult science fiction/romance)
HERE
THERE (December 2012)

The Curse Keepers Series
(Urban fantasy)
THE CURSE KEEPERS (November 2013)

REDEMPTION

DENISE GROVER SWANK

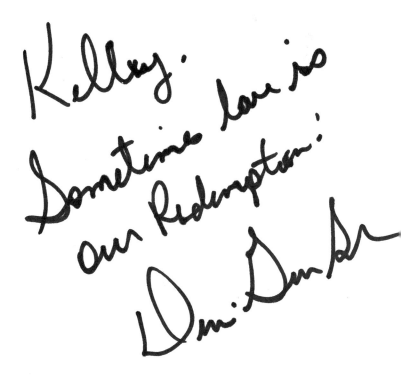

Kelley,
Sometimes love is
our Redemption!
Denise Grover Swank

This book is a work of fiction. References to real people, events, establishments, organizations, or locations are intended only to provide a sense of authenticity, and are used fictitiously. All other characters, and all incidents and dialogue, are drawn from the author's imagination and are not to be construed as real.

For Ryan,
You may not be blond-headed and blue eyed, but you'll always by my Jake.

CHAPTER ONE

SMOKE clung to her nostrils, now an ever-burning constant. Downtown Albuquerque smoldered in the valley below her, but Emma's more immediate concern was above.

Marcus stood on the cliff, the element Water in human form. Emma knew the destruction he was capable of causing, but she'd been searching for him, hoping he would be her savior. Instead, he'd just declared himself to be her worst nightmare.

"What the hell?" Will growled, trying to shield her with his body, a difficult task given that they sat on a tree growing from the rock wall. "You told me to save her. Now you're *threatening* her?"

Marcus leaned over the edge, opening his mouth as though to speak, but abruptly turned and ran out of view.

"We have to get out of here." Will rose to a crouch while he craned his neck to see above.

"No kidding," Emma muttered, searching for an escape as well. The tree trunk they straddled was ten feet down the side of a cliff. The car she had been in lay fifty feet below in the bottom of a ravine.

"*Shit.*" Will growled.

Emma could only imagine the lengths Will would go to protect her now. He had felt protective of her before, when her son Jake had branded him, binding them together with a mystical mark. But only moments ago they had *joined,* which bound their hearts and their powers for eternity. If Will felt half the need to protect her that she felt for him, he could be reckless, and that worried her.

He pointed to a tree several feet away but out of reach. "If we can make it to that branch, then I think we can climb up to the ledge."

"And then what?"

"I guess we'll find out. I'm going first."

"Okay."

Grabbing hold of a rock that jutted out of the cliff, Will pulled himself along the wall while Emma looked above. Marcus might have left, but Emma remained doubtful. The Water elemental had shown up for a reason. While she and Will were half-elemental, the experiences she'd had with full elements had proved them to be self-centered and manipulative. She expected no less from Marcus. She'd hoped, while searching for him, to appeal to their mutual hatred for her father, Aiden.

Will's foot slipped on a small ledge, and Emma's breath caught. Small rocks tumbled to the ravine as he regained his footing.

"Will, be careful." The words were wasted breath, yet it gave her comfort to say them.

"I didn't just find out who I really am to plunge to my death, Princess. Besides, maybe I could whip up a water slide or something." Of course Will would joke about the power he'd just discovered he possessed.

His right hand reached the branch, but he kept his foot on the ridge as he tested its weight, then pulled himself up to straddle it. "Okay. Your turn."

Adjusting the backpack slung over her shoulders, she maneuvered into a crouch on the tree branch she sat on. She glanced up and locked eyes with Will. His mouth pinched in determination.

"Do you think he's still up there?" she asked, reaching for a rock. Her hand slipped on the wet surface. Wet from Will's recent demonstration of his new power.

Will's silence unnerved her and she cast a glance at him for reassurance.

He grimaced. "I don't know. I guess we'll find out."

The book and the laptop in her backpack threw off her balance, but the book was more important than she realized when she and Will had stolen it weeks ago. Written in a magical language that humans were unable to read, the book held the details of the looming confrontation between the elements. The *final* confrontation. Albuquerque had been partially destroyed by Emma, who was half Fire; Raphael, the element Earth; and Alex, the element Air, as they fought for control of the book. She wasn't about to let it fall down into the ravine, and she sure as hell wasn't going to go down with it.

When she was closer to Will, he gripped her wrist and pulled her to the branch with him. Their combined weight made the wood creak.

"Now up?" she asked, her stomach tumbling at the thought of what waited for them above.

Worry filled his eyes. "I'll go first."

She accepted his decision. For one thing, as an ex-Marine who'd been in the Special Forces, Will was a seasoned warrior. For another, although Will had only gotten his power moments before, he'd managed something that had taken Emma weeks to master. And last, Marcus was apparently Will's biological father. Marcus had just found Will, and it was doubtful that he'd sought his son in order to harm him. Even her father Aiden, in all his perverse game-playing, had never tried to physically harm her.

"Be careful," she said again, annoyed at her own redundancy. Yet she couldn't let him go without saying something.

"Always." His mouth lifted into his cocky smile, then he kissed her.

He started to lean back, but she put her hand behind his head and brought his face close to hers. "I love you, Will. If you get yourself hurt, I'll kill you. Got it?"

He grinned again. "I've got quite the honeymoon planned later. I won't be letting anything get in the way of that."

Honeymoon. She guessed technically they were newlyweds. While they might not have gotten married in the eyes of the state or a church, she and Will had just pledged themselves to each other eternally. Their souls had been supernaturally bound with no possibility of breaking it, even through death.

"Does it include the honeymoon suite at the Ritz?"

"No, but it does include a hot shower."

"Even better."

His smile fell away as he glanced to the edge of the cliff. "I don't know what I'm going to find up there, so stay put until I tell you it's safe."

"I should be with you."

He shook his head and determination hardened his eyes. "Marcus just threatened you, not me. It doesn't make sense that he wants to harm you when he was the one who told me to save you. Let me go talk to him and see what that was about."

"If it sounds like you're in trouble, then I'm coming up."

Pausing, he looked up, then back into her eyes. "Okay, but watch yourself in case I'm wrong."

"Okay."

He turned to face the cliff wall, scaling the rock with little effort. When he reached the top he gave her one last look before he climbed over the edge.

Emma strained to hear any conversation, but was met with silence. It struck her that this had become a habit, Will going off to face their enemies while she hung back to wait. It made sense when he was facing armed men—she barely knew how to fire a rifle with accuracy—but the game had moved to another plane. Even though her power might not match the power of the others, it was better than nothing. She could defend herself and possibly Will if necessary. For all they knew, Raphael and Marcus had teamed up to ambush them.

Shifting the backpack, Emma took a deep breath. She wasn't as confident about scaling a rock wall as Will had been, but if he could do it, so could she.

She stood on the branch and grabbed for the handhold Will had used. Her heart pounded. The cliff was wet and she doubted she could survive a fifty-foot fall. Still, she had to shove aside her trepidation and get to the top.

She heard a shout above, and urgency bolstered her courage. A couple of feet from the top, one of her hands slipped, and she fell several feet, releasing a shriek as she grabbed hold of a tree branch at her side. Her body dangled over the ravine.

Marcus's face appeared at the edge, and he reached a hand toward her. "Grab hold."

"Where's Will?" Shifting her gaze to the side, she searched in vain for an escape route or even a foothold.

"Emma, I'm not going to hurt you. Take my hand and let me pull you up."

"Why should I trust you? What have you done with Will?"

"Will ran after Raphael." Marcus released a sigh. "I realize that I sounded confrontational, and I'll explain later. But I assure you that it's in my best interest to keep you alive. Let me help you up, and I'll tell you and Will what I can."

Her eyes narrowed. "I thought you said Will ran off after Raphael." Her hands were wet from the rocks and she shifted her hold to hang onto the branch, her breath catching. A rock stuck out from the wall about a foot, enough for her to stand on if she didn't plunge to her death getting there.

"Trust me, he did, but there's no way he'll go very far from you, especially now that you're joined. He'll be back and then I can explain a few things before I have to go. But all of this will be for nothing if you fall to your death." His voice became more insistent.

Her fingers slipped and the tree branch shook.

Marcus's hand reached down farther, his fingers extended toward her. "Emma, let me help you. Please."

She hated to trust him, but the only way was up and there was no way around him. What if he grabbed her hand and let go?

"I swear to you on the book that you can trust me."

She sucked in a breath and looked up into his face. "You know about the book?"

"Yes, and once you get up here, I'll explain that too." He eyes softened. "Emma, trust me. Will is worthless to me if you die."

What if this was a trick to get the book? What if Marcus had done something to Will?

Will? Where are you?

I took off after Raphael.

Marcus is here.

She felt his worry, then his anger. *I'm coming back.*

The branch she held onto jerked, coming loose from the wall. To her irritation, she released an involuntary shriek.

Marcus plopped onto his stomach, stretching his hand closer. "Emma, please. I understand your concern, but I swear to you I won't hurt you tonight. I only want to help you."

Of course, he wouldn't want her to fall. She had the book strapped to her back. But she had no reassurance that he wouldn't betray her at the top of the cliff, other than his word.

The branch creaked and dropped several inches.

"Emma!"

He said he wouldn't hurt her *tonight*, which for some reason made his promise more trustworthy. Not that it mattered. She only had two choices: fall to her certain death or take a chance on Marcus. She thrust her hand toward him, worried her other hand wouldn't support her weight. Her arms were already quivering from the strain.

Marcus's face filled with relief as he grabbed her wrist and pulled her up with surprising strength—but then, he was an elemental being.

Her stomach scraped against rocks as he tugged her over the ledge. She lay on her stomach, her feet still dangling over the cliff when he released his hold. Panting, she climbed to her feet as Will ran out of a clump of trees toward them. "Get away from her, Marcus."

Marcus backed away, hands raised. "I pulled her up before she fell. I don't want to hurt her."

Will glanced at Emma for confirmation.

She nodded, keeping her gaze on Marcus. "It's true. I slipped and the branch I held onto was breaking. Marcus promised to not hurt me. Tonight."

Stepping toward Emma, Will turned his attention to his biological father. "So any other night she's fair game?"

Marcus shook his head with a scowl. "No, but the time is coming when we won't be able to trust anyone. The game is ending and it will be everyone for themselves. *Everyone.*"

Will grabbed Emma's hand and pulled her away from the edge. "If you're suggesting that Emma and I will fight each other, you have another thing coming."

"You may not have a choice." His grin returned and Emma almost gasped in surprise. She'd seen that grin hundreds of times. On Will's face.

"Bullshit. Why did you threaten Emma after you helped me save her?" Will tried to push Emma behind him, but she shoved his hand away. She was done hiding behind Will.

"I didn't threaten Emma, but I was the one who set this all in motion. I was the one who cursed you both."

Emma lifted her chin. "What are you talking about?"

Marcus sighed. "Years ago, Aiden and I made an agreement. It changed the course of things."

"An agreement?"

Marcus's gaze shifted to Emma for a brief moment, then returned to Will.

Dread knotted Emma's back. "What kind of agreement?"

Marcus grinned again, but it didn't reach his eyes. "Insisting that your father create a new daughter was the second-best idea I've had in a millennium."

Will took a step forward. "What do you mean?"

"I'm the reason there's a new Emmanuella."

"What could persuade Aiden to do something you wanted? Aiden's only interested in himself."

"You."

Sucking in her breath, Emma shot a glance to Will.

Will's brow furrowed. "What about me?"

"While Aiden created a daughter and reincarnated her time and time again, I never sired a child. You were my first."

If Will was surprised by this, he hid it, shifting his weight to the side and raising an eyebrow. "So why now?"

"To end this madness Aiden calls a game. To restore the world to balance."

"What do I have to do with that?"

"Emmanuella's been reincarnated so many times, her power has faded. As has Raphael's and Alex's. By creating you, I've tipped the game to my advantage."

Will shook his head in disgust. "I didn't think you were part of the game."

"It doesn't matter whether I agreed to the game or not. I'm an element. I'm part of it. I'm tired of waiting and I want this done."

Emma crossed her arms. "So why a new Emmanuella?"

Marcus watched her for a moment, then smiled. "To have a fresh start. Emmanuella had a tie to Raphael, an unfair alliance. Raphael had exerted so much influence over her through the centuries, she would never pick anyone else. I merely wanted to even the playing field."

"So why hide my true identity and the fact I have control over water?" Will asked. "Why not tell me from the beginning?"

"It was Aiden's only insistence. I refused at first. How could you enter the game if you didn't know who you were when Emmanuella gained her power? So that's how you became The Chosen One. Aiden said he'd make you her protector, which I'm sure he saw as a safe bet. In over two millenniums, Emmanuella never had any feelings for her protector other than fondness. There was no reason to expect otherwise. On either of our parts."

"So if I was Emma's protector, when was I supposed to find out who I was?"

"When Emma came into her powers, she would no longer need you. She would release you. *Then* you would know who you were."

"So Raphael was right." Emma murmured. "Even if he didn't realize the significance of his advice."

"If Raphael told you that you needed to release Will, yes. You obviously did just that before your encounter with Raphael on the cliff."

Emma didn't answer.

"Your predecessor had an advantage that you don't. She had memories of how to gain her power, who she was. Who Alex and Raphael are. Each time she was reborn, she knew all of this —or at least she began to remember before her untimely demises. Aiden stole those memories from you, but then again, perhaps they weren't yours to remember. They belonged to the original Emmanuella. In any case, in this round you had no idea how to gain your power, nor that you needed to release Will."

"Nor the joining words." Which is why Raphael expected her to know them and why she couldn't remember them.

"Exactly. If you didn't know that you had to release Will, he'd never know who he was. And if you didn't know the words, you couldn't join with anyone. I suspect it was Aiden's fallback plan."

Will shook his head. "Okay, that still doesn't explain how I fit into all of this. Why enter me into the game? How does that benefit you?"

"Because Emmanuella no longer has—"

Emma tensed.

"Emma," Will said, taking a step forward. "She prefers Emma."

Marcus nodded with a slight grin. "*Emma* no longer has a tie to Raphael, which meant she was free to choose anyone. If you were her protector, I had hoped her fondness for you would overshadow any advances from the other two and she would feel a loyalty to you. That she'd pick you. Then Aiden realized that she loved you, and I'm sure he suspected that would give me an unfair advantage when the whole power balance sorted out. So he changed the rules. Again. He stole your memories of Emma, thinking that would stop you two from joining. None of us expected the two of you to be so committed to one another, especially in the short time you were together. Past protectors had months with her, but Aiden insisted the timetable be expedited this time. Probably in hope of cutting any ties on Emma's part to you."

"If you made the new rules, how could Aiden change them?"

"Aiden's a tricky bastard and he's always looking for a way out. A loophole. I thought I had the bases covered. Obviously, I didn't. Let this be a lesson to you: if you enter an agreement with Aiden, think it through very carefully."

Emma didn't need that spelled out for her. And there would be no agreements unless they all agreed Aiden needed to die.

"So he changed the rules." Emma swiped stray hairs out of her face. "Now what? I take it that *you* have a backup plan."

He lifted an eyebrow. "I always have a backup plan."

They watched him for several seconds before Emma groaned. "Care to elaborate?"

"No. Not right now, you'll just have to trust I have things under control."

"The only person I trust is Will."

Marcus laughed. "Then you're smart. But the day is coming when you may not be able to trust Will either."

She cast a quick glance in Will's direction.

Will's eyes burned. "Why did you tell Emma that you were her worst nightmare if you say you don't plan to hurt her?"

"Because in the past, Emmanuella had to choose between Raphael and Alex, and with each new generation it became no longer a choice, but a given. But because of the changes I suggested and I confess, manipulated, she faces a much more painful choice this time." He looked into Emma's face. "The time is coming when you will have to choose, but your choices will be Will or Jake."

The blood in her head pooled in her feet, leaving her lightheaded. "What do you mean, choose Will or Jake?"

Marcus studied her for a moment. "I think you know exactly what I mean. I'm sorry."

Will tensed.

A chill shot down her spine. She'd have to choose one of them. But hadn't her father insisted the same thing? Anger burned in her chest and she shook her head. "You're not sorry. You're an element and all an element thinks about is himself. So don't give me your *I'm sorry* shit."

With a sigh, Marcus lifted his hands at his sides. "Fair enough. And while I'd love to give you more answers, I have an errand I need to run. Go stay somewhere outside of Albuquerque. I'll come find you and we'll discuss our next move."

Will didn't answer as Marcus backed away and then hurried to his car. He opened the door, leaned down and grabbed something, tossing it toward the car parked in front of his. A moment later he drove down the mountain.

Emma turned to Will. "You're not seriously planning on going back to Albuquerque and waiting for him, are you?"

"Hell, no. We're going north. To Santa Fe."

CHAPTER TWO

AS Will watched Marcus drive away, his emotions rolled into in a slow boil of anxiety. Will's entire life was a fucking lie. Every single bit. Everything except for the woman standing next to him, and he had to get her out of here.

"Why is Raphael's car still here?" Emma asked, motioning to the sedan pulled off onto the shoulder, the driver's door standing open. "I thought he took off."

"He tried, but Marcus took his keys out of the ignition. So he ran."

She tilted her head and narrowed her eyes. "How do you know that Marcus took his keys? When did you talk to Marcus?"

It all made sense now. The voice in his head after Will had lost his memory. Still, he found the events of the last half hour overwhelming. He took a breath and released it. "He told me in my head. He was the voice in my head when Kramer and his men took me after I lost my memory." Will looked over his shoulder into the trees. Raphael might have abandoned his car, but that didn't mean he was gone. "We need to go before Raphael comes back."

"You plan to take Raphael's car? How can we if Marcus took his keys?"

"That's what Marcus tossed toward the car. I want to get out of here in case Raphael figures that out."

While he searched for the keys, she stood several feet from the sedan, her feet spread apart in a defensive stance, her hands at her sides. Her still damp, long brunette hair blew about her face in the light breeze. The sun had set and the glow of the fires in the valley behind her created a golden aura that gave her a magical look. The moon overhead cast its light on her face revealing her lifted chin, her dark brown eyes alert. She looked wild and ruthless.

And she was his.

She caught his gaze and smiled. "You going to stare at me all night or are we going to get the hell off this mountain?"

"Get in the car."

Amazingly, she didn't argue with him. She climbed into the passenger seat and he gave her a worried glance as he sat behind the wheel. She looked paler than usual, even in the moonlight. "Are you okay?"

"Let's see, in one day I've faced my megalomaniac father, had my son taken from me again, gotten attacked by two elements and destroyed a city, was forced to tell the man I love goodbye forever, had my car shoved off a cliff by one of the elements, nearly plunged to my death a couple of times, was magically married to the man I just told goodbye, and found out from another element that he was the cause of my impending Sophie's Choice." She gave him a sarcastic grin. "I'm fine."

"It's been one hell of day." He turned the car around and headed back up the mountain. He didn't want to risk of encountering Raphael until he and Emma had a chance to regroup.

"How did you get down to me so fast?" Emma asked. "I left you a couple of miles up the mountain."

"Marcus."

Her eyebrows rose, but she remained silent, leaning the back of her head into the seat.

She'd left Will higher up the mountain after she tried to tell him goodbye forever, at Aiden's insistence. But Aiden would soon find that his plan had not only failed, but literally spawned a new dimension to the playing field. When Emma had told Will goodbye, it had crushed him. Will knew she'd done it to save him from her father, but Will had pleaded with her to think of another way. Her concern for his safety overruled his protests, however, and she'd used her magic to release him to his destiny. And Marcus was right at his heels. "Marcus showed up and offered me a ride. He told me that I had to save you." He snorted. "As though I needed any prompting."

"That makes sense after what he told us. It sounds like he's been doing some master manipulating of his own."

Will's hand tightened on the steering wheel. "He's an element. We know they aren't to be trusted."

"Even though he's your father?"

"Especially since he's my father. He's no better than Aiden as far as I'm concerned. He created me for the sole purpose of winning this fucking game. Just like Aiden created you."

"But why would he do that? What's your purpose in all of this? I was created, or shall I say, my *predecessor* was created, as a game piece. They all used Emmanuella for their entertainment. Why would Marcus suddenly create you?"

"He had no one in the game to swing things to his side. There are big stakes here. You were meant to be not only the prize in the game, but also the deciding factor. You were the one who was supposed to choose which elements survived. Whoever you chose would gain incredible power. Marcus never stood a chance, even though he wasn't officially part of the game. No matter who won, Marcus's own power would be weak in comparison. He must have created me for a shot at surviving, once the game was finished." Will watched her for a moment. "He wanted us together. He needed you alive, which is why after I lost my memory, he told me to protect you when Kramer's men questioned me. Tonight he said that I had to save you from Raphael."

"And that explains why Aiden was so adamant about keeping us apart."

"But now we're together and joined." He grabbed her hand. "Which is what Marcus wanted and Aiden feared, and that gives us an advantage. Together we could potentially be stronger than either one of them. Which makes me distrust Marcus even more. Obviously he wanted the power our uniting would bring, but he has to see it as a threat as well. Not to mention that you are Aiden's daughter. There can't be any love lost there."

"True."

"So that's why we'll head away from Albuquerque. Not that it's a good idea to stay there with the city in chaos anyway."

Pain flickered in her eyes, and he cringed at his remark. Emma felt responsible for the destruction even though she'd had no choice in the matter. She'd kept the book from Raphael and Alex. Thousands may have died and been injured this afternoon, but millions would be at the mercy of the Air and Earth elementals if Will and Emma had lost the book.

With a heavy sigh, she stared out the windshield. "So you really got all your memories of me back? You didn't just say that to get me to stay?"

He squeezed her hand. "No, I got them all back. Everything."

She was silent, watching the road. "I'm sorry."

He glanced at her in surprise. "For what?"

"For not believing in you and me sooner. For not trusting you or your love for me."

His grip tightened. "Emma, you don't need to apologize to me. I had to earn your trust. I'm just glad that I did."

"But if I'd said that I loved you sooner, if I'd just told you how I felt, I might not have lost you. We might not have been betrayed by James. I might not have lost the baby." Her voice hitched before she continued. "Aiden might not have stolen your memories."

"You really think Aiden wouldn't have taken my memories?"

"Could he, if we were joined? We could have fought him together."

"We couldn't have joined that night by the fire, because you didn't know to release me, and I didn't know that I was part Water." He turned to her. "It all worked out. Aiden inadvertently set the wheels in motion when he forced you to release me. In a way, we can thank Aiden for helping me realize who I really am and what I'm capable of."

She scoffed her disagreement. "I'm not thanking that man for anything." She paused. "How did Alex and Raphael not know who you really are? How did *I* not know? We can all sense each other's presence through our power. In the warehouse, Raphael stood right next to you and he didn't sense anything."

"I don't know. Maybe the mark hid my true identity. But I do know that I became fully aware of who I was when you used your power to release me to my destiny. How did you know to do that?"

She gave him a wry smile. "Raphael. Practically since the moment I met him he's been encouraging me to release you. You said you loved me, but I worried that it was just part of the mark still in you somewhere. I didn't want you to suffer any more so I thought if I could release you…"

"Let's make a pact. No more leaving one another. We're a package deal now."

She laughed. "I think that's a given with our joining and all."

"True, but Raphael and Alex wanted you to join with them for a reason. We have an advantage over the others now. And in a world of narcissistic men who will go to any lengths to ensure their own survival, we have to be prepared for anything. Particularly them trying to split us up."

"But is that possible? Our joining is for eternity."

Will's hand tightened on the steering wheel. "Yes, but that doesn't mean they might not try to physically separate us. And for that matter, we don't know anything about the implications if that happened."

"I don't want to live without you. It nearly killed me when I believed you were dead."

"Exactly. We have no idea what the effects are of separation. Or death. We need to study the book. Hopefully, we'll find answers in there."

Emma shook her head. "I didn't see anything about it, but then again, I didn't get to read all of it."

"We can only hope there's something in there to help us understand, but we need to be prepared to experiment with our powers and test their limits."

"You were never fond of my experimenting with them before," she said sarcastically.

"True, but in my defense, we didn't know much about your power, and I was worried about your safety. But now we know we can't survive without using our elemental sides. Plus, now that we both have power, and we're linked, we need to learn how to work together. We're going to need all the help we can get to save the two of us and Jake."

Her hand tensed. "How does that work, Will? *Four shall fight, two shall remain.* How can all three of us survive? Marcus said I'd have to make a choice."

"Fuck Marcus," he growled. "Listen, just because he says he's my father doesn't mean we can trust anything that comes out of his mouth. For all we know, he told you that to psych you out and screw with your concentration. We can trust each other and no one else."

Emma turned to face him for a moment before she returned her gaze to the road, but it was long enough for him to see the fear in her eyes. "I don't know," she whispered. "I think he's right."

"Emma, you can't think like that. All three of us—you, me, and Jake—are going to get out of this. We'll figure out a way. I promise."

"Don't make promises you can't keep, Will."

"I don't." Now he just had to figure out how to keep his word.

***

Aiden wasn't happy.

But it was more than unhappiness. It was rage, and the walls of the house shook with it.

Jake hid in a linen closet in one of the house's many halls, crying for his mother. He wiped his tears with the back of hand in a defiant swipe. Let Aiden yell and scream. The fact that Aiden hadn't found him yet made him smile with pride.

Jake could hide from Aiden. And what that meant excited him.

Scrunching his eyes shut, the first image that popped into his head was his mother's face. The fear and agony in her eyes as his nanny, Antonia, pulled him away from Mommy. Her grief had rippled off her in waves. The thickness of it still stuck in his lungs, making it hard to breathe.

He shook his head. His mother couldn't help him now. Mommy had left him with Aiden.

He knew she had no choice. Mommy would have tried to fight Aiden if Jake hadn't pleaded with her to stop. Aiden might have killed her. But part of him wanted her to fight harder, to find a way to save him.

Because now he was at Aiden's mercy.

Aiden had taken everything he loved away. Before, he would have clung to Rusty, his stuffed dog, but Aiden had burned him to ashes as a punishment. Jake would have given anything to have Mommy hold him on her lap, rubbing his hair and whispering in his ear that everything was going to be okay.

But Mommy wasn't here and nothing was okay.

Now Aiden stomped through the house and demanded *retribution*. Jake wasn't sure what that meant, but he was pretty sure he wanted some too.

"There will be hell to pay!" Aiden's screaming was accompanied by crashing and breaking glass. Jake pushed even farther into the closet corner. If he pressed himself flat against the wall, surely he would become part of it and Aiden would never find him.

"*Jake!*" Aiden's voice carried through the air and through Jake's head.

Jake held his breath, his chest burning for release as he watched the light under the door.

Shadows lurked at the edges of the light, inching closer to him. Weeks ago, he'd been frightened of the moving shadows, but now he saw them as a comfort. They were the only things he could count on.

Maybe he could hide forever. Water had come to Jake in the middle of the night and taught him how to hide small thoughts from Aiden, and so far it had worked. How long could he hide himself completely?

Not long enough.

The door flew open and Jake blinked from the blinding light, fear crashing through his body. Aiden stood in the opening, surrounded by a red glow.

"Did you really think you could hide from me?"

Jake lifted his gaze to Aiden's angry eyes. "No," he answered, his voice loud and strong. He was tired of being afraid.

"Was this something your mother convinced you to do?"

He shook his head, clenching his teeth to keep his chin from trembling.

Aiden reached down and grabbed his arm, jerking him to his feet.

Jake released a squeal of pain and Aiden's mouth lifted into an evil grin. After dragging Jake across the hall, Aiden threw open doors that lead to a balcony overlooking the vineyard. "I've offered you all of this and so much more, *yet you hide from me?* What was your plan, Jacob? Surely you didn't think you could hide from me for long."

Jake jerked his arm from Aiden's grasp and clenched his fists at his sides. "I hate you! You took my mommy away! You promised to give her back to me! You promised! *You're a liar!*"

Aiden's eyes widened in surprise.

Burning filled Jake's chest and rushed through his body, pooling in his palms. "You can't keep me here! You can't make me stay! I'm going to go find my mom and if you stop me I'm going to kill you!" The heat in his hand felt like fire and Jake flung out his fingers.

Thunder rumbled and clouds swirled overhead. The dolphin-shaped hedges around the fountain burst into flames.

A slow smile covered Aiden's face.

"*I hate you!*"

Flames licked at the bottom of the drapes. The wind blew in a gust that made Jake stumble.

Aiden began to chuckle.

"Don't laugh at me." Jake growled through gritted teeth, the pressure in his chest continuing to build in spite of his release.

The chuckling stopped and Aiden's eyes narrowed. "So stop me."

Thrusting his hands forward, Jake forced his energy toward Aiden. Lightning shot from his hands, the bolts striking Aiden's chest and arcing off in all directions, sparks flying.

Aiden smiled and Jake grunted his frustration, reaching one hand into the sky. Fat raindrops pelted the balcony, stinging Jake's skin with their force.

"Is that all you've got, *little boy*?"

Fury burned white-hot, dotting Jake's vision as he rushed Aiden. His shoulder slammed into Aiden's thighs. Aiden's mouth gaped in surprise and he tripped backward, the balcony railing stopping his momentum.

But Jake pushed harder. Aiden's weight shifted backward, over the railing.

Jake released more power. The wind pushed Aiden with greater force.

"Enough!" Aiden's voice filled the air and echoed through Jake's head.

An electrical jolt shot through Jake and he flew backward six feet, crashing into the concrete spindles. A sharp pain stabbed Jake's back and his breath released in a whoosh.

Aiden loomed over him, moving faster than Jake thought possible. Rain continued to pour from the sky, dripping into Jake's eyes as he looked up.

The eerie red glow surrounded Aiden and shone from his eyes. "You haven't seen my full power, Jake. Would you like to now?"

Fear swamped Jake's head and he sucked in his breath and glared. He hated Aiden.

The glow faded and the anger on Aiden's face softened. "Turns out you're more like your mother than I anticipated."

Jake wasn't sure what that meant, but he'd rather be like his mother than Aiden.

"Don't be so sure about that," Aiden said.

In the struggle, Jake had let down his wall, allowing Aiden back into his head.

"Do you know what's coming, Jake?"

The rain puddled around him, soaking through his jeans as he cowered on the balcony floor.

"I'll tell you what's coming. A storm, far larger than anything you or Alex could ever create. Disease and pestilence. Fire and wind and mass destruction. For something to be reborn, it first has to die. The world is about to see its rebirth, Jake, and you are going to be instrumental." Aiden took a step back. "You've had your fun. You've shown me your true potential, but don't *ever* try that again or you will wish you hadn't. Is that understood?"

A lump filled Jake's throat as he nodded. Resentment brewed deep inside him.

"Good. Go dry off, then get ready for bed. We've got a lot of work ahead of us and we need to get an early start tomorrow." Aiden spun around and left Jake in the rain.

He clung to the concrete spindles, staring at the smoldering bushes, rain drops sizzling as they landed. He had created that. He'd made fires, and a storm and stinging raindrops. He'd finally done it. But after a short moment of pride, the full weight of Aiden's words sunk in. Aiden planned to destroy the world and he expected Jake to play a part in it. Jake's temper tantrum had only proved that he was capable of helping with the destruction.

He'd given Aiden exactly what he wanted.

The enormity of his fear and guilt rooted him to the floor. His eyes sunk closed and he called to his mother, no longer worried that Aiden would find her. What did it matter now? *Mommy, I need you. I'm scared.*

Jake only encountered silence. A void.

It was as though she didn't exist.

Desolation swept in and mixed with his fear. Jake was truly alone.

CHAPTER THREE

IN Santa Fe, Will pulled into a motel parking lot and Emma roused from her nap as he turned the car off.

She blinked, trying to focus. "I'm sorry. I tried to stay awake."

He leaned over and kissed her head. "No, you needed the sleep. I'm going to get us a room. I'll be right back."

She nodded, looking around, surprised by all the nice cars. "Where are we?"

"Santa Fe."

"No, I mean the motel. We usually stay in dives. This place looks nice."

He smiled. "It's our wedding night. I think we deserve better than sleeping in a bed that we're worried hasn't had a change of sheets."

She smiled. "I love you."

"I love you too. Now let me get checked in so you can get some sleep in a decent bed for a change."

He got out and disappeared into the office.

Leave it to Will to surprise her by thinking about the accommodations of their first night joined. He called it their wedding night, which wasn't so far off. While there hadn't been a ceremony, the joining words were vows, stronger than any human wedding ceremony.

Human. Funny how a couple of months ago she thought of herself as human and how quickly she had accepted that she was not. But she wasn't full element either, so what did that make her? Would she even survive long enough to worry about it?

Will returned several minutes later and climbed into the car. "We'll park and go inside. We don't have anything to carry in except the backpack. We lost everything when that car fell down the mountain."

"There wasn't much in the car. I had to get out of our last motel room with what I could carry. Aiden put someone who resembled you in our car, and it scared the hell out of me."

"What do you mean put him there?"

"He was dead."

Will's eyes widened.

"I thought it was you and I lost it. Someone called the police and I only had time to grab one bag and the backpack. Now all we have is the backpack, the laptop, and a couple of guns."

"And the book."

"And the book." Her words came out wearier than she intended.

"Come on, Princess. Let's get inside."

They found their room on the third floor, and once the door was closed Will pulled Emma into a hug. "What do you want to do? Take a shower? Go to bed?"

She looked up at him. "Actually, I'm hungry."

He smiled. "Good thing I ordered a pizza while I was checking in. They'll deliver it in about fifteen minutes. Plenty of time for you to take a shower if you want."

Emma looked around the nice room. "Can we afford this place? And aren't you worried they'll track us down through our credit card?"

Will tensed. "I used my persuasiveness to get the room."

"What does that mean?"

His eyes hardened. "Remember how you got Kramer to talk? I used my power to convince the night clerk to let us stay here without a credit card."

"Without paying? That's stealing."

"If it makes you feel any better, I'll pay in the morning when we leave. But we can't risk getting found out tonight."

She nodded. In the scheme of things, it was a minor point. Still, to not pay to stay here made her more like Aiden, Raphael and Alex. She wanted to stay on the side of good, not take advantage of her powers like the other elementals did. But how long could she stay here? Albuquerque had forced her to straddle the line.

"Why don't you take a shower and I'll check out a couple of things on the internet."

"Okay…" She wrapped her arms around his neck. "You don't want to take one with me?"

The corners of his mouth lifted in a lazy grin. "What about the pizza?"

"You said we had fifteen minutes."

He shook his head. "As tempted as I am, I suspect if I get in the shower with you, fifteen minutes won't be enough."

Standing on her tiptoes, she kissed him. "Suit yourself." Her lips lingered over his.

His arms tightened around her waist, pulling her closer. "You fight dirty."

"I learned from the master."

He kissed her, then pushed her away. "You go shower and I'll figure out where we're going tomorrow. Then after you get out and the pizza comes, we won't have any distractions."

"Okay," she said reluctantly, backing toward the bathroom.

She meant to take a quick shower, eager to get back to Will, but the warm water unknotted her tense back and shoulders, and she let it wash over her, taking some of her anxiety with it. When she emerged from the bathroom, wrapped in a towel, Will sat at a desk with the laptop, an unopened pizza box next to him.

"The pizza came? Why didn't you tell me?"

He looked up with a soft smile. "I wanted to let you enjoy the shower." He stood and walked toward her. "I've already had some. Why don't you eat and I'll take a shower."

"Okay."

She was hungrier than she thought, eating several slices before Will came out of the bathroom naked. They'd been together for weeks now, and she'd seen him unclothed many times, but the sight of him now set butterflies loose in her stomach.

He walked toward her without saying a word and took her hand, pulling her to her feet. His other hand loosened her towel and it dropped to the floor.

His eyes were more serious and intent than she was used to seeing when he stared at her naked body. But he wasn't looking at her body. He was searching her face.

His free hand reached for her cheek, pulling her mouth to his, kissing her with more gentleness than she expected.

"Do you have any idea how much I love you?" he whispered, trailing kisses from her mouth to her ear, then her neck.

She closed her eyes and pressed against him.

His mouth returned to hers, more insistent, and her hand looped around his neck. "I feel like I've waited for you my entire life," he murmured. "And now you're really mine."

She kissed him back, needing to be closer to him, but it wasn't enough.

He led her to the bed and lay next to her, staring into her eyes.

"I love you, Will."

Those were the words he seemed to be waiting for, and he resumed his trail of kisses over her body.

They made love with a gentleness that contrasted their usual frenzy and need, and when they were done, Emma lay in Will's arms, her cheek resting on his chest.

***

Will's fingers stroked Emma's arm, as he closed his eyes, committing the moment into memory.

"Will, that was..." She looked up at him and smiled. "Beautiful."

He gave her a cocky grin. "Just making sure you don't regret our shotgun marriage." While he joked, part of him worried that she did regret the decision. Everything about their joining had happened so fast. She'd been pinned by a car to the side of the cliff and the car was falling, taking her with it. He'd joined with her in an attempt to save her using their combined powers. But their joining was eternal, and in hindsight, he wondered if he could have found another way. He was sure the ramifications of their joining had further-reaching implications than either of them realized.

Her smile fell and her worried eyes searched his. "Do *you* regret it?"

"No, Emma. Never."

"But you just got your memories back. Maybe you needed more time..." Her gaze lowered.

He lifted her chin and stared into her face. "I've never been more sure of anything in my entire life." He paused and his voice lowered. "Do *you* regret it?"

She shook her head slightly. "No. Other than Jake, you're the best thing that's ever happened to me. I'd do it again. I love you."

"I love you too." His arm around her back tightened and his mouth lowered to hers.

Emma wrapped her arms around his neck, pulling him closer.

"I bet it wasn't the type of wedding you had hoped for. I suspect you wouldn't want a big one, but at least something more romantic than what we had."

She laughed. "How I got married was never important, and what could be more romantic than you risking your life to save me? It's definitely more memorable. A story to share with our grandkids."

He kissed her again, partly in desperation. Would they live long enough to have children, let alone grandchildren? They were pawns in a deadly game. A game of elemental immortals that had begun millenniums ago, and soon, the final confrontation would begin.

Four shall fight, two shall remain.

Will didn't know how the math of that played out, now that there were seven participants. But Aiden had claimed that he didn't intend to fight. He'd created a loophole to be exempt.

And any world with Aiden still in it was unacceptable.

Will clung to Emma, desperate to protect her and spare her the pain her father intended to inflict. Aiden held Jake as a hostage to force Emma's participation. He'd orchestrated her entire life, from her neglectful, emotionally abusive mother, to sending a then-unenlightened Alex to search her out in college nearly six years ago and rape her to determine if Alex was The Chosen One. She'd lived like a hunted animal when Aiden sent men after Jake, forcing Emma and Jake to hide in one town to the next, always trying to stay one step ahead.

Emma had lived through more pain than a person ought to, and she would face more. Will could do nothing to stop it, and that knowledge tormented him as he tried to fall asleep.

***

Will stood outside. He heard water splashing behind him, but he couldn't see anything. He had no idea where he was, but smoke surrounded him, and fear swamped his senses.

This was a familiar dream.

The smoke parted and the back of a woman's head appeared, her long dark hair hanging down her back. When he was a kid having this dream, Will always thought she was his mother. Now he wondered why. While his mother had had dark hair, it had never been that long.

Fire raged around him and iciness coursed through his veins. Water drenched his body, the fire heating the liquid so that it burned his skin. A little boy's voice screamed, "Mommy!"

Columns of fire appeared, surrounding the woman and the water rushed toward her. But the smoke filled his lungs, choking off his air, and then everything was black.

Will woke with a start. Emma's naked body was draped over his. He pulled her closer and buried his face into her hair. The last thirty-six hours had been a roller coaster, but then again, his whole life had been in upheaval since the moment he climbed into her car. Last night had topped everything so far, and now the dream confirmed his biggest fear.

Will slid his hand down Emma's back. Her hair covered the side of her face, falling across her chest. She looked so peaceful when she slept. He wished she could always look this way, soft and content.

She stirred next to him, a smile lifting the corners of her mouth even though her eyes remained closed. "Good morning."

"Sleep well?"

"No bad dreams. Only good ones."

Will wished he could say the same. Instead, he lowered his voice. "Any include me?"

She opened her eyes and gave him a wicked smile. "I said they were good, didn't I?"

He pulled her against him. "How about showing me?"

She laughed, a low throaty sound. "Is that all you ever think about?"

He lifted her chin and stared into her deep brown eyes, and gave her his cocky grin. "Are you trying to tell me you don't, Mrs. Davenport?"

She scoffed and narrowed her eyes. "*Mrs. Davenport?*"

"You can't get much more permanent than what we have, Emma. We can make if official if you like."

"I think we have a lot bigger things to worry about than a piece of paper that changes my last name."

"Are you saying you'll bind your soul to me for eternity, but you don't want to marry me?"

She propped on an elbow. "Is this seriously that important to you? We're together, Will. Isn't that what really matters?"

He had to admit, he hadn't realize how much he wanted to marry her until he'd brought it up. But she was right. Marriage paled in comparison to their joining.

She leaned over him, her hair draping around the side of his face as her lips lowered to his. "Tell you what. When this whole thing is over, I'll marry you. I promise."

Will knew the significance of her promise. She didn't make them lightly. "And then I can call you Mrs. Davenport."

"Or maybe we'll call you Mr. Emma Thompson." She nipped his lower lip and laughed. "Let's work on surviving, then we can pick out your white dress."

"Very funny."

She started to rise, but he pulled her back down, kissing her with a possessiveness incited by his lingering fear.

Her fingers fanned his cheek. "I'm not going anywhere, Will."

"I know." He knew she didn't have any intention of leaving him, but no matter how much they prepared, they might not survive. The worry was a constant hum in his head. If only one of them survived, he had to figure out how to ensure it was Emma.

Will rolled her onto her back and Emma wrapped her arms around his neck, pulling him down and kissing him with an urgency of her own.

"So what's our plan?"

He laughed. "I'm trying to seduce you and you want to know what our plan is?"

"Women are multitaskers."

Rolling to his side, he grinned. "*Our plan* is to read the book from cover to cover, then test out my new powers and see if we have an advantage together. But I want to get out of here as soon as possible. Just in case anyone's looking for us."

"Good idea."

He trailed his finger over her shoulder and down to her breast. "But we have to take care of more important things first."

An hour and a half later they were on the road after stopping at Walmart for clothes, toiletries and food.

Emma pulled the book out of the backpack. "I've already read part of this, but I'll read it again to see if I can find anything different."

"Good idea."

Will ate a sandwich as she opened the leather book and began reading.

"Aren't you going to eat?"

She shook her head, keeping her eyes on the pages. "My stomach's a mess. I can't eat anything. Add reading in a moving car, and you're asking for a disaster."

He shot her an anxious glance.

Pausing, she looked up with a grim smile. "Don't worry. It's not the nausea that warns me when we're about to be attacked. It's just nerves." She glanced out the window. "Where are we headed?"

"We need someplace we can hide and where I can have water to practice and you have some barren ground so you won't catch the countryside on fire."

Her mouth pinched into a scowl.

"I'm thinking the West Coast. Maybe Oregon."

"The ocean?"

"Got a better idea?"

"No..." She bit her lower lip, looking out the side window. "I've never seen the ocean."

"Really?"

"My mother didn't have much money for vacations. She usually drank away most of her paychecks and gave away the rest to her parade of men."

Will resisted the urge to offer comfort. It would piss her off if she thought he pitied her because of her past. "Then the coast it is."

She was silent for several seconds. "Jake once told me I'd see the ocean. Without him." Her voice broke. "Since that one prediction hadn't come true I used to think that maybe, just maybe, we could change things. Now..."

Will cringed then slipped his fingers through hers. "We're going to figure a way out of this. You look at the book first and then I will and we'll keep reading it until we find something."

She nodded and turned her attention to the pages.

They rode in silence and the last few days filled his head. Will knew he should be more surprised at his true parentage, yet it was as though he'd always known that the Colonel wasn't his father. The Colonel had hated him, no matter how hard Will tried to please him. Now his mother's decision to stay in Morgantown made sense. She'd tried to protect him. Had she loved Marcus? Her reaction when she gave him the ring insinuated that she did, but was it like Emma's mother, Brandy? Had the relationship been one-sided or was it reciprocated? Did it even matter?

Marcus had helped manipulate it all. Insisting that Aiden create a new daughter. Creating a son to compete.

Aiden had known all along that Marcus was Will's father, which was why he wanted to keep Will away from Emma. Will had thought that understanding why Aiden had done what he'd done would make it more palatable, but he'd been wrong. The manipulation from all sides made him angrier.

Marcus confessed that neither he nor Aiden expected them to fall in love. In the end, it didn't matter what Aiden or Marcus wanted. Will and Emma belonged to each other. *Forever.* Not because some egotistical elementals deemed it so, but because Will and Emma chose it.

Will still wondered if joining had been the right choice, more for her sake than his. He had no doubt whatsoever that he wanted to spend eternity with her. He'd known it since Colorado when he worried she would die from her gunshot wound. But would Emma end up regretting her choice? Would she resent him?

Would they even live long enough to care?

CHAPTER FOUR

JAKE sat next to the fountain. The singed shrubbery emitted a burnt smell that made him want to throw up his breakfast. He was supposed to be practicing, but he didn't see the point. He wasn't angry now. He was only sad.

The more he thought about last night, the more he realized that his anger had produced the fire and storms. He'd been angry last night. He'd been angry the day Alex's men had taken him from Mommy. But the night he'd branded Will by the fire, he hadn't been angry. It was like the power was simply part of him. As natural as the heart that beat in his chest. So why wasn't it here with him now?

The night Jake had gotten his power, he'd been near a fire.

Jake's eyes clouded and his heart skipped a beat in surprise. Was this a vision? He hadn't had a vision in weeks. Not since Aiden had shown up.

Everything around Jake faded as he fell into the vision. He stood outside in the dark, choking on smoke that hung in the air. Will knelt on the ground while Jake's mother stood several feet in front of him, her face blackened. Aiden shouted something and then the air was filled with fire, the heat surrounding Jake's body but not burning him.

Power rushed around him in a vortex and he felt his own energy sucked from him. He fell to his knees.

"Mommy!" he screamed.

The fire increased, followed by a rush of water. And then it was gone, replaced by a terrifying nothingness. As sure as Jake knew his mother loved him, he knew that one of the three of them was dead.

The vision faded and Jake fell to his hands and knees, the tiny pieces of gravel next to the fountain digging into his palms.

One of them would die.

No.

Panic flooded his head as he gulped several deep breaths, choking back a sob. He had to stop it. He had to save them, but as soon as the thought entered his head, he knew it was useless.

He'd never changed a vision. Ever.

Sitting back on his heels, he wrapped his arms around his chest as though he could hold his fear inside if he squeezed tight enough.

One of them would die.

Thunder rattled over his head. One of them would die, but he didn't know which one. Did that mean he could decide who? As much as he hated to admit it, that was an easy choice, even if it filled him with guilt.

Voices floated across the lawn and Jake recognized one as Aiden, but not the other. It was a man, and he was upset.

Jake turned to listen. No one but the staff came to Aiden's house and none would ever dare raise their voice to him. This voice had to belong to a stranger. Jake was curious.

The voices came from the other side of the hedges, surrounding Aiden's private patio. Jake hesitated. If Aiden caught Jake eavesdropping, there was no telling what cruel punishment Aiden would give him. Turning his back, he decided to head to the house.

"I have information about Will," the stranger said.

Jake stopped, torn. If he was going to make sure Mommy lived, the more he knew about Will, the better chance he had of saving her.

Still, Jake hesitated. Aiden could sense his thoughts, and would know he was there. But Jake had hidden himself in the closet the night before and Aiden had found him by accident, not because he could read his mind.

Could Jake hide from him again? Last night had been an experiment and he'd been more angry than scared, like he was now. It might not work. If they were talking about Will, Jake was willing to risk punishment to hear what they said. Focusing inward, Jake covered all of his thoughts with a blanket of power, hoping it would work.

He crept to the bushes and crouched, peeking through the branches. Aiden sat in a chair, his legs crossed. His face was pulled into his bored look, the one he wore when he was irritated and about to let his anger out on someone. Most people wouldn't have noticed, but Jake had spent hours trying to read Aiden's face, trying to make him happy. Something had made Aiden unhappy.

And it had to be the man sitting across from him.

The man was about Mommy's age with dark curly hair and dark skin. He wore nice clothes, and he didn't look scared of Aiden.

"You're lucky I haven't killed you yet, Raphael. I told you to never come here."

"Oh, you'll want to hear what I have to say, Aiden. For once, something hasn't gone according to your plan. Someone else is making the rules."

"What the hell are you talking about?"

"Will."

Jake sucked in his breath.

"You've already mentioned you had information about Will, but I don't know what you could possibly have. He's history. Gone."

Raphael laughed, but it sounded ugly.

Aiden's fist clenched slightly. Not enough for Raphael to notice.

Raphael cocked an eyebrow and the corner of his mouth rose. "Are you so sure about that?"

"Yes." Aiden's hand curled over the edge of the armrest. "I convinced Emma she had to give him up for good or I'd kill him."

"And you're sure that happened?"

Aiden sighed with an impatient air. "My men assured me that Emma showed up to tell him goodbye. She knows I'll kill him if she doesn't."

"Will thinks that you *can't* kill him."

Anger flickered in Aiden's eyes before he blinked it away. "And how would you know what Will thinks?"

"Will and I have had several encounters. One of particular interest was in a warehouse about a week ago."

"What Will thinks is irrelevant."

"Is it? What if he convinced Emma otherwise?"

"He couldn't do that."

"Are you sure?"

"Enough!" Aiden's voice filled the air. "You're talking in circles. You think you have information that I don't. Tell me what it is before I strike you dead where you sit."

"Emma told Will goodbye."

Aiden groaned and pushed himself from the chair. "Why the hell are we having this conversation? I know this already."

"But then Marcus intervened."

The color washed from Aiden's face and he sat down, his hands gripping the chair arms.

"That was my reaction too."

Clearing his throat, Aiden lifted his chin. "How do you know this? Last I heard, you were ripping Albuquerque apart."

"True. Emma's a stubborn girl."

A wicked smile lifted the corners of Aiden's mouth. "She is my daughter."

"Maybe more so than you'd like. She defied you, Aiden. Emma is with Will at this very moment."

Jake sat back on his heels. *Mommy found Will.* Jake knew that he should be happy for her. Will loved her and his job was to protect her. But jealousy burned in his chest. It wasn't fair. He was supposed to be with Emma, not Will. Emma was supposed to want *him.*

Red flashed in Aiden's eyes. "You're lying, Raphael. You'll say anything to try to gain the upper hand."

"You don't believe me? Go find out for yourself. Last I knew, they headed to northern New Mexico."

"*Why would she do this?* She knows I'll kill him."

"So why haven't you? Why the games, Aiden? You should have killed him weeks ago. This doesn't make sense, even for you."

"What I do or don't do is my own business, Raphael. You are out of line."

"I wonder if Will might be right. Maybe you *can't* kill him. What if Emma figured that out, eliminating your threat and leaving her free to be with him?"

Aiden stood, his anger sending shockwaves into the air around him. The leaves on the bushes rattled from the vibrations. "Get the hell out of my house before I finish you now."

"Emma figured out who Will really is."

Aiden released a primal growl and the bushes burst into flames.

Jake's shirt singed from the heat and he jumped backward.

"Will is no one. Will is inconsequential."

"Will is Marcus's son. See, Aiden? You don't know everything." Raphael grinned, hatred in his eyes.

Aiden flung his arm and Raphael flew backward and through the smoking shrubs, landing on his back. Aiden stomped over to him and placed a foot on Raphael's chest. "I knew Marcus sired a child before you were even born this cycle, Raphael. Don't you dare presume to think you know what I know and don't know."

The ground shook and Raphael jumped to his feet, making Aiden stumble backward. "You dare to tell me that you knew that Will was the son of Water?"

"Yes, you fucking imbecile! Of course, I knew. That was part of the end game. Marcus asked to insert his son into the mix so we could end this once and for all."

Raphael shook his head, then grinned. "I suspect you don't know this little fact: Will and Emma joined last night."

Aiden's mouth dropped open. "You're lying."

"If you don't believe me, ask Marcus. He witnessed it as well."

Aiden lifted a shaking hand to his mouth. "He did it. Marcus actually did it."

"What the hell does that mean?"

"It means Marcus succeeded in changing the game. He's orchestrated this for centuries."

Raphael erupted into laughter.

Aiden's face reddened and his hand fell to his side. "What the hell is so funny, Raphael? Your chance for survival just dropped from slim to none."

Raphael pointed to Aiden, still laughing. "You. I've never seen someone best you, Aiden, and I've never seen that priceless look of pure shock on your face. It almost makes my end bearable." He stopped laughing and his eyes narrowed. "Almost."

"This changes everything. The Vinco Potentia was supposed to kill him. Emma was supposed to send him away." Aiden turned to Raphael. "She swore to me that she would leave him. Her promise was the one surety I could count on."

"She did leave him. When I found her, she was alone. Will showed up after I'd pushed her car over a cliff and, despite her situation, she kept insisting he leave."

"She couldn't have tried very hard if he found her."

"Marcus brought him."

Aiden scowled. "You pushed Emma over a cliff?"

Raphael shrugged. "She refused to hand over the book."

"Forget the gods-damned book." Aiden growled. "The book is a distraction."

"The book holds answers to what's unfolding now, and I need those pieces to fill in the blanks. But then again, maybe you don't know what's going on yourself anymore, Aiden. Maybe you need the book too."

Aiden's mouth pinched tight.

"Alex and I never stood a chance, did we?"

"You always stood a chance. You had millenniums of chances."

"I'm not slinking off into the shadows, Aiden. I'm going to fight to the end."

Aiden shrugged. "You can try."

"So why did you create a new Emmanuella?" Raphael's voice caught on her name. He cleared his voice. "After centuries and centuries, why replace her?"

Aiden began to pace. "Marcus. He demanded it."

"Since when did you give into anyone's demands, let alone Marcus's?"

"He offered me the one thing I'd coveted since the beginning as a prize. His power."

Raphael shook his head. "*Why* would he do that?"

"To end the game. To restore order to the world, he said."

"And you believed him?"

"Of course not. But his offer intrigued me, as did his terms. I agreed to let his son enter this final round, but in return Marcus requested that I create a new daughter."

"So when you figured out Will was Marcus's son, why didn't you just kill him?"

"Years ago, Marcus killed Emmanuella when she was a small child, before any of you were aware of who you were. He told me that he would kill her every cycle unless I agreed to let him enter his own son at some point. We vowed then that we wouldn't kill each other's children. I can't break that vow."

"Which is why you couldn't end Will."

"I figured Marcus's son would appear the next cycle, but several centuries went by and nothing. It may have seemed that Marcus forgot, but I knew better. Marcus was plotting."

"What does he want, Aiden?"

"What we all want. Not just to survive, but to rule with more power. Marcus has been outcast for a very long time. He wants back what he thinks is his."

"With his son."

"You're sure Emma and Will joined?"

"I'm surprised you missed the light show. You've lost your upper hand, Aiden."

"Emmanuella is still my daughter."

"Who bears no love for you, only hatred. She loves Will, and will do anything for him. Perhaps she'll be fonder of her new father-in-law than her own daddy."

Aiden's stare landed on Jake.

Jake froze, having forgotten that he was no longer hidden.

"I have someone she loves more than Will. She *will* fall in line."

Raphael's gaze moved to Jake and he walked toward him, stopping several feet in front of Jake with his hands on his hips. "So this is Jake."

Jake lifted his chin in defiance, electricity sizzling on his skin. "You tried to kill my mother."

Raphael's eyes widened and he chuckled. "Only by accident."

"I'll kill you on purpose." Jake glared, raising his hand.

Raphael laughed until Jake sent a ball of fire toward him. Raphael ducked in time to avoid contact.

"Enough, Jacob." Aiden's voice boomed. "There will be a time for that, but not today."

"Feisty little guy, isn't he?" Raphael asked.

"That was a very minor demonstration of what he's capable of. Do not underestimate him."

Raphael cocked his head, studying Jake. "He resembles Alex."

"In looks only. His disposition is more like his mother's."

Raphael's eyes narrowed as a smile lifted his mouth. Jake didn't trust him.

"So why are you really here, Raphael? Surely, there's more than your need to gloat."

"I've come to make you an offer."

Cocking an eyebrow, Aiden looked amused. "And what could you possibly have that I want?"

"Information. You've shut yourself up here with Emma's son and I'm out in the world *seeing things*."

Aiden watched Raphael for a moment. "Go on."

"I can track down the two of them to see what they're up to so you won't find any surprises when they show up for the final confrontation."

"And what's in it for you?"

"You and I unite our power."

Aiden rolled his eyes. "I have men to keep track of Emma. They report what they find."

"But they didn't tell you about Will or their joining."

"They would have."

"Would they know what they saw? Would they understand that Will and Emma's joining has tipped the balance for all of us?"

"Their joining means nothing."

"How can you say that, Aiden? Their joining means everything."

"To you and to Alex, of course it does. But it means nothing to me. Emma will do anything to save her son. Her bonding to Will is an inconvenience, but the bottom line is she will have to choose. Will or Jake. We both know the choice she'll make."

Raphael's gaze pierced Jake. "Do we?"

Anger bubbled in Jake's chest. Mommy would always choose him. Wouldn't she? Or would Will make her pick him?

"You underestimate a mother's love, Raphael."

"And you underestimate the strength of Will's."

"Then we shall agree to disagree and see how it all plays out in the end."

"What about our arrangement?"

"We have no arrangement. However, you *have* provided key information my men failed to report. If you find out something else, come to me with it and we'll revisit the idea."

"You seriously think I'm going to just come back and hand you information without a guarantee that you'll help me?"

"Yes."

"You fucking—"

"Language, Raphael. Need I remind you that there is a small child present?"

"I know for a fact you've killed countless household staff in front of him, but you don't want him to hear coarse language? That's rich."

"Killing is a necessary evil. Bad language is not."

Raphael took several steps closer to Jake, bending over to look into his face. "I'm going to see your mother soon." Raphael grinned. "Is there anything you'd like me to tell her?"

Jake gritted his teeth to keep from crying. He wanted to talk to Mommy himself, not give a message to Raphael.

Would Raphael try to hurt her again? "Tell her I tried to kill you for her."

Raphael laughed. "Anything else?"

I love you. Don't forget me. "No."

Raphael turned his back and looked over his shoulder. "I'll be in touch."

Jake watched Raphael walk away, cringing with fear. Aiden had found him listening to their conversation, and he wasn't about to let that go unpunished.

Aiden sat in his chair and crossed his legs. "Jacob, come sit with me."

Head lowered, Jake moved to the chair next to Aiden, placing his hands on his knees.

"Do you know what your mother has done?" Aiden's voice had a softer tone than Jake expected, and he looked up in surprise.

He shook his head.

"Your mother has joined with Will. They have united their power and their souls forever. It's an unbreakable bond. It's like they were married, only permanent. There's no way out of it."

Will loved Mommy and would try to protect her. That was probably a good thing if Raphael was going to find her.

"Do you know what it means for *you*?"

Jake was afraid of that part. What *did* it mean? Raphael thought it meant Mommy picked Will. He shook his head again.

"Your mother will be forced to make a choice when the final battle occurs. Only two can survive, Jacob. Your mother will be forced to pick you or Will."

Was Aiden right? Would she be forced to choose?

"Your mother loves you. She's proved this many times to me. She'd do anything for you. You know that, don't you?"

Jake bit his lip to keep it from quivering, then nodded.

"Your mother would never purposely pick Will over you, but Will forced her to make a choice that gives him an advantage. Will took advantage of your mother."

Jake doubted Will would take advantage of Mommy. He loved her.

"He may love her, but he's going to make sure that things work out in his favor." Jake had let his guard down and Aiden was back in his head. "Will tricked her."

"Will loves Mommy. He would never trick her."

"I know your mother. She loves you with everything in her. If she knew that the joining could affect your survival, she would have *never* agreed."

"Is Will going to kill me?"

Aiden tried to give Jake a reassuring smile but it looked wrong on his face. "All the rules have changed. Thanks to Will's father, Marcus."

Aiden said that Marcus had been planning this for a long time. The night Marcus came to Jake's room, Marcus knew. He knew it all. He knew Emma and Will would join. He knew Jake would be left with no one. Why had Marcus taught Jake how to hide his thoughts from Aiden? Why did he tell Jake that he was the most important player in the game? Will, Alex, and Raphael all wanted Emma. Mommy was the most important.

"She will still choose you, Jake, of this I'm sure."

Jake looked up at Aiden in confusion. Why was he pretending to be nice? He was acting like the Aiden who he used to know, the Aiden who visited him in his dreams before the Bad Men took him.

Aiden's face softened and he smiled. "I've been too harsh with you, Jacob. With all of this end-of-the-world talk bandied around, it's easy to forget that you're only a little boy. A boy who's lost his mother."

Tears sprang to Jake's eyes, and he sniffed angrily.

"You have nothing to worry about, Jake. Will's tie to her will make the choice much harder on Emma, it's true, but in the end she will choose you. I'm most worried that Will has added to her stress. She'll need all of her concentration and focus. I'd hate to think that Will has distracted her and…"

Aiden didn't need to finish his sentence. Jake knew. And he knew what he had to do.

CHAPTER FIVE

EMMA groaned in frustration. She'd been studying the book for several hours and so far she'd found little difference, or anything to help.

"Maybe you should take a break. You look tired."

"I don't have time to take a break." She slammed her palm on the open pages. "Our lives depend on what's in this damn thing."

Will reached over and rubbed her neck. "I know, but if you're tired and frustrated, you might miss something. Just take a few minutes to clear your mind then go back to it."

"How the hell am I supposed to clear my mind? We're going to die, Will, if I don't figure out how to change this." Even as the snide words left her mouth, she regretted them. Will was as stuck in this mess as she was. It was unfair to take her frustration out on him.

She had no idea how they'd get out of this disaster. The math didn't stand up. By her count there were seven players, seven of them who had elemental powers. That meant three wouldn't participate in the final battle, a fact that Aiden was counting on. Aiden had planned all along to be one of those three. So who would be the four? There was no way Will would agree to stand on the sidelines if she were to battle for her life, but if there were some way to trick him into it, and some way to have Jake sit out as well...

Perhaps joining with Will hadn't been the best decision. Before they realized Will was the son of Water, she had to only get herself and Jake out the situation her father had created. But now that Will's powers had been revealed, he could be forced into the ring. And they had to consider their mystical bond. They had no idea what it meant if one of them died. After Will's demonstration last night, it was clear that her powers were weak, weaker than his. Aiden planned to force her to fight, to be one of the four. Even if she could figure out a way to get Will to stay on the sidelines, he still might die. Because of her.

She had to come up with something within two weeks. It seemed totally hopeless, but she couldn't watch them die. She'd spend every spare moment getting stronger and scouring the book for some answers.

She leaned her head on his shoulder. "I'm sorry. I'm just scared. We have no idea how much longer we have to figure this out before the end and we *hope* the answers are in this gibberish."

"We should have at least a couple of weeks. We'll figure it out. Why don't we look at what we do know?"

"Yeah. Okay, that's a good idea." She took a deep breath and flipped to the page with the joining words, her biggest concern at the moment. "The joining words are here. I didn't know them until I read them in the coffee shop, but then it was like they were burned into my brain. When we joined last night, they were just there."

Will put his hand on the book. "Maybe there are some other kinds of oaths in there that can help us."

"I think we should study the joining words more. They may have a clue or insight to help us. Maybe they have another purpose."

"Their purpose was to bind us."

"But the words mean something, Will. They obviously have power."

"The power to bind us for eternity. They did their purpose."

Emma wasn't ready to dismiss it.

With echoes from the beginning of time
To the last ray of light from the stars at the end
I join my heart with yours
onto an endless path that winds through infinity
and sears our souls and power into an unbreakable bond
Through life and death, and all that lies between
I vow to be yours, forever

The shadows on the seat darkened as she read aloud, creeping closer to her.

"Did you see that?" She gripped the sides of the book with both hands.

His shoulders straightened and he looked out the window. "See what?"

"The shadows. They moved while I read the words. They also moved when I studied the book in Albuquerque."

"Maybe you're imagining things."

"No, I'm not. Raphael said we ruled the shadow realm, so it makes sense that they might be affected by these words. And Raphael and Alex both claim that elementals—that *we*—don't die but are instead exiled to the shadow world. I haven't seen anything about that in the book yet."

"First, it's hard to trust anything Raphael says. He would have promised you the moon to get you to join with him. But, we can't dismiss it either, especially if you think the shadows moved."

She leaned over the book again. "'With echoes of the beginning of time.' What do you think that means?"

"Maybe it's power from the beginning of time. It has to be something powerful to bind us for eternity."

"It joins our hearts on an endless path through infinity."

"Another way of saying forever."

"'Through life and death and all that lies between.' That's the part that scares me. What happens if one of us dies? Does it mean that we're still bound or does it mean we die together?"

"I don't know. I'm in no hurry to find out."

"Me either." Emma turned her head, positive that a shadow on the dashboard had moved. "Raphael had access to this book before but didn't seem to know much. In fact, he suspected if we joined that we would know each other's every thought, but he also said he wasn't sure. So far that isn't true with you and me."

Speak for yourself.

She turned to him with a glare.

"Don't worry. I can't read your thoughts. I purposely sent that thought to you."

So you can hear this?

He grinned.

"But can we read each other's thoughts like Jake could?" She tried to push in to Will's mind and met a wall. She tried not to let the relief show on her face. Even though she didn't plan to keep secrets from Will, she wasn't comfortable with the idea of being an open book.

"No, apparently not, although you look relieved at that."

"You can't say you welcomed it."

His eyes darkened. "There's something to be said for privacy."

Emma turned a page. "There's hardly anything in here about the final confrontation. Only this:

"The battle shall end the fight
When all four unite
Four will fight, two will remain.
And the end will restore
The balance again.

"I was reading that part right before Raphael showed up to get the book—I didn't get to 'the end would restore the balance' then." She read the section again. "Four will fight at the end and two will remain."

"It says remain, Emma. Not live. That means the two who don't remain don't necessarily die. There's a possibility we could all survive."

"Not if Aiden has his way. That's not his intention."

"Did you find anything else?"

"Two things. The first is another type of oath, as you called it. It looks like the words give a transfer of power."

"What does it say?"

With the shadows as my witness,
I give to you an irrevocable gift
Power and elemental control,
And all that is mine.

She looked up. "Do you think this is the oath Raphael and Alex took at the beginning of Aiden's game?"

Will shook his head. "It says irrevocable. They hope to get their full power back, and it seems like insanity for them to fight Aiden while their powers are partial. Not only does he have his own full power but part of theirs."

"But you told me, when I first started training, that energy can't be created. It flows from one source to the next. Wouldn't creating children weaken Aiden and Marcus's power?"

Tapping his thumb on the steering wheel, Will shook his head. "It makes sense. I think it would." He turned to look at her. "But we have to take it a step further."

Her face rose to look into his eyes.

"You. And Alex. You had Jake. If this theory is correct, your power would have been weakened. Alex's, too, probably."

She leaned her head back into the seat. "I think you're right. But Jake seems so powerful. More so than I am."

"I don't know. Maybe he is because both of his parents are elemental. It's something to think about."

She suspected he was right. Which meant all the training in the world couldn't help her. She'd have to outthink her father, rather than overpower him. Now she needed the book more than ever.

"You said there was something else."

"Yeah." She sat up and flipped the pages. "It's more like a poem than an oath. Maybe even a prophecy. But I know it's something because I have to use my power to read it."

"What does it say?"

Earth and Air, Water and Fire,
All are meant to rule apart and also as one
The world suffers from imbalance until the end
When one will be overcome
By that which has no price.

Will sat up, excited. "That last part. It's in the prophecy. One will be overcome by that which has no price."

"One of us will save the world?"

"It sounds like it."

Emma's fingertips traced the words. "But which one of us? And what happens to the rest of us?"

"I don't know. The big question right now is who's making the rules? Aiden or some supernatural force? Where did the prophecies come from? I suspect it wasn't Aiden. He doesn't want to restore a balance of power. If anything, he wants more."

She looked up at him. "Marcus said *he* wanted to restore a balance of power."

"Maybe so, but I still don't trust him."

"I'm not saying we should trust him, but maybe he's the one to restore the balance."

"At this point, it could be any of us.

"So basically, we have a book with an oath and a pointless poem. Neither of which helps us very much." Emma shut the book, nausea turning her stomach. "I can't believe I destroyed half of Albuquerque for this. I killed countless people for *nothing*."

"Emma you didn't know. And there still might be something in there you missed. Raphael and Alex were desperate to get it. You did the right thing."

"Did I, Will? It's easy for you to say. There isn't blood on your hands."

He turned her to face him. "Are you so sure? You forget my past, Emma."

Irritation burned through Emma, not at Will, but at herself for making him remember his time in Iraq and what he'd done since. He'd told her about a small portion of his time there, but she was sure there was so much more he kept to himself. "I'm sorry, Will. I'm worried I'm not strong enough." She grabbed his hand and held tight. "Don't get me wrong. I'm not giving up, but we both know my power is weak. Probably the weakest of all of us."

"That's not true. When it's available to you, it's just as strong as Raphael's."

"When it's available. When I'm scared, it's almost completely gone."

"We'll practice. The more confident you feel about using your power, the less scared you'll be. Besides, you'll do it to save Jake."

"And to save you."

Will brought her hand to his lips and kissed it. "I don't need you to save me. I can take care of myself. I need you to focus on yourself, Emma. And Jake." He rested their joined hands on his leg. "We'll do the best we can with what we have. We have two advantages the others don't. First, we're joined, which we already know is a huge advantage since both Raphael and Alex were desperate to join with you. We'll figure out how to use our joining to fight. But we have something else they don't, Emma." He paused and looked at her. "We're fighting for something more than ourselves—we're fighting for each other. That gives us greater power."

"Or becomes our greatest weakness."

"Only if we let it."

She wasn't sure he was right, but she'd humor Will for now. She needed any scrap of hope she could get at this point.

Hours later, she stood barefoot on the beach, sand squishing between her toes and the roar of ocean waves filling her ears. She stared at the expanse of water as the sun began to set.

Will's arm wrapped around her from behind and she leaned into his chest, releasing an exhausted sigh. Even though they'd taken turns driving and napped, she was still tired.

Will brought his lips to her ear. "Is it what you thought it would be?"

She wrapped her arms over his and clung to him. Her entire life she'd wanted to see the ocean and here it was in front of her, larger than she imagined. But the ocean's beauty meant nothing now—all that mattered was that the ocean was a tool that Will could use to test his powers. And a reminder that Jake had been right all those years ago.

"I opened the cabin and put our bags inside. As I suspected, it doesn't look like it's been used for several years. It's musty so I opened the windows to air it out."

"Okay."

"I say we try to get a good night's sleep and start first thing in the morning."

"Okay."

"We're going to win this."

"I know." But she didn't.

She turned to look up at him. His gaze was on the waves, awe in his eyes. "So you really came here when you were a kid?"

"Only a couple of summers, but those two summers were awesome. I always loved the water. I guess I know why now."

Had she loved fire when she was a kid? Not that she remembered, but Jake had always been fascinated by it.

"I know there's a fire pit around here somewhere. I can get some firewood and run up to the cabin and look for something to light it with."

"I just blew up half of Albuquerque. Lighting a fire is nothing."

"Emma…"

"It's done. We need to move on." She knew she had to let Albuquerque go, or at the very least, stop making Will endure her guilt. But the soot-covered and bloodied faces of the people rushing out of the buildings still haunted her. "I'd rather just go to bed."

"Okay."

"But not yet. I want to stay here a minute." There was something soothing about the waves washing over her feet. The way the sand was sucked beneath her feet. She realized she'd spent her life like this—digging her toes into the sand while circumstances rushed in and sucked away every bit of her life that mattered. But she was done. Done reacting to the things thrown at her. It was time to take control and seek retribution from the people who'd made her suffer.

Closing her eyes, she reached out to Jake with her mind, calling his name. Her calls disappeared into nothingness and her heart squeezed with fear. Why couldn't she sense him? Had something happened? She tried to relax, remembering that she'd encountered the same feeling after Aiden had taken Will's memory and his mark. She'd mistaken it as a sign that Will was dead, but she was wrong. If she'd lost her connection to Will because Aiden had erased his mark, both on Will's skin and hers, had the same happened with Jake? Had she lost the fire mark that appeared the night her son was conceived?

She stepped away from Will and jerked down her t-shirt, craning to look over her shoulder.

"What's wrong?"

"I can't feel Jake. Is his mark still there?" Her voice shook with fear.

He tugged her shirt down farther, turning her so the moonlight shone on her back. "It's there. Along with water."

"But not your mark?"

"No, it's still gone. But something new is there."

"*What?*" She stretched her neck, sending a spasm in her shoulders. "What is it?"

"It looks like two triangles. One is upside down and they intersect."

"What does that mean?"

"I don't know, but they weren't there a couple of days ago. Trust me, I would know."

"What does the water mark mean? Is it you? I got it when I discovered your mark."

"I don't know. You said Raphael told you it was gone after you lost my protector mark. I didn't trust him at the time, but maybe he told you the truth. Maybe they both had to do with me. Then the water mark reappeared when I came back."

"Maybe." But she had another theory—and right now, she didn't want to tell him what she really suspected the mark might mean. The thought sent a new shockwave of anxiety through her. Her fire mark had appeared six years ago, when Jake was conceived. The water mark had appeared after she and Will had made love the first time. The night their baby was conceived. And the mark disappeared the night she miscarried.

So a new water mark could only mean one thing...

She cut off the thought, unable to accept the possibility. She could be wrong. Alex was Jake's father, so shouldn't she have gotten an air mark the night Jake was conceived? Maybe the marks had a meaning she hadn't yet thought of.

"There's a picture of the mark of The Chosen One in the book, but no other symbols. It must have to do with our joining."

"But two triangles seem weird when the other marks are symbols, not shapes. Do you have anything?"

"I don't know." He looked down at his forearm, where his protector mark had been. Emma knew there wouldn't be anything on his arm. He'd worn short sleeves the last two days.

"Maybe it's on your back too." She lifted up the bottom of his shirt. On his right shoulder blade were two intersected triangles.

***

Emma's hold on his shirt tightened and Will wasn't sure whether to be relieved or worried.

"I have them?"

"Yes." Her voice was soft and almost lost in the air.

"Nothing else?"

She lowered his shirt. "No, but I think you're right. It has to be related to our joining."

"Agreed." But what it meant was a mystery, along with everything else in this fucked-up production. The other marks had been more detailed and intricate. The triangles were plain. Elemental. Maybe that was the answer right there. "I say we test it all out tomorrow."

"Do you think we're safe out here?"

"Are you worried about someone or *something* sneaking up on us?"

She looked up, worry in her eyes. "Do you think they will?"

"At first, I was concerned, but I've since changed my mind. I think your father will wait until the end. Raphael is too chickenshit to do anything. And the last we saw, Alex was back on the campaign trail for his father."

"And Marcus?"

Will tensed. He'd been asking himself the same question since Marcus had disappeared at the top of the cliff. "Marcus is a wild card."

"You think he'll find us."

"I'm sure of it. The question is when."

Emma's back stiffened.

"Even if he shows up, I don't think we'll have anything to worry about." For Emma's sake, he hoped to God that was true. "You don't need to worry, Emma. I'll protect you."

"No, we'll protect each other."

He smiled and kissed the top of her head, pulling her closer. "Come on. Let's go inside and get some sleep." She would need all of her strength tomorrow.

CHAPTER SIX

JAKE lay in bed, watching the shadows in fascination. They had grown bolder, moving closer to him, crawling across his covers. He tickled one with his fingers and it vibrated then reached for his hand.

"I'd be careful with those, if I were you."

Jerking his head up, Jake found Water sitting in the chair in the corner. "You weren't there a minute ago."

Water grinned. "Are you sure about that?"

Jake hesitated. He was sure no one had been there when he went to bed. While he'd played with the shadows, he was positive the door hadn't opened.

"You're right. I didn't come through the hall door."

Jake shoved his thought into the deeper part of his head. He didn't like that Water had read his thoughts.

"I saw your mother."

Jake's jaw dropped and he sucked in a breath.

"She was with Will."

Jake knew that, but it still hurt to hear. And he shouldn't be surprised Water had seen her. "You tricked me."

Water tilted his head, confusion covering his face. "How so?"

"You didn't tell me you were Will's dad."

Water laughed. "So Aiden's told you."

"*You* should have told me."

"I couldn't. Aiden's rules. If you want to get upset with someone, get mad at him. This could all be over if it weren't for Aiden."

"Your name is Marcus."

Water grinned. "What else did Aiden tell you?"

"That Will tricked Mommy."

With a chuckle, Marcus shook his head. "So that's how he sees it."

Jake looked away. A burning lump filled his throat.

"Do you remember when I told you that you were the king in our game of chess?"

Jake nodded reluctantly.

"I'll give you a hint. Part of it has to do with the shadows."

The shadows on Jake's bed darted to the edges of the mattress and over the sides, as though they were hiding.

"They like you, you know. That's very unusual. But they sense how important you are, and they need you."

"Need me for what?"

Water smiled and leaned over his knees. "I can't tell you that part yet, but play with them. Let them trust you. You'll want them to help you at some point."

"How do you know? And why didn't Aiden tell me?"

"Aiden is threatened by you. You're stronger than he expected you to be. I doubt he thought out the results of the child of two elementals." Water pursed his lips, then grinned. "Then again, maybe he did. Aiden rarely lets details slip by."

"How do you know all of this?"

"Aiden and I are old acquaintances. Ask him about the shadows if you like. I'm sure he'll fill you in to some extent. But he won't tell you everything. Not the important parts."

"Why do I need them?"

Water held up his index fingers and waved them back and forth. "Not yet. Just know they will help you when you need them." His grin fell. "And that time is coming sooner than you think."

Jake watched him, dread creeping up his back. "Can you have visions too?"

"No, not like you. But the proverbial handwriting is on the wall. I know that Raphael told Aiden about your mother and Will."

"How—"

"I have my ways."

Jake narrowed his eyes and focused on Water's thoughts. The man wasn't prepared for Jake's intrusion.

"You followed Raphael here."

"Very good, Jake. But stay out of my head."

"I will if you stay out of mine."

Water smirked. "Fair enough. And yes, I followed Raphael here. Once he realized what your mother and Will had done, I wondered what his move would be. The way I saw it, he had two options. One, go to Alex. Two, he came to Aiden. Frankly, I didn't think he had the guts."

"Why do you care?"

"Because I've put too much planning into this to let anything take me by surprise."

"Did you know Raphael was going to hurt my mom?"

Marcus's lips pressed into a thin line. "Yes, and I warned Will. Even when Will didn't know who she was, he still protected her."

Will loved Mommy. Of course he would protect her.

"Will didn't know her when they captured him. He'd lost all of his memories of her, so don't presume he would have protected her. She meant nothing to him then. Kramer's men questioned him to find out where she was. He had no reason to keep her safe, but I convinced him to."

"How?"

"By talking to him in his head."

"Why would you do that?"

Marcus gave him a soft smile. "I care about you and your mother, Jake. I've tried my best to protect you both."

Jake thought of the years he and Mommy had spent running. All the bad things that had happened. "You didn't try hard enough."

"I did the best I could." Marcus sighed. "There are things I would do differently, but I can't change the past. We need to focus on the immediately important things. Namely, the fact that Raphael and Aiden aren't happy that Will joined with your mother."

"So?" That was no surprise to Jake. He wasn't happy about it either.

Water shook his head. "No, you don't understand. Aiden knows that Will has power now and that he's joined with your mother. He will do anything to try to split them and to keep them from becoming stronger."

"How? What will Aiden do?"

"He won't want them to learn to work as a team. He'll probably try to distract them. And I suspect he'll use you to do it."

Jake's stomach tightened. "I won't do what he wants."

"I doubt you'll have a choice." Marcus's eyes narrowed. "Have you been hiding things from Aiden? Has it worked?"

Pursing his lips, Jake gave him a mean scowl. He wasn't going to give him any more information than he had to. He didn't trust Marcus.

Marcus chuckled, looking toward the window. "Keep practicing. You can't tell Aiden that I visited you, and you can't let him see it in your head."

Jake lifted his chin in defiance. "I could go tell him everything."

"You could, but you won't. You're curious enough to keep me around and frightened enough to not tell Aiden this is our second meeting. Aiden doesn't like secrets."

Jake did his best to turn his irritation into a glare.

"Continue to play with the shadows. Gain their trust, but be careful. Many men have thought they could harness the energy of the shadows. All were deadly wrong. But if the shadows accept you, they'll show you what to do." Marcus stood. "I will return in a few days."

"I don't want to see you again."

"I'll tell you about your mother."

Jake froze.

Chuckling, Marcus moved toward the window. "Maybe I'll even bring back a message."

And then he was gone.

***

Even though Jake knew he was in a dream, it felt so real. Like the dream when he had Will save Mommy.

The air was cool and crisp, and he smelled the musty earth. He was in a valley surrounded by mountains and his bare feet sunk into sand. The sky was dark on one side with more stars than he had ever seen filling the sky, but a hint of pink lined the other side. The sun was getting ready to come up.

Spinning around, Jake found himself alone and a hum of fear filled his chest. He knew something bad was coming.

Two big overlapping circles outlined in black covered the hard ground, forming a sort of oval with an almond shape in the middle. His sight blurred, the image in front of him shifted, like when the cable went out and the picture stopped and jolted in a new place. The circles had been empty and then there were people in them. But not just people—Jake saw Aiden, Raphael and Alex in a circle on one end and Water, Will and Mommy were on the other. Jake's breath caught. *Mommy*.

Without moving on his own, Jake now stood in the middle, where the circles overlapped, his feet firmly rooted even though he wanted to run to his mother.

"*It has begun.*" A voice echoed around him, bouncing off the mountains and vibrating through his body. "*Four shall fight, two shall remain.* This is the rule set by Fire, but the rules are not complete."

Jake looked around at the others. Aiden was furious. Alex and Raphael seemed nervous. Water smiled, but Will and Mommy looked worried.

"Each element must be represented in the fight. The words of transfer are in effect."

What were the words of transfer? Jake wasn't sure but Aiden's grin widened.

Raphael looked like he was about to throw up.

"*All* will fight. Two will survive."

Mommy released a small cry.

"The book contains the rules. The end will occur within two weeks' time, but Fire may determine the place and the time."

Tears streamed down Mommy's face. Anger filled Will's eyes as he stared at Jake.

Jake sucked in a breath. Why was Will angry with him?

The image shifted. Mommy was there and then she wasn't, then she was back again. She reached for him, her mouth forming his name, but no sound came out.

Everyone disappeared and Jake stood alone in the almond shape, the sky still dark on one side, but getting pinker on the other. And then everything went black.

***

Will woke to Emma bolting upright in bed, morning sunlight streaming through the blinds.

"Emma?"

"Oh, God. I had a terrible dream." She looked down at him. Tears wet her pale face. "We were in a desert and all of us were there—Aiden, Marcus, Raphael and Alex. And Jake. A voice from nowhere gave us new rules."

Will's eyes sank closed in horror. "I had the same dream."

She jerked away from him. "*What?*"

He sat up. "I had the same dream, Emma. It was real."

"No! No, it can't be real!" She jumped out of bed and began to pace. "Oh, God."

Will followed her and tried to pull her into his arms, but she shrugged him off.

Her chest rose and fell, and she brought her hand to her forehead, closing her eyes. "Think, Emma. Think."

"You don't have to do this alone anymore, Emma. I'm here now. We'll figure this out together."

Her hand dropped, her eyes full of terror. "Then what are we going to do, Will?"

He didn't have a clue, but he suspected that was the last thing she wanted to hear. He also knew that while she was afraid for herself and for him, her real horror was over what would happen to Jake. "First we're going get dressed and eat something. We'll practice this morning then head somewhere else this afternoon. Now that the others know how important the book is, they'll all come after it. Once we practice and get to a new place, we're going to scour that thing front to back until we figure a way out of this." Will ran a hand through his hair. "It's going to be tricky to practice unless we can figure out a way to mask our power while we're using it. Otherwise, we'll be a beacon, practically inviting them all to find us. So we'll do what we did when you were training before we joined. We'll drive somewhere and sleep then practice and leave."

She nodded. "Will, the voice said only two would survive."

"I don't give a fuck what some voice in a dream said." He pulled her to his chest, thankful she didn't pull away this time. "I won't let anything happen to you or Jake. I'll make sure you two survive."

She looked up at him, biting her lip. "What about you, Will? Do you think I'll just let you die?"

"We'll find something in the book. It will all work out. Now let's get dressed and get started."

She refused to meet his gaze, confirming that she didn't believe him, but she accepted his answer instead of arguing.

A month ago, the fact that he and Emma had shared the same dream would have freaked him out. Now a shared dream was the least disturbing aspect of their situation. All of the players had been present, so they must have all had the same dream.

What bothered Will the most was Jake's position. He was in the center, between the two groups. Did that mean he was the *one that was overcome by that which had no price?* Was Jake the key player in this game? And what the hell did *overcome by that which had no price* mean? Whatever it was, it didn't sound good.

There had to be some significance to their placement in the circles, but damned if he knew what it meant. And who was the voice? He wished he knew if it was a good or bad thing that Aiden was no longer in charge. Did that give

Marcus the upper hand? Or was someone else—something else—in control?

Will's immediate impulse was to read the book again to find out what they could. But if the others were going to come looking for the book, defense seemed the first, most prudent order of business. The more familiar Will was with his new power and working with Emma, the better off they would be.

Emma was the biggest challenge at this point. He had to figure out a way to make her more confident with her power. Right now, she was unpredictable and, although he'd never tell her, that made her dangerous.

A half an hour later, they walked down to the beach. Will chose this section of the coast because it had always been fairly deserted when he was a kid. Of course, things changed, but the inlet cove was still uninhabited.

Emma walked to the water with one hand on her hip, the other shielding her eyes from the rising sun. She'd calmed down after her initial shock, although she'd only taken a few bites of breakfast, saying her stomach couldn't handle it.

"Do you have any ideas what you want to try first?" Her hair was in a ponytail, but the wind whipped stray hairs into her face. She batted away the strands, a losing battle. "I think you should practice using water. I'll practice with fire and later when you've gotten used to your power, we can try to combine them."

He gave her a cocky smile. "I thought I was in charge of training."

She lifted her eyebrows, shifting her weight to the side.

Thank God her fight was back. "I oversaw your training and we're getting ready to fight for our lives, Emma. I was trained half my life for combat. I'm our best chance."

She sighed, her smile falling. "I agree. I want Jake to survive and you're more experienced. But I want to make it perfectly clear that Jake is our number-one priority. Do you agree?"

Will knew she'd accept no other answer. "Agreed."

"Okay."

He didn't want to admit how nervous he was. He'd been in charge of a Marines unit in Iraq and faced the enemy more times than he could count, but the thought of bringing Emma into a mortal battle made Will queasy. Especially since the odds were against them.

"So *general*, what are your orders?"

He smirked. "You practice with fire and I'll practice with water."

She studied him for several seconds, shaking her head, before she turned away. He'd expected a sarcastic retort since she'd suggested the exact same thing.

He watched her walk along the beach, resisting the urge to tell her not to go too far. He doubted she'd leave his sight, more because she worried something would happen to him rather than herself. Especially after he'd been kidnapped. He wished he'd never left her that night in Farmington, New Mexico, but it had all played into their union. If Aiden hadn't forced Emma to leave him, she'd never have freed him, releasing his power. They never would have joined. He never would have known what he was capable of.

Unless Marcus told him.

The thought of Marcus left a bitter taste in Will's mouth. Marcus was an element, and he couldn't be taken lightly. Every element was out for himself and Marcus had admitted that he had a plan for Will. And for Emma. The latter scared Will the most.

All the more reason to find out what Will could do now. Staring out into the ocean, he had to admit that his power was both exciting and terrifying. He felt as though everything in his life finally made sense. As though he were looking through a polarized lens, bringing everything into focus. Will had a purpose. He only wished James were here to share it.

If the thought of Marcus left a bitter taste, the thought of James was acrid. James's betrayal was still hard to stomach. Maybe someday Will would get more answers. If James were even still alive.

Thinking about James was pointless.

Standing at the water's edge, he closed his eyes. Energy flowed from the waves into his body, lapping through him. Was it like this for Emma? He didn't think so. From what she said, she experienced a burning sensation with a surge of power. But this was the opposite of burning. Not exactly cold, but cooling. And the energy ebbed and flowed, along with the tide. That made sense. Water and Fire were polar opposites. It stood to reason they'd be opposites in power.

Will hoped it meant they had an advantage in the battle, especially if they could combine and share their powers.

He tried to remember what using his power had felt like when he'd saved Emma. He hadn't even thought—the power just came to him. Automatic, like an extension of himself. Could he use it now, or did he need emotional distress like Emma needed in the beginning?

Opening his eyes, he lifted his hand toward the water and called to it. It amazed him that days ago he didn't even know his power existed. Now the energy of the water lapped through him like the movement of the waves. The water six feet in front of him bubbled, then swirled, rising into a water-filled tornado. He couldn't stop his grin. What else could he do?

Showoff.

Down the beach, he spotted Emma scowl and turn away.

He understood her irritation. Using her power hadn't come naturally to her, and she'd struggled every step of the way. It had to be frustrating for her to see him do things with little effort. Hopefully, she'd appreciate it since they had so little time to prepare. Especially if it saved her life. And Jake's.

For the next hour, he controlled the waves, exhilarated from the energy of the water and the power, astounded what he could do.

"That's amazing, Will." Emma sat behind him on a rock, knees tucked beneath her chin.

He glanced over his shoulder. "How long have you been there?"

She'd snuck up behind him. He hadn't even realized she was there.

"About five minutes."

He'd been concentrating so hard on his progress that he'd ignored his surroundings. When Emma had practiced, she'd been completely absorbed in the task at hand, while Will kept watch. Now he wondered if he should have her to do the same.

"I didn't know you were there. My carelessness could have gotten us killed."

"It didn't. I was watching."

He couldn't dismiss it so easily.

"I know what you're doing."

His eyebrows rose. "Do you?"

"Right now you're beating yourself up because you were concentrating so hard you lost track of what was around you. But you forget something, Will." She walked toward him. "You're not the only one here. And although you tend to treat me like a fragile flower, I'm not. I can watch over you just as easily as you watch over me. You want to be in charge of planning strategy and attacks, fine. But we're a team, not a military unit. You're not my commander."

Her words burned, mostly because they were true. "Emma, I don't think you understand my strong need to protect you."

"I'm completely aware of your need to protect me, and I appreciate it more than you know. Did you ever think that it goes both ways? But you know, deep in here—" she pointed at his chest, "—that we'll never win that way. We have to trust each other and work together. It will never work if you're just issuing orders."

"I know," he sighed. It was harder than she thought. The thought of losing her filled him with terror.

"So you've got a good handle on working with a large body of water, but what about when a water source isn't available? Like on the cliff two nights ago? You pulled water from somewhere. Where did it come from?"

"I have no idea. I only knew I needed to save you and somehow I just knew what I had to do."

"Lucky you," she grumbled.

"I don't know why all of this is coming to me so easily. And although I wish it had come easier for you, thank God it is for me. If nothing else, to save Jake."

She nodded, a grim look on her face as she looked down the beach. "Visitors."

Will's heart lurched, surprised someone had found them so quickly, but it was a man walking his dog along the shore. The sun had been up for a couple of hours and although their spot was secluded, it was still a public beach. They needed to find somewhere more private.

She kept her eye on the man, her arms crossed. "So where are we going to go next?"

"That's a good question. Got any suggestions?"

Her eyebrows rose in surprise. "It's obvious that a large body of water is a piece of cake. Maybe we should go head to the mountains again and find somewhere with a creek and see what you can do."

"You're liable to catch the forest on fire."

"After you master that, which of course you will, then we'll head back to the desert. Maybe *that* will be a challenge for you."

"Okay, the mountains it is."

CHAPTER SEVEN

AIDEN had been furious all morning, and although he didn't say why, Jake knew it was because of the dream. Aiden was worried and that made Jake happy. He hid it, of course. The satisfaction of gloating wouldn't be worth the punishment. Instead, Jake pretended like nothing had happened, even though the dream had scared him. He hid his fear too.

Today Aiden wanted a storm. Jake gave him one as they stood on top of the hill, overlooking the valley. The clouds swirled overhead and a fierce rain pummeled Jake's shoulders, but he concentrated on the raging mass of chaos over his head. The wind tumbled and he pushed more energy into it until the beginnings of a funnel cloud appeared.

"Keep going."

The funnel whipped wildly as it extended from the sky, touching down to earth. Debris scattered into the air as the funnel ripped trees from the ground and tossed them around like they were sticks.

"Move it in a straight line toward us."

While Jake had some control over the air, the funnel had an energy of its own. He focused on moving the destruction toward them, but the tornado broke free of his hold and swerved to the right. His head pounded as he tried to pull it back on course.

"Don't control the tornado itself. Control the air around it to push it where you want it to go."

Jake eased his concentration from the twister to the molecules around it. The pain in his head decreased and he moved the pressure from one side to the other to keep the tornado in a straight line.

"Beautiful."

A house came into view, near the funnel. Jake pushed the vortex to the side.

"*No. Keep going.*"

Fear swamped Jake's senses.

"Do it."

The funnel moved back into its original path. Jake knew there were kids in that house. He'd watched them playing from on top of this hill, wishing he could play with them too.

"Do it."

Fire burned Jake's skin. Aiden was warning him of the punishment for refusing.

Jake's conscience warred with his fear. Aiden's punishments had become more severe, moving from abusing the servants to punishing Jake directly.

The funnel began to lift off the ground, the dense mass thinning as it moved toward the house. The burning sensation increased.

Tears blurred Jake's eyes, rolling down his cheeks and blending with the rain that coated his face. He shoved his fear away and sent energy into the clouds above, giving strength to the funnel. It veered off path because of the refocus of power.

"The house."

Jake swallowed his horror and narrowed his eyes, pushing the funnel toward the structure. *It's just a house. It's just a building.* For a split second, he considered turning it away, but the skin on his arm began to blister. Jake forced his anger into the storm overhead and the funnel grew denser and widened, smashing into the structure. The house became lost in the darkness and when the tornado moved on, there was nothing. The ground was completely flat, no debris left behind.

The funnel began to thin, but the burning on Jake's arm returned.

"Keep going."

For ten more minutes, Jake manipulated the air to destroy several more houses before Aiden allowed him to stop. He collapsed in exhaustion.

Aiden's face glowed with approval. "Well done, Jacob. I think perhaps you're ready for the next step."

Afraid to ask what the next step was, Jake looked at his burnt and blistered arm, biting his lip to keep from crying. It had been easy to ignore the pain while he concentrated on the storm.

"I could take that away from you, but I think I'll leave it as a reminder that defying me is folly." Aiden turned sideways, taking a step toward the path down to the house. "Stay here and observe what you have done. I'll send someone for you in an hour."

The rain continued to fall as Aiden walked away. Jake no longer controlled it. Maybe the sky was crying for him.

Jake's face scrunched into a scowl as he watched Aiden disappear down the hill. No one cried for him. Not even Mommy.

Closing his eyes, he called out to her, again hitting nothing. Before he at least knew she was out there, but now it was emptiness. He'd been terrified that the emptiness meant she was dead, but Aiden would know. Jake had heard him on the phone with someone about Mommy and Will. They had gone to the ocean in Oregon, then disappeared.

Mommy had talked about Oregon once, when she and Jake were on the run and figuring out where to go next, but she worried their old car wouldn't make it that far.

Jake remembered tracing the path from Oklahoma to Oregon with his finger on the atlas Mommy had bought. It hadn't seemed that far with his finger, but Mommy had insisted it was at least two days of driving. Jake had studied the states around Oregon and he remembered that California was right below Oregon.

Jake was in California now.

Aiden hadn't told him where they were, but he'd found out from one of the staff members. They hadn't told him, of course, Aiden would have killed them for telling him anything. Instead, Jake had found out himself, in a servant's head. He'd begun searching their heads, getting whatever information he could about Aiden, about Raphael. About Marcus. He'd found little about the elements, but he did discover that Aiden's house was in Napa Valley, California. At the time, he thought that information was worthless.

Now he wasn't so sure.

Could he sneak away from Aiden and find Mommy? Would Mommy want him now that she had Will?

Yes. Mommy would always want him.

She'd kept him safe from the Bad Men until she'd fallen down the hill in Colorado. Will had been the one who kept her from saving him. The Bad Men might have killed her if she'd tried. Will had saved Mommy's life. But lost Jake's instead.

Jake knew that was wrong. He'd seen it all in his head before it happened. Jake knew that the Bad Men would finally get him. He'd known it for a long time although he kept it from Mommy. But what if Will had let her climb the hill? No, Will was supposed to keep Mommy from trying to save him. But what if this one time things could have changed? Jake shook his head, choking back his sobs. The bad things in his head never changed. But was he with Aiden because that's where he was supposed to be or because Will didn't help him?

Will would always pick Mommy over Jake. Jake needed to remember that.

He lay on the hill, his head resting on his right arm as he looked at the destruction he had caused. He knew he should feel bad about what he'd done and he did, but not as bad as he thought he should. This wasn't his fault. He had no choice. Besides, the people had seen the storm. They would have gone to their basements. No one was hurt.

I didn't hurt anyone.

No, Jake was the one who was hurt. His left arm stretched out in front of him, the skin blistered and black from his wrist halfway to his elbow. His cuts and scrapes usually healed fast, but this burn didn't seem to be healing. Aiden must have done something to make it stay. Who knew what Aiden would have done if Jake hadn't obeyed him? Now Jake was the one suffering.

A shadow inched toward his left hand and Jake reached out a finger toward it, pain shooting up his arm.

Ever since Marcus had visited several nights before, Jake was more curious about the shadows. Marcus was right. They seemed to like him, following him wherever he went. The only time they stopped was when Aiden was around.

They had grown bolder since Marcus's visit, as though they had gained permission to play with Jake. Or maybe it was because Jake was more open to them. Jake didn't care which one was the cause; he loved the result.

He had friends.

Splaying his fingers into the mud, Jake watched as the shadow touched the tip of his middle finger. Icy coldness stabbed his fingertip and Jake sucked in a breath as he jerked his hand backward. Pain shot up his arm and he cried out as he sat up and grabbed his wrist. The burn throbbed and fresh tears blurred his eyes.

The shadow scurried backward, settling next to a bush.

"I'm sorry," Jake whispered. "I'm not scared of you. You just surprised me. I didn't expect you to be so cold. Come back."

Jake extended both arms in front of him, pressing his palms into the earth. Spreading his left hand shot a fresh wave of burning pain up his arm, but he ignored it. "See, I want to be your friend. It's okay."

The shadow slid away from the bush.

"I'm nice. I won't hurt you."

The shadow moved closer while other shadows formed a circle around him, curling and uncurling in a coordinated rhythm as though they were dancing.

The air around Jake cooled. His wet clothes clung to his body, raising goose bumps on his skin. The throbbing in his arm increased, and he bit his lip to keep from crying out and scaring the shadows.

He was so close.

The shadow was less than an inch away from his left arm.

"It's okay," Jake whispered. "I'm your friend."

Darting forward, the shadow touched Jake's finger again. He was prepared for the cold, forcing his body to remain still. It reminded him of jumping into a cold swimming pool. Mommy always told him he would get used to the temperature after he jumped.

But the coldness remained as the shadow spread out around his other fingers. The iciness crept upward, making his fingers numb. Jake closed his eyes at the assault, refusing to break contact, determined to see this through.

Stabs of cold touched him everywhere and Jake's eyes flew open. The shadows around him had moved closer and now touched his body on all sides.

The sun poked a hole in the clouds, sending a beam of light in front of Jake, brighter than the sun should have been. He squinted into the beam.

A new shadow crawled out of the light, darker than any shadow he'd ever seen before.

"Jacob." A deep voice echoed softly around him.

Fear washed through Jake as he sat up straight, crossing his legs in front of him.

The shadow rose from the ground, shimmering, almost see-through, taking the shape of a person. Only it was just a blob and had no face, and was about as tall as Jake.

"We have found you worthy." A voice came from the figure although it had no mouth. It was the voice from his dream.

Fighting to catch his breath, Jake wheezed. "Thank you."

"You only have to call upon us and we will help you if we can. You shall be our champion."

"Who are you?"

"We are the spirits of the shadow realm. Aiden and his kind have trapped us for eternity, but you have the power to release us and help stop his hold upon the earth. You are the key."

Marcus had told him the same thing. Maybe it was true.

"What do I do?"

"For now, nothing. Know that we are always watching and we wait."

How could the shadows help him? "Can you help me save my mom?"

"Perhaps."

"And Will too?"

"Four shall fight. Two shall remain. There is no changing this."

"So one of us will die? Will, me, or Mommy?"

"Yes, it is etched into the future. At least one of you will die before it's all over. Possibly two. "

"Who will die?"

"That part is unwritten."

"I can change it?"

"No, not change, for it has not been determined. You have the power to create the future."

"I can pick who dies?"

"Yes."

Who would die was an easy choice.

"We wish to give you a gift." The shadow's form shifted, the vague shape of an arm rising from its side and extending toward Jake.

Jake knew he should be frightened, but he was fascinated instead.

"Do you accept our gift?"

Jake nodded.

The tip of a finger unfurled from what should have been a hand, reaching for the burn on Jake's arm. A tidal wave of cold rushed into the wound, sweeping through his body, coursing though his blood. The brutal iciness burned but eased into a slight chill as it settled in his chest. The shadow moved its finger and the intense cold was gone. And so was the burn on Jake's arm. In its place, the skin was swollen and darkened.

"My burn is gone."

"It is only part of our gift. On your chest is a sign of our protection."

"But if Aiden sees it…"

"Aiden is too arrogant to see what's in front of him."

"What am I supposed to do?"

"Wait."

The shadow dissolved into the air and the beam of light faded, the clouds shifting to cover the sun.

"Jake?" a voice called behind him. Antonia.

Jake looked over his shoulder, wondering what she had seen, but her gaze seemed intent on the path, her chest heaving to catch her breath after her climb.

"*Señor* Aiden has sent me for you."

Jake stood, looking up into the clouds where the light had come from. Finally, he had someone on his side. Someone who really wanted to help him. For now, Aiden might be able to boss him around and hurt him, but the time would come when Jake would kill him for everything he had done.

And he would kill Will too. The coldness surrounding his heart helped him accept it even more.

***

As Emma drove toward the Oregon mountains, fear and guilt rushed through her head, but it wasn't her own. It came from Jake, although she didn't know how. She'd tried multiple times to contact him the last few days without success. But she had no doubt she was sensing Jake's emotions. He was doing something he didn't want to do. Something bad.

Before Will had lost the mark of The Chosen One, he had the ability to sense her, but only when she was afraid. Maybe it was the same with Jake now. She wasn't sure whether to be grateful or horrified. Aiden was making Jake do something he didn't want to do, and there wasn't a damn thing she could do about it, which only added to her fears. And her imagination.

But it also led her to consider the future. Suppose Jake lived through the coming trial, and Aiden did too. What kind of hell would her son be forced to endure?

Emma had to make sure that didn't happen.

She glanced at Will. He sat in the passenger seat, reading the book again to see what had been added. Emma had no doubt that Will was stronger and more powerful than she was. There was no telling how much more he would grow over the next week. His power, added to his convictions and his love for her, made him the perfect choice.

Will and Jake had to be the two who remained.

The surety of it filled her, quelling any fear over what that meant for her own life. The moment she'd become a mother, Jake's safety had superseded her own. It wasn't conscious, more instinctual. Her job was to ensure that her son not only survived but had the best possible future. And of all the other elementals, Will was the only acceptable choice. Not only would he be a good father, but he actually had a shot at beating Aiden. Much better than she could hope for. The question was how to make sure that happened.

She could use their new connection to her advantage. Will had taken her power and added it to his own to free her from the car. What if she pushed all her power to him to help him win? The trick would be to do it without Will realizing she was sacrificing herself in the process. She needed to use their practice time focusing on her new goal.

Not telling him about her plan was the same as lying, and it crushed her. She didn't want to lie to Will anymore. But Will was so protective that he'd never agree. In the end, she had to decide what held the most importance: providing the best possible outcome for Jake or having a clear conscience.

A heaviness settled in her chest. There was really no choice at all.

Reluctance crept in to her resolve when she thought about how she might be pregnant again. By throwing the battle and assuring her death, she may be ensuring the death of an innocent life. But it wasn't as if she stood a chance anyway.

CHAPTER EIGHT

WILL studied the book while Emma turned on the television in their cabin, flipping channels with a groan. "What kind of motel only has ten stations? I hope they at least have a news channel."

Will looked up. "This place is cheap and remote. They figure people aren't here to watch TV."

Three days after the dream, they had found in the book the new rules that the mysterious voice had mentioned, and nothing else new. But the fact that the text changed meant that the book remained important. Just because there wasn't something in it today didn't mean they wouldn't find something tomorrow. Which only reinforced that the others would come to claim it.

"I just need a news channel," Emma muttered. The image on the television stopped on a man at a news desk and she sat on the bed, the remote still in her hand.

Although she hadn't said what she was doing, Will knew she was searching for Alex's whereabouts. He was the one element they could keep track of through the media, and although they could have tracked him on the laptop, they hadn't had internet service for a couple of days.

After clips about earthquakes, volcanic eruptions and wars, Senator Phillip Warren's face appeared on the screen.

"Senator Warren is on the campaign trial this week, making his way up the East Coast," the newscaster announced. "Rumors run rampant as to the whereabouts of

Alex Warren, Senator Warren's son, especially after his disappearance earlier this month." Film of Alex walking next to his father and shaking hands with the crowd filled the screen. "Several of the younger Warren's recent campaign appearances have been cancelled, causing widespread speculation, including rumors that he's doing a stint in rehab for substance abuse or that he was abducted during last week's terrorist attack in Albuquerque. In any case, security detail around the Senator has been increased."

Scenes of Albuquerque flashed across the screen, the burning and collapsed buildings. The bloody faces and limbs of people in the street.

"So that's how they're explaining it," she mumbled.

"Turn it off, Emma." Will's voice was harsher than he meant, but she'd finally begun to let the incident go and this would only reopen the wound.

She ignored him.

"No group has claimed responsibility for the attack, but the White House has suggested it was carried out by an extremist militia group that supports a one-world government, the Cavallo."

Emma's head whipped around to Will, her eyes wide. He moved next to her on the bed.

"Information has leaked that the secret group has specifically targeted Senator Warren by attacking while Alex Warren was in Albuquerque for a fundraiser. The younger Warren hasn't been seen since the attack, raising speculations that he was either killed by the terrorists or he was one of them. A spokesman from the Warren camp called the speculation ridiculous."

A man appeared on the screen. "Alex Warren is not part of a radical terrorist group and to suggest otherwise is ludicrous. These rumors are being spread by Senator Warren's political enemies."

The news anchor's face returned. "The missing Warren is only fueling outrage in both camps. No further information is known about the Cavallo at this time."

Phillip Warren's beaming face lit up the screen and he stood on a stage, waving to a crowd. "Since the attack, Warren's numbers continue to soar, giving Warren a previously unheard of twenty-point lead."

The newscast broke for commercials.

"Who would have linked the Cavallo to Albuquerque?" Emma asked. "Isn't that a little too close to Warren? Won't it eventually be tied back to him?"

"Maybe, but it probably wasn't Warren's camp who leaked their name. It could have been Raphael or Aiden. Hell, it could have even been Marcus."

"How can they call what happened in Albuquerque a terrorist attack?"

"How else would they explain it? Things like that just don't happen, Emma. People will reach for the easiest explanation."

"But what about the earthquakes? Terrorists can't do that. How do they explain those?"

If he told her much more, he'd give away that he'd known about the media's explanation of the incident. And that he'd withheld the information with her. But she deserved to know. "They called it a new high-tech weapon. The national security level has been raised to imminent."

Emma's eyes widened with understanding. "You knew this and you didn't tell me?"

Will reached for her arm, but she shrugged him off. "Emma, what good would it have done?"

She stood, taking a step away from him. "That wasn't for you to decide, Will!"

"I knew what you would do. Just what you're doing now."

She glared. "I'm not a child, Will! You can't protect me from the truth."

"I know. I'm sorry." Sighing, he ran a hand through his hair, leaning his elbows on his thighs. "Look, I suspected they would pin what happened in Albuquerque on a terrorist group, but I worried it would get pinned on some fringe group who had never caused any real trouble. At least with the Cavallo, we know that not only do they deserve the incrimination, but the members probably aren't even alive to care after Aiden and Alex finished with them."

Emma shook her head, looking away from him. "That's not the point, Will!"

"What *is* the point, Emma? That you don't think you've beaten yourself up enough over what happened? Does it ease your pain to smother yourself in guilt?"

"That's not fair! You didn't destroy half that city!"

Will sat up and said with an icy calm, "No, Emma I didn't. I just murdered forty kids and listened to them scream as they burned to death."

She sighed, her shoulders relaxing as she closed her eyes. "You didn't murder them."

"And you didn't murder those people in Albuquerque."

He could argue with her about this all day long and it wouldn't change a thing. Nothing could take away her guilt but the passage of time. Unfortunately, time was a luxury they didn't have. Will stood and eased toward her, grabbing her hands. "Do you remember that night in the cornfield when you asked me if you would ever stop seeing the face of the man you shot?"

"Yes." She choked on the word, looking down.

He dropped her hands, and tilted her chin up, staring into her eyes. "I told you it would always be there, but it would ease with time. Remember?"

She nodded, tears filling her eyes.

"This is the same thing. What I did in Iraq is always with me. Every day. But something makes the pain more bearable. Do you know what it is?"

"No."

"You. Your love for me. Your belief that I'm worth saving. You make the pain bearable. Let me do the same for you."

She buried her face in his chest.

"All of this is going to get worse, Princess," he whispered into her hair. "You have to find a way to accept the pain and the guilt and move forward, otherwise it's going to eat you alive. If you can't do it for yourself, do it for Jake. You'll never save him if you don't."

The newscaster's voice broke into their moment. "Meteorologists are still trying to explain yesterday's freak storm in Napa Valley."

Emma pulled away from Will and turned her attention to the screen.

"A tornado touched down yesterday afternoon in the Napa Valley, killing twenty-five people. While the tornado itself is an odd occurrence, the path it took is particularly unusual." Footage of rubble strewn across the landscape appeared. "The tornado appears to have jumped from an F2 to an F5 within a matter of moments right before destroying a house. Then it returned to an F2 status until it struck another home as an F5. And as though that wasn't strange enough," —the footage switched to an aerial view— "after the tornado destroyed the first house, it's almost as if the funnel cloud's path purposely sought out the homes it destroyed. Then just as abruptly as the storm appeared, it disappeared." A meteorologist's face filled the screen. "We've never seen anything like this. There were no colliding fronts, no indication that anything like this would happen and consequently no warnings were issued."

Will tensed. "Alex."

Emma's face paled. "No, it was Jake."

He paused for several seconds. "Why do you think Jake did this?"

"Because this afternoon, right about the time that tornado touched down, I felt Jake. He was afraid and he felt guilty."

"You know Jake would never purposely hurt people."

"No, he'd never do something like this on his own, but he's with Aiden. Aiden might have forced him to do this."

"Why?"

"Maybe as practice, like you and I have been doing? Testing his abilities?" She grabbed Will's arm. "But we know where he is now! And we know that the two of us together are more powerful than Aiden. We can go get Jake."

"Emma, think this through. I know that sounds like a good idea and you know I want nothing more than to go get Jake, but what if that's Aiden's plan? What if he's trying to lure us out and separate us before the end and steal the book? This could be a trap. "

"I don't care, Will! He has my son!"

He gripped her arms. "I know and I want to get Jake too, but we have to be smart about this. We think we're stronger together, but we don't know for sure. We need more practice before we try to attack. Otherwise we might get both us killed, and that won't do Jake any good."

She nodded but refused to look at him.

"Let's get some rest, wake up in the middle of the night, practice and then move on. We'll move closer to Napa Valley so if we think we're ready, we'll be close enough to strike."

"All right."

"Don't get your hopes up, okay? You know I'll try, Emma, but I can't promise anything."

"I know."

***

The sounds of bird calls and the trickling stream were amplified in the dark forest. The sun wouldn't rise for another hour, but Will stood next to the creek, manipulating the water. It was safer this way. They were less likely to have someone stumble across them, and they could practice then leave in the daylight, driving to the next location. They'd done this two nights in a row without problem, but Will had a feeling they were pushing their luck.

Emma had practiced some, but Will still wasn't satisfied with the amount of practice they'd done combining their power. While Emma wasn't either, she knew their choices were limited given her desire to stay in Northern California now. Also, she insisted he needed more practice since his power was so new to him. But his practicing had been at the expense of hers, and Will planned to change that tonight. He wasn't sure how happy she'd be driving out of California into Nevada in a few hours. He needed to test his ability to find water when none seemed available, and she needed to use her power without fear of creating a forest fire. Not to mention, they need to practice together without limitations. Of course, using their powers in the real world would come with a higher price, but they'd worry about that when they got there.

Emma sagged against a tree with her eyes closed, clutching her stomach. The backpack with the book hung on her back. She'd been practicing making small fires in a straight line using the undergrowth but had stopped several minutes before.

"Emma, are you okay?"

Her eyes opened, but shadows covered the rest of her face. "I'm fine. Just tired."

"You look like you're more than tired."

She pushed away from the tree with a start. "I'm fine. Can we leave it at that?"

But she wasn't fine. She was exhausted and sick more often than not. She claimed it was nerves, but Will was worried. Her supernatural healing properties should have cured her of any virus or infection, leaving him to wonder what was really wrong.

"Emma, why don't you go back and lay down for awhile? You've done pretty much all you can. I'll practice a little while longer, then we can go."

She hesitated. "Are you sure?"

He expected more of a fight from her, so her response made him even more anxious. "Yeah, we need to move somewhere more open for you to practice next. You go back and rest so you'll be ready to work hard tomorrow."

She hesitated again, looking toward the cabin then Will. "Okay."

"Can you get back all right?"

"I'm not six years old. I know where I'm going."

"I meant finding your way in the dark."

"I can find it just *fine*." She started to stomp off, but Will ran after her, the underbrush crunching beneath his feet.

"Emma, wait."

She stopped and turned around to face him, a hand on her hip. "What?"

The darkness hid most of her face so he had trouble reading her emotions. "Maybe I should go back with you."

"Why? So you can baby me some more? I'm fine. Stay and practice. We need you to know what the hell you're doing."

"Do you want to leave the book here?"

"So you can get it all wet?" She turned and headed for the cabin. "I'll see you later."

He watched her disappear into the darkness, worry needling the base of his skull. She was probably right. He was being overprotective. Returning to the stream, he began to practice again. But he couldn't shake the feeling that something was wrong.

***

Emma shook her head as she trudged back to the cabin. She had no idea why Will put up with her temper. She hadn't meant to snap at him, but her frustration had gotten the better of her.

Their schedule was wrecking havoc with her hormone-riddled body, exacerbating her already raging nausea. Although his coddling irritated her, Will was probably right. She needed to go back to the cabin and sleep. She didn't want to be dead weight, but that was what she had quickly become. She might have the power of fire at her disposal, but it did her little good if she was too busy throwing up to use it.

The nausea hadn't been this bad with her last pregnancy and she knew that it was a good sign for the health of the baby, but she wondered whether it mattered. She was doomed. Her goal was to make it to the end just long enough to help Will and Jake become the two who remained. The way her body had betrayed her the last few days, she now wondered if that was possible.

When she emerged from the edge of the woods, twenty feet from the cabin, she stopped, her senses on alert. An undercurrent of power rippled toward her.

Someone was there.

She let the energy wash over her as she decided on her best course of action.

Alex.

Surprise over the fact that she could recognize him lasted a fleeting moment, before succumbing to a spike of fear. Then the fear faded—not fleeing entirely, but not overwhelming her. Of all the elementals, Alex was the best possible one for her to face. If she got close enough to touch him, she could subdue him since her power overrode his.

"Alex, I know you're there."

He stepped away from the shadows of a tree, his hands stuffed into his front pockets. "Long time no see, Emma."

"Not long enough." Should she keep him close to her cabin or draw him into the woods?

His eyes fell on her backpack. "You have something I need."

She put a hand on her hip, hiding her fear. "That again? This is getting old."

"Didn't your mother teach you that it's nice to share, Emma?"

"My mother was a drunken whore whose middle name was *selfish-bitch*, so guess again. And then you've met my father."

Laughing, Alex slid his hands from his pockets in a slow, smooth movement, taking several steps toward her. "Come on, Emma. You're wasting your time with Will. If you really want to save Jake, join with me. I'm his father. Who better to have by your side helping you?"

She kept her surprise in check. Alex obviously didn't know that she and Will had joined. Would it be to her advantage to keep it a secret? Did Alex even know that Will was Marcus's son? "I take it you had the same dream explaining the new rules for the end. That's why you're here for the book."

"While that was an informative get-together, I'd like to see it for myself, if you don't mind."

"I don't have it."

Alex's gaze landed on her back. Grinning, his eyes rose to hers. "Where's Will?"

Emma forced a low chuckle. "With the book, I'm afraid. So you're out of luck."

"Hmm...."

She was going to have to fight him, something she didn't relish, but Alex wasn't going to leave until he had the book or he was forced to go. Where was the best place for this to happen?

She took a step toward the cabin. "Alex, I'm tired. It's the middle of the night and I just want to go to back to bed. So maybe we can pick this up tomorrow."

He blocked her path, standing ten feet in front of her. "Not a chance."

A sudden wind blew against her, slamming her sideways into a tree. Pain shot through her side. Damn it, why hadn't she been prepared for that?

Emma?

Alex is here. But it pissed her off that she needed his help while if he were in this situation, Will could most likely handle it on his own.

She held onto the tree for several seconds before pushing away. "I don't want to fight you, Alex. Please, just go away and we'll meet at the final battle."

"You seriously don't think that's going to happen, do you?"

Emma sighed her disappointment. "No, but you can't blame me for hoping."

Alex took several steps toward her.

Emma's power burned in her chest. She was ready to defend herself this time.

"This doesn't have to be difficult, Emma."

"I don't have the book, Alex."

"Don't lie to me, Emma." He shifted his weight, his eyes searching the trees before he looked at her again. "You know, I'd love nothing more than to work something out with you. But it has to be a compromise. We can work together."

"I never said I wanted to work with you. I said I didn't want to fight you."

Alex's face softened. "It's not like you have a choice. You'll have to fight me in the end."

Damn, he was good. The compassion on his face was believable. Too believable. He might be an element, but he also took after his human father, a politician used to duping people. "What kind of compromise are you talking about?"

He grinned. "It depends on what you're considering. Sharing the book or sharing power?"

"Let's start with the book."

"You've already read it, I presume."

She nodded.

"Then you don't need it anymore. Just hand it over."

"And if I want to keep it?"

"Then consider option two. Come with me and we'll join. We can share the book."

"You know I won't do that."

"I was afraid you'd say that."

She was prepared for the wind this time, countering it with a burst of energy.

The gust stopped and Alex reached a hand toward her. "Emma, I'm just asking you to be reasonable."

"None of this is reasonable." She waited for his next attack, knowing she should attack him first. But when she reached for the energy to do it, images of Alex saving her from Raphael and taking her to Will flashed through her mind. It didn't matter that he'd had selfish motives. He'd helped her all the same.

Will was trained to be a soldier. Battle was second nature to him. Over the past three years her instinct had been to run, and although she was done running, part of her wasn't ready to become a cold-blooded murderer either.

Albuquerque had left a festering wound on her soul. Now she stood at the edge of an abyss that she wasn't ready to jump into. While she would do anything to ensure

Jake's survival, she was also conscious that her actions from this point on would outlast Jake's memories of her. The moment was coming when she'd drench herself in filth, but that that moment wasn't today.

Alex's hand stretched toward her a little more. "Just come with me, Emma. We'll save Jake together."

Will stepped to the edge of the trees, to Emma's left. "She's not going anywhere with you, Alex."

There was no way Will could have reached her this quickly unless he'd gotten a head start. Emma wasn't sure whether to be relieved or annoyed.

Alex's arm dropped and he spread his feet apart. "Ahh…Will. I knew you couldn't be very far away."

"And here I am. Nice catching up. We'll see you at the big showdown."

Alex turned to Emma. "I'm surprised to see you're still keeping him around, Emma. Especially this close to the competition. Everyone's going to need a buddy to have a shot at winning this thing and Will's no help to you there."

A slow grin covered Will's face. "You still don't know, do you?"

The confidence left Alex's eyes. "Know what?"

"Why do you think I was in the dream, Alex? Did you think I just happened to be Emma's plus-one?"

Alex's eyes narrowed. "Why don't you save us all the tedious guessing game and tell me what you're talking about."

"I have two surprises for you Alex. First of all, I'm Marcus's son." Will paused to let the full effect settle over Alex.

"You're the son of Water?" Alex cleared his throat. "How? That's never happened before."

"There's a first time for everything."

"Why?"

Will shrugged with a lazy smile. "You'll have to ask Marcus. Your guess is as good as mine."

"So let me guess the second surprise." Alex turned to Emma, despair in his eyes. "I take it congratulations are in order?"

Why did she feel sorry for him?

A strong wind blew Will back into the woods, and the cracking and splitting of the tree trunks sounded in the night air. Logs piled up to block his return. Emma felt a swift breeze and raised a hand to defend herself, but Alex was next to her, his hand lifted in surrender.

"I need that book, Emma. Please." Alex's voice was low, but not threatening. Fearful. "You have Will. Jake has Aiden. Raphael won't side with me and I know Marcus won't. I'll never survive this on my own. I need the book."

She looked up into his anxious face. There could be only two winners and she couldn't afford for Alex to be one of them. Could she look this man in the eye and condemn him to death? But giving him the book might harm Jake and Will's chances.

"Alex, I can't." Her voice broke.

"Emma, I helped you. I'm begging you. Just give me this."

Emma? Are you okay?

Yes.

I'm trying to get to you. Alex blocked my path.

I'm okay.

If she touched him, Alex would be under her control. His power would flow to her. But if she did that, she was no better than Raphael, and she hated Raphael for what he had done to her. Could she live with herself if she manipulated Alex? Could she live with herself if she didn't?

Before she could react, Alex grabbed the backpack strap on her shoulder and jerked it down. Emma reached for his arm, but he pulled back, tangling the pack in her arms. Twisting behind her, Alex wrapped the straps around her wrists and yanked up. She gasped in pain. The backpack zipper opened and the weight of the pack lightened.

She pushed power through her hands, hoping to hit Alex, but he ducked. The trees overhead burst into flames, raining burning embers over them.

Alex twisted her palms so that they touched her back. If she tried to use her power now, she'd catch herself on fire.

"I know you don't believe me, Emma, but I don't want to hurt you. If I did, I'd kill you now. If you change your mind about Will, let me know." He pushed her to her knees and a wind threw her forward, her face hitting the dirt.

She heard the trees cracking again as she strained to move her palms away from her back and shot energy behind her. More trees burst into flames as she shook her arms, freeing them from the straps.

"Emma!" Will shouted.

The wind eased and, spitting dirt out of her mouth, Emma climbed to her feet. She ran toward the parking lot, but it was empty. No sign of Alex and no sign of a getaway car.

Will reached her, scrapes covering his face and arms. "Where is he?"

"I don't know," she mumbled trying to catch her breath and looking around. "It's like he disappeared." Pausing, she sought out the energy from Alex's power. "I can't even feel anything from him. He's hidden his power."

"He could be anywhere."

"Yeah."

"Are you okay?" Will asked without looking at her.

Was he mad? Did he realize she'd hesitated when Alex asked for her help? "I'm fine."

"I take it he got the book." He still didn't look at her, his eyes focused on the gravel road leading away from the cabins.

"I'm sorry."

Will didn't respond for several seconds. "It's not your fault."

But it was. She should have attacked Alex instead of waiting for him to retaliate. Yet given the chance to do it over, she wasn't sure she would have done it differently.

CHAPTER NINE

WILL was furious. Alex had found them and taken the book, and it was Will's fault. He'd sent Emma back to the cabin alone and left her to face Alex. Then when Will showed up, instead of just killing the fool, he'd talked to him and given Alex the advantage. For all Will knew, Alex was still out there waiting to attack. And even if he wasn't, if Alex had found them, that meant the others probably weren't far behind. "We have to pack up and go. Now."

"I'm sorry."

Will leaned his head back, staring into the star-filled sky. "This isn't your fault, Emma."

"It is. I didn't stop him."

He released a heavy breath and leveled his gaze on the destruction Alex had left behind. "We can stand here all morning and argue over who's to blame, but it's pointless. It's done. Go inside and pack up and I'll make sure Alex doesn't come back to finish the job."

She hesitated, then walked toward the cabin without answering.

How the hell had Alex found them? Will had been so careful, leaving within an hour of practicing, making sure they drove somewhere at least four hours away. It was possible that Alex had realized where they were the night before, then tracked them and waited to sense their power today. What range did Alex's sensing ability have? Will had been practicing for over an hour and they'd been making a steady path from Oregon into Northern California. All the more reason to head to Nevada.

Fires still smoldered in the trees. Why were the branches over his head burning? Why had Emma been aiming that high? And why hadn't Alex tried to kill her?

He swiped a trickle of blood that slid down his cheek. While Alex had incapacitated Will to get to Emma, trapping him under a pile of trees, Alex hadn't staged a full-fledged attack and he hadn't tried to kill Will. Once Alex realized Will's true potential, he must have decided his best course of action was to get the book and run.

Will was now sorry he'd told Alex that Marcus was his father. Since Alex hadn't known that Will was a water element or that he and Emma had joined, Will could have used it to their advantage later. Raphael and Marcus had been there to witness the event, but what about Aiden? Will found it hard to believe that something so important would have slipped Aiden's notice. In the end, it probably didn't matter if Alex knew or not. Will suspected Alex was the weakest of them all. *Except for Emma.* The thought popped into his head before he quickly banished it. She was capable of great destruction. When she could make her power work.

"You were lucky."

Will's head jerked up to see Marcus at the edge of the woods. Will's temper flared. "Goddammit. We're not hosting a fucking party here."

Marcus shrugged and took several steps closer. "Maybe not, but you and Emma should expect to see more visitors."

Will tilted his head with a glare. "We don't have the book, if that's what you're looking for. Alex took it."

"No, I'm looking for you."

While Will wasn't surprised, he wasn't happy about it either. He spread his arms at his sides. "And here I am. What do you want?"

"We need to talk."

"So start talking. You have less than five minutes."

Marcus's eyes widened in surprise. "Don't you have questions about me? You just found out I'm your father."

Shaking his head, Will grunted. "You're not my father. I don't even know you."

"I'd like to change that."

Will spread his feet apart, braced for a possible attack. "I think it's a little late to play daddy, given our timetable with the end of the world and all. How about you say what you have to say, then leave?"

"I want to help you. Why won't you hear me out?"

"My entire life you've known who I was, so the way I see it, you've missed plenty of opportunities. I found out the truth on my own, no thanks to you. If I'd known weeks ago, we might not be in this situation right now. Emma would have Jake and we'd have the advantage over Aiden."

"I told you it couldn't happen that way. There were rules."

Will shook his head in disgust. "You people and your fucking rules."

Reaching a hand toward Will, Marcus's eyes softened. "*We* are your people, Will. Like it or not. You're one of us."

With a glare, Will pointed a finger at Marcus. "No. I'm nothing like you egocentric dickheads. I have one goal: save Emma, Jake and myself."

Marcus's voice lowered. "You can't save all three of you. You know that."

Panic threatened to swamp Will's senses before he shoved it away. The dream had told him there would only be two, but he'd hoped to find a way around that rule. If there was an answer to this, it was probably in the book. The book that Will had let Alex take. The sooner he found Alex, the better. "We're all caught up, so I've got to go."

"Patience, Will. This game has lasted millenniums."

"True, but you've have thousands of years to get used to it all. I've got about a week to figure this out and save the world."

Taking a step backward, Marcus glanced toward the cabin. "I'm glad you finally see the bigger perspective." His gaze swung to Will's face. "I know you love Emma, but she's one life. Thousands, *millions* are at stake."

While he'd suspected it was true, Marcus's confirmation chilled his blood. "This game has gone on for centuries with little consequence to humanity. Why would that change now?"

"Aiden's a showman. He likes the big bangs and the flashy lights. He wants a large-scale production. Not to mention he wants more of a fresh start than just a new daughter. He wants to recreate the world. Then there's Tweedle Dee and Tweedle Dum to consider."

"Raphael and Alex."

Marcus smirked. "They have their own agendas, besides saving their own skins. They're both thinking long-term here. Are you?"

The question caught Will by surprise. "Long-term?"

"You need a goal besides survival. You need to be prepared for after the battle."

"Prepared for what?"

"Prepared to rule the world."

Will laughed. "You've got to be kidding me."

Marcus's face twisted into a scowl. "I'm deadly serious. The winners, the survivors, rule. It's best to have a plan in place so you can implement it immediately. After a major battle between the elements, the world's liable to be out of whack."

"So you say I need to fight for the survival of the world. What if I say my priority is Emma's survival?"

"And of course your own."

Will hoped to survive, but he wouldn't tell Marcus that his long-term plan focused on keeping Emma and Jake alive. "I still don't get why you created me. After all this time. What's my purpose?"

"To double my chances of succeeding."

"You mean taking over the world."

"I mean restoring balance."

While that might be partially true, Will knew there was more to it. "Nice try, Marcus, but you'll need to do better than that."

Marcus leaned his shoulder against a tree, the leaves overhead still smoldering. "I met Jake, did I mention that?"

That caught Will by surprise. "When?"

"He was with Aiden."

"Why are you bringing Jake into this?"

"Not only do you need to think about after the game is done, but also who the players will be. Everyone will be forced to participate but each element must be represented."

"What does that have to do with Jake?"

"How will Emma behave if Jake is one of the four? What if it's down to the three of you?"

Will didn't want to consider it. If he could ensure that the three of them were in the final battle, he'd only have to eliminate the fourth participant and convince Emma or Jake to kill him.

"Jake is the son of two elements. And every element must be represented."

"He's taking Alex's place," Will whispered.

Marcus's eyes lit up "Of course, technically he could take Emma's place instead. But then that would mean that Aiden would be eliminated by the final battle. How likely is that?"

The blood rushed from Will's head and pooled in his feet. "He's just a little boy."

Marcus shrugged with a frown. "Some of us are unwilling participants."

"So three elements have children to be their stand-ins, but what about Raphael? He's on his own?"

"Unless he dredges up a child somewhere, but that would surprise me. He truly did love Emmanuella. In his own twisted way."

Will swallowed his fear. "*Four shall fight, two shall remain.* You're telling me I either have to kill Emma or her five-year-old son. What kind of sick monster are you?"

"I told you that I didn't make those rules. That's not how I prefer it."

"But the voice in the dream said that *all* would fight and two would remain."

Marcus's mouth twisted into a grimace. "Yes, even the best-laid plans get altered. While the original intent was to have children represent the elements, the shadow realm intervened."

Will's back stiffened. "So who represents Water?"

"If one of us kills Raphael, he could stand in his place. Or one of the other elements. Who knows what will happen between now and then?"

"Who spoke in our dream? Who changed the rules?"

"The shadows. They rarely insert themselves into such matters, but when they do, they are not to be ignored."

"I thought you ruled the shadow world. If you rule them, how can they issue rules?"

"Some things aren't governed. The best you can hope for is to keep them in check. There is no ruling the shadows. Our goal is to keep them contained."

"And if they're let loose?"

"That's part of the reason Aiden conceded to my demands. With the weakened powers of the elements, the shadows are close to escaping. If they're let loose, gods help us all."

Will shook his head in disgust. "I don't believe a word that comes out of your mouth. I don't trust you."

"I've never given you reason not to."

"You've never given me a reason that I should."

An exaggerated sigh heaved Marcus's chest. "I'm not the only one you should question. Why is Emma still alive? Why didn't she try to kill Alex?" Marcus's voice lowered. "I saw their encounter. Emma had the chance to attack Alex and she didn't take it. Instead she practically handed him the book and he let her go. That doesn't make sense. His best offense for the end is to eliminate all competition, yet he let you both live. You, I understand—he hadn't tested your powers yet. But Emma..."

"Shut the fuck up, Marcus."

"I'm not saying Emma did anything wrong. Maybe she froze up with fear, but at least consider the alternatives."

"What possible reason would Emma have to join forces with Alex?"

"I can name one. Jake."

Will shook his head. "What the hell are you talking about?"

"Emma has made no secret what her main goal is: Jake. Alex might try to use that to his advantage."

"You obviously don't know Emma. She wouldn't side with Alex after what he did to her."

"I wouldn't be so sure of that." Marcus shrugged. "Just something to think about." He took a step toward Will. "I think that's enough for one night. Be careful from here on out." Turning, he walked away, looking over his shoulder. "Watch out for the shadows. They aren't to be trusted."

"The shadows?"

But Marcus left without an explanation.

***

Antonia found Jake under an oak tree after his morning practice session with Aiden, tears streaming down his face. She settled on the ground next to him, resting her hands in her lap. Jake liked that she didn't ask him questions. She was probably afraid of the answers. She was smart.

"I miss my mom."

Keeping her gaze on the field below them, she took his hand in hers, placing it on her open palm so her hands made a sandwich out of his. Mommy used to do that sometimes. He sniffled and more tears fell down his cheeks.

"Your mother misses you just as much. Probably more."

"She has Will. And the new baby. She doesn't need me anymore."

Antonia's fingertips lifted his chin so that he looked into her face. Love filled her eyes. "You are her first baby. She will always need you."

His shoulders lifted in indignation. "I'm not a baby."

She chuckled and her hand dropped, covering his again. "No matter how big you are, you will always be her baby." She sighed and a sadness crept over her face, puckering her mouth so lines crinkled around her cheeks. "Your mother would have died for you that day in Albuquerque if you had not have stopped her. You saved her life."

Jake hadn't considered that before, but it didn't make him feel better. "She won't love me anymore when she finds out the bad things I've done."

"Your mother will always love you no matter what you do. She will know that you are forced to do these things. And it will make her even more angry at the horrible man who forces you to do it. Just like it makes me."

Jake felt numb with terror. What if Aiden knew she was saying those things? What if he knew she was *thinking* them? "Antonia, you can't say that! Aiden—"

She covered his mouth with her index finger. "Saying it or not saying it does not change what it is."

"But Aiden, he knows things."

A smile lifted her mouth into a soft grimace. "The truth is like a rare flower in this place, lost in the choking weeds of deceit. The garden must be pruned, Jake."

Jake didn't know what that meant, but he couldn't let Aiden find out how she really felt. Maybe he could hide her thoughts from Aiden like he hid his own. Was that possible?

He closed his eyes, breathing in the scent of the lavender soap she used. He searched her mind and found her hatred for Aiden buried deeper than other thoughts, like what Jake should eat for lunch when they went inside. Did Aiden pay attention to what the staff was thinking? Would he notice if some of Antonia's thoughts were missing?

"Do you see the vineyards?"

Jake opened his eyes and looked up at her in confusion.

She tilted her head toward the fields. "The grapevines in the vineyards? Those grapes are grown to make wine."

He nodded. "I like to look at them. I like the way they grow in straight lines, but then the lines go in different directions."

She smiled, staring out into the fields on the hill below them. "I like that too." Her hand squeezed his. "Grapes grown for wine are a higher quality when they are stressed. If you withhold water or rainfall, the grapes will grow smaller, but the juice is more concentrated. The wine is better." Pausing, she looked down at him. "If it were in his power, the vigneron would withhold as much water as possible, doling out only small amounts to force the vine into making smaller grapes. But the grapevines need water to survive so it is a careful balance."

"How do you know so much about grapes?"

"My father owned a vineyard."

"Where is it?'

She hesitated then waved her hand toward the valley. "This is it."

Was this Antonia's vineyard? If so, then why was Aiden in charge? "Where's your dad now?"

"He has been dead for many years. He was killed by a *demoñio*." Her free hand found the beads in her pocket. "Aiden is like the vigneron and you are the grapes. He wants you to grow stronger by withholding what you need most. Love."

Jake's eyes widened in surprise.

"He thinks if you learn to hate that you will be more powerful. You will be his weapon." She paused. "Hate is an easy trap to fall into, but you are a strong boy." She kissed the top of his head. "And you are also brave. Your mother's love is more powerful than your grandfather's hate, but you must be strong too. You must keep love in your heart."

Her thumb stroked the back of his hand as the wind tickled his neck. Her words were pretty and for just a few moments, Jake let himself believe her.

***

The desert had never looked so good. The earlier events only proved that Will had wasted valuable time testing his own powers when they needed to concentrate on honing Emma's.

Will watched her from the corner of his eye as he drove. Emma had been unusually quiet during the drive and hadn't put up a fight when Will announced they were headed to New Mexico. Marcus's words rattled around in his head.

I'm not saying Emma did anything wrong. Maybe she froze up with fear, but at least consider the alternatives.

That was Marcus's plan. Divide and conquer. Destroy from within. It only meant one thing: Marcus wasn't to be trusted, but then Will had already known that. So why was he still thinking about what he'd said?

Marcus had been right about one thing. Will needed to come up with not only a plan for when the battle was over, but how to make the outcome swing his way.

"I've been thinking about the final battle."

Emma's head lifted and she turned to him. "What about it?"

"What if we can manipulate who's in it?"

She sat up. "What are you talking about?"

"The four elements have to be represented. All the big boys represent their elements, but three of them have children, the three of us, who could stand in their place. That leaves Raphael on his own."

"Okay..."

"What if instead of waiting until the end, we eliminate our competition before the battle starts? We decide who we want in the battle and eliminate everyone else."

She stared out the windshield. "You're talking about murder."

While he understood her reservation, he had to get her past that if they were going to survive. "Emma, there are seven of us, and only two will survive. In the final battle or before it, five of us will die."

Her face turned gray. "Pull over."

"What?"

"I'm going to be sick. Pull over."

He swerved over to the shoulder, and she had the door open before he stopped, throwing up on the side of the road as she leaned out the opening.

Will looked around them for any sign of being followed. "Is it the Cavallo?"

She held onto the car door with one hand and the back of the seat with the other, her head hanging over. "No."

"Are you sure?"

"Yes." Her back rose and fell as she took several deep breaths. "Now can I barf without carrying on a conversation?"

He watched her dry-heave for nearly a minute then handed her a bottle of water. She took a swig, spitting it onto the ground, then shut the door, leaning her head on the back of the seat. Her eyes sank closed, her lashes dark against her pale skin. "Eight."

"Eight what?" But even as the words left his mouth he knew, the knowledge dropping the ground out from beneath him and sucking his breath with it.

Her eyes opened and she turned her head to look at him, her dark hair fanned around her face. "You said there were seven of us. There's eight."

He froze in his panic, sorting through the implications of what her pregnancy meant. While he'd been excited at the thought of having a baby before, now was the worst possible timing. "Are you sure?"

Her eyebrows rose as her mouth twisted into a sarcastic grimace.

After hiding the confirmation of her last pregnancy for so long, he was surprised she told him this time. But then, she could no longer hide this one.

What did it mean for her ability to fight for her life? At least before, when her nausea had been an early warning sign of danger, it disappeared when the Cavallo showed up. Now it was bound to hit her at any time, making her vulnerable. Could she train hard enough without harming the baby? Did it even matter? Without Emma, the baby couldn't survive. And Emma couldn't survive if she didn't train.

As much as he hated to admit it, Emma was Will's primary concern. The baby would have to come third, after Jake. He only hoped she survived so the baby did too.

Her dark brown eyes watched him, her mouth pinched into a tight line as she waited for his reaction.

No matter what he thought or felt, she needed his reassurance. He pulled her against his chest, his arms tight around her back. "It's going to be okay."

Her face buried in his shoulder, she said, "No, it's not. I'm tired of pretending it is. No matter what happens this won't turn out *okay*."

Will grasped her shoulders and eased her back to look into her face. "I'll make sure you, Jake, and the baby are okay."

"Will, we know I'm not strong enough to win this."

He released her, gripping the steering wheel and looking out the window at the passing traffic. "That's why we're going back to the desert. So you can practice. Maybe we can rework the way you get your power."

"It's taken me weeks to get to this point. You've surpassed me in days." She rested her cheek on his shoulder as her hand rubbed his arm. "You're right. We need a plan for the battle and for after it's done. But we need to consider all the factors. We need to be realistic."

He shook his head, not trusting himself to speak.

"We don't have to do it right now, but before it all begins, I'd like to know you have a viable plan. You can even have a Plan B and C. I just need to know before…"

She sighed, her body sinking into his. "I just need to know."

CHAPTER TEN

JAKE woke to light streaming in his window as Antonia parted the curtains. He was groggy from staying up so late playing with the shadows.

"Get up, *corazoncito*," Antonia said, moving to the side of his bed. "*Señor* Aiden says we are going on a trip."

The last time Jake went on a trip, he saw Mommy. But then Aiden made her go away. Jake's excitement faded. "Where?"

"He didn't say, only that you must hurry and dress."

Jake didn't want to leave. What if the shadows didn't go with him? He looked down at the gauze wrapped around his arm.

Antonia's gaze followed his. "I will bandage your arm for you."

"No!" Jake shouted, then took a deep breath. "I mean it's not that bad and it sticks so I like to take it off myself."

Antonia frowned. "I must look at it, *corazoncito*. *Señor* Aiden said it was a bad burn."

"It's not really. I'll let you look at it tomorrow."

She clicked her tongue as she handed him a pile of clothes and pushed him toward the bathroom. "I would like to see for myself. I'll be careful not to hurt you."

Jake shut the door behind him and locked it.

"*Señor* Jake!"

"I'm already naked!" Jake shouted. "I'll be out in a minute."

He heard her mumbling Spanish as she walked away, probably asking God to bless his soul like she did many times a day.

Jake didn't need her god to bless his soul. He'd already been blessed.

When he was sure she had really left, he unwrapped the thick padding of gauze and studied the inside of his arm. The burn was really gone. If Aiden found out, he'd want to know how. And if Jake told him, Aiden would discover what the shadows had put on Jake's chest.

A symbol.

Jake's arm had been completely healed by the time he got back to the house after his meeting with the shadow figure. He knew Aiden had done something to stop Jake's fast-healing ability, so that the burn would heal at a normal rate. Not wanting to defy Aiden's expectations, Jake had pretended the burn was still there. It had been easy to find bandages and wrap his arm himself, but Antonia had caught an earful from Aiden the next day for not dressing Jake's wound. Jake had almost jumped to her defense until he remembered what happened to his first nanny when he'd defended her. Now Jake watched in silence when Aiden disciplined the staff.

Maybe that would change soon.

The real surprise was under Jake's shirt. His chest had been swollen and red the first day, but it had gone away to reveal the symbol from his dream—two circles, overlapping in the center and making a weird-looking, sideways eight.

Mommy had marks on her back and Jake had given Will his mark of The Chosen One, but now Jake had a mark of his own and it made him happy.

Except Aiden couldn't know anything about it.

Aiden would be furious if he found out Jake had talked to the shadows, let alone accepted their *gift*. The fact that Marcus had encouraged him to befriend the shadows was proof enough. He needed to keep his mark hidden as long as possible and although Antonia would never get him in trouble on purpose, if she knew about it, there was no way she could keep it from Aiden. Jake had been practicing hiding her thoughts when Aiden was around, but Jake couldn't be sure it actually worked. He couldn't take the chance.

Jake liked Antonia. Since he couldn't have Mommy, Antonia was the next best thing. Jake didn't want anything to happen to her, a fact he kept buried deep in his mind so Aiden wouldn't use it to punish him. He had to hide the mark on his chest from Antonia. Thankfully, he didn't have much longer to hide it.

Jake knew that time was running out. Raphael had come back last night. Jake had snuck down to hear them talking in the living room. Even though he couldn't hear everything, he'd figured out that Raphael was frustrated because he couldn't find Mommy and Will.

Raphael had shouted at Aiden about having a little over a week until the end. Aiden mumbled something to make Raphael stop shouting, but Jake still felt Raphael's anger rippling into the hall. Leaning against the door frame, Jake let a smile lift the corners of his mouth. He was glad

Raphael was mad. Jake hated Raphael and someday he'd kill Raphael for what he'd done to Mommy. Sometimes when Jake practiced, he pretended he was fighting Raphael.

The other times he pretended it was Will.

Will was harder. Jake mostly liked him. Will had been nice to Jake, teaching him how to play the peg game and buying him a book. But most of all Will loved Mommy almost as much as Jake did. While that should have made Jake happy, the mark on his chest turned icy with jealousy instead. Part of Jake had changed since the shadow had given him his gift. Everything was darker and cold. So cold his insides sometimes burned, like the walk-in freezer in one of the restaurants Mommy had worked at once.

"*Señor* Jake!" Antonia stood outside his door, pounding on the wood. "I have a key and I will open this door if you do not do it yourself."

"I'm naked!"

"I have cared for other little boys. You have nothing I have not seen before."

Jake traced the circles on his chest before lowering his pajama shirt and wrapping his arm with clean gauze.

The door opened and Antonia's face peered in the crack. "I thought you said you were naked. You are still in your pajamas."

"I put them back on."

She scowled, then shook her head. "You are hiding something from me, probably what's under that bandage. I would check right now, but your *abuelo* is in a hurry to leave." Her hand reached into her pocket, her rosary beads clinking. "We do not want to make him angry."

If they were late, Aiden would blame it on her. "I'll hurry, Antonia."

She kissed his head. "You are a good boy." Her hand ruffled his hair then she turned to leave.

Fear squeezed Jake's lungs, making it difficult to breathe. Antonia didn't know what was under his bandage, but she knew he was hiding something.

It didn't matter if she knew his secret or not. The fact she knew he kept a secret meant that Antonia wasn't safe.

***

It has become a daily ritual. After she and Will drove for hours, they checked into a motel and Emma searched the news channels. She wasn't even sure what she was looking for. Signs that the world was in chaos? Signs that it wasn't?

Even though she was exhausted, she felt stronger. Her nausea had lessened and to her relief, Will rarely acknowledged the pregnancy, focusing on her training instead. He was relentless, pushing her harder than she'd ever been pushed before. She had made progress—but whether or not it was enough remained to be seen.

They'd tried sparring, but their joining must have triggered a protective failsafe that kept them from harming one another. Whenever they tried, their power faded, which worried her. They still didn't know what would happen if one of them died. Did the other die too?

But what worried her most about their joining failsafe was that it meant they couldn't kill one another in the final battle. If the final three were she, Will, and Jake, then Jake would have to kill one of them to end the game. Not an acceptable alternative.

She had to trust Will to come up with something, but whenever she quizzed Will about his plan he refused to tell her, although he swore he was working on one.

Alex Warren's smiling face appeared on TV. "And now in political news, Senator Phillip Warren's son is back on the campaign trail."

Will looked up from his laptop. "What the hell?"

Turning up the sound, Emma scooted next to Will.

"The younger Warren has several stops planned in the Midwest. Alex Warren will attend a function in Cincinnati tomorrow morning and then move to St. Louis for a fundraiser dinner tomorrow night."

Leaning over the keyboard, Will's mouth pursed. "We're going to St. Louis."

"*What?*"

"Alex has the book and we need it."

"Will, there's nothing in the book."

Will kept his eyes on the computer screen. "There wasn't the last time we looked, but there might be today. That thing changes to reflect the most current rules and we need it."

"Will—"

His head jerked up, his eyes hard. "You said you wanted a plan. Do you still want one?"

She did, but his tone suggested otherwise. "Yes."

"The first part of our plan is to go to St. Louis, steal the book, and kill Alex."

The blood rushed to her feet, leaving her light headed. "Kill Alex?"

"We should have done it the morning he found us in California. It would save us this aggravation."

"I don't know if I can kill him."

"Then *I'll* kill him, but we need the experience of fighting him. I still think he's the weakest so he'll be good practice." He typed on the laptop keyboard. "It's a fifteen-hour drive and the political dinner is at seven. It's almost three o'clock now. We have plenty of time if we drive straight through and it'll give us a chance to check out the hotel."

She stood up, lifting her hand to her forehead. "You're serious?"

His eyes were cold and calculated. "You really thought I wasn't?"

This Will scared her. She'd seen a glimpse of him in Colorado when the Cavallo had sent men to kill her while they hid in the cabin in the woods. But he did this for her and the baby and for Jake. That had to mean something, didn't it? And in the end, Alex would try to kill them too.

But wasn't most evil birthed from justification?

This was a game with only two winners and it was inevitable that Emma would bloody her hands. She'd never do it to save herself, and she wasn't sure she'd even do it for the baby. Emma felt a mixture of horror and self-recrimination about that, but there were only two people who could compel her to throw herself into the mire of perversion. She knew less than a week ago that she'd lose her soul in the process of saving them. But it was one thing to know it was coming and another to actually do it.

"So do you want to leave now?"

"I need to do some research first."

She flipped channels hoping to find something to take her mind off the situation, but only came across soap operas and talk shows. Closing her eyes in frustration, she reached out to Jake, surprised that she actually felt something when she concentrated. He was worried and scared.

"Okay, I think I have something."

Will jolted her back to the present.

"When we get to St. Louis, we'll canvass the area where he's staying. His schedule shows that he's spending the night at the Crescent Hotel, although from what I've gathered, schedule changes on the campaign trail aren't that uncommon. That means we'll have to keep a close eye on his itinerary. In a perfect world, we'd draw him away from the city, but I don't see how that's going to happen since he's back in the public eye."

Emma sat down on the bed. He talked about this so matter-of-factly.

Will looked up from his laptop, his face expressionless. "You might not like the next part, and neither do I, but I think it's our best option."

While she didn't like the sound of that, she nodded. "Okay."

"I want you to contact him and tell him that you've changed your mind about me and that you want to talk to him about what your options are."

"You're asking me to lie to him?"

His steely eyes held hers. "Yes."

She shook her head. "Not only no, but hell no."

"Emma, I know how you feel about lying and promises—"

"Then how can you ask me to do this, Will?"

His voice hardened. "Because we are at war, Emma. When you are at war, you use every trick in the book to win. Where do you think the term *all's fair in love and war* came from?"

"I'm sure Hitler saw it the exact same way when he built all those concentration camps."

Will released an exasperated sigh. "That is not even close to the same thing, Emma. Alex is a monster. He raped you. He kidnapped your son. He's killed the previous version of you over and over again." He ran a hand through his hair, closing his laptop. "Honestly, I'm scared to send you to him. For all I know he'll try to kill you the moment he sees you."

"Then why do it?"

"Because the odds are greater that he won't. He didn't kill you in California—he didn't even try. If he thinks he has a snowball's chance in hell at getting you to help him, he'll give you the time to talk to him."

"So then what? Alex and I sit down for tea and you sneak in and slit his throat?" Her words were harsher than she meant.

His eyes cold, he remained silent, watching her.

"Oh, my God."

Will groaned. "Emma, we're going to St. Louis to kill him. You know this."

"It doesn't mean I have to like it," she said through clenched teeth. Why was she getting angry with him? This wasn't Will's fault and although the logical part of her knew this was a good plan, the decent, humane side of her screamed in protest.

"It doesn't mean I like it either. I've already told you that. But it has to be done. And for the record, I'd do this even if I wasn't the son of Water and had no stake in the outcome other than your and Jake's survival."

"You'd kill him because of me?"

"It's not the first time I've killed for you and I guarantee it won't be the last."

How did her life get so fucked up that she would let the man she loved pledge to kill for her? She reminded herself that none of this was her fault, but she also knew the nightmares Will lived with and the coming days would only add to them. If he was willing to do this, who was she to stand in judgment? "So, my job is to set him up. Your job is to kill him. Do you really think it will be that easy?"

Relief flickered in his eyes before the hardness replaced it. "While I hope so, I doubt it. Look what you did to Raphael in that warehouse in Morgantown, and it didn't stop him."

"That night in the woods after you had lost your memory, Raphael told me that we could be killed by Kramer's men and if we died, we weren't coming back. It might be *harder* to kill elementals since they can heal themselves, but they can obviously be killed. Maybe if they're weakened, they won't have the energy to repair their wounds."

He studied her, raising his eyebrows in surprise. "You've actually given this thought?"

She shot him a glare. "Thinking about how to kill them? No. I've been thinking about how to help you if you're injured and weak. I think I can use my power to help you."

"No, it took too much out of you when you healed James back in Morgantown. We can't risk you being that weak in a fight."

"I'm stronger now. I can do it."

"Let's hope it won't come to that. We'll get rid of him and he—"

"*He* has a name. His name is Alex. If we're going to kill him, at least say his name."

Will's temper snapped. "Goddamnit, Emma. I'm not your enemy here. For fuck's sake, stop treating me like I am. We have to work together on this and we won't make any progress if you're fighting me every step of the way. If you have another idea, I'm all ears. If not, then agree to help me."

She closed her eyes. "I *know*. I'm sorry."

"I'll do anything I can to save you, even if it's ugly. But know this: If I wasn't sure we needed to do this, we wouldn't. You know yourself that killing someone comes with a price you pay with your soul."

"That's what I'm afraid of."

CHAPTER ELEVEN

JAKE stood next to Aiden on a busy street corner. The sun burned the top of his head and sweat dripped down his neck, making his t-shirt stick to his back. The skin under his bandage itched, but he resisted the urge to scratch.

"This is an experiment," Aiden said, a happy tone in his voice, a clue that something bad was about to happen. "It's a test to see what we can do together." He wore his grin that looked all wrong.

Dread prickled the back of Jake's neck. He and Aiden had only practiced dangerous things. With so many people around, someone would probably get hurt.

Aiden lowered his gaze and smiled. It looked more real, but evil filled his eyes. "There's no reason to be afraid, Jake. I assure you if you cooperate, you will be safe and sound. Perhaps you'll even get to see your mother sooner."

Was Aiden tricking him? Jake kept the thought buried deep in his head and Aiden squinted in confusion.

Aiden expected a reaction and Jake hadn't given one. He quickly let himself think of seeing Mommy, the happiness at the possibility, the sadness he wasn't with her.

Aiden's face brightened. "I knew that would make you happy."

They continued to wait on the corner as people brushed past, hurrying to where they needed to go. Although Jake was glad to put off causing destruction, he was confused about why Aiden was waiting.

"Patience, young Jacob."

Ten minutes later, Raphael appeared around the corner, his black curls stuck to his forehead and irritation wrinkling his nose. "You couldn't pick somewhere cooler? We have to go to the godforsaken South." He swiped the sweat off his brow. "You know I hate it here."

"Then why do you have your estate in Tennessee?"

Raphael's jaw clenched. "I don't want to talk about it."

"The sooner you let Emmanuella go, the happier you'll be."

His mother's name got Jake's attention.

Raphael's eyes widened and filled with rage. He took a step closer, his hands clenched at his side. "She was your *daughter*, Aiden. How can you be so callous?"

Aiden shrugged. "She was no longer needed. Everyone is replaceable."

Jake didn't understand. Aiden had another daughter?

Putting his hand on Jake's head, Aiden lowered his voice. "Little ears, Raphael. No need to talk about such unpleasantries around Jake."

"Why not? He has a right to know that his mother is your replacement daughter."

"Enough." Aiden's voice wasn't loud, but the tone made it clear the subject was closed.

Jake buried his thoughts deep in his head. Mommy was a replacement? And if Aiden replaced his other daughter, did that mean he'd replace Mommy? Or Jake?

Putting his hands on his hips, Raphael walked in a circle, his anger washing over Jake. "Okay, whatever you say, Aiden. So why Little Rock?"

"I have my reasons."

Raphael looked around the street. "The city seems a little small to get much attention. I take it that *is* your intent."

"It's a good start. Emma will appreciate the significance."

Raphael turned to Aiden with a scowl. "If she even finds out. I suspect they're in the middle of nowhere."

"I don't expect Emma to show up today, and it may take her a few days to figure it out, but I expect her to see the correlation. And she will. Trust me." Aiden looked around, scrunching his face in disgust. "This really is a small city, but it'll have to do. Raphael, I want to see what you and Jake can do together."

Jake took a step back, stumbling on a crack in the sidewalk. He didn't want to do anything with Raphael.

If Aiden picked up Jake's thoughts, he ignored them. "Let's begin." Aiden clapped his hands together. "Jacob, Raphael is hot. I think we should cool him down with a nice storm."

Jake focused on the molecules in the sky, pushing his rising terror aside. Fear always made it harder for him to do what Aiden asked. But his worry was like tiny pinpricks poking his insides. There were too many things he didn't know, too many dangers lurking about. He didn't trust Aiden and he sure didn't trust Raphael, yet he had no choice but to do what he was told. There was no way Jake could stop Aiden, not yet. Trying would only get himself and other people hurt.

The shadows were his only hope. They were his friends now. He glanced down at the bandage on his arm. Someday they would help him show Aiden who was boss. Someday soon.

With Jake's purpose renewed, clouds appeared overhead, puffy white wisps that swirled into thick gray clouds. Within moments, a wind blew, dropping the temperature ten degrees.

Raphael's eyes glowed and he held his hands at his sides with his fingers spread apart. The ground vibrated under Jake's feet, building from a gentle hum to a steady shake. People on the street screamed and fumbled around, trying to stand. They held onto buildings and light posts, parking meters and cars.

Aiden's smile deepened.

A hairline crack split the sidewalk, spreading toward the street and widening until it was big enough to suck in cars.

Jake was scared as he struggled to stay on his feet, but the panic of the crowd frightened him more. Their screams filled his ears and set his nerves on end. They scrambled over one another trying to hide in stores and offices, though Jake wondered how safe that was since the buildings swayed. Across the street, the corner of a building split with a loud crack. Large pieces of concrete slid off, crushing a man on the sidewalk. His screams joined the others as his blood covered the concrete, running into the gutter.

Jake watched in horror, his mouth gaping. He'd never seen anyone die before. Well, someone who didn't deserve it. The men Will had shot trying to protect him had deserved it. And the men Aiden killed to take Jake away from the Bad Men had deserved it. But the man on the sidewalk was just walking down the street. Probably going home to his own little boy.

Jake's unbandaged arm began to burn and his gaze jerked up to Aiden's angry face.

"Concentrate." Aiden growled.

Shuddering, Jake focused on the air above him. His distraction had caused the storm to lessen. Jake pushed more energy into it and the wind increased as the sky darkened.

The burning sensation went away.

A little girl ran past Jake, her face red and wet with tears. Her long blond hair swung in the air as she swiveled her head. "Mommy!" she screamed over and over again.

Jake's tummy tightened and his breath caught in his throat.

She ran up to him and grabbed his hand. Blood trickled down the side of her face. Jake tried to pry himself out of her grasp, but she held tight. "I want my Mommy!"

A building across the street collapsed. Dust filled the air and Jake's lungs.

"*Mommy!*"

A woman ran up and snatched the girl into her arms. The girl still held Jake's hand, pulling him with her before she let go. Her mother cradled the girl to her chest, tying to cover her head from the falling debris.

Mommy.

The ache in Jake's heart exploded, and he gasped as pain and sadness rushed through his body. The little girl's mother saved her. Why didn't his mother save him?

Because of Will.

Anger mushroomed, filling his head until he saw red. The wind increased and a funnel cloud appeared, swooping down from the sky.

The screaming grew louder.

The earth continued to shake as rain fell, pounding the earth and stinging Jake's skin. People fell to their knees every time they tried to get up, yet Jake no longer had trouble standing. Jake looked down in surprise.

He was hovering inches off the ground.

Another building collapsed, smashing more people. Jake cast a worried look toward the girl and her mother, losing them in the crowd.

The tornado moved toward them, destroying stores and apartments in its wake. There were people in those buildings. *I'm killing people.* He sucked in his breath at the horror and the tornado began to lift off the ground.

Jake's arm burned.

Gritting his teeth, Jake fought back, in spite of the pain. He couldn't kill people. Killing people was wrong.

The heat moved up his arm.

Tears filled his eyes. Fear washed through him in thick, suffocating waves. How much longer could he hold out?

The tornado disappeared and the wind decreased, but Jake's entire body burned before the pain just as quickly vanished.

He fell to his knees, the ground shaking violently under him.

Do not defy me, Aiden said in his head.

Climbing to his feet, Jake ignored the people around him, not even caring when buildings and cars began to blow up. Aiden laughed, his eyes glowing. A man ran down the street screaming as flames licked up his back. Jake turned away. There was nothing he could do.

They continued their destruction until there was nothing left for as far as Jake could see. No building remained standing. Every car was smashed. Bodies littered the street.

Jake released the storm, his shoulders slouching from exhaustion. He'd never sustained one that long. He tried to ignore what his power had done.

His storm hadn't been nearly as harmful as Raphael's earthquake. But he couldn't deny he'd played a part.

Aiden grinned, a genuine smile of delight. "Yes. I believe this will work."

"So you'll join with me?" Raphael asked.

Snorting, Aiden shook his head. "Me? No. This was a test to see how well you and Jake work together."

Raphael stared at him for several seconds. "You expect me to join with a *child?*"

"Join? No, but fight with, yes. I want you and Jake to team up in the final battle."

Raphael narrowed his eyes and pointed at Jake. "First of all, destroying a city is one thing. You just work your magic with no one to stop you. But the battle will be entirely different. Someone's going to actually fight back and he's a child. What does he know about fighting?"

Aiden lifted an eyebrow with a grin.

Jake needed no prodding. He hated Raphael. He sent a strong wind toward him and Raphael flew backward, his body bending forward before he crashed into a pile of rubble.

Scrambling to his feet, Raphael lifted his arm and his eyes glowed. A crack split across the asphalt, sucking in the smashed cars and pieces of buildings in its path, heading for Jake.

Jake was tired from his storm but his hatred made him strong. He jumped out of the way of the crack, throwing fire at Raphael as he leapt into the air.

A gust of wind caught Raphael in mid-leap, tossing him against a partially collapsed wall. Raphael growled and the ground shook beneath Jake, and he fought to remain upright.

"Enough."

Ignoring the command, Jake continued his onslaught.

"*I said enough.*" Aiden's voice filled his head as well as the air.

Jake stood with both feet apart, his hands clenched at his sides, and his chest heaving as he struggled to catch his breath. It had felt good to release his hatred with his power, but he was frustrated that Aiden made him stop.

Raphael lay sprawled on the ground, blood trailing down the side of his face.

Aiden laughed. "Still consider him a defenseless child?"

Jake couldn't help gloating, but he wished that Aiden had let him finish Raphael off.

Casting a glance at Jake, Aiden pursed his lips. "All in good time, Jake."

Raphael pushed off the ground, spitting a mouthful of blood onto the street.

"Tomorrow we shall do this again."

"Why the hell would I do that?" Raphael bent over, resting his elbows on his thighs.

"Because you need me and Jake and if you don't show, you'll lose any chance of aligning with us."

Raphael shook his head and groaned, raising his hand to his temple. "Maybe I'll just team up with Alex."

Aiden crossed his arms. "Doubtful. You hate him more than you hate me, which is saying something. Then there's the fact that Jake has more power in his little finger than Alex ever dreamed of possessing."

"There's three of us here and only two will survive. It's not hard to figure out which two you're planning to make it to the end with you."

Shaking his head, Aiden laughed. "You'll be dead if you don't. But if you help me, there might be a way for you to survive this with us."

"What the hell are you talking about? Only two survive."

"Oh, Raphael. Haven't you figured out by now that I always have a backup plan? Who do you want to be on your side at the end? Me and Jake? Or Alex?"

"And if I refuse you all?"

"Good luck surviving on your own. You'll have chosen a side. And it won't be mine."

Raising an eyebrow, Raphael winced and reached up to the cut on his forehead. "And how is that different than what we are now?"

"Because right now we're more like adversaries working toward the same goal."

"And that goal is…?"

"To keep Emma on her toes, to distract her from strengthening her power with Will. To hopefully create animosity between them."

"And Marcus?"

"Wherever Will is, I'm sure Marcus won't be far behind. Now that everything is out in the open, Marcus won't want to lose his precious leverage." Aiden looked at Jake with a grin. "And perhaps Jake will see his mother sooner."

Jake was scared about what else he'd have to do to make that happen.

Raphael traveled with them on the plane to their next city. He and Aiden sat at the front of the plane, on separate sides of the aisle, talking in hushed tones. Jake sat several rows back with Antonia. Her hands shook in her lap, clutching her rosary beads. Jake stared at the back of the seat in front of him, the little girl's face appearing in his mind as soon as he closed his eyes. Was she dead, smashed under some giant pieces of building? Did her blood run into what was left of the street? His insides crawled with unseen bugs, then they moved to his head, and he felt like he was going to scream.

Antonia took his hand and cooed soothing sounds into his ear. Jake leaned his head on her shoulder, pretending she was Mommy. He needed Antonia and that scared him.

The plane landed and Aiden told Raphael, Jake and Antonia to wait on the tarmac while he talked to the pilot.

Aiden didn't tell Jake where they were going, but if he didn't want Jake to know, he must have forgotten that Jake knew how to read. *Jackson, Mississippi* was on a sign over a building at the airport. The name seemed familiar.

"The fucking South again?" Raphael stood next to the plane, wiping his brow as Aiden climbed down the ladder. Sweat dampened his shirt.

"There's a reason," Aiden said in monotone.

"Want to share it?"

"Not especially."

Raphael's eyes hardened as put his hands on his hips. "You expect me to just blindly follow you around like a puppy?"

"Yes."

"I could leave right now."

"Then go."

Raphael's face pinched in hatred and frustration.

Jake wished he *would* leave. Being with Aiden was bad enough, but the anger and hostility coming off of Raphael was suffocating.

Raphael cursed in a language Jake didn't understand and stomped off to the building.

Aiden told Antonia to take Jake to the car waiting out front and to check into the hotel. They walked in silence, Antonia holding his hand in a firm grip. Jake glanced over his shoulder. Aiden stood outside the airport watching them, a blank expression on his face. When they climbed inside and the car door was closed, Jake watched out the back window, glad to see Aiden was gone.

Antonia's face relaxed and she pulled Jake into a hug. Jake was even more scared. As hard as he tried to hide his feelings for Antonia, Aiden knew.

"Antonia," he whispered. "Let's run away."

Her mouth dropped.

"We're alone. We can do it. We can go find my mommy. She'll take care of us."

"Shhh!" She clasped her hand over his mouth. "If *Señor* Aiden knew what you were saying—"

Jake pulled her hand down and lowered his voice. "Aiden's not here. He could be gone a long time. We can do it, Antonia. This is our chance."

"Jake, you must not say this. People are listening." She lifted her chin toward the front.

Jake looked up front. The driver's face was in the mirror, watching them with narrowed eyes.

Jake's body stiffened as his hatred rose, and he felt the need to hurt someone. "I can kill him."

Antonia's mouth dropped open as her face paled. "Jake, you cannot say such things."

"I'll protect you, Antonia. I won't let Aiden hurt you."

She pulled his head to her chest. "You are a brave boy. You have seen many things a boy your age should not see."

She didn't believe him.

He leaned back and stared into her eyes. He had to make her understand. "I can do it, Antonia. I can do it right now."

Her face softened and she brushed the hair off his forehead. "I know you are able to do this, Jacob. That is not the question. We are given many gifts in this world, but we must learn how to use them. You have much too much responsibility for a boy your age. You are asked to do things no one should do." A tear fell down her cheek. "I met your mother, even if only for a few moments, and I know that she loves you very much. I promised her that I would take care of you and that means that I must take care of you *in all things*. I cannot let you do this."

"But…"

"If we try to leave now, *Señor* Aiden *will* find us and he will hurt you. We must stay for now."

She was right, but he didn't have to like it.

Aiden wasn't back by dinner time, and Jake was grateful. He and Antonia ordered room service and ate in the hotel suite while he watched TV.

Jake was almost done eating when Aiden walked in the door, grinning. "You did very well today, Jake."

Jake didn't want to listen to Aiden gloat. He faked a yawn. "I'm tired. Can I go to bed?"

"Of course. You have another big day tomorrow."

Jake's stomach twisted into a pretzel. He stood and Antonia pushed him into one of the bedrooms. Shutting the door, she crossed herself and muttered something in Spanish as she unpacked his pajamas. She read him stories even though she knew he could read to himself. Her shaky hands jiggled the book. He didn't care that she treated him like a baby. It triggered fuzzy memories of Mommy. Before all the bad things happened.

When she finished, she cradled him in her arms and sang to him in Spanish as she brushed his hair with her fingers with one hand, the rosary beads clinking in her other.

He closed his eyes and pretended it was Mommy even though Antonia's lap was softer and she smelled different. Was Aiden tricking him? Would he let Jake be with Mommy again? Jake didn't trust Aiden. He needed to figure out how to get Mommy back on his own.

He knew how to make it happen.

Antonia sat in a chair next to the bed as she waited for him to fall asleep. He made his breath slow and steady and lay still even though he felt twitchy. He thought of his stuffed dog Rusty and how he'd make Aiden pay for burning him up. He'd make Aiden pay for a lot of things. And Raphael too.

And Will.

But he couldn't think about Will right now, because the good memories of him flooded Jake's mind and he needed the bad ones. He counted on the ugly ones to do what he needed to do later. He didn't want to kill Will, but he had to. It wasn't his fault. It was Aiden's.

He was back where he started.

After several minutes Jake's legs grew stiff from holding still so long, Antonia finally seemed satisfied he was asleep and left after placing a kiss on his forehead. When he was sure she was really gone, he sat up and ran to the door, locking it. He threw open the heavy curtains covering the window, then returned to his bed, sitting cross-legged in the middle. His bandage was still on his arm and he was surprised Antonia hadn't insisted on checking it again, but Antonia had been nervous and shaky since they left Little Rock. When Jake read her thoughts and sifted through the Spanish, he realized that Antonia knew that Aiden and Raphael had destroyed Little Rock, but she was unsure about Jake's involvement. She prayed Jake would be delivered from the *demonio* and his sweet soul would remain uncorrupted.

It was too late for that.

Stripping off his shirt, Jake stared at the mark on his chest, two black outlined, intersecting, sideways circles barely visible by the light coming through the window.

He smiled. He had a mark like Will.

His smile fell just as quickly. Will was one of the reasons he needed the mark.

The shadows on the wall didn't move. Since the shadow figure had marked him, they'd been quiet and still. Jake worried that they had forgotten him, then he remembered that the figure said he was supposed to call them.

"Shadows, move."

They started slowly, creeping around the room, then swirled faster and faster until they became a blur of motion. Jake covered his mouth and giggled with happiness. They hadn't forgotten him.

"Stop."

They instantly halted their movement, as though waiting for his next command. Moving shadows were a cool trick, but how would that help him get his mommy?

A shadow crept toward him and he heard a voice in his head. "We can do more…"

He was counting on that, but what more could they do?

"Watch."

The shadow moved across the floor and up to the window ledge. A bird sat outside the glass, snapping up an insect on the bricks.

Jake stood and moved closer to the window, careful not to startle the creature.

Fingers of gray reached toward the bird until shadows covered the animal's foot. The bird flapped its wings in a frenzy but remained on the ledge. Then it stopped moving and fell on its side.

Gasping, Jake ran to the window and cranked it open, expecting the bird to fly away. Instead it lay unmoving as he reached through and touched the bird with his finger, surprised by the icicles clinging to its feathers. That was impossible. The sun had set, but it was still hot outside.

When the shadow figure had given him the mark, it had felt cold. The shadow killed the bird with its coldness. Could it kill people too?

Could it kill elements?

CHAPTER TWELVE

THEY stopped for breakfast outside of St. Joseph just after sunrise. Will found a restaurant that advertised free wi-fi so he could check on the latest news about Alex's whereabouts.

The drive from Utah was grueling, and he was worried about Emma. After she'd told him she was pregnant days ago, they'd rarely acknowledged her condition. The way he'd pushed her to practice her power had to have been hard, but she never complained. They got up in the middle of the night, practiced, then drove hours to a new location, with Emma collapsing in the car and sleeping most of the day. Thankfully, her nausea seemed to have eased. But she hadn't had a decent night's sleep in a bed in over a week and now she'd just slept in the car.

They hadn't discussed their plan since they left Utah, and he knew she wasn't happy about it. He wished he could ease her into this, but there wasn't time. Planning Alex's assassination reminded Will of his tenure in Iraq, and he found it surprisingly easy to slip back into the role. He had to remind himself that they weren't a Marine unit. Emma had no training for this, and he needed to help her emotionally prepare for this because once they started, there was no room for wavering.

Emma sat across from him, looking out the window.

"Are you okay?"

Irritation flashed in her eyes but just as quickly faded. "Yeah, I'm fine. Sorry I haven't been very good company. I'm trying to adjust to the idea of—"

"Emma."

She shook her head. "Will, don't. I know you're right. I'm just trying to figure out how to do this and live with myself. But that's not your problem. It's mine."

"Your problems are mine, Emma." He leaned across the table and covered her hand. "I wish you didn't have to do this."

"There's no reason to rehash my feelings. Now tell me what your plan is."

He turned the laptop so she could see the screen. "Phillip Warren's campaign site says Alex gets into St. Louis mid-afternoon and stops by a school. The fundraiser dinner is scheduled for seven at the Crescent Hotel. He's spending the night in the same hotel, one of the reasons I picked this stop in his campaign. His next overnight stop is on the East Coast. Since it's too far to drive and neither of us can fly on a commercial plane without getting arrested, that rules that option out. So St. Louis it is."

"You want me to just pick up a phone and call him?"

"He gave you his number in Tennessee for a reason, Emma. Trust me. He wants you to call him."

"But he knows we've joined. Won't he suspect something's up?"

"Tell him we've had a fight. Tell him that I want to kill Jake. Tell him whatever it takes to make him believe you want to find a way to break our bond and team up with him."

She snorted. "You think I'm an actress now."

He grinned. "You fooled me into thinking you didn't like me when we first met."

Shaking her head, she laughed. "Sorry to disappoint there, player. I really didn't like you."

"Then pretend I'm that guy. Pretend I really do want to kill Jake. You'll have to be convincing."

Fear leached the color from her face. "You have to promise me you won't kill Jake."

His heart skipped a bit. "Emma. I would never kill Jake. You know that."

If possible, she turned even more pale. "You might face a choice, him or me." She gripped his hand, her nails digging into his skin. "You have to save him. Promise me."

The pancakes in his stomach revolted against their confined space. She was asking him to kill her. And as much as he wanted to save Jake, he wasn't sure he could do what she was asking. Was it even possible, considering their bond?

"I know that we're bound together now and I'm worried what happens to you if I die." She shifted in her seat and looked away. "The next time Marcus shows up, you need to ask him what would happen. His loyalty is to you, not me. But while I think he does want you to live, if nothing else so he can use you for whatever he has planned, I'm worried he sees you like Aiden sees me. Expendable."

"I'm not naïve enough to think Marcus is glad to have the son he's waited millenniums for, Emma. I know he's using me."

"But he wants you to live as long as possible. He'll sacrifice me to save you. We need to be sure that you'll survive."

"Emma, stop being so fatalistic."

"I want Jake to live. Will, you have to promise me."

"No. I will not promise to kill you. I can't." He raised his voice louder than he intended and a man two tables away glanced over with alarm. Will smiled and patted Emma's hand. "You take those video games way too seriously, sweetheart."

The man turned his attention back to his omelet.

Emma leaned forward, lowering her voice. "There's no point in doing any of this if Jake's going to die. I won't help you with Alex if you refuse to promise."

Will turned to the window, taking a breath. He understood her need to protect Jake at all costs, but her ability to dismiss him so easily because he refused to promise stung. "Don't be stupid, Emma. Let's say you don't help me and Alex and Raphael survive. You really think they're going to go easy on Jake because he's just a little boy? Hell, Emma. They're going to specifically target him."

Her eyes widened. "No."

"Yes." He took her icy hand in his. "The look on your face tells me that you know it's true. It's all the more reason to eliminate Alex and Raphael first. To make sure Jake survives."

Her face turned gray and she covered her mouth with her hand. "I have to go to the bathroom."

She stood, bumping into the table. The silverware rattled and Will grabbed a glass of water before it fell over as she bolted to the restroom.

Her nausea was probably morning sickness, but he groaned when he realized that he'd just told her that two grown men were going to target her son to kill him. What did he expect?

He laid cash on the table, packed up the laptop and headed down the hall. Knocking on the door, he pushed it open a crack.

***

"Emma? Are you okay?"

"Yeah." Emma retched again, trying not to think of all the germs covering the toilet she was trying desperately not to touch.

"Are you sure?" Will asked.

The nausea still rolled in her stomach and she gulped a deep breath of air.

"Emma?"

She threw up again until she dry-heaved. When she finished, she realized Will had come into the bathroom and was crouched behind her, rubbing her back. "This is the women's restroom, Will. What are you doing in here?"

"Checking on you." His hand worked a light circle on her back. "It's going to be okay."

He couldn't assure her of that, but it meant so much to her that he'd do anything to make her feel better. Even go into a women's restroom. She leaned back into him with a sigh.

He wrapped an arm around her waist. "Do you think you're okay now?"

Her stomach had seemed to settle. "Yeah, I think so."

Will helped her up and kissed her forehead. "I've got to check out one more thing on the computer before we go."

"I'm fine. You go do what you need to do and I'll clean up."

She watched him walk through the door, then rinsed out her mouth, refusing to look at her reflection in the mirror. She didn't need the reminder of how terrible she looked. Even though she'd napped in the car, she hadn't slept well in weeks. The now-constant dark circles under her eyes were hideous, and she sometimes wondered why Will still found her attractive. But she knew that his love for her ran deeper than her looks—it had even from the beginning. She'd thought he loved her because of his mark. Turned out that he loved her in spite of it. There was no doubt his life would have been a hell of a lot easier if he'd never accepted his assignment from the Vinco Potentia. And while she wished the entire nightmare had never happened, she was glad that if she had to live through it all, at least she had him to go through it with her.

Could she do what Will asked her to do? Could she lie to Alex and pretend to want to team up with him while Will snuck in and killed him? Could she watch him die in cold blood? Did she have a choice?

Will was right. Alex and Raphael would target Jake right away in a confrontation of power. And for Jake to make it to the final battle, Alex had to die so Jake could take his place. She couldn't wait for that to happen. Her job as a mother was to protect her son. At all costs.

Nausea bubbled in her stomach again and she knew it had nothing to do with her pregnancy. The thought of killing someone with premeditation made her physically ill. But she needed to suck it up. It had to be done. Maybe if she remembered the night Alex raped her she could go through with this. She forced herself to remember the cruelty in his eyes. The way he threw her to the ground and used her, leaving her laying there, half-undressed as he walked away. That man was a monster. He was the man she would kill. Her resolve returned until she remembered the Alex by the creek, giving her information about her power that no one else would. Or the man who helped her escape and took her to Will. That Alex seemed completely different.

No, he's the same man. He's his father's son. Manipulative and calculating. He was used to siding with the winner. Alex saw her as the winning side, even that night at the creek. Maybe especially that night by the creek when he realized how strong she was. He was using her. Just like everyone else in her life.

Everyone except Will.

She'd stayed in the bathroom too long. Sure her guts were under control, she found Will at their table, hunched over the laptop. His drawn mouth was her first clue something was wrong. He glanced up at her and forced a smile, reaching for the computer's lid to close it.

Reaching for his hand, she stopped him. "What don't you want me to see?"

"Nothing."

She slid in next to him on the booth seat, and he moved to make room for her while keeping the screen turned away.

"It's a wonder you made a career out of playing other people, because you are so fucking obvious right now. If this were a real job, you'd be dead."

His grip tightened as she tugged on the computer. "Wow. That was harsh."

"I order you to let me see what you were looking at."

Will chuckled, but his eyes were serious. "Princess, your ordering powers disappeared when my mark faded."

"Then respect me enough to stop hiding things from me."

His hold loosened, but he still held the screen at an angle. "Emma. Trust me. You don't want to see this."

Her heart plummeted to the floor. Whatever he was looking at had to do with Jake. She grabbed the laptop, and Will released his hold.

Photos of rubble filled the screen, columns of smoke scattered across the debris. The headline read *Downtown Little Rock Destroyed by Earthquake and Freak Storm.*

Her mouth dropped open as she tried to put the information together. What was the likelihood of an earthquake and a storm at the same time? And, according to the information in the article, the damage had been neatly contained to a four-block area. Earthquakes didn't behave that way and neither did storms. And they sure as hell didn't behave that way together.

"What were Raphael and Alex doing together in Little Rock? Was Alex at a campaign stop there? That's a little risky, isn't it? Won't the media put it together?"

"Emma…Alex was in Boston yesterday."

"Then how did he pull this off? Have they teamed up? Is our trap for Alex going to work now?" Hysteria made her voice an octave higher.

"Emma. You know this wasn't Alex."

The muscles in her shoulder blades knotted, shooting spasms down her back. "The earthquake was Raphael. This has his name all over it. The storm must have been a fluke. Or…" She struggled to catch her breath. "He timed it to coincide with a storm. To make it look like Alex was there."

Will didn't answer, pity in his eyes.

"No." She shook her head. "*No.*"

He closed the laptop and stuffed it into the backpack. "Let's go. You can rest in the car and we need to get moving."

She stood, trying to pull herself together. "But it's my turn to drive."

"It's okay. Let's just go." He took her hand and led her out the doors into the parking lot. Her reactions were a half second off and she stumbled at the curb.

When Jake was born, she'd promised to make his life better then hers. She promised that he'd know love and security. Now he had neither. Her son had destroyed a city. He'd been forced to kill innocent people. She'd failed him over and over again. And she was done.

She jerked out of Will's grasp. "No. We're not going to get into the car and pretend like everything is okay. *Everything is not okay.*"

"Emma, don't."

"*Don't?*"

He closed his eyes.

She ignored the exhaustion that covered his face. She didn't give a fuck how exhausted he was. "What the hell is my son doing with Raphael?"

"I…" His mouth opened then he closed it. "I don't know."

She brushed past him. "I'll drive. I know how to get to Little Rock from here."

"No, Emma. We're not going to Little Rock." His voice was soft but firm.

She spun around to face him. "*Excuse me?* Did you just say *no?* That monster has my son! Jake gets passed from evil being to evil being and what the hell am I doing about it? Nothing. I'm sitting around doing *nothing!*"

Will closed the distance between them. "Emma, I know you want to go to Jake, but think about this for a minute. What if Raphael somehow knows our plans? He obviously wouldn't want us to create a truce with Alex. Maybe this is his way of keeping us from doing that."

"Then he got his wish. Let's go." She spun to open the car door.

"No." He pulled her back. "We're going through with our plan."

She jerked out of his hold. "Fuck our plan. I'm getting my son. You can do whatever the hell you want."

His shoulders slumped in frustration. "Emma, *stop* and think this through. What if it's a trap? What if Raphael is thinking like you and I are? What if he decided to eliminate his threat? He could have staged this to draw us to him."

"Then it's working. Let's go."

"Emma." He reached a hand toward her but she took a step back.

"How did Raphael get Jake?" She hated that her voice broke. She couldn't fall apart. She had to be strong.

"You don't know that Raphael has him."

"Yes. I *do*." Did he really think she was an idiot? "Do you think Aiden handed him over? Did they have a fight? I can't see Aiden just giving Jake up." She choked on her frustration and fear. "*How did this happen?*"

He ran a hand through his hair. "I don't know." He reached for her arm again and pulled her to him.

She leaned into his chest. Fear swept through her, washing away all thought. "Raphael is angry with me. What if he's taking it out on Jake? What if he's hurting him?"

"Don't do this to yourself, Emma."

How could she not do this to herself? That psycho had her son. Did he have the power over Jake that he'd had over her? Had he forced Jake to join with him? A gasp of horror escaped her, then she squared her shoulders. "We have to go to Little Rock. We have to get him from Raphael." Before it was too late.

Will's face hardened. "He won't be there and you know it."

"But what if he is?"

"Raphael's not going to stick around with Jake and all that media. He seems more like a hit-and-run kind of guy. So if he's not there, where do we go?"

She tried to think like Raphael, what little she knew, but her mind was lost in a fog. Why hadn't she paid closer attention when she was with him? "I don't know. Tennessee? He took me there after you lost your mark." Her panic bled into her words.

"What if he's not there? What if he's gone west? Then we've just traveled farther away from him, Emma. I know you're upset. I know this is killing you, but we can't find Raphael or Jake if we don't know where they are."

"What am I supposed to do?" Her voice rose from her anguish. Raphael hated her now that she'd joined with Will. Raphael might hurt Jake just to make her suffer.

Lowering his face to hers, Will spoke softly. "Let's just go after Alex first. Raphael needs Alex more than ever. There's a good chance Alex might know where he is."

Every part of her screamed no. Once again, she was abandoning her son. But as hard as it was to admit, Will was right. She had no real choice. What if Alex knew where Jake was? What if he was part of it? For the first time since Will came up with his plan to confront Alex, Emma was completely on board. Fighting back tears, she nodded.

She'd torture Alex herself if it meant finding her son.

CHAPTER THIRTEEN

WILL was amazed that they'd made good time getting to St. Louis. Construction was always an issue on I-70, but it was as if the gods were favoring them today. Will almost snorted at the thought. The manipulative elemental men controlling their lives were the only gods he knew, and they were definitely not favoring him or Emma.

If Raphael really had taken Jake from Aiden and forced him to destroy a city to upset his mother, it was not only effective, but a move Will admired as a military leader. Emma was distracted and distraught—two things neither of them could afford at the moment. It not only weakened their bond but also their defenses. The move was the perfect sabotage, not that he'd confess such a thing to Emma. He'd rather that she continue focusing her anger on something else. Or in this case, someone else.

Jake's possible change of captors was the perfect excuse for her to see Alex. She was more than eager to talk to him now. While Will was grateful he didn't have to worry about her forcing an excuse to see Alex, at the moment, he was more worried that she'd cause a scene. He doubted that killing Alex would be easy, but he'd hoped to use Emma's energy control over the Air element to subdue him until Will could complete the job. He hadn't told Emma that part of the plan yet, unsure she'd go along with it. But now he wouldn't put it past her to subdue Alex and kill him herself.

Will had no problem with that, but it needed to be done as quietly as possible so they'd have time to escape. Emma's emotions could be a double-edged sword.

He checked them into a hotel several blocks from where Alex was staying. It was nicer than their usual accommodations, but it was close to Alex. If it came to a chase, Will hoped they'd be able to lose their pursuers on foot without having to resort to guns or using their powers. He planned to make his move in the middle of the night, his goal to have only one fatality. But if it came to a chase, he wanted as few people as possible in the line of fire.

In South Dakota, it had been easy to avoid civilian casualties. The compound they broke into was in the middle of nowhere. But Albuquerque was proof of what happened when elements were let loose to fight, and apparently Little Rock too. He didn't want a repeat in St. Louis. He was sure Emma couldn't handle the guilt, and he wasn't sure he could either. The memories of the fire in the Iraqi school still lurked at the edges of his mind.

For the first time since coming up with his plan to kill Alex, Will began to question his decision. Not the death sentence for Alex, but where to carry it out. St. Louis was far from ideal, but it was the least populated area Alex would be in for the next few days, as well as the closest. He had to look at it from a military perspective. If he didn't kill Alex now, the death count could rise much higher. And killing Alex would put Jake into the final four.

What if the final battle happened in a densely populated area like Atlanta? Or New York City? Or even Hong Kong? Who was to say they'd stay on the North

American continent? Every military operation figured in the possibility of collateral damage. This was no different.

As soon as she entered the hotel room, Emma turned on the television and sat on the edge of the bed. It only took a couple of clicks of the remote for her to find news coverage of the Little Rock disaster. Reports flooded all the major networks.

Will sat next to her and wrapped an arm around her back, relieved that she didn't shrug it off.

The footage showed more of the same destruction, news crews filming as everyone speculated about what had happened.

The camera cut to an older man behind a desk. "While seismologists are attributing the quake to the New Madrid fault line, no one can explain how a 7.6 magnitude quake could be isolated to a four-block-square area. For answers we turn to Dr. Renee Sever with The Simmons Institute."

The camera cut to a woman standing in front of a geological map.

"Dr. Sever, can you explain what happened in Little Rock?"

A grim smile tightened her mouth. "This is unprecedented. We have no scientific explanation for this occurrence. It goes against the laws of physics for a quake of this magnitude to be restricted to such a localized area."

"But there was damage and additional quakes miles away from the epicenter."

"True, but we would have expected the ripples of a quake this size to be larger in both intensity and distance.

It's as though very specific energy was centralized in one area."

The camera cut to the news anchor. He leaned forward on his desk, toward the camera, resting his weight on his arm. "But how do you explain the storm?"

The doctor's eyes widened. "I'm a seismologist, not a meteorologist, but I would say this was a once-in-a-trillion incident. It was purely coincidence, plain and simple. Call it bad timing or extremely bad luck."

"Doctor, you call this a one-in-a-trillion incident, but this same thing happened in Albuquerque a week ago."

She crossed her arms over her chest. "Both locations are known to be close to fault lines. It's not uncommon for quakes to occur on multiple faults."

"Some experts are suggesting terrorist warfare was used to create the devastation in Albuquerque. Surveillance footage taken from a bank shows a man and a woman standing still in the middle of the destruction while everyone else is running away."

They didn't show the footage, and Will wondered how clear the images were. Did the authorities know it was Emma? Did they have a clear image of her face?

"There is no technology in existence capable of creating such devastation."

"How do you explain the storms in both locations at the same time?"

"Conspiracy theorists are having a field day with this, but I assure you that this is a fluke. It's Albuquerque's monsoon season. Sporadic storms are a common occurrence in August."

The coverage continued, with reporters interviewing credentialed experts, all offering different theories. The news team cut to images of groups standing on street corners with signs reading "The End is Near" and "Sinners Repent. Judgment Day is Here." Some attributed the disasters to the devastation predicted by the ancient Mayan calendar. Others cited aliens.

Emma's back was rigid as she watched with a glazed look. Will took the remote from her clenched hand and turned off the TV. He expected some protest from her, but she sat still for several moments. He would have preferred an emotional outburst to the icy silence.

She stood. "What do we need to do to see Alex?"

"Do you want to talk about what happened in Little Rock?"

Lifting an eyebrow, she stared at him. "What the fuck is there to talk about? Raphael not only had my son but forced him to help kill hundreds of people. I need to find Jake, and Alex might know where he is. Tell me what we have to do to get to him, and what I need to do once we find him."

Will heaved a sigh and grabbed the laptop. "Ideally, we would have gotten here at least a day earlier and checked out the physical location. I've tried to find some schematics online but haven't been able to find anything yet. If James were here…" He cleared his throat. "He might have been able to find them. We could consider calling James to see if he could help."

"No James."

He didn't blame her. The last time they were together, James had wanted to hand her over to the Vinco Potentia, but Will knew James had tried to keep him safe. In fact, James had put his life on the line to help Will and Emma escape from the parking garage. He'd dragged James into this mess back in July when he'd shown up on his driveway with broken ribs, but James was far from an innocent victim. He'd been working with the Vinco Potentia the entire time to hand Emma over. Nevertheless, Will couldn't ignore the only reason James had done any of it.

To save Will.

He didn't want to involve James, but Will and Emma were facing threats from lots of fronts and there were only two of them. Granted, they hadn't seen the Vinco Potentia in over a week, but he wasn't naïve enough to stop considering them a threat. He hoped to get more information about them from Alex too. "No James for now."

Anger flashed in her eyes.

He was prepared for another fight, but she waited in silence. *Choose your battles.* It looked like Emma had chosen hers.

"I'd like to examine the property in person, but I'm concerned they will be watching for us and know what we look like. For all we know, they have footage of you from Albuquerque with Raphael. But I need to know the weak points in Alex's security team, and you and I can't go together. One of us in a disguise could likely get away with it, but Alex is sure to have given our physical descriptions and photos to his men. If we're together, they're bound to discover us, but if we split up, we might be able to pull it off."

"So then we split up."

He hesitated.

She rolled her eyes. "Don't you pull that macho caveman shit on me now. I've pulled your ass out of more than one frying pan, and you know it. I can take care of myself."

Emma was right, but the thought of letting her walk alone into a potentially dangerous situation scared the shit out of him.

"What do we need to do?"

He made himself ignore his fear and treat this like any other mission. Booting up the computer, he loaded the page with a rough diagram of the hotel layout. "The dinner is going to be in the grand ballroom. We obviously don't want to try anything then. I need to find out what room Alex is staying in, and for security reasons that's going to be a closely guarded secret. The best way to find that out is for one or both of us to dress up as hotel employees."

"But I thought you wanted me to contact Alex and tell him I want to talk. Why don't I get him to tell me his hotel room?"

"For one thing, I'm not sure he'll tell you. He won't exactly trust your motives. Second, it would alert him to our presence. If he's smart, he'll put out extra security. I suggest we get some information on his room first, then you call him."

"So you want us both to dress up and sneak around the hotel first?"

"Yeah."

"Why don't you just pull out the Will charisma and charm the pants off some female employee?"

His jaw dropped. "You can't be serious."

"I don't want you to literally charm her pants *off*, but yes. Why not channel that power?"

He processed her suggestion for several seconds. It might work. "You don't care?"

"You're coming back to me, right? I have a mark on my back that says you are. Just don't take it too far."

Pulling her against his chest, he lifted her chin to look into his eyes. "You know there's no one but you."

Her eyes softened for the first time since that morning. "I know, and I'm counting on that. Otherwise, I wouldn't have suggested it."

"So you'll stay here while I go do this."

"No. I'm going to do my own snooping. We just won't be together."

"Wait—"

"Look, we both know how persuasive you can be, but it won't hurt for both of us to do this. Plus, I plan to look around so I'll know the layout of the hotel in case something goes wrong. And we've learned from past experience that things tend to go wrong. If I've gone through the stairwells and backdoors myself, I'll have a better chance of getting away if it comes to that."

"Emma, I'm going to be with you when we go after Alex."

"I know, but we might need to split up. I want to be able to do this on my own if I have to."

He wanted to argue with her, but she had a point.

"But I'm going to shower first. I've been in a car for a day and a half. I stink and I look like crap." She walked into the bathroom and shut the door.

He was glad she wasn't as distraught and angry as before, but her one-eighty was a concern. What was going through her head? He wanted to ask, but the closed door told him a discussion wasn't an option. He knew she wouldn't tell him until she was ready.

Forty-five minutes later, Emma was eager to leave the room, but Will held her back with last-minute instructions.

"I don't know what they'll be expecting from either of us, but I doubt they'll be expecting you to look like this."

Will had gone to the hotel gift shop while she showered and bought her a floppy hat, sunglasses, and a purse. She dressed in a skirt and button-down blouse, with a little makeup and her hair loose. She looked different than Alex was used to seeing her. Will was counting on that.

"You walk the hotel, get familiar with the exits, and then come back."

"I'll be fine, Will."

He put a handgun in her purse. "I know, but I can still worry."

She reached up on tiptoes and kissed him on the lips. "I'll be fine."

He slipped an arm around her back, holding her close to him. "You're not trained for this. This isn't a game. The Vinco Potentia's men could be waiting for you." His voice lowered. "I can't lose you, Emma."

"And I can't lose you, but we both know this is the right thing for me to do. They don't know we're here. Alex probably thinks you and I are hiding somewhere preparing for the final battle. Or going after Raphael. Don't worry." She kissed him again. "*You're* the one who needs to be careful."

"I'm the one who's trained for this."

"Still…" Pulling away from him, she reached for the door. "I'll see you back here in about an hour."

If you need me, call.

She nodded and left the room.

***

Emma walked through the lobby of the Crescent, displaying an air of confidence she didn't feel. She'd stuffed her fear for Jake into the recesses of her mind, focusing on the one thing that might help her find him. Alex.

Alex would most likely be staying in a suite and she knew the suites in most hotels were on the top floors. She headed for the elevator bank.

The doors opened and a couple emerged, arm in arm and obviously in love. Emma ignored the thought of Will that popped into her mind. She brushed past them and examined the elevator panel. As she suspected, the twentieth and twenty-first floors needed a key to gain access, so she pushed the button marked nineteen. The doors closed but a hand stuck through the crack, forcing them back open.

A man in a gray suit walked onto the elevator and turned to face the front. He ignored her, but his actions seemed too purposeful.

She tensed, the hairs on her arm tingling. He hadn't pushed a button on the panel.

The elevator stopped on the second floor and a family in wet swimsuits got on, dripping water onto the floor. The man in the suit wrinkled his nose and took a step closer to Emma. A little boy pressed for the fifteenth floor. The children shivered and chattered until they got off.

Emma considered getting off with them but knew it would look suspicious. She needed to see this through. The man didn't move away from her as the family exited.

The doors opened on her floor and he indicated she should go first. She hated to put her back to him but saw no other way around it. Stepping into the hall, she opened her purse and pretended to look for her room key. The man walked past her down the hall without looking back before he entered a room.

Relieved that she had overreacted, she headed the opposite direction, taking note of a utility closet halfway between the elevator and the end of the hallway. She saw the door to the stairwell, managed to slip inside without anyone noticing, and went up. The door to the twentieth floor was locked, but at the twenty-first, the knob turned. Hesitating, she peered through the crack and found an empty hall.

Emma doubted she'd be stopped if someone found her here. Then again, security might be tight with Alex's visit. She could just say she followed someone else off the elevator and got lost. Taking a deep breath, she eased through the door, half-expecting men with guns to jump out and attack her. All that greeted her was the soft hum of the air conditioning blowing from the vents overhead.

The muffled thud of her shoes echoed in the hall, and her heart rate sped up in anticipation. Of what, she wasn't sure. This was too easy. Too effortless. Surely if Alex was here security would be tighter, but he might be on the floor below. She'd stroll through the hall, make note of the closets and niches, and exit through the stairwell at the opposite end. Then she'd head down to the lower levels and check escape routes to the street.

The elevator dinged and the doors slid open as she approached. A quick glance inside the car revealed it was empty. She forced herself to calm down. Panicking wouldn't help anything. But what were the chances an empty elevator would open on a floor that required a key?

Three doors from the stairwell she felt a wave of power. The door to one of the rooms opened. Emma stopped in her tracks when she saw the man in the doorway.

Alex.

CHAPTER FOURTEEN

ALEX stood in the doorway wearing gray pants and a blue shirt, several buttons undone at the top. Leaning into the frame with an air of nonchalance, he gave her his television smile. "Hello, Emma. I've been expecting you."

She froze, her brain scrambling to form a coherent answer.

He took a step back. "Come on in."

"I…" None of the scenarios that she'd prepared for included this situation.

"Don't be shy. I take it you're here to see me?"

Honesty seemed the best way to go, to a certain extent. She took two steps toward him. "I didn't think it would be this easy to find you."

His eyes twinkled. "You knew right where to go."

"Lucky guess."

Motioning into the room, he grinned. "Lucky indeed. Come on in." He stepped into the suite as she approached, probably worried that she'd touch him.

He headed to a counter, turning his back to her. "Can I get you a drink?"

"No thanks." She walked inside, surprised to find she and Alex were the only people in the room. While she didn't know much about campaigning, everything she'd seen on TV or in movies showed lots of people working. "Where is everyone?"

"They're in our conference room wrapping up my speech." Alex grabbed a bottle of water from a mini-fridge and gestured to a chair. "Have a seat."

Emma sat next to a small table, folding her hands in her lap to hide her nerves.

"Where's Will?"

"How did you know I was here?"

Laughing, he unscrewed the bottle. "Are we playing this game again? I ask a question and you answer with a question of your own?"

She tilted her head, raising her eyebrows.

He took a long sip then studied her with an expressionless face. "You might be careful there. You no longer hold any bargaining cards, Emma."

"And yet you invited me in."

Grinning, he leaned back and crossed his legs. "I was curious."

"About...?"

"Why you would risk so much to see me."

Will had his own purpose for visiting Alex, but her reason trumped his. Other than the incident in Albuquerque, Alex had been semi-reasonable as of late. Of course, he'd hoped to join with her and that hope was gone. But even after he'd found out, he'd told her to come find him—so he must think her good for something. She hoped that something wasn't dead. Still, her questions wouldn't be unexpected. "I want to know where Jake is."

He opened his palms and tilted his head. "Haven't seen him since Montana."

"I think Raphael has him."

"What makes you say that?"

"I take it you weren't in Little Rock yesterday?"

"No. But you already know I was on the East Coast or you wouldn't be here."

"I think Raphael has Jake and together they destroyed four square blocks of Little Rock."

"The earthquake was caused by the New Madrid fault, Emma."

"You don't really believe that, do you?"

A boyish grin lit up his face. "No, but I've been practicing it for the media, trying to keep a serious face. They've been quite skeptical after Albuquerque." He winked.

"How could Raphael have gotten Jake from Aiden?"

Alex rolled his eyes. "I don't see how he could. Aiden is much stronger than Raphael, stronger than any of us. There's no way. Are you sure Raphael has him?"

"If you weren't in Little Rock, they have to be together. Otherwise, how do you explain what happened?"

"It was a freak storm."

Emma groaned. "A freak storm that just happened to occur when the earthquake hit?"

"Stranger things have happened."

"You know it was the two of them."

"What makes you think I know anything about it?"

"Raphael needs you now."

He shook his head. "Nope. Raphael has another plan."

"What is it?"

Alex's eyes narrowed. "How does it feel to think I have something you want, yet you're completely at my mercy?"

"I'm not completely at your mercy."

"Are you suggesting that you can touch me?" Alex leaned forward. "Go ahead and try it."

Indecision wound around her spine. Why would he suggest she touch him? If she still had power over him, the moment she touched him he'd be under her control. Was this a test?

She smiled and gave him a half-shrug. "I think I'll save it for when I really need it."

He sat back with a grin. "Suit yourself. Where's Will?"

"Not here."

He snorted. "Always one to state the obvious. Where is he?"

"I don't know." Technically, it was true.

"Why are you here?"

"Have you teamed up with Raphael?"

The corner of his mouth lifted into a lazy grin. "Sizing up your competition?"

"More like making a proposition."

His lips twisted as he looked out the window then back at her. "Go on."

Time to go with the original plan. She knew she should let Will know she'd found Alex, but she knew he'd be worried and possibly come search for her. She wanted to see what she could find out first. "I want to team up with you."

Alex laughed, then stood, shaking his head. "That's a little difficult given the fact you're already *taken*."

"Will and I don't see eye to eye on things. Since he found out about Marcus, his alliances have changed."

"How so?"

"I've never made a secret of my main goal: find and save Jake. Will's goal has never been certain. The only reason he wanted to find Jake was for me, but once he realized that his father was Water, his priorities changed. He now wants to rule with Marcus."

Alex rested his hands on the chair back, leaning forward. His eyes had a hard edge. "There's no way Will would leave you."

"He didn't. I left him." Also technically true.

"Why on earth would you do that when you moved heaven and earth to find him?"

"I told you—"

"Yeah, yeah." He scowled and waved his hand. "His priorities changed. I call bullshit."

Her breath stuck in her chest. Could she beat him in a fight? He'd insinuated that her touch no longer had an effect. Without that advantage, was she strong enough? Perhaps it was his way of psyching her out. "He wants to kill Jake."

Alex's face paled and he sat on the chair edge.

Did his reaction mean he actually felt some concern for Jake's safety? "I came to you because even though you haven't been part of Jake's life, you're still his father. And while you might be a full element like Aiden, I hope to God you're a better father than he is. We can't let Aiden use our son as a pawn, and I can't let Will or Raphael kill him."

"I'm surprised you thought to include me in this."

"You *are* his father."

"You made it pretty clear about a month ago that I didn't have the right to claim that title."

"I'm desperate." She was amazed how easily this came to her. Did she really mean it?

"I'm surprised you're being so honest with me."

"I'll do anything to save Jake, even if that means including you."

Alex's eyes glistened with unshed tears. "Thank you. You won't regret this."

Was his reaction genuine? Did he really care about Jake?

A grim smile lifted his mouth. "You look surprised."

"I am." Her voice choked on the lump in her throat. "You kidnapped him to use him against me."

"No to use against you, Emma. To get to you. I never would have hurt him." His eyes seemed to be pleading with hers. "I screwed up the first time I met you. You have no idea how much I regret that night. I knew there was no way you'd have anything to do with me unless I had something you wanted."

"He's just a little boy. How could you put him through that?"

"No, Emma. He's much more than that. I'm not sure you know what he's capable of."

She wiped a tear from her cheek. "I know he can make storms."

Shaking his head, he grimaced. "That's only a part of it. When he was with me in Montana, he hurt people."

"*No.*"

Alex's face lowered to hers. "Yes, Emma. He did. I'm not sure if he fully understood the implications of what he did. He's only five, so how could he? But he *killed* multiple men, Emma. On several different occasions."

Hysteria rose in her chest. Jake wouldn't do such a thing. Not sweet Jake.

Emma? Will's frantic voice filled her head.

"He didn't mean to." She had to believe it.

"Yes, he did mean to. But he was defending himself. It wasn't done out of malice."

Emma! She felt Will's panic.

I'm fine. Just give me a minute. She couldn't concentrate on both conversations at the same time and Alex was more pressing. "So you'll help me?"

"I wish you'd asked me a month ago."

Her anger flared. "Why didn't you tell me you wanted to help Jake after Aiden took him?" One more reason to be skeptical of his motives, although his concern seemed believable.

"I didn't think you'd believe me. Plus, you loved Will. I couldn't compete against that. Or Raphael. Are you telling me you no longer love Will?"

Even for the right reason, saying she didn't love Will felt like a betrayal. Her voice broke. "No, I'm saying I love my son more."

Alex took a deep breath as he considered her answer. "Fair enough."

"What are we going to do?" She wasn't sure she trusted him, but Jake was his son too. Could she count on any kind of fatherly bond from him or was he too much like Aiden?

He looked at his watch. "I have to go to a dinner in about an hour." Alex lifted his gaze to her face. "I'm not sure how we get around your bond to Will. Is it true that you know everything he thinks and vice versa?"

"No. Only what we chose to share."

He lifted his eyebrows. "Past tense?"

"The man wants to kill my son. You think I'm going to share what I'm doing with him?"

"And what makes you think he won't try to find you?"

"He made his choice very clear. And so did I."

"You two are connected now whether you want to be or not. I'm not even sure you're capable of harming one another, let alone living if one of you dies."

"I guess we'll find out." She released a half-laugh.

"Not funny." He remained silent for several moments. "He's not going to let you go so easily. He's going to come find you."

She didn't like where this was going.

"You need protection, Emma."

She glared at him and stood. "I didn't come here seeking protection for *me*. I want it for Jake. Are you going to help me save him or not?"

"Yes. I am."

"How are you going to do that, Alex? You're on the campaign trail shaking hands and holding babies. Why are you even doing this anyway? The end of the world as we know is about to happen and you're on the campaign trail. What the hell are you doing?"

His eyes softened. "I'm helping my father."

"What does that mean?"

He sighed and rubbed his chin. "Why do you think I stole the book?"

"To get an advantage over everyone else."

"Yeah, because I need one. Do you know why? I'm all alone in this. Aiden has Jake, and now Aiden's adopted Raphael into his fold. Then there's you and Will and Marcus. And that leaves me high and dry."

"Am I supposed to feel sorry for you?" Yet she did, even if she couldn't acknowledge it.

"For some reason I always thought you were the one with a heart."

"Maybe I was until you threw me on the ground and raped me." She needed to remind herself of that but antagonizing him wasn't going to help things. "I'm sorry."

He shook his head and took a gulp of water. "I deserve it." Putting the cap on the bottle, he looked up at her. "I took the book to see if I could find anything, some small rule or loophole, to help me beat you all. But there was nothing. So, I came back to help my father. In all the times I've been reborn, my human families have been unique. This time, my human father really loves me. Maybe I won't make it through the final battle, but perhaps I can help my father win the election. If there's anything left of the world once Aiden gets done with it." Sadness filled his eyes and his mouth twisted into a wry smile. "I bet you're finding that hard to believe, that I'd help someone."

She scooted closer to him. "No. It doesn't surprise me."

He leaned back, closing his eyes. "Part of me is glad this is almost over. I'm tired."

She stretched her hand across the table toward him. "Has it been hard?"

"It's been endless."

Thousands of years were such a big number it was hard to put it in perspective until she began to think about how many lifetimes that encompassed. Countless.

"How are you going to be able to help me? The cameras are on you twenty-four-seven. I'm not sure it's a good idea for the media to watch what we might be up to."

Alex sat up with a frown. "You underestimate me, Emma. But then again, you always have." He stood up and headed for the bedroom.

She started to protest that she'd never really had an opportunity to underestimate him, but she stopped. He was referring to Emmanuella, her predecessor.

"I have to go shower and get ready. We'll discuss this more after I finish with my political responsibilities."

"What time should I meet you back here?"

Alex smiled, and for the first time since she'd entered the room she felt unsafe. His eyes had an evil glint. "Oh, you're not going anywhere, Emma. I told you that I'm worried that Will is going to come find you and I intend to make sure you're safe. I'll have guards posted outside the door while I'm gone."

Her heart jumped into her throat and she forced her words to come out slowly. "Just the door?"

He laughed. "No, two guards at the door wouldn't even stop a human Will, let alone a Will with elemental power. But don't you worry about a thing." He walked toward her until they were inches apart and leaned his face next to her ear, his cheek brushing her hair. "You just relax and let me take care of Will."

With a chuckle, he walked into the other room and shut the door. The sound of running water soon following.

Lightheaded, she sank into the chair, releasing the breath she'd held.

What had she just gotten herself into?

***

Jake had an ache in the pit of his stomach before they even reached their destination. He knew what they were doing before Aiden told him. Aiden had insisted that Antonia stay at the hotel when they went out. She'd clasped his hands in hers and whispered in Spanish as she leaned down into his face with tears her eyes. *"Que dios me lo bendiga, mijo."*

Thankfully, Aiden was silent in the car as their driver took them downtown, away from the hotel and Antonia. Jake tried not to think about what Aiden wanted him to do. He hoped this time he wouldn't see any children, a thought he kept buried deep, next to his love for Antonia. They were secrets that needed to be kept hidden in the dark.

The car stopped and they climbed out into the heat. Jake had eaten lunch a couple of hours before, but what was left in his stomach threatened to come back up. Could he call the shadows to help him stop Aiden? Or Raphael? It was late afternoon, in the middle of a busy street. He doubted the shadows could help now. While their demonstration the night before had been impressive, Jake realized a bird was *nothing* compared to Aiden or even Raphael's powers.

The sun was hot and within a minute sweat trickled down Jake's face, but he refused to wipe it away. A man hurried around them, talking on a cell phone. How long did the man have to get away before Raphael showed up and Aiden told them to begin? He wanted to yell at the top of his lungs, to warn everyone to run, but what would Aiden do to him if he did? What would Aiden do to the people close by? Images of Jake's first nanny dying rushed into his mind, along with the images of several other employees who had disobeyed Aiden. Jake bit the inside of his lip to remain silent.

Several minutes later, Raphael strolled up, looking fancy in his dress pants and a stiff long-sleeve button-up shirt. He looked hot too, sweat dampening his shirt and sticking his curls to his face.

"You're late," Aiden growled.

"Well, *you* try finding a cab in this place. New York City, it's not."

"I'm counting on that."

"Please tell me we're not going to stay in the South." A whine crept into Raphael's voice.

"You'll go where I tell you to."

Jake knew Raphael would, no matter what Aiden threw at him. Aiden had something Raphael really wanted, but even Jake knew Raphael never had a shot at getting it. Too bad Raphael was too stupid to figure that out.

Raphael grumbled for several moments then looked serious. "Same as yesterday? Except for the toddler fit at the end?"

Jake's anger ignited in his chest, his mark burning icy cold. He'd show them a fit. He wished Aiden hadn't stopped him yesterday. Maybe next time he'd ignore Aiden and finish Raphael off.

Aiden chuckled. He'd read Jake's mind. Jake had let his guard down, but it was probably good that Aiden saw those thoughts. If Jake hid too many, Aiden would become suspicious.

Aiden looked from Jake to Raphael. "Let's get to work."

CHAPTER FIFTEEN

WILL left the hotel room ten minutes after Emma, but those six hundred seconds chewed at his already strained nerves. As much as he hadn't wanted her to go, she needed to be prepared for tonight. No one had any reason to suspect they were here. Even if something happened, she was more valuable to Alex alive. Will was counting on that fact.

There was no sign of her as he entered a side entrance to the lobby, which was no surprise, but he wouldn't have minded the reassurance. Dread hummed in the back of his head.

His first order of business was to find a hotel uniform of some kind. He didn't care if it was a janitor or bellhop. He headed to the basement and found a deserted employee locker room. With his lock picking set, he opened several lockers until he found a maintenance uniform in the right size. He could get damn near anywhere wearing this. There was even a name tag. *Perfect.*

After he changed, he snagged a toolbox from a maintenance supply closet. He hid his clothes in the chest and headed up the nearby stairwell. He'd only gone up a couple of stairs when Emma's terror slammed into his chest.

Emma?

He stopped on the landing and waited for a response, calling again in panic. *Emma!*

I'm fine. Just give me a minute.

Her fear eased and Will allowed himself to take a breath. Maybe she'd been startled. He almost convinced himself until her fear seeped through again. Where was she? Concentrating on their connection, he could tell that she was above him somewhere. He started climbing the stairs, waiting for her to tell him what happened. After several minutes, she hadn't answered, but her anxiety persisted.

Emma. What's going on?

She hesitated before answering. *I found Alex.*

The way she said it made him think she wasn't watching Alex from the distance. *Are you upstairs? I'm coming to get you.*

NO! Her panic returned stronger than before. *Alex has men posted to watch for you.*

Will's stomach knotted. *He's keeping you prisoner.*

She paused. *No. I'm here on my own. Alex found me in the hall outside his suite and invited me in. I told him that I came to see if he could help me get Jake back.*

And what did he say?

He seemed upset that Raphael had him. But more upset when I told him that you wanted to kill Jake.

Sweat beaded on Will's forehead. He knew that was all part of the plan but it made him nauseated to hear her say it anyway. *Did he buy it?*

I think so but he wanted to know where you were. Since we've joined he's suspicious that I'm not with you, but he seemed to buy my reason. I told him you sided with Marcus and want to rule the world with him. But Alex says that you wouldn't let me go that easily and you'd come to get me. So he's posted guards at the door and other places to protect me from you.

Will's hand clenched around the toolbox handle. *Alex is right about one thing. I'm coming to get you.*

No! I'm in with Alex now, which is what you wanted. Right? Just wait until after the fundraiser dinner and I'll tell you when it's safe to come.

Will didn't like the idea of leaving her in Alex's suite, but he had to admit that she was right. This was going better than he could have hoped. And that worried him. *Okay, but the first sign of trouble and I'm coming to get you.*

I'm counting on that.

Be careful, Emma.

I'm fine. He's been well-behaved and he's left me alone while he gets ready for his dinner.

What room are you in?

She didn't answer for several seconds. *I think I'm in 2146.*

You think?

I wasn't exactly paying attention to the number on the door when Alex invited me in.

Will sighed. That was the difference between the two of them, further proof he was an idiot to let her do this. He would not only know the room number but the location of the air vents, the supply closet, and the fire hose. *Can you find out for sure? Check the phone?*

There is no phone.

Fear mixed with Will's dread. *He's not protecting you, Emma. He's keeping you prisoner.*

I'm not an idiot. I'm willing to see this through for a bit to get more information from him.

While it went against Will's instinct, it seemed the smartest thing to do. *Okay, but if he acts like he's going to hurt you, just touch him.*

I'm not sure that works anymore.

He paused. *What are you talking about?*

He insinuated it didn't work. Maybe it's because you and I joined.

He told you that to make you think you'd lost your upper hand. He's bluffing, Emma. You should have just touched him.

I want him to trust me.

You really think he's going to trust you?

He's not going to if I'm trying to touch him.

I don't like the idea of you being with him for so long. Tell him you have to leave.

He's going down to his dinner. I considered telling him that I need to get my things from my room, but I don't want to lead his men there. You know I'll be followed.

Will ran his fingers through his hair. *Yeah, you're right. But he'll think it suspicious if you don't want to get your things.*

I'll snoop around after he leaves and see if I can find anything.

Be careful, Emma.

You too.

She was in. That was the plan, even if it was hours earlier than expected. The guards by the door didn't surprise him. He'd figured he would encounter them when he found Alex. But if he had to dispose of them now, Alex and his security team would be alerted to his presence. Emma needed to stay.

***

Jake knelt on the cracked pavement and vomited into a puddle. A puddle of rain he'd just created. He'd held in his nausea as long as he could, but this city was worse than last. There were more people. More kids hurt by Raphael's earthquake. And because of the wind in his storm. Jake tried to close his eyes, but Aiden burned his arm and forced him to watch.

There had been so much blood.

He threw up again, but there was nothing left to heave out. His stomach clenched in spasms, and tears stung his eyes. His wet clothes clung to his body and he shivered uncontrollably in spite of the heat.

"Get up, Jake. We need to go." Aiden's voice was cold and distant.

Hatred exploded in Jake's head. He hated Aiden. Hated Raphael. Hated Will. If it weren't for Will, Mommy would be here saving him.

Mommy! he screamed in his head.

Nothing.

He choked back a sob.

"Calling your mother is a waste of time. I told you that Will forced her to choose. He blocked her from you."

"*No.*" Jake pushed the word through his gritted teeth. His body ignited, heat building until he was sure he'd burst into flames.

"Jake."

Aiden's voice angered him even more, but he added it to the energy growing inside him. The power he'd used to make the storm was nothing compared to this.

Raphael slowly backed away, fear in his eyes.

The smile left Aiden's face and his tone softened. "I know this is hard for you, Jake. But your mother is coming. I promise you that. In fact, I expect that she'll make the connection tonight and find you tomorrow."

Jake's mouth dropped open and his anger oozed from tiny pinpoints all over his body.

"Come with me. I'll take you to Antonia and she'll make some of those pancakes you like so much." Aiden leaned over and held out a hand.

Jake released his energy in a violent wave. The trees in its path burst into flames. Cars exploded. The asphalt in the road bubbled and the grass turned black.

Aiden knelt down, his hand still extended. "It's okay, Jake. Let's go see Antonia."

Was this a trick?

A warm smile covered Aiden's face.

Jake reached for him, expecting pain or a jolt of some kind. Instead, Aiden gently pulled Jake to his feet. "I've pushed you too hard, too soon. But it's almost over."

They walked through the rubble, Aiden still holding Jake's hand.

Raphael fell into step beside them. "Aiden, we have to talk."

"Later."

"No. *Now*."

Aiden's hand burned Jake's before he dropped it and turned to Raphael.

Sirens blared in the distance, and people outside of the damaged area continued to scream and run from the destruction.

"We don't have time for a discussion, Raphael. Unless you feel like confronting humans."

Raphael snorted. "I don't give a fuck about the humans. So they discover it was us now or later. It makes me no nevermind. But we need to discuss Jake. Now."

"This can wait, Raphael."

"No. It can't. Do you realize that you have only begun to tap into that boy's power? What he just did—"

"Was nothing." Aiden looked down at Jake. "Why don't you go wait for me in the car?"

Jake hesitated.

"Now, Jacob." No-nonsense Aiden was back.

He turned around and took slow steps to the car. Raphael and Aiden lowered their voices but he heard snatches.

"You're wasting his power…"

"…what I'm doing…"

"…strength is fire..."

Their voices faded as a man opened the back door and let Jake in. The air-conditioned car seemed wrong. Like it was a different world. There was the nightmare outside, full of death and blood and evil. But inside was just as bad. It was cold and sterile and empty.

Just like Jake.

CHAPTER SIXTEEN

WILL had searched several floors and found scant security. After some conversations with hotel employees, he'd discovered the twenty-first floor was off limits to everyone, including the staff. All food and amenities were carried to the room by security.

While he had powers at his disposal, he wasn't sure he wanted to rely on them to deal with Alex's men. He was much more comfortable with guns and bare hands. Funny how he'd been encouraging Emma to rely on her powers, yet he couldn't do the same. He was going to have to get over his reluctance or he'd be a dead man in a week.

After checking the pool maintenance room, he took a short cut next to the indoor pool, passing a fully clothed man who sat in a lounge chair. The man turned to Will and grinned.

"Marcus."

"I figured I'd find you here."

Will was about to ask him why, until he glanced at the pool.

"Have you always been drawn to water, Will?"

"Don't we have more important things to discuss?"

"Such as?"

"Such as the fact that Raphael has Jake and they destroyed half of Little Rock."

Marcus scowled. "It's nothing. You need to focus on other things."

"It wasn't *nothing* to Emma. Or Jake, I'm sure. How did Raphael get him? What's his purpose?"

"What do you think?"

Will sat in the chair next to Marcus. "To get to Emma."

"And it's working, I take it."

"Of course."

"Are you here to kill Alex?"

Marcus asked so matter-of-factly, he took Will by surprise. "And if I was?"

"I'd say it was a smart decision. Eliminate as much competition as possible before the battle to ensure you and Emma make it to the final round."

Will's chest tightened. "Is that Raphael's goal? To kill Emma? Jake would never go along with that." But it made sense, especially if killing Emma killed Will in the process.

"I'm sure Jake has no idea. Jake is a pawn." Marcus turned to him. "Where's Emma now?"

Will hesitated. How much should he tell him?

"I'm not your enemy, Will. What purpose would it serve for me to have created you, only to betray you?"

"Why don't you ask Aiden?

"I understand your distrust and appreciate it. It helped make you a decorated soldier. But I'm nothing like Aiden. You and I are on the same side, Will."

Will had to admit he could use the help, but could he really trust Marcus? "Emma is upstairs with Alex."

"Interesting." Marcus was silent for a moment. "I wished this could have all unfolded differently. I wish I could have told you who you were years ago."

Will stared at his folded hands. "Would it have made any difference? Emma only found out about a month ago. I'm just a few weeks behind. What's strange is I've managed to accomplish in days what has taken her weeks."

"Your power is more pure than hers." His voice softened. "Do you know why I chose you?"

Will shook his head and released a bitter laugh. "That's an interesting choice of words. I thought this was all about genetics. And destiny."

"True. You are who you are because of genetics, but I assure you that you and I aren't anything like Aiden and Emmanuella. Don't you wonder why you're my first child?"

Will turned to look at Marcus. "Okay, I'll bite. Why *am* I the first?"

"Because of your mother."

Will expected Marcus to tell him revenge or destiny or a whole cosmic host of reasons. He hadn't expected that.

"There was something about her. Something special. In thousands of years, I'd never felt what I felt with your mother. I loved her. I still do."

The stone on Will's ring swirled as sorrow washed through him. "She's dying."

"Will…" Marcus looked into the pool, his voice turning to a whisper. "She died last week. I was with her at the end."

Will's grief exploded in his head and he choked on a sob. He knew his mother wouldn't last long after he saw her, but hearing the confirmation still caught him by surprise.

"When she became pregnant with you I knew I couldn't stay with her." Marcus rubbed the side of his index finger. "I knew I couldn't raise you. She had no idea who I really was and she never would have believed me if I told her. How would I explain the fact that I never aged?"

"You could have tried. You were a coward. Instead, she ended up with the Colonel, the bastard." Will snorted. "I guess I was the bastard."

"Will." Marcus cleared his throat and leaned forward. "That was my fault too. After I discovered your mother was pregnant, that's when I approached Aiden and told him I was ready to initiate the final round. Maybe I couldn't raise you and provide for you that way, but I could give you an inheritance."

The revelation caught Will off guard. Marcus hadn't created Will for the game. Instead he'd changed the game to accommodate his son. Still, Will wanted no part of his *inheritance*. "*This*? Are you shitting me?"

"It wasn't supposed to be this difficult."

"What the fuck, Marcus? How could it not be this difficult?"

"It was supposed to be you and me against Aiden. My plan was for you and Emmanuella to join for practical purposes and then we could use her and her power against Aiden. She was just another piece in the game."

Anger rose until Will's ears burned. "Emma is not a pawn."

"I see that now, and it's a huge complication. I told you, Emmanuella had never fallen for her protector before. I didn't expect it."

"Maybe because she's not Emmanuella. She's Emma."

"Fair enough. But the bottom line is your end goal. I know what Emma's end goal is, which Aiden is counting on to weaken you. I'm asking you to rethink yours."

"What the fuck does that mean? Do you expect me to throw Emma and Jake to the side because my real daddy shows up?"

Marcus leaned closer. "No, Will. It means I need you to think logically. This is about more than you or me or Emma or even Jake. This is about the fate of the world. What do you think is going to happen if Raphael gets more control than he already has after years of exile as a human? Or Alex? What do you think Aiden will do if his power increases?"

Will's breath came in short bursts. "I will not let anything happen to Emma or Jake. I'd rather die myself than let that happen."

Marcus covered Will's hand with his own. "I know. I felt like that with your mother."

"So you deserted her and she married the Colonel. If you really loved her you wouldn't have let that happen. He treated her like garbage."

Releasing a heavy sigh, Marcus's grip tightened. "I encouraged her to marry him."

Will clenched his fists to keep from punching his father. "You fucking bastard."

"I knew he was destined to be a great soldier. I hoped he would be a good influence for you. I needed you to be a warrior."

"What the hell do you want me to say to that? *Thanks?*"

"No, Will. I watched over you as you grew and I realized he wasn't the father to you that I'd hoped for. But there was no doubt that he did influence you. You're a great soldier with good instincts. They'll serve you well."

"You watched me and never thought to visit Mom? Or see me?"

"How could I explain that I looked exactly the same as I had twenty years ago?"

"Plastic surgery? Good genetics?"

"The longer I waited the more impossible it became."

"You tell yourself whatever you need to, to make yourself feel better." Will stood. He didn't want to hear any more. "What do you want? Obviously, you're here for a reason."

"You need to trust your instincts." Marcus rose to his feet and put a hand on Will's arm. "Emma's not a soldier. She's a mother. There's nothing wrong with that, but you need to trust *your* instincts and not hers. You're the one capable of saving you all—and the world. Not Emma. You may have to go against her wishes and force her to do your bidding."

"Even if I were to believe that, she'll never go along with it."

"You are bonded, Will, and you are the stronger of the two of you. You can influence Emma to do what you want her to do. You can use her power to accomplish what you need to do."

Ice rushed through Will's veins. "Why are you telling me this?"

"You need to be prepared. Your love for her is already a handicap. You need to know your options."

Will shrugged off Marcus's hand. "I've heard enough."

"Just remember what I said. All I ask is that you make your decisions based on your military expertise and logic, not your emotions. You know that's the best advice anyone could give you."

Will released his anger into the pool, the water rushing up and breaking the glass walls. The roar of the water filled the room and half the pool ended up in the adjoining courtyard. Marcus stood to the side with his lips pressed together.

Shoving the hallway door open, Will tried to pretend his rage was a result of Marcus's bad advice.

It was easier than acknowledging that Marcus was right.

***

Alex emerged from the bedroom, knotting a tie around his neck. "You're still here." He sounded amused.

She lifted her eyebrows. "I told you that I need you. Why would I leave?"

Stopping in front of a mirror, he finished the knot. "So you say. It just seems too good to be true, Emma."

He watched her reflection as she approached, distrust in his eyes. She stopped and held his gaze in the mirror. "I've told you why. I'm not going to try to convince you otherwise. But you of all people know the lengths that I will go to, to protect and save our son."

His eyes softened, his skepticism fading. Could he really care about Jake? She thought he'd faked it before, but now she wondered.

He's a politician, Emma, she told herself. *His job is to convince people to believe him.* But Jake was his son. Was it so farfetched to think he cared about him?

"Alex..." she hesitated, unsure she really wanted to know the answers to the questions she was about to ask.

He turned toward her, waiting with a patient expression.

"If I hadn't been hiding the last three years... I mean...If Aiden hadn't interfered..."

Alex sighed. "I wanted to be part of his life, Emma. In spite of his conception. But even if Aiden hadn't interfered, I wouldn't have contacted you. *Because* of his conception."

Could she really believe that? She lifted her chin, hardening her gaze. "That's not the impression you gave me in South Dakota."

Indecision clouded his eyes. "It was all a game. I suppose it still is. A game of power and control. You were simply a part of it. But that was then."

Her back stiffened. "And now?"

"And now my priorities have changed." He turned from her toward the door.

She put her hand on her jutted out hip. "Yeah, the speech you're about make proves how much they've changed. Instead of finding your son, you're campaigning for your father."

Alex stopped, his shoulders slouching before he spun halfway around. "If you doubt me, Emma, you're free to leave." He waved to the door. "The men outside this room are there to protect you, not keep you prisoner." Sighing, he shook his head then stared into her face. "I'll be gone several hours. If you want to work with me, stay. If not, then leave. No hard feelings."

He walked out of the room before she had a chance to answer, not that she knew what to say. Was it really that simple? She wasn't naïve enough to believe it was. The closer they got to the end of this thing, the higher the stakes became. Alex knew she'd joined with Will. If he thought killing her could kill Will, it might be worth his effort. So why hadn't he tried it yet?

The real question was: Could she still follow through with Will's plan? While she understood Will's reasoning, she wasn't sure she could actually do it. What if Alex really *would* help her get Jake back? What if there was some strategy Will hadn't thought of?

She sat in a chair, looking out the window at the St. Louis arch, the sun reflecting off the metallic structure. She needed to remember her primary goal. To save Jake. Everything and everyone else came second. Even Will, as much as it pained her to admit it. And if she really could count on Alex's motives, she couldn't dismiss his help.

This was a decision she couldn't make lightly. Will was the trained expert. She had to trust him, as hard as it was to do. He loved her and loved Jake by default. He was on her side and perhaps she didn't agree with his methods, but she had to trust them anyway. Still, she'd just had a civil conversation with the man she planned to help murder. If that didn't make her a cold-hearted bitch, she didn't know what did.

The fact was that she was going to have to perform many evil acts before this all was over. Emma would pay whatever it cost her to insure Jake and Will survived. She'd worry about the redemption of her soul later.

***

Will had gone largely unnoticed by the hotel guests and staff for the last two hours, and that worried him. Sure, he'd been stopped by Alex's security team a couple of times, especially after the damage at the swimming pool was discovered. Will could have kicked himself for losing control. The deeper they dug into this mess, the more important self-control became.

Thankfully, the security team didn't seem suspicious of a lowly maintenance worker. They'd matched the name on his stolen name tag to their lists and let him pass. If they had patted him down, they wouldn't have found any weapons, but an inspection of his toolbox would have been a different matter. He had determined that the Secret Service was nowhere in the vicinity, an oddity unless he took into account the fact Alex had secrets he didn't want leaked to the voting citizens. The fact that his father came off looking like a hero, with his campaign providing their own security and saving tax dollars, was a bonus.

The fundraiser dinner was being held in the hotel's ballroom. Five hundred bodies filled the space, all waiting for Alex Warren to give a mesmerizing speech. Will didn't have access to the ballroom, but he got close enough to the entrance to see Alex get off the elevator and walk toward the doors.

A crowd of people stood in front of Will. Girls called out Alex's name. Will could see why. He was the first to admit that Alex had movie-star looks and charisma—even without his elemental powers, he could charm anyone. If only he'd tried to use that charm six years ago. Will was sure Emma wouldn't have fallen for it, but it might have made her life just a little easier.

Alex paused less than six feet away, his eyes shifting to the crowd. Will stayed in the back, lowering his face and moving behind a tall man. The security team tightened around Alex, and he leaned into one of the guard's ear before resuming his trek to the ballroom.

Had Alex known Will was there? Will decided not to press his luck and headed to the stairwell, passing a couple of security men at the entrance. They gave him a glance, but otherwise ignored him, which Will took as a good sign. He couldn't imagine them letting him walk free if Alex knew he was here. But Alex might realize that it would be more difficult to contain Will now and want to handle it himself.

At the moment, Will needed to concentrate on how to get onto the twenty-first floor with as little incident as possible. Emma knew about two men at the door. Will had to figure out how many more there were and where were they located.

Emma, is there any way you can get a count of the security men outside Alex's room? Go out and get a bucket of ice or something?

I can do better than that.
What are you going to do?
Take a walk.

***

Emma was going stir-crazy sitting around the hotel room so she was happy to have an excuse to get out. Alex had told her that she was free to go, which in theory meant she could wander the hotel. When she opened the door to the hall, two men turned to face her.

"I'm going to get some fresh air."

"If you could wait a moment, miss, we'll call someone to go with you."

"That's not necessary."

"Mr. Warren insists that someone accompany you when you go out. For your protection."

More likely to watch her and see what she did, but she had no intention of doing anything suspicious. She gave them a look of helplessness. "Are you sure that it's not any trouble?"

The guard relaxed. "It's no trouble at all. It will take a few moments to get someone up here. We'll let you know when he arrives."

"Thank you." She considered leaving anyway, but she wanted Alex to trust her. That meant accepting his protection.

Several minutes later the door opened, and the guard poked his head in the crack. "Excuse me, Miss Thompson. Mr. Warren says he needs to speak to you as soon as possible. Unfortunately, he's unable to get away. We have two men to escort you downstairs to see him."

Her heart jolted into her ribcage. Had they found Will? Did they find it suspicious that she wanted to walk around? "All right." To her irritation, her voice trembled.

"Right this way."

She picked up her purse and headed into the hallway. Two new men waited for her, another by the open elevator. She laughed nervously. "You overestimate my need for protection."

The two men fell into step next to her. "Mr. Warren insists, miss."

So they kept saying. What if Alex found out her and Will's plan and he was taking her downstairs because it would be easier to dispose of her there?

Will? They're moving me.

Moving you where?

Downstairs. They sent two men to take me to Alex.

He's in the ballroom. I just saw him go in about thirty minutes ago. Are they taking you to the fundraiser?

I don't know.

I don't like this. Where are you now?

In the elevator, going down.

I'm headed down now. If they're really taking you to Alex, you're headed to the second floor.

The *two* button lit up overhead, and the doors slid open. The men led her into a large lobby-type area filled with people who stood behind a padded rope.

The words *Fundraiser Dinner* above an arrow emblazoned a sign, pointing down the hall. Maybe they really were taking her to see Alex. But why? They hadn't caught Will and she couldn't think of a single reason, good or bad, that Alex would drag her down here. Surely he didn't want her known by the media.

They led her down a side hall and stopped in front of a door with a plaque reading *Magnolia Room* on the side, then ushered her inside. Other than rows of chairs facing the front, the room was empty. There was another door on the back wall.

Always know your exits, Will had told her once. She hoped she wouldn't need to run.

One of the guards left the room, but the other closed the door and stood in the doorway. "If you want to take a seat, Mr. Warren will be right with you."

Emma paced instead. She knew it made her look weak and nervous, but after everything she'd been through, she was past the point of caring.

Will, I'm in the Magnolia Room. Down the hall from the ballroom.

I'm in the stairwell on my way.

I have men guarding me. Stay back.

I'll be close by if you need me.

Okay.

Several minutes passed before the door opened. She half-expected Will, but Alex slipped through the opening instead.

"Leave us," he grunted. The guard brushed past Alex and he shut the door behind him.

Alex's face was pale and his hands shook. "Emma, I think you need to sit down."

Her breath caught and she forced out, "Why?"

He gestured to the chair. "Please."

Emma? Will had sensed her fear.

What could make Alex so nervous? Something that he thought would upset her too? "Oh, God. Jake." Her legs gave out and she sank onto a chair.

Alex sat next to her, worry in his eyes. "It's not what you think. He's safe, but I'm worried he won't be safe for long."

A metallic taste coated her tongue. "What? How do you know?"

His gaze held hers. "They attacked another city about an hour ago."

She shook her head. "No."

He grimaced. "This one had more damage. The death count is much higher."

Oh, God. "How many?"

"Little Rock had a couple of hundred fatalities." He paused. "Today's incident looks like it might be a thousand. Or more."

Jake had been forced to participate in killing a thousand people. Nausea rolled in her stomach.

Emma, I'm coming now.

No. Wait.

"Are you okay? You look like you're about to pass out."

"Just give me a moment."

Alex stood and poured a glass of water from a pitcher on the table.

Emma rubbed her forehead. "Don't you have to get back to your dinner?"

"Not yet." He took a sip, watching her.

She took a deep breath and her stomach settled. "What city was it this time?"

Alex set his glass on the table. "Jackson. Jackson, Mississippi."

The blood rushed from her head. "*What?* Are you sure?"

"Emma, it's all over the news. My security team came in to tell me and I had them bring you down since I couldn't get away for very long. I wanted you to hear it from me first."

She narrowed her eyes. "Why?"

"I already told you that I want to work with you on this. You need to trust me. Maybe this is one way of me proving it." He leaned toward her. "I've sent men out to see if they can track Raphael and Jake to their next location."

Raphael was leaving a trail in neon lights. Could it really be so easy? "I know where to find Jake."

"Emma, they've left Jackson. Raphael has no intention of getting caught."

She shook her head. "No, not Jackson." Should she tell him? "I know what they're doing, but what I don't understand is how Raphael would know. Jake wouldn't know. He was too little to pay attention, and I purposely kept some of the names of the places we lived from him."

"Emma. What the hell are you talking about?"

The room spun and she lifted her hand to her forehead. "They're destroying cities I lived in. They started with Little Rock. I lived there when the Cavallo first showed up. Then we moved to Jackson."

Alex rubbed the back of his neck. "You think they're following a pattern. Why?"

"I have no idea. To distract us? Maybe they are trying to keep Will and me from preparing for the end."

His body tensed and he lowered his voice. "I thought you weren't with Will."

"How would they know that? You didn't."

"Well, good job on their part. However, I don't think Raphael is orchestrating this. He's not smart enough."

"You can't be saying Jake would—"

Alex looked grim. "No. Not Jake. Aiden."

"*Aiden?*" Would Aiden really work with Raphael? "*Why?*" She had no doubt that Raphael would agree to whatever Aiden wanted. But the fact that they dragged Jake into this sickened her.

"You think they are going to the cities you lived in starting from the beginning when you went on the run? In order?"

"Yes."

He gazed down at her for several seconds. "Isn't it obvious? They want you to come to them."

Her pulse thrummed in her temples. "I don't understand. Why?"

He sat down in front of her again. "You said it yourself. Maybe they're trying to interfere with you and

Will. But we'll have the element of surprise. They won't expect the two of us."

"You'll help me?" Her disbelief drenched her words.

Alex's face softened. "Emma, he's my son too. Now tell me where they're going next so I can have my men make the arrangements. We'll leave as soon as I'm finished here."

"What about your schedule?"

He stood and waved a hand. "Let me worry about that. Where are we going, Emma?"

She hesitated. While it seemed like insanity to trust Alex, she couldn't deny he was convincing.

The door opened. "Mr. Warren, you need to get back."

"Emma. I have to go," Alex pleaded.

He said he'd help. Three against two were better odds, right? Even if Will would never agree to work with Alex, and Alex would be furious when he found out Emma lied about Will. But the most important thing was Jake.

"*Emma*." He stood at the door, his eyes imploring.

"Shreveport. They're going to Shreveport."

CHAPTER SEVENTEEN

EMMA, what the fuck is going on? Will shouted toward her. He was about to burst into the room, whether Emma wanted him to or not.

The door to the Magnolia Room opened and Alex exited, then walked toward the ballroom.

I know where Jake is.

Will paused. *Alex knows? That's why he wanted to talk to you?*

No. He told me Jake and Raphael destroyed part of Jackson, Mississippi this afternoon.

Will held his breath. Another city? So soon? Marcus had to be right about their motives, and the timing of the attacks suggested urgency. *Emma, by the time we get there, he'll be gone.*

I know. Raphael's targeting cities I lived in with Jake while I was on the run. In order.

You're saying that you know where they're going next?

Shreveport. We need to go now.

What to do with this information? Alex was so close that Will couldn't back off now. Especially if Alex really trusted Emma. Will might not have this opportunity again until the end, and they couldn't afford to leave Alex alive that long. Getting to Shreveport would take eight to ten hours. Raphael probably wouldn't stage another attack until tomorrow. They had time. *No. Not yet.*

He felt her confusion, then her fury. *No?*

We need to finish what we started.

Let's be clear, Will. You and I have two very different objectives at the moment. You've known mine since the day we met. I came here to find out where Jake is and now I know. Alex wants to help and I want to let him. Three of us stand a better chance of saving Jake than two.

Will leaned against a wall and closed his eyes. Shit, Marcus had been right.

Her anger poured through their connection, prickling at his nerves. What the hell was he going to do? There was no way he would agree to work with Alex. Will came here to kill him and he wouldn't leave until he'd accomplished that task. But she'd never agree to any of it, so he'd have to keep her in the dark. *You said Alex wants to help you get Jake?*

Her irritation faded. *Yes.*

Did he say what he wants to do?

He says as soon as he finishes his fundraiser, he plans to go to Shreveport.

And he wants to take you with him.

Yes. He thinks I left you.

Then stay with him for now. Emma was going to be furious once she realized what he was planning. He hoped he could make her see this was the rational course of action. Marcus was right. Emma was thinking with her heart when they needed to be using their heads.

You want me to go with Alex to Shreveport?

Hell, no, he didn't want that. He'd never let it get that far, but he couldn't tell her that now. *I need to figure this out. For now, unless you're in danger, stay with Alex.*

How easy it was to slip into the callous, heartless man he'd been years ago, but he didn't have time to think about the ramifications now. Jake had once told him that good and bad were just words. Who was to determine what was good and bad? The consequences were what mattered in the end.

Will was counting on that.

***

Antonia had fussed over Jake from the moment she saw him get out of the car at the airport. She stood next to the waiting plane, her lips moving without sound, her hand in her pocket. He walked to the steps and she approached, tsking in her nervousness, the rosary beads clinking in her skirt. She tried to wrap an arm around his shoulders, but he jerked away. He didn't want anyone to touch him. Not even her. Especially her.

He didn't want her love. Love never helped him. Love had only hurt.

The plane took off within minutes of their boarding. Jake and Antonia sat in the back row by the restroom and Aiden and Raphael sat in the front, just like last time.

The plane flew past the smoke that covered part of the city, flying far, far away and leaving the ugliness of the afternoon behind. Jake had watched a Superman movie once after Mommy fell asleep on the sofa after working late. Superman had flown so fast around the world that he made the bad thing that happened to his girlfriend not happen. Maybe their plane could do that too. Fly faster and faster so that the buildings didn't fall and the wind didn't blow and the people on the streets weren't covered with blood.

But that was a movie and this was real life. Besides, even if the plane could do such a thing, Aiden would never let it happen.

Jake hated Aiden.

He kept the thought buried deep in his mind, so deep it dug a tunnel to his heart. He kept it hidden close to the mark on his chest. The spot that was always cold, no matter how hot it was outside.

Antonia fretted next to him, mumbling under her breath and driving him crazy. He ignored her and stared out the window. The fires were gone, but now there were squares of land that reminded him of a mixed-up quilt. He leaned closer to the glass and saw tiny houses and trees. Jake imagined he was a giant and stomped on the houses, smashing them into the ground.

That was what he'd done this afternoon.

He hadn't done it with his feet, but Raphael's earthquakes made the buildings collapse and Jake's wind had destroyed the rest. Maybe Jake was looking at this wrong. He wasn't weak because he did what Aiden made him do. No. He was like a giant. Jake could do things most people couldn't. Not even Will.

Jake was powerful.

Marcus had told Jake that he was special, but he didn't believe it. Not really. Grownups were always telling kids they were special, but they didn't really mean it. But Marcus had meant it.

What else had Marcus said?

He'd said that Jake was the key to winning the game. Jake was the king. He liked the sound of that.

We can help. The shadows tickled his ear as they whispered.

Marcus had told him that too.

Antonia tried to shovel a spoonful of food into his mouth. To Antonia, the answer to anything was food or hugs. Jake wasn't hungry, but he couldn't stand the thought of her hugging him right now so he opened his lips. Soup slid down his throat, warming everywhere in his chest except for his mark.

As if reading his mind, Antonia reached over and brushed some crumbs off his shirt. She jerked her hand back when she touched the place where his mark was.

Her eyes widened with fear. "*Demonio.*"

He shook his head. "No, Antonia."

She lowered her face to his, tears in her eyes. "Let me see your chest, Señor Jake."

What would she do if she saw his mark? Tell Aiden? He couldn't let that happen. He looked deep into her eyes, his mind reaching into hers. "You are going to forget about the cold spot on my chest. You aren't going to ask about it anymore."

Her eyes glazed over. "*Sí,* Señor Jake." She sounded like a robot.

Jake grinned. "It is nothing."

"*No es nada.*"

But it was everything.

***

Emma had resumed pacing. The guards had taken her back to Alex's room and soon after someone had brought her a tray of food. Her anxiety made her too nervous to eat, but she forced herself to choke down some of the sandwich. She needed her strength to fight for Jake. She needed nourishment for the baby.

There wasn't time to think about the baby. She had nothing but time to think at the moment, but she needed to figure out Will's sudden change of mind. Had he really decided to let Alex help him? Should they actually trust Alex to help them?

She needed to be productive. No harm doing a little snooping as long as she didn't get caught. She flipped through a stack of papers on a table, finding nothing but information on Senator Warren's campaign and poll results.

There was a knock at the outside door and a moment later, it opened. A maid entered the bedroom, ignoring Emma as she placed a suitcase on the bed and began to pack Alex's clothes.

She watched the maid folding shirts. *Alex told the truth. A maid is packing his clothes.*

But no sign of Alex.

No.

Any sign of anyone else?

Human or elemental? *Other than the maid and the man who brought me food. No.*

The fundraiser is wrapping up. Alex should be back soon, so be ready.

Ready for what?

Two seconds passed before he responded. *Ready for anything.*

What did that mean?

We don't know what Alex is really up to so you should be ready for anything he throws at you. Will paused. *He just left the ballroom. He's on his way up.*

And then what?

Be ready.

Be ready. She would never be ready for any of this, even if she had a hundred years to prepare.

Several minutes later, Alex came through the door, loosening his tie. He stopped several steps inside the room and studied her. "You're really still here."

"You keep saying that."

"That's because I'm surprised every time I walk in to find you."

"Why would you be surprised? You said you'd help me get Jake."

His mouth twisted into a frown before he walked into his room. "So I did."

Emma followed Alex and stopped in the doorway. "Does that mean you're not going to help?"

He released an exaggerated sigh. "No, Emma. It's a reminder that I shouldn't expect anything more from this arrangement than getting Jake to safety."

Her back knotted. "What else do you expect?" Sarcasm hardened her words.

He unbuttoned his shirt, shaking his head. "Not what you're thinking. I meant at the battle. I hoped we could work together."

"So that's why you're helping get Jake?"

His fingers stopped and he squinted in irritation. "Why can't you accept the fact that I want to save Jake? I took him from the Cavallo and kept him safe until Aiden found him in Montana. He's *my son*, Emma."

Confused, she didn't answer. Her head told her not to trust him, but he seemed so sincere. He was dropping everything to go find Jake. But surely he knew that keeping Jake safe now wouldn't guarantee anything in the final battle. Only two would survive. Maybe he planned on himself and Jake being the survivors and he was using Emma to make that happen.

Would that be so bad? If Jake survived?

Alex looked down, his fingers resuming their task. "I'm not going to lie to you and tell you that I don't want you to team up with me, but why can't we treat this as two separate things? Jake's safety first, the battle second."

"So we're leaving tonight?"

Alex pulled a dark t-shirt out of his suitcase and shrugged out of his dress shirt. "As soon as I finish changing, we're flying to Louisiana. I have my team checking for a location. Aiden and Raphael have been targeting downtowns, so we'll stay in a hotel in that area." He glanced up. "In adjoining rooms, just like Kansas City." His gaze lowered to his suitcase as he pulled out a pair of jeans. "We'll register under different names, of course. But I still wouldn't be surprised if Aiden figures out we're there."

"And then what?"

"Then we wait."

"Can't we try to find them first?"

"Sure, if you have any ideas how to do that, I'm all ears." Alex unzipped his pants and started to pull them down.

Emma turned her back and went into the other room. *We're getting ready to leave.*

Leave to where?

Why did he sound so surprised? *Shreveport.*

A pause. *Stall him.*

Why?

Trust me.

Trust him. It worried her that he had a plan and wasn't sharing it with her. But in the past she hadn't trusted him and it had nearly killed them both. *Okay.*

She felt his relief before he shut off their connection.

Alex came out of the room carrying a suitcase.

She pointed to his bag. "Somehow I expected you to have someone else do that for you."

He set the case down and packed his laptop into a messenger bag. "I usually do, but I decided the fewer people who knew about our departure, the better."

She watched him gather a stack of papers and stuff them in his bag, thankful he hadn't noticed they were out of order. "Do you have the book?"

He looked up in surprise. "Is that why you're here?"

"I don't give a damn about the book. But I presumed you would keep it close."

He gave her a tight smile, but his eyes were cold. "Don't worry about the book. It's safe. Somewhere else." Alex slung his laptop bag over his shoulder. "Let's go."

Will had said to stall Alex, but how could she do that without looking suspicious? Especially after she'd been so eager to go get Jake since the moment she'd walked in the door hours ago. *Will, he's ready to go.*

Go with him.

Did Will expect her to go to Shreveport with Alex?

Alex's eyebrows lowered in confusion. He looked suspicious.

She resisted the urge to tense. "What?"

"I asked if you have a bag somewhere that we need to pick up. You showed up without one."

"Um…yeah." What was she going to say? The truth. She was sick to death of the lies. "It's in a hotel a couple of blocks away."

"We can swing by and pick it up. I should have had someone go get it for you. I wasn't thinking."

She tried to hide her surprise. "That's okay."

He released a derisive laugh. "You think I'm incapable of thoughtfulness?"

She scoffed. "Do you really have to ask that?"

Alex opened the door and motioned for her to go into the hall.

Emma expected to find the two guards incapacitated and Will waiting, but they remained on watch and there was no sign of Will. She wasn't sure whether to be anxious or relieved.

Alex led her to the elevator and they waited in silence until the doors opened. Alex motioned for her to step inside.

The guards remained at the door to Alex's room.

She eyed them and raised her eyebrows. "We're going alone?"

Walking into the elevator, he motioned for her to follow him in. Alex lowered his voice. "They work for my father. The less they know the better."

The doors closed and Alex pressed the button marked B.

Her heartbeat pounded in her ears. "The basement?" Was this a trick? Had he made her think he was going to help her, intending to kill her somewhere they wouldn't be discovered?

"I have to get out unnoticed."

We're going to the basement. Alone.

No guards?

None.

I'll meet you there. She heard the smile in his voice.

Was Will still planning to kill Alex or use him to help find Jake? She wanted to ask but was afraid of the answer.

Alex stared straight ahead, adjusting the strap over his shoulder. His gaze shifted to her and he smiled.

If Will carried through with his original plan, the man standing next to her would be dead within a few minutes. And she would be an accessory to his murder.

Her chest tightened and she forced herself to take slow breaths.

"Emma, are you okay?"

Whether she faced him now or in another week, did it matter? Either way, she'd fight him to the death. That fact didn't make her feel any better. The light over the door flashed fifteen.

When the elevator opens in the basement, I need you to touch Alex.

Panic gripped her. It was the perfect plan. The basement was probably empty. Alex was unprepared and off guard. She would touch him and put him under her control and steal his power. Then Will could kill him.

Ten. Nine. Eight. The remains of her dinner rose and she swallowed it back down, coughing from the bile in her throat.

"Emma. You really don't look well. Do you need to sit down when we get out?"

"No." Tears burned her eyes. She had to get herself together.

Three. Two.

If she did this, she crossed a line she could never uncross. When she'd killed men before, she was fighting for their lives. She was protecting Jake and herself.

But wasn't she doing that now? Protecting Jake?

Except the man next to her said he was taking her to save Jake.

One.

She only had seconds before she had to choose. She had to trust Will.

B.

The doors slid open and the florescent lights flicked. The hallway appeared empty.

Emma froze.

Confusion filled Alex's eyes. "Emma?"

Touch him, Emma!

She lifted her hand and reached for his arm, her hand trembling.

"Emma…"

Goddamnit, touch him!

Concern darkened Alex's eyes. He was genuinely concerned about her.

She shook her head.

EMMA! The force of Will's anger sent pricks of pain into her skull.

"No," she whispered.

Alex cocked his head, confusion covering his face. "What are you talking about?"

She stabbed the button for the first floor on the elevator panel, then repeatedly punched the door-closed button.

Alex reached for her hand, trying to intervene. "Emma, what the hell are you doing?"

The doors were almost closed when a hand stuck through, wrenching them open.

Dropping his bags, Alex jabbed a button on the panel, freezing the doors in place. Will's face appeared in the six-inch opening.

"Touch him!" Will shouted, straining to open the doors.

Alex's eyes bulged as he glanced from Will to Emma. "You set me up? You made it all up?"

Emma shook her head frantically. "No! I swear! I want your help!"

Hatred danced across Alex's features. "You have a funny way of showing it, Emma."

A gust of wind filled the elevator car.

"*Touch him!*"

Emma's chest involuntarily constricted, forcing the air out of her lungs.

Alex grinned, but his eyes were colder than she'd ever seen. "Granted, having control over air isn't as handy as I'm sure fire is, but it does have some advantages."

Fear swamped her as she fought for breath. "Will," she wheezed.

Hatred oozed from Alex, flooding the elevator. "Will can't help you now."

With a gasp, Emma concentrated on her power and grabbed Alex's wrist, forcing heat into his flesh. Smoke billowed off his arm and pain flashed in his eyes.

Her chest still refused to expand. Her vision faded.

Gathering her energy, she pushed it toward Alex, igniting his shirt. His hold on her lungs vanished and she fell to the floor, taking in deep breaths.

"Blast the control panel!" Will called through the crack.

She concentrated on the control panel. Sparks shot into the air and the elevator was plunged into darkness before a dim emergency light switched on overhead.

Climbing to her feet, she watched Will still working on the doors before she was slammed into the elevator wall by an unseen force. A vortex of air spun in the enclosed space, sucking her into its center.

Will was no longer at the door. *Will?* she cried out to him in terror. He wouldn't have left her. What did Alex do to him?

The air currents pulled harder and she grabbed hold of the bar on the wall.

Alex stood in the corner, his contempt palpable. "You'll regret that decision, Emma."

"Alex, please. I couldn't do it."

"But you knew about Will. You knew the whole time. You stood in my room. You let me tell you..."

"I'm sorry!"

The wind stopped and Alex took a step toward her.

"I couldn't do it. Alex. I swear. I tried to stop him."

"Where is Will now? He's run off and left you all alone with me. Coward."

She backed into the elevator wall. "Alex, I know you're angry."

"Am I?" His hand reached for her neck.

She waited for the rush of power she'd felt before when she touched him by the creek, but there was nothing except the pressure of his fingers on her throat.

Alex grinned. "Sur-prise."

"How can you touch me?" This changed everything, but then again, if she was about to die, it didn't matter.

Alex laughed. "Lost your advantage, huh? Didn't you know? Will's power counters yours, making your control over me neutral. Evens the playing field a bit. The good news is that you're immune to Raphael, just like you wanted. If you live long enough to see him again."

She gave Alex a hard shove. To her amazement he dropped his hold and took a step back.

"How did you know that would happen?"

"The book." He grinned. "See? I don't need you for anything."

"I didn't—"

"Save it for some idiot who will listen," Alex sneered. "I'm not falling for your *help me save Jake* act anymore. I can't believe I ever did. You know," he rubbed the back of his neck, shaking his head. "I actually believed you." His hand dropped. "I really did. Bravo, Emma. You fooled even me, and that's saying a lot."

His words ripped her heart into shreds. "I swear to God, Alex—"

His voice lowered. "Haven't you figured out that there is no God? The only deities are the sadistic bastards you're about to face. Is Shreveport really the next city? Did you make that up as part of the trap?"

"It's real. We lived there next." Where the hell was Will? Was he so angry with her for not touching Alex that he left her here? Maybe he thought she was getting what she deserved for not following through with his plan.

"I think I was a little hasty when I said I don't need you for anything." An evil grin lifted Alex's mouth. "I'm curious if killing you kills Will. But for now, I wonder if he feels what you feel." He took a step toward her again and grabbed her wrist. "If I hurt you, does it hurt Will?" His hand tightened, the pressure intense.

She gasped from the pain. "Alex, please." *Will!*

"Don't beg me, Emma. It only pisses me off." He bashed her arm into the handrail, pushing her hand backward until her arm bent at an unnatural angle.

Intense pain shot through her wrist and her knees buckled.

Alex jerked on her broken hand and she screamed.

"Can you tell if it hurts him, Emma? Don't you have a connection?"

"I can't... feel him..." Her vision was fading. No, she couldn't pass out. She tried to find her power but only came up with small sparks.

"Try harder."

Will!

"Maybe the pain wasn't strong enough." His hand cupped her head, striking her right temple into the wood panel.

Lights flashed in her eyes, but she clamped down on her feelings, trying to keep them from going out to Will. If he was going to help her and he *did* feel her pain, it would incapacitate him.

"Can he feel that, Emma?"

"No," she groaned, leaning against the side of the elevator car and sliding down.

Alex gripped her arm, pulling her upright before he slammed her hard against the steel handrail. The rod shoved into her ribs, an intense pain blazing across her side. She screamed.

"I hear broken ribs are painful. Is that true? Can Will feel this one?"

"Alex," she sobbed. Fear and pain were all she could feel. She tried to push through it. She needed to think. Alex wanted to hear that Will would feel her pain. She knew she should lie but her pain-numbed mind couldn't respond.

The elevator car shook and Emma's legs gave out. She fell to the floor, pain slicing through her side and arm.

Alex's head jerked up and he grinned. "Will's back."

A stream of water shot through the metal doors, gouging a hole that grew larger and larger. Alex jumped to the side, out of harm's way. Droplets of water rained down everywhere.

Emma tried to get up, crying out from the intense pain. Her chest froze, stealing her breath. Her right hand hung at an awkward angle, and she tried to push up with her left hand while water collected in the bottom of the elevator car.

Her lungs struggled to breathe, and she realized Alex was using the limited air in the box to combat Will's water stream. Will had almost completed cutting a large circle into the door, but Alex's efforts slowed him down.

Emma had to stop Alex, but her pain muffled her power.

Anger. She needed to focus on her hatred. Her power burned brighter, but was it enough?

Steeling herself, she ignored the agony in her side and climbed to her knees.

Alex turned to look down at her, irritation on his face.

Lunging forward, she reached for Alex's arm with her uninjured hand. She forced her energy into his skin. Alex jerked back, and she dug her fingers deeper. The smell of burnt flesh filled her nose. Her stomach rolled, but she held on, determined to buy Will more time.

A gust of wind threw her across the floor. Her head hit the wall, the piercing pain adding to her hurts. Black spots obscured her vision as she looked up at the elevator door, hoping Will had made it through. The stream of water had stopped and Will was pushing the cut section into the car. Her eyesight faded as a face appeared in the opening and she realized she was hallucinating from her head injury. The person trying to help her wasn't Will.

It was Marcus.

CHAPTER EIGHTEEN

EMMA'S stunned face was the last thing Will saw as the elevator doors shut.

Son of a fucking bitch.

He tried to grip the doors, forcing his weight into the opening, but he knew enough about elevators to know it was helpless. Panic swirled in his head, before he quickly shut it off. Emma was trapped in the car with Alex. She might have been safe if Alex still believed that she'd left Will to seek Alex's help, but Will had blown any chance of continuing that charade. And now she was at Alex's mercy.

Will swiveled around trying to find something to open the doors until he remembered the maintenance closet down the hall. When he got there, he threw the door open, rummaging through the contents.

"You need to use your power."

His heart jolting in alarm, Will glanced up to find Marcus standing in the hall.

"Will, you need to learn to rely on your elemental power, not your human skills."

"I'm all ears, Marcus, but we're in a basement. Where am I going to get enough water to help me do anything?" Will picked up a mop. It had a long handle but would break in half if he used it as a lever. Throwing it across the closet, he swore. He'd wasted close to a minute and was no closer to helping Emma than before. What he really needed was an elevator key.

"Will, you need to trust your powers. They'll tell you what to do."

"Right now, they're telling me nothing."

Will! Pain stabbed his arm and he looked down in surprise. His arm bore no wounds—then he realized that Emma was the one being hurt. He was feeling her pain through their connection. "I have to get her out of there!"

Marcus grabbed Will's shoulder. "You go to the floor above and get into the elevator shaft. Climb down and go in through the trap door on top. I'll draw Alex out."

"How can I trust you? She's Aiden's daughter. How do I know you won't kill her if you get the chance?"

Marcus put a pair of gloves and a long piece of metal into Will's hand. "Because I *can't* kill her, remember? Plus we need her. *Now go!*"

Will hesitated until she screamed his name into his head again, the pain in his arm sucking his breath away before it vanished. Alex was going to kill her.

He ran up the stairs, taking two at a time, to the floor above. Exiting the stairwell, he was grateful the hall was empty. He threw the gloves onto the floor and examined the metal object Marcus had given him. It was an elevator key. He didn't stop to wonder what Marcus was doing with one. Instead, he inserted it into the hole in the top of one door and let the end drop, twisting the tool to unlock the door mechanism. When he felt it release, he pulled the doors open.

The shaft was pitch black. Groaning, Will realized he'd left the flashlight with his toolkit in the basement. At least he had his gun tucked into the back of his pants—he'd gotten it out of the toolbox in preparation for his encounter with Alex.

Emma, I'm coming. It was too far to jump without risking an injury. He remembered the gloves Marcus had handed him and put them on. Standing at the edge, he hesitated for only a moment before he jumped into the shaft, grabbing the cable and wrapping his legs around it.

Emma's muffled scream rose up for the elevator. His heart raced as he realized that she'd closed their connection. Why?

Another sound filled the space, something Will couldn't determine. It sounded like a drill. He shimmied down the cable, quickly found the trap door and tried to open it, surprised when it didn't budge. He managed to lift it an inch before the suction in the elevator pulled it closed.

Goddamn, Alex.

If Will had thought to find a fire hose, he could have brought it down and manipulated the water pressure to open the door. That didn't do him any good now.

The drill sound stopped. Will tried the trap door again, caught off guard when it flew open, all resistance gone.

Alex stood directly beneath him, emanating a blue glow. Emma lay on the floor in an awkward position.

Rage consumed Will and a guttural sound rose in his throat as he directed his power toward Alex.

Alex's eyes widened as he looked up. The pooled water on the floor swirled up to Alex's face and into his mouth and nose. Will felt Alex's power push the water out, but Will held on. Water whirled around the car, stinging Will's face as he leaned down.

Not in the elevator, Will. You're going to hurt Emma even more. Let me get him out.

Marcus was right. Will dropped his hold on the water.

Alex bent over, coughing and gasping for air.

Marcus's hand reached into the opening and pulled Alex out of the elevator.

Will jumped through the trap door, landing in several inches of water, soaking his shoes.

Emma's face was pressed to the floor, her mouth and nose submerged.

Fear bearing down on him, Will pulled her onto her back and found a weak pulse on her neck. Had she inhaled water? Without even thinking, he called to the water in her lungs and throat, drawing it out of her in a rush of fluid.

Emma gasped and coughed.

Will, I need you. Marcus shouted in his head.

Emma was breathing now, but she obviously wasn't okay. Will didn't want to leave her, but Alex was in the hall, and he was the one who'd done this to her. Will glanced toward the opening in the doors, and Emma touched his arm.

"Go."

He hesitated for a moment before he jumped to his feet and climbed out the hole into the hall. Alex had cornered Marcus against the wall. While anger darkened Marcus's eyes, he wasn't defending himself.

Water flooded the hallway floor. Will didn't think, he just called up his power and forced the water into Alex's back, tearing through his right shoulder blade and exiting through his chest.

Crying out in pain, Alex turned to Will. "*You.*"

The air around Will stirred.

Blood poured from Alex's wound, plastering his dark t-shirt to his chest. "Three against one is hardly fair odds. Somehow I figured you were more *honorable* than this, Will."

"Nothing personal, Alex, but I'll do whatever it takes to protect the people I love."

"You didn't protect Emma in the elevator now, did you? Tell me, did you feel it when I broke her arm and her ribs?"

A rage burned deep within Will, and he tried to dampen it. Alex wanted him to get angry.

Trust your power. Marcus stood behind Alex, staring at Will. Why the hell was he just standing there?

"You worried about fighting an unconscious woman and an old worn-out element, fine. Let's make it you and me, Warren. What do you say?"

A slow smile formed on Alex's face, his eyes squinting. "Are you sure you don't need Emma's skirt to hide behind? She does have a mighty fine ass underneath." The wound on his chest, visible through the hole in his shirt, was almost healed.

Could Alex heal himself if he was using his powers for offense? Will let his energy build, intending to find out.

The air began to swirl.

"I could have had her in the elevator, especially when she was nearly unconscious from the pain I gave her. But don't you worry. After you're dead, I'll be sure to screw her before I kill her, and this time she'll beg me for it first."

Will took slow shallow breaths, trying to ignore Alex's words, but the thought of Alex touching Emma enraged him more.

He was in a basement. Where was he going to get more water? Emma had always called out to things that gave her power. Could it be that simple? He let his power search for a moment and he nearly staggered with the results. He felt energy swishing in the pipes in the walls. He heard it running in the pipes in the street. He felt the water droplets in the air, all waiting to do his bidding.

The sound of clanging metal in the air behind Will drew his attention and he turned to see tools flying through the air toward him. Thinking that he needed to stop them, he called to the water in the wall. The pipe burst, spraying water into the air and forming a wall. Will ducked as the tools slammed into the water and stopped, except for a hole that allowed a pair of pliers and a screwdriver to pass through.

The pliers hit Alex in the temple while the screwdriver embedded in his chest. His eyes widened in surprise. He pulled out the screwdriver, tossed it to the floor and laughed. "That all you got, Davenport?"

The air in the room began to churn, picking up tools down the hall. They circulated around Will and flew at him one by one. He ducked and weaved to avoid the first two as he reached into his power. Water rose and slammed into the air current, whipping the tools into the wall and floor. Will beckoned more water, from the ceiling and the floor, flooding the room more quickly than he thought possible.

Emma was still in the elevator.

Marcus, get Emma out of here!

Marcus, who had been in the corner, moved to the elevator opening and ducked inside.

The water level rose to over the tops of Will's feet. He bent, grabbed the screwdriver from the floor and held it in a defensive stance.

Alex laughed. "You think you're going to *stab* me, Will? All of this power and you resort to your human resources. This is why you don't stand a chance."

A gust of air slammed Will into the wall. He gasped. When he tried to take a breath, his chest constricted.

"You're a child playing in the big leagues, Will." Alex slinked toward him, his eyes glowing with power and hate. "This is nothing. I can create tornadoes and hurricanes. I can destroy towns and cities. It's all within my control. Yet, we're in a basement playing with tools."

Will tried again without success to suck in a breath. He forced a wave of water up, intending to smash it into Alex, but Alex sent a gust of air to intercept it, sloshing the water into the wall.

Alex took a step forward. "It's too bad it had to end this way. I was hoping you'd be more of a challenge."

"What about me?" Emma called from the hole in the elevator. "I suppose I wasn't much of a challenge either."

Startled, Alex turned toward her, and his hold on Will loosened. Will took a deep breath and rammed the screwdriver between Alex's ribs.

Alex's mouth dropped open.

Will stabbed him again, holding the handle flush against Alex's chest. Alex's blood pumped onto Will's hand in massive amounts. He'd pierced Alex's heart.

"That's not enough." Marcus stood behind Emma, his face grim.

Alex fell against Will, his legs buckling.

Marcus moved closer. "It's not enough for him to bleed to death. He still might recover."

Blood poured down Will's arm, into the water.

Terror filled Alex's eyes, but Will steeled himself. This had to be done.

Emma stepped through the hole, holding her hand against her side with a grimace. "What do we have to do?" Her voice was cold and distant.

"To disconnect his power, you'll have to make sure his brain is no longer functional."

"Like a zombie?" she asked, her voice expressionless. She kept her gaze on Alex's face.

"Not exactly like a zombie." Marcus paused. "If he has enough brain damage, he won't be able to regenerate. Even though you feel your power in your chest, the true source is your brain."

"Emma," Alex pleaded. His voice was weak and his face pale. "Do it. Kill me and you'll get my power."

She froze.

Will watched in horror. That was the last thing he expected Alex to say. Was it a trick?

Emma's eyes hardened. "Why would you offer that?"

"If I die now, I'll live in the afterlife. If I die later...you heard the shadows." His voice was raspy and he coughed, spitting up blood. "I have to say the transfer words first. The words to give you my power. You can use it to save Jake."

This didn't make sense. Why would Alex do this? "Don't trust him, Emma," Will growled.

She ignored him. "You found the words in the book?"

Alex grinned, blood running from the corner of his mouth and down the side of his face.

Emma looked over at Marcus. "Is it true? Can he do that?"

Marcus's face hardened. "Yes, but…It can't be you. It has to be Will."

"Fuck that." Emma pulled Will's gun out of the back his jeans before he could stop her. She turned off the safety and slid back the rack, pointing the gun at Alex's head. "Start talking."

Alex's eyes narrowed with hatred. "I thought you were the decent one of all of us." He closed his eyes and a glow emitted from him.

"With the shadows as my witness,
I give to you an irrevocable gift
Power and elemental control,
And all that is mine."

Alex closed his eyes and mumbled in a language Will didn't understand.

The glow around Alex faded and Emma's knuckles whitened as she gripped the gun. "Now?"

"Emma, wait!" Marcus took a step forward. "It's a trick!"

Alex grinned but hatred darkened his eyes. "You don't have the guts."

Emma pointed the gun at Alex's head and pulled the trigger twice in rapid succession, her hand jumping with the recoil.

Alex fell from Will's grip, landing on his back in a pool of water.

She stared down at him, the gun still in her hand. "Is that enough?"

Marcus shook his head. "Let Will do it."

Her hand still extended, she continued to stare at Alex. "I asked if it was enough."

Will reached for her hand. "Emma, I'll—"

She looked up at him, anger making her eyes glow with power. "You'll what? You'll do it? The fuck you will." She shot Alex in the head three more times. "Is *that enough*?"

"Yes, Emma," Marcus said softly. "It's enough."

"Good." She threw the gun onto the floor.

Will bent down to pick up the weapon. Alex lay on his back, his eyes wide open, blood swirling in the water around him. "Thank God he's dead."

Emma looked into Will's face with dead, vacant eyes. "There is no God, Will. Only cold-hearted elemental deities. And now I am one." Emma spun around and walked down the hall.

"Emma, where are you going?"

"To get my son."

***

Jake sat on his bed, playing with the shadows. *Shreveport*. He was sure he knew this place. He'd lived here with Mommy.

The shadows crept onto the bed and tickled Jake's fingers, but Jake sighed, bored with this game. Tickling shadows didn't make Aiden pay. And more than anything else in the world, he wanted to make Aiden pay.

Not more than everything. He wanted one thing more.

Mommy.

Pushing himself off the bed, he looked out the window. He watched the cars driving down the street past the hotel. There weren't many at this time of night. He wondered what he could do to them from up here in his room. Could he blow them off the road? Could he blow them up?

The door opened and Antonia walked in, startled to find Jake out of bed.

"*Jake*. You need your rest, *mijo*."

"I'm not tired."

"I will sing you a song."

He almost argued with her, but after he'd turned her away earlier in the day and made her forget his mark, he'd felt bad and needed her comfort. He needed her to love him even though he was bad. Because he was bad.

She helped Jake climb back into bed, tucking the covers around him with loving hands.

A tear fell out of Jake's eye, down his cheek, and into his hair. "I'm a bad person, Antonia."

Her eyes widened in surprise, but she leaned forward and kissed him on the forehead. "No, *mijo*. You are not bad. Your *abuelo* makes you do bad things, but you are a good boy. A sweet boy. I know this in my heart."

Jake wished he knew it. He wasn't so sure anymore.

"No more talk of this. You must sleep. I will stay with you if you want."

He wanted her to stay, almost as much as he wanted his mother, but she couldn't. He had work to do. "Just one song. Please."

A soft smile lifted her mouth. "You have always been such a sweet and polite boy." She brushed his hair as she started the tune that she always sang. He never understood the words, but her soft voice and the fingers in his hair always made him feel safe and loved. He basked in her love and pretended he was safe, even if only for a few minutes.

When she finished, she kissed his forehead again.

He wrapped his arms around her neck and whispered into her ear, "I love you, Antonia."

She pulled him into a tight hug, rocking him to her body for several seconds. "And I love you. I will do everything in my power to keep you safe, *mijo.*"

He nodded, tears burning his eyes. There was nothing she could do to keep him safe. But he might be able to save her. He pushed her away. "I'm ready to sleep now."

"*Sí,* Jake." She left the room, closing the door behind her.

He waited a few minutes before sitting up again and calling to the shadows. "I need to learn more," he whispered into the darkness. "I need to become stronger."

A ray of moonlight shone through the window, onto a spot in the middle of the floor. The shadow figure that had given Jake his mark grew out of the light.

This was even more than Jake had hoped for.

"You are about to get your wish," the shadow cooed.

The other shadows circled around the figure, dancing in and out.

"What do you mean?" Jake whispered.

The figure lifted an arm from its solid form, holding up a finger. "Shhhh, you must wait. It is almost done."

"What is—"

"Shhhhhhh."

Jake sat cross-legged on the mattress, growing impatient, until a soft light glowed from the figure.

"It is happennnninnnngggg…"

Shadows weren't supposed to glow. *What* was happening?

A bright light, brighter than anything Jake had ever seen before burst from the figure, blinding him. Something sharp stabbed into Jake's chest and he flew backward onto the bed, his body becoming white-hot with energy.

Energy that came from the shadow.

He felt stronger as raw power rushed through his blood. He had to release it or he might combust. "I… I…"

"You will become accustomed to it."

"But… how…" The flow of energy made it difficult for Jake to speak. "How did this happen?"

The shadow bowed. "It is a gift and has been passed on to you."

"A gift? From who?"

"From your father. But it comes with a steep price. Do you accept?"

Jake had never felt so alive. He could do anything with this energy. Even destroy Aiden. "What is the price?"

"You must take the life of the person who took your father's life."

Jake's heart thudded. "Alex died?"

"Yes. He gifted his power to you."

"He can do that?" Jake wasn't sure if he should feel sad or not that Alex was dead. He didn't feel sadness, just a weird emptiness in his chest.

"Yes, but you must agree to destroy the person who took his life. Do you accept?"

Jake paused. "Who killed him?"

"It is a secret until the end."

Jake stuck his tongue out of the corner of his mouth as he thought this through. The end? Was that the final battle Aiden had talked to Raphael about? And who could have killed Alex? It couldn't be just anyone. The person had to be strong. Alex had power. So much power. That meant that the killer had to be Aiden. Or Raphael. Maybe even Will. Jake had already decided that he'd have to kill all of them.

"Okay."

"You accept? Think long on this. Once it is done it cannot be undone."

"Yes. I accept."

The shadow nodded, then lowered its head. "Then tomorrow we begin."

CHAPTER NINETEEN

WILL followed Emma out a back door into the alley behind the hotel.

Marcus fell into step beside Will. "She's not handling this well."

Will blew out a breath, his anger simmering under the surface. "No shit. She just killed a man. What do you expect?"

"I told you she's not a soldier—"

Will clenched his fists at his sides, trying to keep his frustration and fear in check. "If you don't mind, spare me the lecture. I don't want to hear it." Will's pace quickened until he was next to her. "Emma, stop."

She ignored him, walking toward the street corner. The vacant look in her eyes scared him.

"Emma." He grabbed her arm and pulled her to a halt.

She stopped but didn't face him. Her clothes were drenched, and water dripped from her hair onto her face. The bruises had already begun to fade, but she held her hand against her side. Her physical wounds were almost healed, but her emotional wounds ran much deeper.

"Emma, you did the right thing."

Her chin trembled and her voice broke. "I can't talk about this right now."

"Okay." But it wasn't. Emma was far from okay. Will wasn't sure she'd ever be able to live with what she'd done. And Alex was just the first.

She resumed walking, toward their hotel.

Will lagged back to talk to Marcus. "We're headed to Shreveport. They're taking Jake there next."

Marcus nodded. "I figured."

Will's anger exploded. He shoved the heels of his palms into Marcus's chest, slamming him into the wall. "*You know*? How the hell do you know about Shreveport?"

Marcus's face remained stoic. "Aiden's not the only one who kept an eye on her."

The fact that so many people had stalked her for so long made Will sick. And even more furious. Will grabbed Marcus's shirt and shoved him again. "Stay the fuck away from her."

Marcus didn't fight Will's assault. "I can't, Will. We need her. Especially now."

Will released his hold and spun away. "So why didn't you tell me what Aiden was doing when I saw you this afternoon? You could have saved us from all the drama." He rubbed his forehead. "You could have saved her from *this.*"

"Because I didn't know this afternoon when I saw you, but when I heard about Jackson…"

Will swallowed, overwhelmed with the events of the last half hour. Why was he taking his frustration out on Marcus when it was Aiden and Raphael he needed to worry about? "If Alex had…Thank you for saving her."

Marcus grimaced. "I'm not sure I saved her or delivered her to hell."

How right was he? If Emma were angry or upset, or exhibiting any kind of emotion, Will would have felt better. "I'm not sure she'll recover from this."

"It's only going to get worse."

That's exactly what Will was afraid of. He wasn't sure Emma could handle worse, but there wasn't anything he could do about it. Will's frustration rose once more.

"There's something you should know."

Will was afraid to ask, but he'd had enough surprises to last a lifetime. "What?"

"Emma didn't get Alex's power."

"What are you talking about?"

"At the very end, Alex transferred it to someone else."

"Who?"

"I don't know."

If things weren't bad enough, they'd just gotten ten times worse. "Could he have sent it to Aiden?"

"Your guess is as good as mine." Marcus's gaze trained on Emma, twenty feet in front of them.

"Who do you plan on representing Water at the final battle?"

Marcus grimaced, turning back to Will. "That's an excellent question. And the answer lies in the fact that I insisted *you* kill Alex, not Emma. If you had gotten his power, you could have taken his place."

"So now Emma will stand in for Air?" That would assure her a position at the end, but what about Jake?

"I don't know. The fact he transferred his power might mean the person he sent it to could fill his vacancy."

"Are you planning on going to Shreveport with us?"

Marcus raised his eyebrows. "If you and Emma will have me. Alex was a cakewalk compared to what you're going to face in Shreveport. You're going to need all the help you can get."

"So you think we should knowingly fall into Aiden's trap?"

Marcus's mouth twisted. "No. It's definitely a trap, but we need Emma and she's determined to do this. If we can reunite her with Jake and bring him to our side it's a double victory. She'll be more focused and we'll gain Jake's power. It's worth the risk. Let's get to Shreveport, scope it out and see if we can swing it to our advantage."

While Will wasn't fond of Marcus talking about Emma and Jake so matter-of-factly, he was right. And it only proved how right Marcus had been earlier. And it also proved Marcus's point about Will needing to think with a clear head and not with his emotions. Damn, he wished he could leave Emma out of all of this, but the reality was that Emma *was* all of this.

As Emma neared the hotel, Will hurried in front of her and opened the door. They walked in soaking wet and received odd looks from the people in the lobby. Will wasn't thrilled that they drew so much attention, especially since the son of the presidential candidate lay dead on the basement floor of the Crescent Hotel. How would Warren's staff play that one off? They'd probably pin it on some political extremist group.

Will opened the door to their room and Emma brushed past him, her face still an empty mask. She opened the bag, pulled out some clothes, and headed for the bathroom.

Marcus stood at the doorway. His gaze shifted to the bathroom door, then to Will. "I have to get my things. Do you want to meet in the hotel parking garage in thirty minutes? I'll pick you up at the exit."

Will ran a hand through his hair. "Yeah…"

"Will." Marcus's voice lowered. "I know you're in a difficult spot here, but we need to leave St. Louis as soon as possible."

Nodding, Will looked at the bathroom door. "I know. We'll be there."

Will bolted the door after Marcus left. He found Emma sitting on the side of the tub in her wet clothes, staring at the blood splatters on her splayed hands.

"Emma," he said softly, squatting in front of her. "Let me help you get undressed." He slipped her shoes off first then reached for her shirt, pulling it up carefully over her bruised arm, thankful she didn't resist his help.

Helping her to her feet, he tugged off her skirt and tossed it onto the floor. "Why don't we take a shower before we go?"

She looked up, wide-eyed. "I have to go to Shreveport. I have to get Jake."

"We will, I promise." He kept his voice gentle and calm. "We're just going to wash off first. We have a long drive ahead of us and you'll feel better if you wash off all the… grime."

Her chin trembled. "You mean blood. So I can wash off all of Alex's blood." She crossed her arms and rubbed her hands along them.

Will didn't answer. Instead, he turned on the water, then stripped off his own clothes before removing Emma's undergarments. He helped her into the water and she closed her eyes. Will washed her hair and her body, being gentle when he noticed the bruising on her side before washing his own. When he was done, he wrapped his arms around her back and pulled her to him in an embrace.

"I thought you left me," she mumbled against his chest.

Will leaned his head back to look down at her, pain crushing his chest. "Emma, how could you think that?"

She looked up at him with teary eyes. "I didn't do what you asked. I didn't touch Alex."

"Emma. *No.* I would never leave you. *Ever.* I'm sorry. I should have prepared you more or made sure you'd practiced or not had you do it all. You weren't ready. I should have recognized that." The truth was that he had, he'd just hoped she'd come through in the end. Now she paid for his mistake. Will knew she had broken her arm and he suspected her ribs from the bruising she still had. What else had she endured? "What did he do to you in the elevator? Why didn't I feel all of it?"

"I blocked it from you."

"*Why?*"

"Did you feel pain in your arm?"

"Yes, but—"

"Alex wanted to see if he could hurt you by hurting me. If you felt half of what...I needed you to be strong enough to get me out of there so I couldn't let you feel it."

"What did he do, Emma?"

She closed her eyes and shook her head. "It doesn't matter now. Once I get some sleep, I'm sure I'll wake up and be fine."

"I should have been there."

"You were. You got Alex out and away from me."

"No, Emma. Marcus got him out."

"Oh." She pressed her cheek to his chest. "Yeah, I that remember now."

"Marcus wants to come with us to Shreveport."

Several seconds passed. "Do you want him to?"

"I think he can help us. I think..." He hated to bring this up now, but she needed to be prepared. "Shreveport is bound to be an ugly mess. I think we need all the help we can get. Marcus helped us today and it's in his best interest to continue to help us."

"But for how long?"

Will released a long sigh. "I don't know. But he could make the difference in getting Jake back." He felt like an ass pulling that card, but there was truth in his words.

"Okay."

They had to go soon, but he knew she wasn't ready. "Emma. We need to talk about Alex."

She tried to pull away, but he held her close.

He brushed a wet strand of hair plastered to her cheek. "You saved me. You know that, right?"

She squeezed her eyes shut.

"Alex would have killed me. I was about to pass out until you distracted Alex and he released his hold on me."

"I killed him."

"You may have pulled the trigger of a gun, but he was nearly dead from my stab wound."

"He may have begged me to do it, but I killed him out of hate and revenge. I shot him in cold blood. And then I did it again. And again. And again..."

"Emma, he was already dead."

She shook her head, rubbing her cheek on his skin. "No. Not the first time. I murdered him."

"If you hadn't done it, he might have recovered, as difficult as that is to believe. You did the right thing."

"I know. That's just it. I know." Her face rose as she searched his eyes. "So why does it feel like I didn't?"

"He would have killed us both, Emma. Jake too."

Pursing her mouth, tears filled her eyes again. "No, he wouldn't have killed Jake. I'm positive of that. I made him trust me, and I led him to his death." She shook her head. "I'm as bad as they are. Worse. At least we know what we're facing when we see them."

"Emma, don't do this to yourself."

Her eyes hardened. "I murdered a man. I have to be honest about it."

He knew her lack of emotion was from shock, but it worried him. At some point the dam would break. It made her unpredictable. Nevertheless, time was running short. "We need to get dressed. We need to meet Marcus."

She dried off and dressed in a t-shirt and jeans, then pulled her hair into a ponytail. Her attire, along with the hard look in her eye, reminded Will of the first time he met her. *That might not be a bad thing.*

***

Marcus's sedan idled at the curb by the parking garage exit. It was new and shiny and exactly like something an element would drive. Raphael had once given her a Lexus. Emma scowled in irritation. Did they all drive luxury cars?

The trunk popped open and Will loaded their bags as Emma reached for the back door. She looked back at him, suddenly unsure that going with Marcus was a good idea. "I don't know if I can do this."

Will closed the trunk and moved next to her. His eyes softened. "Do what?"

"Go with him."

He leaned toward her, lowering his voice. "This is your call, Princess. If you don't want to go with Marcus, we'll go alone."

Her breath hiccupped in her chest. This was all happening so fast. Marcus had saved her from Alex, but did that mean she could trust him? Alex's vacant eyes flashed through her head and panic rose from the pit of her chest, but she shoved it down. She didn't have the time nor the mental stability to think it through. "You really think we need him? We can trust him?"

Will hesitated. "I think siding with Marcus is our best shot at getting Jake."

"But what about later?"

"Honestly? I don't know about later. Let's just concentrate on now."

She nodded, a lump burning her throat. Who knew if they even had a tomorrow? They'd get Jake, then go from there.

Sirens wailed in the distance.

Will looked over her shoulder at the street. "We need to go. Things are about to get ugly here soon, and we have a long drive ahead of us. You're sure you're okay with going with Marcus?"

"Yeah." No, but she didn't have a choice.

"If you change your mind at any point, just let me know, okay?"

Her panic rose again. "But we won't have a car. We're leaving ours here."

"Then we'll get another one. If we leave with Marcus now, we're not stuck with him."

She wasn't sure she believed that, but she trusted Will, especially now. "Okay."

Emma climbed in the back seat and Will slid in next to her.

Marcus turned around. "You have two choices. We can drive straight through, or we can take my plane, which will be much more comfortable and faster." His gaze turned to Emma. "The choice is yours."

"Fly." She wasn't a fan of flying, but it would get her to Jake faster.

Marcus pulled the car into the street, passing several oncoming police cars. Their flashing lights filled the street with a red glow.

Will took Emma's hand and squeezed.

What had she done?

Every time she closed her eyes she saw Alex's face. Alex carrying his suitcase and telling her he'd help her find Jake. Alex in the elevator when he realized she'd betrayed him. Alex with blood oozing from his chest, his pleading eyes. Right before she pulled the trigger.

She couldn't hide from what she'd done. She could close her eyes and see it all play out on an endless loop in her head or she could face the results. She trained her gaze on the circus outside Alex's hotel. She deserved to watch. She deserved the pain. She deserved so much worse.

What had she become?

Jake. She did it all for Jake. The end justified the means.

Marcus pulled into a small airport parking lot, and Will helped her out while Marcus grabbed their bags and headed toward a small jet waiting on the tarmac. Arm around her waist, Will led her to the plane, treating her as if she would fall to pieces at any moment.

Didn't he know she was already broken?

The plane had three rows of seats and was so similar to Alex's plane that she stopped in the doorway and took a step backward.

Will stood behind her, blocking her exit. "Emma. Are you okay?"

She covered her mouth with a trembling hand. "I…"

The memory of Alex picking her up from Raphael's house and saving her from Raphael's mistreatment rose up in her mind.

"I can't…I …" She spun around, pushing past Will, stumbling down the steps. She stood on the tarmac, frozen.

Will raced down behind her. "Emma, what's going on?"

Chin trembling, she looked into Will's worried face. "I see him everywhere."

"Alex?" His eyes narrowed. "You mean his ghost?"

She shook her head. "No. Memories. He saved me from Raphael. He came to Tennessee and helped me escape and flew me to Kansas City so he could take me to you on a plane just like that." She jabbed a finger toward the aircraft. "And how did I repay him? After I lied to him and betrayed him, I blew his brains out."

"Emma." Pity filled his words.

"Oh, God. What have I done?" Her breath caught in her chest and she forced herself to take a breath.

He took her hands in his. "Just take slow deep breaths, okay? After you feel a little calmer, if you decide you want to drive to Shreveport, we will. Okay?"

She gulped air and nodded.

Marcus stood at the top of the steps, watching and making her even more anxious.

She tugged her hands, but Will held tight. "Marcus is ready to go."

Will's eyes hardened. "Fuck Marcus. He can wait."

She wondered, for what seemed like the millionth time, how she'd ever gotten lucky enough to be blessed with this man. Inhaling a deep breath, she leveled her chin. "Okay, I'm ready."

"We can drive."

"No. I'd rather fly. I'm sorry. I promise I won't freak out."

"Emma, you have nothing to apologize for."

Tell that to Alex.

Will led her into the plane again, and she blocked out all memories of everything and everyone, concentrating on the here and now.

Alex was everywhere. She couldn't escape the image of his vacant face, his blood seeping into the water. She didn't know she was hyperventilating until her face began to tingle.

Will handed her a glass. "Drink this. It'll help you calm down."

She took it with shaky fingers, bringing the glass to her mouth and gulping in two swallows. The alcohol burned her throat, and she fought to keep from choking.

He pried the glass out of her hand, then pulled her head to his shoulder, stroking her hair.

The alcohol worked its way into her bloodstream, relaxing her muscles but not her mind.

"Not much longer, Princess. We're almost there."

When the plane landed, she sat up, furious with herself. Will had killed countless numbers of men, some because of her. Will had stabbed Alex, and his hands had been covered in Alex's blood. Will wasn't freaking out and losing his mind. He'd sucked it up and moved on.

That's what she would do.

No more expecting Will to pick up the pieces of her heart that she left in a trail behind her. She needed to stand on her own two feet.

Will eyed her suspiciously but remained silent.

She refused to take his offered hand when they descended the steps in the sticky, humid heat. A two-story glass structure glowed on the other side of the asphalt.

Marcus moved down the steps. "We're far enough from downtown that our plane will be safe."

So they could destroy the city, kill who knew how many people, and fly out safe and sound. Emma felt like she was going to throw up.

A car waited for them outside the terminal and Emma had to admit that having money made traveling easier. She and Will had spent almost twenty hours driving from Utah to St. Louis. It would have taken only a few hours in Marcus's plane. But she suspected that his perks came with a price. Was she willing to pay it?

Hadn't she just proved she was?

Will sat beside her again, but she refused to hold his hand. She didn't deserve his comfort. She had no idea how Will could be so strong and yet so vulnerable with her. When she met him, he'd been hard and jaded, but the more time he spent with her, the more he began to soften. Perhaps that was the secret. She had to harden her heart and then learn to let him in again. But was that fair to Will? Did they even have time?

The hotel was less opulent than Emma expected, but then Marcus was going for low profile while Aiden was too arrogant to care. Emma was relieved to find that Marcus's room was down the hall from theirs. Although Marcus had been well behaved, and had admittedly saved her life, she didn't trust him. He might be helping them now and he might be Will's father, but he was still an element. Elements might try to disguise themselves as normal people but they were monsters underneath.

She was half element.

She sank onto the edge of the bed.

"Emma?" Will had been treating her as though she were a grenade ready to explode at any moment. "You don't look well. It's late. Why don't you lie down and get some rest?"

"I can't," she whispered.

He knelt in front of her and put his hands on her knees, looking up into her face. "Why not?"

"It's all I see. Blood. On his face. In the water. On my hands." She held her hands out and rubbed the back of one of them. "It's everywhere."

Will swept her off the bed and into his arms, cradling her to his chest.

"I can't... I can't live with this. I can't live with what I did."

"Oh, Emma." His hand brushed her cheek. "You can. I promise." Will leaned down and kissed her, his lips soft and gentle on hers while his thumb stroked her cheek. If he'd kissed her with possessiveness or lust, she could have handled it, but his gentleness was her undoing. Tears flowed down her cheeks.

"I'll help you through this. Trust me."

Trust me. He'd said that before, and look where she was now.

No, she put herself here. Not Will.

"Emma, I'm so sorry. I wish to God I never asked you to do it."

"Will." Her body racked with sobs. "I'm a monster. I've become one of them."

Anger rose up in his eyes and he held her face. "You are not a monster. You are not one of them. You were forced to do something terrible, and I take full responsibility for that."

She closed her eyes and shook her head. "No. Jake is my son. I can't leave it all for you."

"Oh, Emma." His voice broke. "This isn't just about Jake. It's about all of us."

"I'm one of them. You're going to realize that and leave me."

"I will *never* leave you. Ever. Don't ever think that I would. We are joined together by this bond, but our tie goes so much deeper than that. We were bound together with love before we joined. I love you more than I've ever loved anyone in my entire life." He wiped her tears with her thumbs. "You are the most important thing in the world to me. I would do anything for you. I would die for you and I most likely will. I would give anything to take this all away, but I can't." Possessiveness burned in his eyes. "But I swear to you that I will defend you to my death because life without you is not an option. Do you understand?" His grip on her cheeks tightened.

Her guilt was suffocating, but somehow she knew he was the only person who could help her. Standing on tiptoes, Emma wrapped her hands around his neck and pulled his mouth to hers in desperation.

He kissed her with passion and possession. *Don't shut me out.* Will reached under her shirt, running his hands up her back, pressing her body to his.

It wasn't enough. She needed more. Desperate, she grabbed his face and captured his mouth with her own. When she felt him try to slip into her thoughts, she put up a barrier.

Open up to me, Emma.

Will pulled her shirt over her head and tossed it on the floor, then reached for her bra hooks.

I can't.

She tugged his shirt off and dug her fingers into his back, drawing him closer. How many times had she made love with him in desperation? How many times more?

Emma. Let me in.

Will tugged off her jeans.

She wrapped her arms around his head, frustrated over the loss of contact. "Will." She needed more than this, but she couldn't name what she needed.

He laid her on the bed, leaning over her. "Emma, I think I can help you, but you have to let me in your mind."

"I'm scared."

He stared into her eyes. *That's the best reason why.*

Will stood up and took off his jeans, watching her with love in his eyes. He lay down next to her and rolled her sideways, flush against his chest. "Emma, close your eyes."

Her vision blurred with tears. "I can't. Every time I close my eyes I see his face."

He kissed her, soft and gentle, rubbing her shoulder with light caresses. "Do you trust me?"

"I…"

"It's a yes or no question. Do you trust me to help you?"

Did she? He'd asked her to trust him with Alex and that had ended badly. But she hadn't done what he asked either. Will would give his life for her. How could she not trust him? *Yes.*

He rolled Emma onto her back and kissed her so thoroughly she lost herself in him and the moment. *Open your mind to me, Emma.*

She opened the barricade and he eased himself in. She gasped.

Close your eyes.

Pulling back, she looked into his face for reassurance.

Trust me.

Her eyelids fluttered closed, and the terrible images appeared but this time Will was there with her, pulling the pain away, easing her guilt.

How?

The same way I felt your pain in the elevator.

They made love with a gentleness that took her breath away, while Will searched her mind for all her anxieties, siphoning off the pain.

Emma cried with gratitude. She'd never felt more loved and cherished. When she fell asleep in his arms, she wished this moment would never end because from this minute forward, it could get nothing but worse.

CHAPTER TWENTY

WILL woke up the next morning, watching Emma sleep, amazed that she'd opened herself to him. Amazed that it actually worked.

She stirred, looking up at him. "What time is it?"

"Still early. How did you sleep?"

"Better than I've slept in years. How did you know we could do that?"

"Just a hunch."

"Didn't I hurt you?"

"Not that much. I guess our bond means we can share the pain. It evens out between us. It could come in handy in a battle."

She pushed up on an elbow. "What else can we do with this?"

"We know we can share our power. Maybe we can heal each other if one of us is hurt. Like you suspected."

Emma twisted the sheet between her fingers. "I hope we don't need to use that today. Do you know what we're going to do?"

Will sat up and leaned against the headboard. "No. We have no idea what to expect. We have to be prepared for anything." He paused and brushed her hair off her shoulder. He was sure she would be upset over his next subject. "After what happened last night, I don't want you to be there when we confront Aiden and Raphael today."

Emma sat up next to him cross-legged. "Of course I have to be part of it. We're doing this for Jake."

He took her hand and laced their fingers together. "Emma, part of what got us into the situation with Alex is that I asked you to do something you weren't trained or prepared to do. I've spent my entire life learning how to fight. Let me and Marcus do this."

She tried to pull her hand away, but his grip tightened. "Is this about the baby?"

"This has nothing to do with the baby. You can search my mind if you want to."

She gave him a small smile. "No. I believe you. It's just that I should help. Jake is *my* son. I can't let you be at risk while I sit back and do nothing."

"You're telling me you want to fight?"

Fear flashed in her eyes. "No. While I wish Aiden would give Jake back to me, the reality is that I'm going to have to use my power. But I've tried to fight Aiden before and I wasn't strong enough. You saw that. And although I'm stronger now, I know I'm not strong enough."

"You don't have to be strong enough. You have me. We're joined now. We share power. We can do it together."

She tilted her head to one side. "You just admitted that you need me."

Leaning back, he closed his eyes and groaned. "That doesn't mean you have to be there, Emma. It doesn't mean you have to *fight*."

"We have no idea how close we have to be to make our powers work together, Will. I have to be there and you know it."

He did, but it didn't mean he had to like it. "Look, I'll agree because if nothing else, it will be good practice. A test of what we can do and what we're up against for the final battle."

"And we'll get Jake."

"I'll do everything in my power to get him back. And to stop Aiden from destroying any more cities. But if I think Jake is in danger, or if I think you are in danger, I will call a halt."

She shook her head. "I'll never agree to that."

Heaving a sigh, Will sat up straighter. "Then I won't do it."

Scrambling to her knees, she grabbed his shoulders, her nails digging in. "You can't do that, Will!"

"I told you that your safety comes first. Above all else, Emma."

"You promised me that you would save Jake."

"And I will. But if we run into any trouble here in Shreveport, we stop."

"No!" She dropped her hold and sat back.

"Emma, if you or I die trying to save Jake now, what good will we be at the end? Jake is lost. You have to trust me on this. We try our best today, if it doesn't work out, we regroup and concentrate on saving him at the final battle, but we've gained valuable insight into how they work and their plan of attack. We'll be better prepared to face them the next time."

Indecision washed across her face before she looked away. "Fine." Climbing over his legs, she headed for the bathroom.

"Emma..."

She stopped in the doorway and held onto the jamb, looking toward the wall. "Just because I agree with you doesn't mean that I have to like it." The door closed behind her and he heard the shower turn on.

He felt like an ass. But he wouldn't waver. He knew how much she wanted Jake back, but he wouldn't risk getting any of the three of them killed to do it. Still, a confrontation was good. He and Marcus could assess the strengths and weaknesses of both sides. They were going to need every bit of information they could get for the end.

Little Rock and Jackson both suffered four square blocks of destruction. Both happened west of Main Street in downtown. The first attack was at three p.m. and second was at five. Did that mean the next one would be at seven? What little information he'd gathered suggested that Aiden, Raphael, and Jake were positioned one block from the western edge of town in each of the previous incidents. The earthquake epicenter was in that position and all storm damage was to the east, with the brunt of the damage on the far eastern border.

Jackson differed from Little Rock in one key way. One small section outside the ruined area had a narrow band of damage caused from intense heat. Either Aiden or Jake had produced it, but there was no way to tell which one. Will wasn't sure it made any difference. The storm was proof enough that Jake was involved, evidence that Aiden hoped to lure Emma here.

The question was how to detain Aiden and Raphael long enough to get Jake. Hopefully, Marcus would have some ideas.

Emma emerged from the bathroom, wrapped in a towel, her wet hair hanging down her back. Her face was still pale and he couldn't stop his gaze from traveling to her abdomen as she dropped the towel and slipped on her panties.

It had been easy to ignore that Emma was pregnant again, but now it was heavy on his mind. What seemed like a minor issue weeks ago came back to bite him in the ass. She'd developed her powers carrying the first baby, so he knew she could use them. And she'd lost the first baby from a physical beating, nothing supernatural. But her power was so much weaker than his. Why hadn't she used it in the elevator to fight Alex? Was her pregnancy possibly weakening her powers? Would this baby interfere with Emma protecting herself?

Pulling a t-shirt over her head, she caught him watching her. She raised her eyebrows with a smirk.

He leaned back in the chair, putting his hands behind his head, and gave her a cocky grin. "Hey, you can't fault me for enjoying the view."

Shaking her head, she bent down to pick up her towel.

"We haven't eaten since last night so I thought I'd order room service."

"I'm starving. I want pancakes. And bacon. Don't forget the bacon."

"Lots of bacon. Got it."

She walked in front of the window, drying her hair with the towel.

Will ordered their food while watching her. "It'll be here in about twenty minutes."

"Okay."

He moved his chair to face the bed. "I need to talk to Marcus."

She parted the curtains, looking down onto the street. "Just like old times, huh?"

"What are you talking about?"

"You, me and James. South Dakota. Me caught between the man I love and the man in his life who sees me as expendable."

Will swallowed, caught by surprise. "Emma..."

"I wish..." Her fingers fidgeted with the edge of the curtain. "I wish things had worked out differently with me and James. For you. That's one of my biggest regrets."

He hadn't expected that either.

She turned to face him. "He's your best friend for a reason. I wish that he'd given me the chance to find out why."

He'd tried not to think about James since he'd left him in the parking garage in Morgantown.

She sat on the bed, cross-legged in front of him. "Did he ever get along with any of your girlfriends?"

"Now that you mention it..." Will ran a hand through his hair and grinned. "Not a one."

"That's what I thought." She leaned forward and kissed him. "I want to be the first."

Will's back stiffened. "For all I know he'd dead."

Her soft laugh tickled his cheek. "I don't think James can be disposed of that easily. What do you say we go look him up when this mess is all over?"

"We have bigger things to worry about, Emma."

She pulled back, meeting his eyes. "But maybe that's what makes us different than them. Aiden and Alex and Raphael, they're so wrapped up in themselves and what *they* want. Maybe they're evil not because of their power, but because of their priorities." Her fingertips feathered down the side of his face. "Maybe the thing that will save us is what *we're* fighting for." Her thumb stroked his lower lip. "They fight for greed and control. We fight to save the ones we love. Which is more powerful in the end?"

She was wrong, even though he'd told her the same thing days ago. Might was what determined the winner of a battle. Not intentions. History had proven it time and time again.

But for the first time she sat in front of him hopeful that they had a chance. He refused to take that from her.

"I love you, Emma Thompson." He pulled her onto his lap, consumed with emotion. He never thought it possible to love someone this much.

He froze, his hand partway up her shirt, when he heard a knock at the door. "It's probably room service, but I want you to go into the bathroom until I know for sure."

She moved without protest, picking up her towel off the bed on her way.

Will grabbed his handgun out of the bag and moved to the peep hole, surprised to see Marcus outside. He opened the door. "Marcus."

Marcus walked past Will and looked around. "Where's Emma?"

Even though Will knew that Marcus had a vested interest in her, it still worried him. "She's in the bathroom." He put his gun back in his bag.

"How is she today?"

Will knew what he was asking. What good would she be to them in a battle? If she hadn't let him in to help take away part of her guilt, he doubted she would have been useful at all. Marcus was bound to notice the difference, but Will wasn't sure whether to tell Marcus what they could do with their bond. At this point, it seemed better to keep quiet. If Marcus questioned the change in her, Will could chalk it up to elemental healing ability. "She's better."

"Really?" Marcus raised his eyebrows in surprise. "Will she be of any use to us today?"

Marcus was more like the Colonel than Will cared to admit. Always thinking of the bottom line. Perhaps Emma had a point. "I want to protect her from this as much as possible, but she's motivated to rescue Jake."

Marcus seemed to think about Will's answer. "Okay. That's good to know. We need to talk." He looked toward the bathroom door. "But in private."

The bathroom door opened and Emma stood in the opening. "Worried I'll run off to my Daddy Dearest with your secrets?"

Marcus's face hardened. "He has your son. Who's to say he won't manipulate you to get information by dangling Jake in front of you?"

Fury darkened her eyes and she stepped out of the bathroom, hands on her hips. "First of all, I don't like the mental image of my son 'dangling,' so I suggest you refrain from using that phrase again. Second, I love Will with everything in me, so like it or not, we're a package deal, never mind the fact that we're forever joined. And third," She moved in front of him, staring into his face with contempt. "I would sooner die than betray Will. So don't you *ever* suggest that I will again."

A slow smile spread across Marcus's face. "I can see her appeal, Will."

Will had never been more proud of her, but Marcus's comment made Will uneasy. "What do we need to talk about that can't be said in front of Emma?"

Marcus continued to study Emma with a smirk. "Casualties. Acceptable risk. I thought it best to spare Emma the worry."

Emma's face hardened.

Will cleared his throat. "That's an easy discussion. There is no acceptable risk regarding casualties. We will attempt to rescue Jake, but if he or Emma are in imminent danger, we pull back."

"And Will." Emma added. "If Will is in danger, we pull back. But then, I hope *he* wouldn't be an acceptable causality to you."

A current of power filled the room and Marcus's eyelid twitched. "Don't presume to know what I want, Emmanuella."

Will's jaw clenched. The Colonel had bullied and manipulated the people Will loved for years. He wasn't going to let Marcus get away with it too. "Marcus, what you want or don't want is irrelevant in this case. These are the conditions. If you don't like them, you can leave." Will couldn't afford for Marcus to take off, but he couldn't afford to let him stay if he didn't take Emma and Jake's safety into consideration.

Anger flickered over Marcus's face and he glanced at Emma before turning back to Will. "Then we need to make a plan with the stipulated conditions."

There was another knock at the door, and Marcus's eyes narrowed on Emma.

"It's probably room service." Will looked through the peephole. A man in a uniform stood outside the door.

"That was incredibly stupid, Will."

"It's called eating, Marcus." Will opened the door and signed for food, then took the tray. "I haven't eaten since yesterday afternoon and I have no idea when Emma ate last." He put the tray on the desk.

Marcus grimaced but remained silent.

Will grabbed a piece of toast and took a bite. "I figured out a pattern to their attacks. We need to determine the center of downtown Shreveport and I think we'll be able to pinpoint with about a block of accuracy where they'll be."

"That's a good start. It would be even better if we can manage to locate them before they start the attack."

Emma had taken several bites before she jumped up and ran into the bathroom.

Marcus studied the door at the sound of her vomiting. "Is she sick?"

There was no way he was going to tell Marcus about Emma's pregnancy. He had no idea what Marcus would do with that information. "She used to get sick when the Cavallo was close, but lately it's been from nerves."

Marcus didn't look convinced.

"Why don't you go back to your room and I'll be down in a bit. After I make sure she's okay."

"Are you comfortable leaving Emma alone?" Marcus asked in a dry tone.

"I'll be a few doors down. She'll be fine." Will pushed him toward the door. "I'll be there in a few minutes."

After Will got Marcus out, he opened the bathroom door and found Emma hanging over the toilet. "Are you all right?"

She looked up, her face pale. "Never been better." She cast an anxious glance toward the door.

"I sent him back to his room."

Her back relaxed and leaned her head on her arm. "I don't want him to know."

"Agreed."

She released a derisive laugh. "More James déjà vu."

"This is different."

"Is it? I'm not so sure." She sat up. "I'll agree to team up with Marcus in this instance, but I can't commit to anything else."

"Fair enough. I'm not sure I'll even want to. Let's see how today goes and then we'll discuss it."

"Okay." Her color had returned as well as the spark in her eyes.

"You feeling better?"

"Yeah."

"We need to keep your pregnancy between us. Who knows what Aiden or Raphael would do with this information?"

"Or Marcus."

Will grabbed her hand and pulled her to her feet. "Or Marcus."

She bent over the sink and rinsed her mouth. "Will, you have to promise me that you won't make any decisions based on the fact that I'm pregnant. You've done really well until now, but …"

He wrapped his arms around her stomach, watching her in the bathroom mirror. "I can't promise that."

Closing her eyes, she sank back into Will's chest. "Will," she pleaded.

"Princess," he whispered into her ear. "I can't promise because you're far more important to me than the baby. I wouldn't make any decisions because of the baby that I wouldn't have already made because of you."

She wrapped her arms over his. "I wish this was all a nightmare I could wake up from, but then I wouldn't have you. I love you, Will."

"I love you too." He kissed her temple and led her out of the bathroom. "Why don't you rest while I go make plans with Marcus, then I'll come back and tell you what's going on."

Nodding, she sat on the bed and grabbed the remote. Will covered her hand with his. "Be careful with that. What you find is bound to upset you."

"I have to face what I've done."

"And you have so there's no sense beating yourself up about it more." He packed his laptop in his bag. "This meeting could be good. Marcus was hesitant around you so I might get information from him that I might not have gotten here."

"Good idea." She lay back on the bed.

He checked his handgun to make sure it was loaded and placed it on the nightstand. "I'm surprised you're not fighting me more on this."

"I have no desire to be around the man any more than necessary. I trust you."

She trusted him. He'd tried to gain her trust for weeks and they'd nearly lost each other because she couldn't give it. "Thank you."

"But I expect you to tell me everything when you get back."

He smirked. "No problem." He rested a hand on the doorknob. "Call to me if you need me."

"I'll be fine. Go."

***

After Will left the room, she sat on the bed and flipped on the television. She needed to know more about Jackson and she wanted to know what the media was saying about Alex.

Alex. What she'd done still haunted her, but not nearly as much last night. She'd never be able to repay Will for what he'd done to help her and she wasn't sure that she believed it hadn't hurt him very much. She should have questioned him about it more. The likelihood that they'd need to channel one another's pain again was high. She wanted to be prepared for what to expect.

The first channels were the usual hotel information stations, but it only took a few clicks more to find what she was looking for. The Jackson devastation seemed to have top billing on the news station with Alex's death scrolling across the bottom of the screen: *Senator Warren's son killed by terrorists.* Alex would have hated being second in importance.

He'd spent most of his life in that position.

Emma tucked her knees under her chin as she watched the television. Could she really fault Alex for his behavior? Sure what he'd done six years ago was inexcusable, but the rest... It had been about survival. What made her more deserving to live?

She shook her head. This was pointless. Alex had proven time and time again what an ass he was. A few weeks of good behavior didn't change anything. He would have killed her at the end and probably wouldn't have thought a thing about it. It was self-preservation. Pure and simple.

The screen showed the head of Homeland Security telling the nation not to panic but to be on high alert and report any suspicious activity. Jackson was now being called a terrorist attack, and Albuquerque and Little Rock had been called the same. They weren't far off the mark.

Could the authorities stop an attack on Shreveport? She would love nothing more than to make an anonymous call to the police, alerting them to the threat. But that would tip off Aiden and then what would he do? Go destroy Tyler, Texas?

No, as selfish as it was, she had to keep the information to herself and hope that she, Will and Marcus could stop Aiden in time. She was fully aware that she was placing the life of her son over the lives of thousands of other people. She'd deal with the ramifications of that later.

CHAPTER TWENTY-ONE

JAKE smiled. He had not one, but two secrets. He ate breakfast with Aiden and Raphael while they talked about Alex getting killed the night before. Raphael's forehead wrinkled, and he looked pale. If Alex could die, that meant Raphael could die too. Jake squeezed his hand into a fist in his lap. He hoped he was the one who would kill Raphael. Jake lowered his face to hide his smile. He might be able to do it now.

Jake felt powerful, more powerful than he'd ever felt. He wished he could gloat about knowing that Alex died before Aiden did, but he couldn't risk him finding out about the shadows. Aiden would know soon enough. While Aiden might be able to control fire and the people around him, Jake could control air as well as fire. With Jake's increased air power, who knew what he could do.

Still if Aiden and Raphael didn't know about Alex being dead, that meant neither one of them killed him. Unless the one who killed Alex was hiding it. That wouldn't be a surprise.

"It had to be Will or Marcus," Raphael mumbled over his coffee cup. "There was water everywhere."

"And yet no signs of a fire. Emma wasn't there."

Jake's heart fluttered several beats before settling down. He hadn't considered his mother. Thankfully, she wasn't part of it. Killing Marcus or Will would be hard since they'd been nice to him, but Jake couldn't even think about killing Mommy.

Aiden paused, tilting his head as he watched Jake. "There's something different about you, Jacob." He tapped his index finger on his coffee cup. "What is it?"

Jake blinked. "What?"

Setting his cup down, Aiden leaned forward. "I can't quite pinpoint it. What have you been up to?"

What did Aiden suspect? The mark the shadows gave him or his extra power? Jake looked down at the table. "Nothing."

"Nothing, is it?" His fingernail tapping on the cup was the only sound in the room.

"No, sir."

"Raphael," Aiden's voice rose. "Don't you agree there's something different about Jacob?"

"Do you mean his attitude? Did you ever punish him for his outburst yesterday? Or the day before in Little Rock?"

"Is it really your place to question my judgment, Raphael?"

"No…"

The tapping resumed. "Still…Perhaps you're right. Perhaps it is his attitude."

Jake sat in tense silence, holding his fork over his plate.

"I'll let it go for now as long as you don't defy me, Jacob. You would regret that very much."

Jake nodded as he watched Aiden under hooded eyes. Was he strong enough to kill Aiden yet? Should he try it right now? Raphael was here, but Jake suspected Raphael would side with whoever he thought would win.

His power rumbled deep in his bones, like an electric current charging his skin. It made him feel so full that he thought he would burst. If he caught Aiden off guard....

The shadows, normally still around Aiden, slid closer to Jake. "Don't do it," they whispered in his head.

"Did you see that?" Raphael shouted, jumping up so fast his chair fell backward.

"See what?" Aiden asked in an exasperated tone.

"Those shadows just moved."

Aiden shook his head, rolling his eyes. "What the hell are you talking about?"

"The shadows moved. Could the ancient prophecy be true?"

Jake sat up in his chair. "What's that?"

Aiden scowled. "It's childish nonsense."

"Maybe not so childish." Raphael looked scared. "Indulge the boy. Tell him."

Heaving a sigh, Aiden pushed his plate away. "The prophecy says that one day the shadows will come back to reclaim their realm. A very long, long time ago, the four of us elements banished the shadow creatures to the otherworld. Needless to say, they weren't very happy about it. Long ago, humans believed in ancient gods and the shadows convinced the humans that if they helped them escape, they would be rewarded."

"Did they do it? Did they help them escape?"

"No, of course not. But the shadows told the humans that one day they would return to save them from the elements. We destroyed the civilization of course, so there's no human record to prove it, but apparently Raphael has childish nightmares about their return."

"Did Marcus help too?"

Aiden's eyes narrowed. "Why the interest?"

Jake widened his eyes to look innocent. "It's a story. Mommy used to tell me stories all the time. I miss them."

"Well, soon you will be reunited with you mother and she can tell you stories to your heart's content." Aiden stood up. "Someone bring Antonia."

Antonia had been nervous all morning, and Jake worried Aiden would sense it and become angry with her. Jake searched her out in the other room and covered most of her thoughts with his power. He had no idea if it would work, and he worried what Aiden would do to her if he realized what Jake had done, but it seemed worth the risk.

Thirty seconds later, she hurried into the room, lowering her face to hide the fear in her eyes. Now Jake was really worried and readjusted his power so Aiden could only sense the words she spoke.

"Antonia, I need Jake to be ready to go around twelve-thirty today. At that time, have all of his things packed and taken to the car. We will leave as soon as we are done with our errand."

Jake's stomach twisted. Not again.

Antonia bowed her head and nodded. "*Si, Señor* Aiden."

"Jake, you may go for now."

"Yes, sir."

"*Señor* Aiden." Antonia's voice shook.

Jake froze next to his chair, his fear for her turning his feet to stone.

Aiden grinned with a wicked twinkle in his eye, amused that she dared to address him. "Yes, Antonia."

"May I take *Señor* Jake outdoors to play this morning? He's a little boy and he needs fresh air and time to run."

Aiden chuckled. "He'll get plenty of fresh air this afternoon. Besides, it's hot outside."

"I will make sure he's back in time to shower and be presentable before your outing."

The silence that filled the room was deafening.

"What about you, Jake?" Aiden asked. "Would you like to go outside to play with Antonia?"

Jake glanced up at her, unsure what she was doing. She never dared approach Aiden with anything. "Yes, sir."

"Very well, then." Aiden waved his hand. "But don't be late or you *will* regret it."

"*Gracias, señor.*" Antonia nodded.

Jake moved toward her, careful not to go too quickly and rile Aiden's anger. When they entered Jake's room, Antonia's hands shook as she grabbed his backpack. "We shall leave now."

"Okay."

He was curious what she was up to, but prepared to wait. The blanket he'd put over her thoughts kept Jake out as well. If they discussed her plan, there was a good chance they would be overheard.

Antonia picked up his pack and held his hand, leading him from the suite to the elevator bank. When the doors open, she pulled him inside, her grip tightening and making his fingers tingle. He looked up at her, but she kept her eyes on the numbers over the door, her mouth pinched in a tight line.

The doors opened to the lobby and apprehension tumbled in Jake's tummy. None of this was right, but he trusted Antonia.

The air was hot and sticky when the left the hotel. They walked down the street, through the crowd of people. Jake's feet dragged, the crowd reminding him of Jackson and what he'd have to do this afternoon. His stomach twisted and he thought he was going to throw up.

"Jake, we must hurry." Antonia's pace picked up the farther they got from the hotel. Soon Jake had to run to keep up, hoping he didn't barf on the street.

"Antonia, wait."

She halted, tears in her eyes. "We must hurry. We don't have much time."

"Where are we going?"

"You must trust me."

He had no reason not to but couldn't figure out what she was up to. This was so unlike her it made him anxious.

She waved to a passing taxi and the beat up yellow car pulled to the curb. Opening the back door, she pushed Jake onto the backseat, climbing in behind him. "To the airport, please."

Jake's heart lurched. "Where are we going?"

She took his hands in hers, her chin quivering. "I am saving you."

His mouth dropped open. "What? How?"

"There is a plane that leaves in the next hour, but we must hurry if we are to make it in time. It is our only chance."

"But Aiden... if he finds out... he'll..." Fear screamed in Jake's mind.

"That is why we must hurry. We must be on the plane before it leaves. It is our only chance."

He wanted to be far, far away from Aiden, but Aiden knew everything. "He'll find us," he whispered, wishing he wasn't so afraid.

She shook her head. "No. I will use different names. He will not find us. No more talk for now." She turned to the front, still holding his hand.

The drive to the airport was short but long enough for Jake's terror to build. Could she really save him from Aiden? Did he allow himself to hope?

The taxi dropped them off at the curb and Antonia entered the airport, her hold on him so tight he didn't think anything—not even one of his storms—could pull him from her. She stopped at a machine and entered a credit card, tapping the screen furiously, mumbling prayers under her breath. The machine spit papers out and Antonia's fingers fumbled to pull them from the machine.

One fell on the floor, and Jake bent over to pick it up. He handed it to her, looking up into her anxious eyes.

"Antonia, we don't have to do this."

She knelt in front of him, a tear falling down her cheek. "It is the only way I know to save you."

"If he finds out..."

Pulling him into a hug, she buried her face in his hair. "Then we shall make sure he doesn't find out." Still kneeling, she pulled him back and looked into his face. "You are Tony Rodriguez. You live in Monroe, Louisiana. You are six years old. I am your Aunt Barbara and we are going to visit your grandmother in Houston. Now repeat."

She was really doing this. His voice shook as he chanted. "I'm Tony Rodriguez. I live in Monroe, Louisiana. I'm six years old. You are my Aunt Barbara and we're going to Houston."

"Why are we going there?"

"To see my grandmother."

"Good boy." She kissed his cheek before she stood up and took his hand. They headed to a long line of people waiting to go through machines. Jake looked up at her, gnawing on the inside of his cheek with worry.

"This is the security checkpoint. If we can make it through this line, we are safe."

The line moved slowly and Jake eyed every man around them suspiciously. He couldn't believe it could be this easy. What should he do if Aiden showed up? Or Raphael?

Antonia stood in front of a podium and handed her papers to the man in the uniform. Jake's hand turned cold and clammy. Mommy had always warned him that men in uniforms were usually enemies. This man glanced over the papers, then eyed Jake up and down with a frown.

"What's your name, little guy?"

"Tony."

"Tony what?"

"Rodriguez."

"How old are you?"

"Six."

"When's your birthday?"

He tried to keep his eyes from widening. Antonia hadn't told him that answer. "July."

The man grinned. "You just had a birthday, huh? Did you have a party?"

Jake's breakfast rose in his throat. "No."

The man looked at the papers again, then from Antonia to Jake.

"So you're going with your mom to Minneapolis?"

Sweat broke out on Jake's neck. "No, sir. This is my aunt and we're going to visit my grandmother in Houston."

He cocked his head. "Why do you have blond hair and your last name is Rodriguez?"

He didn't know what his question meant. "My dad had blond hair."

"Had?" The man shook his head. "I'm going to have to have you step aside, ma'am."

No! Jake screamed into the man's head.

The guard jerked, his eyes widening.

You will let us in.

The order was so harsh, the man shook.

Jake stood on tiptoes and whispered to Antonia. "What does he have to do?"

"Hey, that guy's not looking so well," a man in line behind Jake said.

Antonia's eyes were wild with confusion. "He has to stamp our tickets and make a line through them."

Stamp our papers and put the mark on them. Do it now.

The man in the uniform stabbed his stamp onto the tickets, then marked through them with his pen.

Hand them to my aunt and forget about us.

He handed the papers to Antonia and turned to the next person in line.

Antonia crossed herself.

They took off their shoes and put them in bins to run through a machine along with Jake's backpack. Jake was nervous until they made it through the line and out the other side.

Antonia took his hand again. "We must hurry. We only have thirty minutes."

They half ran down a hall, stopping at an area with lots of chairs. A long tube extended from the building attached to a plane. It was much bigger than the ones he'd flown in with Aiden "Is that our plane?"

"*Sí.*"

She sat in a chair, tugging him next to her. His nerves had him jumpy and he fidgeted. She covered his hands with hers. "You must be still. For just a little longer. If we are too nervous…"

He nodded, trying to sit quietly.

She leaned over to his ear. "What did you do to the security man?"

"I told him to let us through."

"I didn't hear you say it."

I said it in his head.

Her eyes widened and her rosary beads jingled. She cupped his cheek and searched his eyes. "Are you a *demonio*? You do not look like one."

Maybe he *was* part demon after everything he'd done. "I don't know. Aiden and Alex said that I am a mix of elements. My father was air. My mother is fire. Does that make me a demon?"

"*Mi dios.*" She crossed herself.

The images of the dead bodies flashed into his mind. "Aiden makes me do terrible things. Terrible, terrible things. I don't want to do them anymore."

She kissed his cheek. "I know. This is why I must save you, *mijo*."

"I would never hurt you, Antonia."

"I know this, *mijo*. You are a good, sweet boy."

He wrapped his arms around her neck. "I love you."

"And I love you."

She wiped the tears from his cheek and gave him a warm smile. "When we know that we are safe, we will find your mother."

He squeezed her neck tight again, choking on his tears. "Thank you, Antonia. Thank you."

She pulled him back and smoothed his hair. "A boy belongs with his mother."

A voice crackled on the intercom overhead. "Now boarding for American Flight 7027 to Houston."

Antonia smiled. "That is us." She rose and Jake followed her to another line. A woman next to a door took the tickets and let the people into the tube.

There were only four people in front of them when two men in a police uniforms hurried down the hall in their direction. Jake tried not to watch, instead facing forward.

Two more people left in line, handing over their papers. Jake's heart raced making his breath come in short bursts. He glanced down the hall.

The guards cut through the chairs, determination on their faces.

Antonia handed their tickets to the woman and the machine beeped twice.

Almost there. Almost there.

One of the men wrapped his hand around Antonia's arm. "Excuse me, ma'am. We're going to need you and the little boy to come with us."

The other guard stood to the side, his eyes on Jake.

She tried to break free from his hold. "No! We are on this flight. We need to get on this plane."

"I'm sorry, ma'am, but we need to question you in a suspected kidnapping."

"What? There is a mistake."

"Jake, you'll need to come with us too."

"I don't know what you're talking about." Jake's voice rose in panic. "My name is Tony. This is my aunt."

People gathered closer, watching with curiosity.

The guard to the side stepped forward and gripped Jake's arm as the first man pulled Antonia from the line.

Terrified, Jake unleashed his power. He had to save Antonia. "No!" Jake screamed. A strong wind whipped through the long hallway. The man holding Antonia's arm dropped his grasp and reached for his throat, his face turning a purplish-blue. The other guard's eyes bulged and the veins on his neck popped out. People in the crowd gasped for air, some falling to their knees and to the ground.

Antonia squatted in front of Jake. "Stop! You're hurting these people, Jake. You must stop!"

Jake held his tight fists at his side. "They're going to hurt you. I won't let them hurt you."

"You cannot hurt these innocent people for me."

He stopped the wind and listened to the sounds of choking and gasping.

Antonia took his hand. "Run!"

They ran through the terminal as fast as Jake's legs would stretch, but as the people began to recover, they pointed and shouted. Antonia pulled Jake into a restroom.

Shaking, she covered her mouth with her free hand. Her rosary beads dangled from her fingers. "We must think. We need a plan."

Jake looked up at her, clenching his fists. "I can use my power."

Her eyes widened and she shook her head. "No! You must not. Your power makes you more like Aiden than like your mother."

Tears filled Jake's eyes as fear replaced his anger. "But he'll catch us."

She leaned her back against the wall and closed her eyes. "*Sí.*"

"No." His anger billowed inside him, making him glow.

Instead of her usual fear, Antonia's eyes filled with love. "Do not give him this. He wants you to use your power for bad things."

He swallowed the lump of fear in his throat. "Saving you isn't bad, Antonia. Saving you is good. I love you."

She squatted in front of him, clasping his hands in hers. "You are right, Jake, saving me is not bad. Wanting to save me is done with love. Love is the most pure gift of all. But you are clouding it with anger and hate, and it will destroy you."

"I don't know what else to do if I can't use my power," he sobbed. "I can't let them hurt you."

She dug into her purse, pulled out a handful of money, and reached for his shorts pocket.

He tried to back up, shaking his head. "No! No!"

Tugging gently on his arm, she brought him closer and stuffed the bills into his pocket. "Hush, *mijo*. Hush. Listen to me." She grasped his shoulders, tears streaming down her cheeks. "When they find us, you must run. Do not wait for me. Do not look back. Run. Do you understand?"

He shook his head, trying to catch his breath through his tears. "No. I can't."

Her grip tightened. "Do you love me, Jake?"

"Yes! You know I love you!"

"Have I ever asked for anything from you?"

"No," he whispered. The mark on his chest was icy cold and it seeped into his insides.

"Then do this for me. It is the only thing I will ask of you. If you love me, you will give it to me."

"Please, Antonia. Don't make me do this. *Please*." He clung to her, knowing that if he ran, Aiden would kill her.

"It is the only way." She stroked his cheek. "Do you know why I tried to take you away?"

"Because you love me?"

"Yes, very much so. You are the little boy I never had. But I tried to take you away for another reason. I wanted to save your soul. You are a good boy. A sweet boy. Do not let your *abuelo* turn you into the *demonio* that he is."

Jake sobbed, knowing she was right. But Aiden would kill her. Because of him.

"Remember when I met your mother? In Albuquerque?"

He nodded, trying to catch his breath.

"I promised her I would watch over you for her. Promise me..." Her voice cracked. "Promise me that you will tell her that I did the best I could."

He nodded. "I promise."

Her hands tightened on his face. "Love is the most powerful thing in the world, Jake. More powerful than any evil. Remember this."

He nodded barely seeing her face through his tears. "I'll remember, Antonia."

Sirens blared overhead and shouts echoed in the hall outside the restroom.

"Be brave for me." She stood and looped his backpack over his shoulders, buckling the clasp over his chest, her fingers lingering on the strap. Then she stood and led him to the restroom exit. They made it ten feet before the guards spotted them. Antonia dropped his hand and shouted. "*Run!*"

He could kill them. There were only five guards. He could easily do it and not hurt anyone else. He'd just panicked before. But Antonia shook her head, her eyes filled with love. He searched her mind.

Do this for me. It is the only thing I will ask of you. If you love me, you will give it to me.

The only person he loved more than Antonia was his mommy. Even though every part of him protested, he would give her anything. Even this.

Stumbling as he spun around, he found his footing and ran. He ran faster than he'd ever run, trying to outrun the nightmares that lived in the real world and not just his dreams. He ran past families and workers and old men and women. Small children watching from their mother's arms. He ran out through the exit next to the security gate and made it out the doors into the oppressive heat, the sun blinding him.

Jake jerked to a halt when noticed a shiny black car stopped at the curb. The back door opened and Aiden climbed out, narrowing his eyes. "Hello, Jacob. Looks like you've had a busy morning."

For a split second, Jake was sure he could defeat Aiden, but Antonia's face rose up in his thoughts and her words washed over him. *Love is more powerful than evil.* He had to believe her.

The guards brought Antonia through the doors behind him. Jake turned his head. Seeing the men hold her arms so tight hurt Jake too much.

"What was the meaning of this, Antonia?" Aiden asked in a bored tone.

"This is all my fault. *Señor* Jake had no knowledge of what I intended to do."

Jake's mouth dropped open.

"Is this true, Jake?"

Antonia's eyes pleaded with Jake.

I can't do this, Antonia.

Her beaming face, full of love, told him that he could.

Jake looked at concrete sidewalk. "Yes, it's true."

"I'm very disappointed, Antonia. You were such a model employee until this incident. You provide such excellent care for Jake. Perhaps I should give you another chance."

Jake looked up hopeful, but Antonia's face remained stoic.

"However." Aiden paused with a tight smile. "What kind of example would I give it I let you get away with this blatant infraction? You must be a model for others." Aiden's gaze turned to Jake.

Jake knew Aiden meant him.

Antonia lifted her chin, looking braver than Jake had ever seen her. She fixed her gaze on Aiden. *"Pudrete en el infierno, demonio por lo que le haces al niño!"*

Aiden looked amused. "Interesting choice of words, Antonia."

Her skin turned red and she moaned.

"Do you have anything to say now?"

"Que Dios maldiga tu alma para siempre!" she cried out, her eyes rolling back into her head.

Fear crawled across Jake's skin and he looked away.

"No, Jacob." Aiden's voice was harsh. "You will watch this."

Lifting his chin, her face was blurry through his tears.

"Disobedience will not be tolerated. Remember."

Antonia's mouth moved but nothing came out until she screamed.

Please, Antonia. Please let me save you.

She shook her head. "Only God can deliver me."

Aiden snarled, his lips curling back to reveal his shiny white teeth. *"Yo te libraré."*

Her clothes burst into flames and her hair caught fire. Screams pierced the air as she fell to the ground, screaming and screaming until she finally stopped and then…nothingness.

Jake loved Antonia but she had been very, very wrong.

Evil was stronger than love.

CHAPTER TWENTY-TWO

MARCUS leaned against the desk in his room. "There's a problem with Emma."

Will sat down in a chair in the corner, his mouth suddenly dry. Had Marcus figured out that Emma was pregnant? "What the hell are you talking about?"

"Emma's power is weak and unreliable."

Relief washed through him as he shook his head. "Alex told Emma that she was stronger than Emmanuella."

Marcus pushed away from the desk and sat in the chair next to Will. "Knowing the previous incarnation personally, that's not saying much."

"I've seen her do some powerful things."

"Yes, I agree that she's capable of a great deal, but unfortunately, she's not able to manage it every time she needs to. Her power is sporadic at best. Why didn't she use her power in the elevator? She should have been able to put up more of a fight."

Will released a heavy exhale. Marcus was asking the very questions Will had been asking himself. "She was probably afraid. She gets her power from anger. Fear tends to put a damper on it."

"That's a huge problem, Will."

His statement was so obvious, Will saw no point in answering.

"She needed to ground her source in something free of emotion when it was developing. I'm not sure there's time for her to relearn it."

"From what I've heard, her predecessor instinctively knew how to ground her power in previous lives and her protector helped her." Will didn't try to hide his defensive tone. "Emma had neither. She did the best she could, and I didn't know any better."

Marcus held up a hand in defense. "No one is chastising her. Or you. I'm merely pointing out the facts."

Still guarded, Will rested his hand on the armchair. "Alex told her that the emotional source was what made her stronger than Emmanuella."

"True, but you've also seen that it makes her much weaker when it doesn't work. This is good to know, though." He paused for a moment. "We just need to rile her anger in a battle. You know as well as I do that we can't rely on her in a fight, which will work out today but not at the end."

Will had worried about that as well. "Emma and I can share power. We already have. I can share mine with her."

"You're going to need every bit of your own. You can't share it with Emma or you'll get both of you killed."

"So what are you proposing?"

"I'm not proposing anything at the moment. I'm merely assessing the situation and suggesting we come up with a solution before the end."

Will agreed with everything Marcus said, but the fact remained that only two of them would survive. Marcus had to be trying to swing this to his own advantage. "I take it you have a plan for today?"

"Given the information you've untangled, I suggest we scout out the area starting at five, a full two hours before we expect them to strike."

"And what do you propose for our plan of attack?"

"We need Emma close, but I don't think she should participate in any fighting today."

"Agreed."

"We should plan on both Raphael and Aiden being there, along with Jake. And I think you're correct about their positioning. Given the damage patterns, they're sticking close together. That should make them more vulnerable. We, on the other hand, should split up and come from different directions."

Will would have suggested the same thing. "I think we should engage Aiden and Raphael to get a true sense of what they can do."

Marcus folded his hands under his chin. "And Jake."

"*What?*"

"We need to engage Jake as well. In case we don't rescue him today, we need to know what we're up against later."

Will shook his head, furious that Marcus could suggest such a thing. "Have you lost your mind?"

"You know this is a good idea."

"No. It's a terrible idea. We need to rely on the element of surprise to capture him, especially since our goal is a recovery, not an assassination."

"That's shortsighted on your part, Will."

Will studied Marcus for several seconds, gripping the sides of his chair. "If I didn't know any better, I would think you plan to kill Jake."

Marcus pressed his lips together. "I want no such thing. Do you take me for a monster, Will?"

"Honestly, Marcus, I'm not sure what to believe."

Marcus held his gaze for several seconds before he sighed and looked away. "I don't intend to kill Jake or Emma myself, but we need to face the reality that only two will survive. So while I will not kill them, someone else will." Marcus leaned forward, intensity burning his eyes. "We need Jake to be there at the end, but when we are in the final battle, I won't intervene on his behalf. Or Emma's. And know this: I intend to win and I plan for you to be with me."

Will rolled his eyes in disgust. Marcus was casually dismissing the only reason Will was fighting. "*Why?* Because you loved my mother?"

"Yes, but also because you are my son. I do not take that lightly."

"Forgive me if I'm not falling for this family bonding moment," Will shifted in his seat, uncomfortable with the change of topic but glad to get it out in the open. "I've never seen you in thirty-four years and suddenly you show up and want to play daddy."

"I've been in your life, Will. You either didn't notice or you simply don't remember."

Will snorted. "Yeah, right."

Marcus fingered the fold of his pants. "When you were nine, you, James, and your sister Megan snuck down to the river to swim. You didn't ask your mother's permission so you had no adult supervision. The current pulled you under, and a man saved you."

"That was a fisherman."

Marcus looked up and smiled. "And then the time when you were seventeen and you and James drank too much and planned to drive home, but you couldn't find the keys—only to find them the next morning in your jeans pocket."

Will's breath caught. "Shit."

"Or when you came home for your sister's wedding and James told you he wasn't going to re-enlist. You considered not signing up again too. Until…"

Closing his eyes, Will took a deep breath. "A man in the café convinced me to stay." His eyes opened with alarm. "You told me that I'd find Emma."

"That was the night the final version of this game all began."

The hair on Will's arms stood on end. "What do you mean?"

"Really? You never put it together? That was the night Jake was conceived."

"The feeling I had that something bad had happened…."

"Something bad did happen. You were right."

Will's head felt fuzzy and he tried to focus on Marcus's words. He knew that Marcus had orchestrated events, but he had no idea the scope of his involvement.

Marcus leaned over and placed a hand on Will's leg. "All of this is to prove to you that I've been looking out for you since before you can remember. Why would I go to all that trouble if you weren't important to me? Why would I tell you that you'd find Emma if I didn't want to help you protect her? I want you to have as much time with her as you can before you lose her."

Lose her? Will couldn't face the possibility and he sure wouldn't agree to Marcus's plan. But if he had Marcus's word that he wouldn't harm Emma or Jake today, then he could assess Marcus's power in the coming fight as well as the others. He checked his watch and stood up, needing some space to think. "I need to get back to Emma."

"I have a favor to ask."

Will paused. If Marcus had to ask, it couldn't be good. "What?"

"I'd like to speak to Emma. Alone."

Shaking his head, Will glared. "No way."

"I swear to you that I won't hurt her."

"There's no way in hell I'm leaving you alone with her."

A small grin spread across Marcus's face. "I think that should be her choice and not yours."

"She'll never agree to it."

"Maybe not, but ask anyway."

Will hurried to his room, suddenly anxious to get back to Emma. Either Marcus was one hell of a master manipulator or he truly cared for Will. He suspected the truth was a mix of both.

He knocked with their usual pattern before opening the door. She sat on the bed, cross-legged, her eyes glued to the television, which showed coverage of Alex's murder.

"Emma." he sighed. "Why are you doing this?" He sat next to her, reaching for the remote.

She leaned away from him, keeping it out of his reach. "I'm a grown woman perfectly capable of making my own decisions, Will Davenport. I did pretty well the first twenty-seven years before you showed up."

"Yes, you did." He took her hand in his. "I just don't want you to torture yourself out of some need for punishment."

She moved toward him and brushed his lips with her own, then sat back. "No, that's not why I'm watching. I think we need to know what the media's saying. Or at the very least, find out if we're implicated."

"Good idea. Learn anything?"

Her mouth twisted into a smile. "Actually, yes." She picked up a notepad with a hotel logo at the top. "They're blaming Alex's death on the Cavallo."

"You're kidding."

"Nope. They even have a bit of information about them, which is similar to what we know."

Will shifted closer to look at the paper. "I wonder if Warren and the Vinco Potentia really think the Cavallo are responsible. Maybe they're just throwing the media a bone with a little meat on it."

Emma shrugged. "Phillip Warren may be an egotistical bastard, but he's no Aiden. He loved his son. I'm sure he wants to find who's responsible."

"Not if he thinks it was us. Then he'd want to keep the attention elsewhere."

She sighed. "True."

Will wrapped an arm around her back. "What else?"

"They are trying to tie the attacks on the cities to the Cavallo now, too. They have actual member names."

"Have they found any members to question?"

"Yeah, a few, but many are dead. Which of course reeks of a conspiracy."

Grinning, Will shook his head. "America loves a good conspiracy."

"True."

"But still, the Cavallo is in the Vinco Potentia's backyard. I'm surprised Warren would want the press and authorities snooping that close."

"Maybe it was all they had to throw out to keep themselves from being discovered."

"You might be right."

She pushed him on his back and straddled him. "What was that?" She cocked an eyebrow. "Could you repeat that?"

He chuckled. "You mean that you were right?"

"Yeah, that part."

"It's not the first time I've said it, Emma."

"Just remember it won't be the last." She leaned down to kiss him.

He rolled her to her side, letting his lips linger on hers. "God, I love you."

She pulled her head back, eyeing him suspiciously. "How'd it go with Marcus?"

"It went fine. He's just worried about you."

Her eyebrows rose. "Worried about me? Somehow I think there might be some paraphrasing in there."

"More specifically he's worried about your source of power and that it might be unreliable. I know you don't want to talk about what happened in the elevator, but I need to know. I caught bits and pieces last night, but I need all of it."

She sighed and rolled on her back.

"If it's too painful, I can help you. In fact, I can just search your mind to get the answers if you want me to."

"No," she sighed. "I'll tell you." She stared at the ceiling. "When the elevator reached the basement, the doors opened and you told me to touch him, but I was torn. I really believed he wanted to help me save Jake so I realized I couldn't do it. I couldn't betray him like that." She took a deep breath. "But then you appeared and when he heard what you said, he was sure I'd tricked him. The truth is, even if I changed my mind in the end, I did betray him. I played on his sympathy for Jake and lured him to his death." She sat up and closed her eyes.

"Emma, you don't have to say this out loud. I can find it out on my own."

She looked over her shoulder at Will, resignation in her eyes. "I should own up to what I did, Will. I need to hold myself accountable if I have any hope of redeeming myself for the terrible things I've done." She turned to the television. "For the terrible things I still have to do."

Will sat up and wrapped his arm around her, pressing his chest against her back. Wasn't it his job, originally as her protector and now as the man who not only loved her but had bound himself to her forever, to protect her and save her from all of this? But he couldn't protect her at all, no matter how much it ate at his soul. All he had to give her was his love and support. He kissed the side of her head. "Okay."

She paused for a moment. "Alex was furious, justifiably. To retaliate against both of us, he wanted to make you feel physical pain through our connection. We both know that worked until I blocked it from you." She rested her hand on his arm. "I tried to use my power, but my fear prevented me from doing it in the beginning. The pain...the pain overwhelmed me after that. I burned his arm at some point and set his shirt on fire."

Will knew the physical pain that Alex had caused from searching her mind for it the night before. "Emma, I'm sorry. What happened was my fault. I will never put you in a position like that again."

She turned to face him and her eyes softened. "You can't promise me that, and I don't expect you to. I'm sorry I wasn't stronger."

"You were strong enough."

"I wasn't, and we both know it. Pretending that I was won't help anything, and it might get the three of us killed. We need to figure out what to do in spite of my limitations."

Will's arm tightened around her. He wasn't sure how many days they had left for him to prepare her for the battle and even then, he wasn't sure what else to do. What if Marcus wanted to talk to her so he could help her? It was doubtful, but Marcus was right. Emma should decide for herself. "Marcus wants to talk to you. Alone."

Her body stiffened. "Why?"

"He didn't say but he's sworn that he won't hurt you."

"What could he possibly want?"

"I have no idea."

Leaning the side of her head into his neck, she sighed. "Okay."

"You don't have to do this."

"I know. But I'm curious."

"If you're going to see him, it should probably be soon."

Pushing herself off the bed, she gave him a brief, tight smile. "Let's get this over with."

They walked to Marcus's room in silence. Will stood next to her, wanting to say something but unsure of what. She knocked and within seconds Marcus opened the door.

"Thanks for coming, Emma."

Emma didn't answer.

Leaning a hand against the door frame, Will lowered his voice. "I swear to God if you hurt her or scare her in any way—"

Stepping away from the opening, Marcus gave Emma a soft smile, then turned to Will. "I only want to talk. I promise."

Anxiety prickled Will's nerves. *Are you sure you want to do this?*

Yes. She walked into the room without a backward glance as Marcus shut the door.

CHAPTER TWENTY-THREE

EMMA told herself that Marcus wouldn't hurt her, but her heart still raced. She spun around to face him, spreading her hands at her sides, she spoke with a cocky attitude. "Well, here I am, Marcus. What do you want?"

"It occurs to me that you have questions."

Her mouth almost dropped open before she recovered. "I'm here because you think I have questions." She put a hand on her hip and shook her head with a half-laugh. "Are you serious?"

"I suspect no one has really been honest with you in all of this. Everyone has their own agenda, and they've told you the version of the truth that they want you to hear."

"What makes you any different?"

"Our mutual love of Will. And our mutual need of Jake."

"Which is why you wanted to talk alone." She understood their mutual love of Will, but not Jake.

"Yes."

"Okay, start talking."

Marcus brushed past her and sat in a chair in front of the window and waved to a chair next to him. "Have a seat."

"Thanks, I'll stand."

He shrugged. "Perhaps I'll start with the prophecy."

Her stomach tightened. She hadn't expected that. "What about it?"

"I suppose you wonder what it means."

"It's gibberish."

"Maybe. Maybe not."

She snorted. "The funny thing about prophecies is that people read into it what they want. Everyone has their own interpretation."

Marcus rested his hand on the chair arm and ran his finger along the seam. "After millenniums of observation, I'd love to share mine."

She knew he had to have an underlying motive for this, but she had to admit she was curious. Sitting on the edge of the bed, the closest seat to the door, she cocked her head. "I'm listening."

"I'm sure you know by now that the prophecy the Vinco Potentia believed is wrong. The real one was written in code in the book. Once you heard it, it should have burned itself onto your consciousness."

"Jake told the correct one to Will when he marked him."

"So you know it?" Marcus grinned. "The first part is fairly obvious.

"The land will fall desolate and cold
As it waits for the promised ones.
God resides within the queen
While she hides among the people of the exile land
Hunted for that which she must lose
One who is named protector, The Chosen One,

Shall be a shield, counselor, companion."

'I'm the queen. Will is the protector. I was hunted for Jake." She didn't try to hide the irritation in her voice.

"Yes." He smiled but his eyelid twitched. "I told you it was fairly obvious. It's the second part that is elusive." He recited again:

"The elevated one will arise from great sorrow
In the full moon after the summer solstice
His powers will be mighty and powerful
He will rise up to rule the land
The supplanter will challenge him
But only one will be overcome
By that which has no price."

Marcus cleared his throat. "Aiden believes that Jake is the elevated one. I believe it's Will. He received his mark and found you around the summer solstice. You have to admit that his powers are much stronger than yours and probably stronger than Raphael's."

"What difference does it make at this point?"

"The prophecy still applies, in spite of the rule changes."

"So Will is going to rise up and rule the land?" She refused to admit it to Marcus, but the idea of Will winning and ruling wasn't that farfetched.

With a look of earnestness, Marcus leaned forward, clasping his hands. "Yes, and you have to understand the significance of this. The world has been in chaos for eons.

If Aiden gets complete control, he's liable to wipe out half the human race, just for the fun of it. Raphael is a mini-Aiden. But Will..." Marcus's eyes lit up. "Will has been training for this his entire life. He is not only destined to rule, but he will be fair and levelheaded. Will is just what the world needs to set it back on course."

"With you by his side. Of course."

Marcus didn't answer.

"So where does Jake come into this? You said you need him."

"Jake is the supplanter."

She nodded slowly, raising her eyebrows. "Of course, he is."

"He's necessary for the end to play out."

Her heart lodged in her throat. "And the supplanter is overcome."

Marcus nodded once.

"You want to sacrifice my son. So that you can save your own. Do you realize what you are asking?"

"Yes. I'm sorry. Jake is a child and he's not prepared to rule anything. Can you imagine the consequences to mankind? We must put our own selfish motives aside and think of the good of the world."

"And it just so happens that the good of the world is for *your* son to survive." Her nausea returned and she resisted the urge to run to the bathroom. This man was discussing the murder of her son. She clenched her hand into a fist so he couldn't see it shake. "And that which has no price? What is that?"

"You."

Her heart stuttered. "What?"

"Emma, you must kill Jake. It has to be you."

Icy fear flowed through her veins. "I can see why you wanted to talk to me alone. Will would never agree to any of this."

"His love for you blinds his thought process. If you take a step back and look at the situation without your emotional investment—"

She stood, shaking her head. "I've heard enough."

Standing, Marcus reached a hand toward her. "Emma, wait. There's something else."

"I can't wait to hear this."

He released a heavy breath and lowered his hands. "There's another prophecy. One more ancient. It's so old that the specific words have been lost but the legend remains."

Putting a hand on her hip, Emma gave him a sardonic smile. "Let me guess, it has to do with a mother butchering her child?"

"It's about a child. A boy who restores the powers of the world by uniting two realms. Our own and the shadow world. He has a mark. Does Jake have one?"

"Jake has no mark, so forget your crazy idea. Besides, wouldn't that make Jake the elevated one?"

"The legend says the boy does it at great sacrifice."

"And you think that's Jake's death?"

"Death is the ultimate sacrifice, isn't it?" He paused. "Jake's power is growing. He can use it to defend himself against Aiden at some point, but it's becoming malevolent.

There's nothing more frightening than an out-of-control five-year-old with unlimited power."

Emma's stomach rolled. "Thanks for sharing." Her tone was as snotty she could muster with fear crawling down her spine. "I'm done."

Marcus took several steps toward her. "I'm sure you don't believe me, but this isn't personal, Emma. I really do like you, and Will is going to be devastated to lose you. Sometimes I wish I'd never insisted Aiden create a new daughter. The old one had become selfish and petulant. She would have been…an easier loss."

With a sarcastic laugh, she took a backward step toward the door. "You're quite the smooth talker. Thanks."

She threw the door open and stormed down the hall to Will, confusion jumbling her thoughts. Will would want to know what Marcus had to say and while she knew she should tell him, what if Marcus was right? What if that was how things were supposed to work out? Emma had learned from Jake's visions that some things couldn't be changed. Sometimes fate just intervened. Should she shield Will from the pain of knowing that her death might be foretold?

But in fairness, hadn't she already known? In the end, there could be only two, and she couldn't kill Will even if she tried. Their bond prevented it. She refused to kill Jake. That left her to die.

Will sat in front of the bed, his eyes glued to the television. The strained expression on his face told her something was wrong. When she walked in, he looked up at her with pity and fear in his eyes.

Her heart fell to the floor. "What now?"

"The news…"

An announcer's voice came from the television. "We have more word on what might have been another terrorist attack at the Shreveport Regional Airport."

Emma moved closer to the TV.

"At approximately ten-thirty an incident occurred at the Shreveport Regional airport. Travelers in the terminal report that they suddenly lost their breath, as though the air had been sucked from their lungs. Reports suggest this lasted anywhere from twenty seconds to a minute, and many collapsed. There are a few reported fatalities, no confirmation on numbers yet. After the incidents in Albuquerque, Little Rock, and Jackson officials are treating this as a terrorist attack."

"No earthquake," Emma whispered.

"Not that they've reported."

"The breath thing… Alex did that to me in the elevator."

Will put his hand on her arm. "And to me."

"Alex is dead." Her tone was flat. Only one person had control over air now.

"Jake would never knowingly hurt people, Emma. You know that."

"So what? Aiden forced him to? What are they doing in an airport? I thought they were attacking downtowns."

Will sat down on the bed and pulled his laptop in front of him. "I don't know. The airport is nowhere near downtown."

Emma's feet rooted to the floor. "We know that Albuquerque was a fluke. That was me and the wonder boys fighting over the worthless damn book."

He glanced up at her. "Yeah, go on."

"Then Aiden took that idea and used Raphael and Jake to destroy Little Rock to fuck with my head."

"I'm sure he got a perverse pleasure out of killing a few hundred people too."

"Then Jackson, so he could fuck with me some more. All downtowns. All had earthquakes. All had storms. There was a pattern even if Albuquerque wasn't originally planned that way."

"Okay, so what's your point?"

"Why change now?"

"I don't know. Maybe it had something to do with Alex."

"But Little Rock and Jackson were meant to draw me here. Why would he change the location and the way it was done?"

"To fuck with you more? To get you this close and frustrate you that you're so far from getting Jake?"

"Why not kill everyone in the airport? It would have been easy. Look." She pointed to the TV. "It's small. Raphael could have easily ripped it down while Aiden had Jake make a storm to finish everyone off."

"True."

Excitement bubbled up within her chest. "What if it wasn't Aiden?"

Will cocked his head. "What do you mean? Who could it have been?"

"Jake."

"We already know it's Jake. Alex is dead and no one else could do this."

"I'm saying Jake did this without Aiden."

Will leaned back, watching her carefully. "You're right that it doesn't fit with the pattern at all. But what if Aiden decided to switch things up?"

"There's no way you really believe that."

"I'm just playing devil's advocate here. How could Jake do this on his own?"

How could he? Had Aiden taken Jake to the airport? "Maybe he escaped." She gasped. "He was at an airport! What if he was trying to get away?"

"Emma, he's a smart little guy, but there's no way he could have done this on his own."

"Maybe he had help."

"At this point, we need to determine if this was their strike, and if they're moving on to the next city or if we need to continue on with our plan. Where would they go next?"

"Tyler, Texas. But what if Jake was at the airport because he escaped? If he's run away from Aiden, then we need to go find him."

Will reached over and snagged her hand, pulling her to sit on the bed. "Okay, let's go with your theory. Let's say that Jake escaped somehow and with or without help, he got to the airport. To what? Fly somewhere?"

"Yes."

"Okay, he would have needed someone to get him a ticket somewhere and get him through security."

"Can't we do a search to see if he got a ticket?"

"In theory, but it's outside the scope of my capabilities. James could do something like that, but that's not relevant at the moment. Let's presume Jake has escaped from Aiden. And let's say Jake gets through security because obviously he was inside the terminal. Why would he do this?" Will pointed to the television.

"I don't know."

"He's in the terminal, maybe getting ready to board a plane, then he sucks the breath out of everyone at the airport. Why?"

She realized where Will's questions were going. "To fight."

"Fight whom?"

She closed her eyes, defeat washing over her. "Aiden must have found him."

Will rubbed the back of her hand with his thumb. "I think you might be right."

"You think I'm right that Aiden got him back?"

"I think you're right about all of it."

"What difference does it make if Aiden still has him?"

"A ton. First, we know there's still a good chance that they plan to attack Shreveport. Second, we know that Aiden's liable to be pissed so the destruction might be greater. And third." He brought her hand onto his lap. "Jake might be less likely to cooperate with Aiden, making it imperative that we rescue him today."

"If Aiden hurt him…" Her voice broke.

"Aiden needs him, Emma. Jake is his insurance policy."

But they both knew it didn't mean Aiden wouldn't cause Jake pain.

A news reporter stood in front of the airport, sirens and flashing lights behind her. "Bill, we have something new to report. Something different from the other cities." She looked to the side then touched her hand to her ear. "Multiple witnesses are reporting a woman bursting into flames outside the terminal while several men and a small boy looked on."

The blood rushed from her head. "Jake."

Cursing under his breath, Will grabbed his laptop. "We'll still follow through with our plan to get to downtown by five to prepare for a seven o'clock attack."

Who had burst into flames and who had caused it? Jake or Aiden? "What makes you think it's going to happen at seven?"

"The first attack was at three. The next at five."

"Will, wait. Why would they target the downtown areas of cities?"

"To injure and kill more people in a concentrated area."

"Exactly. So why would they attack at night when downtown has cleared out?"

"Oh fuck."

Emma glanced at the clock. "It's 11:03."

"Start packing. I'm going to tell Marcus."

"So when will they attack?"

"I don't know. Three again? Five? What if he goes two hours earlier this time? That's one o'clock, less than two hours from now and we don't even know anything about the buildings there." Will ran to the door. "Pack everything up. We've got to go."

CHAPTER TWENTY-FOUR

MARCUS looked completely out of place on a street corner in Shreveport, Louisiana. But then again, Emma doubted he would fit in anywhere. He was too good-looking. The Elements had a beauty that was almost too perfect. Will, with his rugged handsomeness, was believable as half Element. Even Jake had a beauty unusual for a boy his age.

Although she wasn't unattractive, she wasn't beautiful either. Sweat stuck her hair to her face and neck. She'd never felt more unattractive in her life, making her difference so obvious that she wondered why she'd never seen it before. There was a direct correlation between their beauty and their power. The true Elements were the most beautiful and the most powerful. She was the least attractive and least powerful. Where did that leave her?

Her hand brushed the gun tucked into the waistband of her jeans. St. Louis had proven that power wasn't necessarily what would win her this thing. Perhaps Aiden didn't intend it to go that way, but she needed whatever weapon would work for her. If it was twenty-first-century technology instead of timeless elemental power, so be it.

Will and Marcus had discussed the best vantage points as well as where to have Emma wait. They considered putting her on top of a building, but Will worried she'd be injured if the structure collapsed. "I don't think we can stop them from damaging the city," Will warned her. "It's a matter of keeping the damage to a minimum. I want you to have a clear escape route if you need it."

Anxiety prickled the hair on her arms. She'd effectively blocked out the fact that people would most likely die here soon. Innocent people who had no stake in this at all. Will's words made it all too real. "What about you?"

"Don't worry. I have no intention of getting killed today. If we get separated, just remember that we'll meet at the corner of Olive and Cleveland."

In the end, the best place he could come up with was to put her in the corner of a parking garage. She was in a covered structure, could see the action, and had an escape route.

And it pissed her off.

Jake was her son. She should be fighting for him, not Will and not Marcus. But even in her anger, she knew she would be more of a liability than an asset. She didn't want to be the one who prevented Jake from being rescued—or worse, the one who got him killed. Her pride would recover.

At twelve-forty-five, they were all in position. Will and Marcus were a half block apart, on separate sides of the street. Emma was a half block down from Will. She had a clear view of him from where she sat.

Will had slipped into full military mode. He was always ready for anything, but whenever she saw him like this she could see that he must have been a great leader in Iraq. She wondered what he was like before he became the man she first met weeks ago. Before he'd come home jaded and broken. Some of the original Will had resurfaced, the Will with integrity who believed in justice. The one who wanted to help the underdog. Will had lived for three years wallowing in his guilt until he met her. Perhaps her own soul could be saved in the end.

The more she thought about her chat with Marcus, the more she believed he was right about Will being the elevated one. All of his life experiences would make him a compassionate and selfless ruler. If only she turned out to be the supplanter instead of Jake.

Her fear over the prophecy and what it meant to Jake consumed her. She knew she had to push it aside if she was going to be effective today. Anger was what she needed, but the more she thought about how the next ten minutes could mean the difference between getting Jake or not, the more fear continued to build until she found it difficult to breathe.

Will sensed her discomfort. *Emma?*

I'm fine. Just worried.

Take a deep breath. It'll be okay.

She would have preferred to shut down her connection to him, but he insisted it remain open. He wanted to know if she was okay and she had to admit that she liked knowing if he was all right. If he ran into trouble, she might be able to help him.

At twelve-fifty-nine, a car pulled up at the corner across the street from Emma and stopped, the back door swinging open. Waves of overwhelming power came from the car.

They're here.

She cloaked her own power, realizing she should have done so half an hour ago to maintain the element of surprise.

Raphael emerged first, dressed in khaki pants and a long-sleeved pale blue shirt rolled up to the elbows. He looked like he was going to a social function. Aiden was next, his arrogance shining from his face as he surveyed the area. For a second, Emma wasn't sure Jake was with them. Part of her hoped that if he'd caused the incident at the airport, he'd actually gotten away. But he got out of the car, his face an expressionless mask. Her stomach lurched. He looked so lost. So hopeless.

Jake, Mommy's here!

But he didn't hear her, moving like a robot, stiff and unyielding. The car pulled away and Raphael and Aiden stood in the middle of the sidewalk, blocking the pedestrians, forcing people into the street to get around them. Jake stood between the two men, looking in Emma's direction, but his eyes were lifeless.

Will! Jake's here!

Don't. Do. Anything.

Doing nothing was easier said than done. There was no doubt that if Emma tried to fight Aiden and Raphael, it wouldn't end well, but there were other means. She pulled out her gun and slid back the rack, placing Aiden in her sights.

Emma, don't you dare! You know it won't work on him.

She felt Will's aggravation through their connection. He and Marcus had carefully calculated where they'd be positioned, but knowing Aiden, he expected Will and

Emma to be here and purposely moved a block to the north.

Emma, I've got to move. Stay there and do not engage Aiden. Will disappeared from his spot, moving to the back alley.

Do not engage was easier said than done. The man who'd made her life a living hell stood thirty feet in front of her and she wasn't about to let him get away. Maybe all it would take was a combination of her power and her gun.

No, she needed to wait for Will. And Marcus.

Raphael shook his hands at his sides as though he were preparing for a ping pong tournament. Aiden's eyes began to glow and Jake stood between them, unmoving.

What had Aiden done to her son?

It was clear that Raphael and Aiden were preparing to inflict their damage, but they seemed to be waiting for something. Or was it someone?

Where the hell are you? she screamed into Will's head.

I'm coming.

They're about to start. Panic brewed in her stomach. Will had stressed that they needed to catch Aiden and Raphael off guard before they began their carnage. Will and Marcus were losing their element of surprise.

Which way are you coming? She had to intervene. She didn't have a choice.

Emma, don't do anything stupid.

You'll intercept Jake when you round the corner. I can create a distraction and you get Jake while Marcus and I keep them busy. Where the hell is Marcus?

He's coming, but let the two of us handle this, Emma.

You said yourself we need to test our abilities. No better time.

The ground vibrated gently. Raphael had begun.

Focusing on the pain Jake had endured, and the horror Aiden had put him through, Emma let her anger build until her body burned.

Emma, please. Will begged, his desperation bleeding through their connection. *This isn't what we planned.*

When the fuck has anything ever gone as planned?

Throwing off her inner cloak was like sending a draft to kindled fire. Her anger and power mushroomed until she could hardly contain it.

Aiden sensed the change, lifting his chin as if testing the air. A grin spread across his face.

Emma realized what he'd been waiting for. He'd been waiting for her.

Trust your instincts. Will's voice had calmed and become soothing. *You fight it too much. Trust your power to know what to do.*

Closing her eyes, she focused on the burning mass in her chest. She needed more. Her body called out, searching for energy sources. Electricity ran over her head and in the ground. Drawing from those sources, her power increased, nearly doubling, until her body begged for release.

The ground had begun to shake and people in the street screamed.

I see Jake. Don't tell your power what to do, tell it what you need. When I say go, release it.

Tell her power what she needed? She needed Jake. Was it really that easy? No. She could tell it to eliminate Aiden, but that's not what she needed.

Release it now!

She thought of Jake, releasing her energy and a fireball blossomed in the street. The rumble of water followed on its heels. The screams grew louder and higher-pitched as the sky overhead darkened with storm clouds.

Will? Did you get Jake?

The smoke cleared and Aiden stood in his position, a grin on his face. Raphael and Jake were nowhere to be seen.

***

A massive ball of flames raged in the street with a flash so bright, Will was forced to close his eyes. When the smoke cleared and he regained his sight, Raphael and Jake were gone.

Will! Did you get Jake?

Son of a bitch. *I've lost him. He's with Raphael. I'm tracking them now.*

Aiden was moving across the street toward Emma as rain began to pour from the sky, but if Will went to help her instead of finding Jake, she'd never forgive him. Aiden needed Emma—he wouldn't kill her. That was the only reason Will left her and took off running down the street. He hoped he didn't regret it later.

Marcus ran across the street half a block from Will but with all the confusion of the people on the street, it was hard to tell if Raphael and Jake were there as well. Marcus seemed intent on something ahead of him. Will hoped he had Raphael and Jake in his sight.

The ground began to shake again and the sky darkened overhead. Raphael must have found a place to resume their destruction. Which, ironically, was the spot where they were originally supposed to be.

Fuck. It was a setup.

***

Will lost Jake? She couldn't focus on that now. Aiden knew where she was and he was crossing the street toward her, a grin spread across his face.

"Emmanuella, you came."

Rain began to pound the pavement, drenching Aiden, though he didn't seem to notice.

She stayed in the garage, partially hidden behind a pillar. *You're a coward*, she told herself. She'd spent the last three years of her life hiding and she was sick of it. Taking a deep breath, she moved away from the concrete support to stand directly in front of her father.

Aiden stood on the sidewalk, ten feet in front of her, his feet spread apart.

"How could I miss your invitation?" She kept her tone light. The gun was still in her hand at her side, but the wall around the garage hid it from Aiden's view.

His smile was friendly, as though he'd happened to bump into her on the street instead of orchestrating their meeting. "Before we get to the important part, I'm curious. Who killed Alex? Was it Marcus or Will?"

She snorted. She wasn't sure whether to be relieved or insulted that he didn't suspect her. "How would I know? The media says it was the Cavallo."

He laughed, but it wasn't a pleasant sound. "Please, Emmanuella. I used to help spin those stories. Which one killed him?"

He seriously thought her incapable of killing Alex? "What difference does it make? He's dead. There's one less contestant for your little game."

"It makes all the difference in the world. The one who killed him inherited his power."

Alex has said the words, but she didn't feel any stronger. Had Will inherited the power instead? At the moment, it didn't matter. "I want Jake."

"And you shall get him. Tomorrow night."

"Don't screw with me, Aiden. What the fuck is tomorrow night?"

"The final battle."

"*What?*" Will and Marcus thought they had more time. "When were you going to tell us this piece of information?"

He spread his hands wide and smiled. "Emmanuella, what do you think this elaborate scheme is? It's your engraved invitation to the final battle. Tomorrow night, at ten p.m., show up at Buckingham Fountain in Grant Park in Chicago."

Outrage washed over her. "You played mind games with me, destroying cities just to tell me when and where the final battle is? Using my son? What kind of fucked-up bastard are you?" Her voice was a screech, but she was past the point of caring. "And then what happens at the big showdown? A cage match?"

"While your show of hysterics is entertaining, let's get down to business." Aiden's smile fell away. "Four shall fight, two shall remain. Obviously you'll be siding with Will, but then what will happen to Jake?"

Fear of that very unknown variable sapped her power. "Why don't you just kill me now and be done with it? You and I both know I'm no match for you."

"Oh, Emmanuella. The drama again. You're my daughter. I have no intention of killing you."

She shook her head. "I find that difficult to believe."

"Why? Because I haven't made things easy for you? You'll thank me later when you gain control and even greater power."

"I don't want it. I never did. I just want Jake and Will and to be left alone."

"Fortunately for you, we don't always get what we want."

She scanned the street, which had erupted into chaos. "Where's Jake?"

"I believe he's running for his life right now."

"What have you done to him?"

"Nothing, my darling daughter. It's what Will and Marcus are attempting to do that you need to be worried about."

***

Will grunted in frustration. Aiden was with Emma while Raphael and Jake destroyed the city over a block away, with Will and Marcus chasing after them. Should he go back to Emma? Rain poured from the sky as the ground rolled. People on the sidewalk screamed and ran, stumbling in every direction as they shoved and pushed one another in their flight.

Raphael came into view on the street corner, emitting a glow. Next to his waist was a little blond head.

Jake.

Will felt Emma's power build and his fear froze him in place, torn between his job and what he wanted to do. Aiden wouldn't hurt Emma. He might scare her, but he wouldn't hurt her. Will had to trust that. Emma would be furious if Will got this close to Jake and turned back for her. He could easily take Raphael, get Jake, then go back for Emma.

Marcus stood in the middle of the street, surrounded in a glow. A pillar of water appeared from the ground, and shot toward Raphael.

The water hit a wall of nothing, dispersing into the air in tiny droplets.

Jake.

A thin crack appeared in the street, moving toward Will, then spreading wide. Will jumped out of the way.

The rain fell in sheets, stinging Will's face as the wind whipped it around. Jake's storm produced the rain, but Will could control it. He sent it darting toward Raphael, hoping it missed Jake. Raphael kept the boy close to his side, most likely as a defensive strategy. Fucking coward.

Will, where's Jake?

He remained silent, not wanting to tell her that Jake was caught in a skirmish.

Emma's power grew again and he wondered what mess she was in. If she needed help, she would ask. But then again, she knew he was after Jake. She might not.

He tried to move closer to Raphael but a large group of people poured from a building, blocking his path. Squeezing through the crowd, Will gasped for breath as Emma gathered more power. He had to get Jake and get back to her.

Emma's power exploded, and a few seconds later reverberated through his head as though he had been slammed into a wall. Worry caught his breath, but he felt her through their connection, reassured that she wasn't in any pain.

The ground shook violently, knocking Will to his knees. When he looked up, the crowd had thinned and Raphael and Jake were gone. Son of a bitch.

***

Her fear siphoned off her power. *Will? Where's Jake?*

"Did you know that they are hunting him down like he's a rabbit, and they are hounds hot on his scent? Very animalistic, don't you think?"

"Will would never hurt Jake." Why wasn't he answering?

"Perhaps not." Aiden raised an eyebrow. "But what about Marcus?"

He sensed her uncertainty and grinned. "You need to be very careful who you choose for your friends, Emmanuella."

Her anger climbed again. He was so close to her...

Aiden winked. "Well, you have things to do and so do I."

She needed to stall him. "That's it?"

"You want more?" He grinned. "Perhaps a demonstration of our power. That seems to be what you are building up to, isn't it?"

She stepped sideways, away from the pillar. "Wouldn't you like that? A little demonstration on my part? A chance to show off yours?"

He laughed, more genuine this time. Amusement filled his voice. "You never cease to amaze me."

"Let's hope I don't disappoint." She knew he'd wait for her to make the first move, then knock her down. What if she could trick him first?

Trust your power, Will had said.

Was it that easy?

Her finger curled around the trigger of her gun. It was an option too.

"Change your mind?" Aiden laughed.

She focused on the mass in her chest, calling to the electricity around her. *I need to distract Aiden*, she thought before releasing it.

A glowing ball shot to his side, blowing up a car behind him.

He released his power toward her, but her energy became a barricade, blocking him.

"Very good, Emma." He sounded genuinely impressed as he advanced toward the low concrete wall.

Getting trapped in the parking garage was insanity—both of their powers contained in an enclosed space would be devastating. Not to mention all the cars that could be used as weapons.

Plus, he would see her gun.

Backing up, she moved her hand behind her back, tucking the weapon into her jeans.

She needed more power.

The storm outside raged at full force, the wind blowing trash down the street. Emma was thankful she saw very few people.

The ground beneath her feet began to shake, the cars around her jiggling. Pieces of concrete rained down on top of her head.

Oh shit.

CHAPTER TWENTY-FIVE

WILL took off running again as pieces of the buildings broke off, falling into the street. Marcus was nowhere to be seen. Will only hoped that Marcus had Raphael in sight. Dodging several stopped cars, Will was sure he spotted Jake's blond head a half a block away, although the rain poured so heavily that he could hardly see.

Emma was uneasy and worried.

Raphael was close. Will was sure of it from the feelings that rolled toward him. But fear came at him in slick waves.

Will!

He was about to answer her when a violent quake rippled the asphalt under his feet, throwing him to the ground. Lifting his face from the pavement, he saw Marcus bolt across the mangled street. He climbed to his feet, jumping over a gaping hole in the street. Marcus had disappeared down an alley and Will followed.

***

Jake had been terrified when he realized they were under attack. He'd seen the wall of water coming toward them on the street corner, and he knew who made it. Where was Mommy? Aiden said she'd come. His head swiveled searching frantically for her when Raphael grabbed his hand and started to run.

Raphael was faster, and Jake struggled to keep up. Raphael's quakes had broken the road into pieces and Jake's shoe caught on a raised part. His hand slipped from Raphael's hold, and he fell face first on the pavement, the asphalt stinging his hands and knees. Tears stung his eyes, but he shoved the hurt into the mark on his chest. He struggled to catch his breath. His heart still ached from what had happened to Antonia.

Pulling him to his feet, Raphael hissed, "You think Will likes you? Well, think again. He just tried to kill you."

Raphael yanked him around a corner and Jake stumbled as he sorted through the thoughts in his head. Still angry and grieving over Antonia, he was eager to take his frustration out on someone.

Will was the final straw.

Jake sent a wave of power into the storm. The rain shot like arrows from the sky, stabbing his skin, but he welcomed the pain. It only added to his anger. The mark on his chest was so cold his wet shirt froze to it.

"Is that the best you can do, Jake?" Raphael curled his upper lip in disgust, but then worry wiped his smugness away, and he ran again.

***

Aiden had Emma backed up inside an enclosed structure with three floors of concrete and cars over her head. He hopped the wall, walking toward her. She backed down the aisle, toward the wall behind her.

"Now would be a good time for your next move, Emmanuella. Have you really been so poorly trained?"

"Who the fuck was going to train me, Aiden?" She ground the words through her clenched teeth. "Will didn't know shit. Raphael was intent on stealing my power. Alex was intent on—"

"Yes, what was Alex intent on?"

"Gaining control and power. Just like the rest of you. *No one* trained me." She held her hands at the sides. "What you see is what you get."

Aiden looked pensive, then spoke. "I'm about to make a one-time proposal. No second chances."

"I can't wait to hear this." His amusement scared her, sapping her power. Aiden's entertainment always came at the expense of others. And if his proposal involved her, she was sure there was nothing good about it.

He continued to advance, determination now on his face. "You're right. No one has trained you. Marcus made sure of that. He's the one who took away your natural instincts. He's the one who made sure that Will was The Chosen One and knew nothing of his role. You've been a mewling babe thrown out among the wolves, that are even now ready to rip you apart and eat the flesh from your bones."

"I'm not sure I have enough meat on my bones to be passed around."

He tilted his head and smiled. "Even now, you fight with sarcasm."

She was backed up against the five-foot wall cutting her off from the street outside. The parking garage continued to shake, small chunks of concrete falling around them.

"Here is my proposal: I will give you Jake. We will go find him and I will immediately give him to you."

Her breath stuck in her chest. "Why?" she choked out.

"Emma, must you ask? I'm your father."

"Ha. Like that means anything. There's a catch. You told me it was a proposal. I don't believe you'll just let me have Jake."

"You're correct. There is a stipulation, but not as bad as you might think. I realize what a disservice I've done to you. You needed proper training and I failed to make sure that you received it."

"What does that have to do with Jake?"

"I will provide your training in the day and a half we have left. I will prepare you as best I can to make you strong enough to defeat Marcus."

Her eyes widened.

"Make no mistake, Emma, he is your enemy. He may pretend to have your best interests at heart, but he is thousands of years old and he wants what he lost millenniums ago. He's no different than Raphael. Or Alex. Or me." He took a step closer, bending his knees so that his face was level with hers. "Or even you."

Her mouth dropped open, but Aiden placed a finger on her lips. Power rippled through her body in electrical currents.

"Shhh... Do you feel it, Emmanuella? Do you feel the raw current of energy? You can have this too." He pulled his finger away.

She shook her head. "No, I'm different than you."

"Not as much as you think. You have power, Emmanuella. You just need to find it."

This was all too perfect. Much too easy. "And you're going to help me do that?"

"Yes."

"And you're going to give me Jake?" She didn't hide her skepticism.

"Yes. There's only one stipulation."

"Well, of course. I would have been disappointed if there wasn't."

"I will teach you all that I can in one and a half days, and I will give you Jake, but you must leave with me now and stay with me until the final battle."

"Why?"

He looked annoyed. "You're not stupid. I've presented it all to you in perfect English."

Why would he do this? A month ago she might have taken him up on his offer, so why not present it then? And then she knew. Will. He was threatened by her bond to Will.

Will! Why hadn't he answered her?

She took a deep breath to clear her head. "And if I refuse?"

Disappointment clouded his eyes. "I expected you to be smarter than that."

"What's in it for you?"

"The satisfaction of helping my daughter."

Her pulse pounded in her head. "You're a liar, Aiden, and we both know it, so cut the cheesy, protective daddy shit."

Aiden's mouth hardened, and a muscle in his cheek twitched. "Does it really matter what my motives are? I'm offering two very precious gifts. Are you telling me you refuse?"

Jake. He was offering her Jake. Not on her terms, but still, it was a chance to be with him. To hold him and let him know he wasn't alone.

The opportunity to learn more about her power was a bonus. But if she had Jake, would she still need her power? Whether she had him until tomorrow night or not, there was still the final battle. What was Aiden really after? She was sure this proposal was an afterthought. His main purpose in luring her here was to tell her when the final battle would happen and where.

It all boiled down to Will. Aiden had done his damnedest to keep them apart since this all began and this was just another attempt. But did it matter? Aiden was giving her Jake. Wasn't that the sole purpose of this fight for her? To get her son? Could she afford to turn his offer down?

Impatience twisted his mouth into a frown.

The parking garage began to sway.

"I need your decision, Emmanuella."

No, she wanted more. If she went with Aiden, she had no guarantee he'd really let her be with Jake. Besides, he wasn't letting her have Jake. He was letting her be imprisoned with him. They wouldn't be free to leave. She would be at Aiden's mercy.

Part of her screamed that it didn't matter. Jake was her son. Who cared about the terms? She'd get to be with him and comfort him. The rest of today and tomorrow.

Two days.

Two days to comfort him.

Two days to prepare to save his life.

She'd told Will that she'd never betray him. To go with Aiden would be the highest betrayal. Will loved her more than she deserved, and he'd do everything in his power to save her and Jake.

Only two more days.

She swallowed, sick to her stomach, afraid that she was possibly making the worst mistake of her life. "No."

He titled his head forward in surprise. "*Excuse me?*"

"No. I'll wait."

"I offer you your son, and *you refuse?*"

"I want to be with him so badly, but I want him to be free from you more. This is the only way I know to do that."

"You fool," he spat, his rage making him glow. The pure power coming off him burned her skin. "I've offered you everything you could possibly want, but you throw it away for what? That simpleton of a man?"

"No. Because I love Jake, and I want him to be free. You're asking me to put my trust in you or Will. I'll pick Will every time."

"Are you that naïve? Will is with Marcus now. Marcus will stop at nothing to destroy you and destroy Jake. You will truly pick sides with that man over me?"

"Will loves me, a concept you obviously don't understand. He will never betray me or Jake. You, on the other hand, do it without a backward glance."

Aiden growled, then released his power into a row of cars to Emma's right. They exploded and the shockwave threw her backward, crashing her head and back into the concrete. Her vision faded as the heat of the flames overwhelmed her.

"Can you do that, Emma?"

She climbed to her feet, using the wall to support herself. "Yes."

"Then do it!"

Her body was a sea of pain and her brain struggled to focus. Where the hell was her anger? Her energy had become a shriveled ball.

Get mad, Emma! Will shouted in her head.

Where the hell have you been? She choked on a sob. What had she done? She'd just sentenced her son to eternity with Aiden. She was going to die in vain in this parking garage. It would be a total waste. She'd done nothing to save Jake or Will.

"You've made the wrong choice, Emmanuella." Aiden's voice boomed in the parking garage. "You'll never save your son. You can't even save yourself."

She was dizzy and the room spun, the quaking ground not helping her disorientation.

Stop feeling sorry for yourself and fight the bastard!

The front of the parking garage caved in, a cloud of dust rushing toward her.

Coughing, she couldn't concentrate, her head a fuddled mess. A wave of energy swept through her skull and her senses returned, along with a rush of power to her chest. Will had given her part of his power.

And now her father was going to pay.

Lightning crashed nearby and she pulled energy from it, filling her chest until she was sure she would spontaneously combust.

Trust your power.

She sent it rushing toward Aiden, who gaped in surprise. The cars on either side of him erupted in flames, engulfing Aiden.

Now get the hell out of there.

The entrance had caved in and flames blocked her escape to the back exit. The wall behind her was open at the top but it was five feet tall. She grabbed the edge with her fingers and tried to jump up but lost her hold, the concrete scraping her fingertips raw. Her choices were to try it again or find another escape.

If she could get to the next row, the wall was low enough for her to crawl over. But she had to pass through a wall of flames to do it.

I am fire. I can walk through flames.

The electrical source overhead was gone. The collapse of the garage must have shut off the electricity. If only lightning would strike again, but she had no guarantee that it would.

Fucking Aiden was keeping her from Jake and he had no right. She shouldn't have to become his prisoner to get her son. Rage burned in her chest, but it wasn't enough. She needed more.

Let me help you.

Will's power flooded her again and the ball of power gave her a surge of confidence. She could do this.

Trust you power. And trust in yourself.

Cloaking herself with her energy, she walked toward the flames, amazed that when she passed through them she only felt warmth, not burning. When she made it through, she ran to the lower wall, the parking garage swaying with renewed effort. Taking a running jump, she climbed over the ledge, falling on her knees when she landed. She scrambled to her feet and ran into the street, and the pounding rain soaked her within seconds. As she scanned the street to get her bearings, the parking garage collapsed, covering her with dust and debris.

***

Giving Emma his power had weakened Will more than he expected. *Emma?*

I'm fine. I'm safe.

He'd fallen to his knees when he'd sent her enough power to heal her and help her defend herself, but in the process, he'd lost Raphael.

A broken fire hydrant across the street sprayed water into the air and Will absorbed power from the gush. Jumping to his feet, he headed in the direction he'd last seen Marcus run.

Following Raphael's energy waves, Will found them in an alley. Jake's face was pale from fear and exhaustion, his chest heaving as he fought to catch his breath. Marcus rounded a corner behind Will, taking in the sight of the three of them as he walked toward them.

"Let him go, Raphael!" Will shouted over the roar of the storm. "Send Jake over to me, and I'll let you go."

Raphael clutched Jake in front of his body as his eyes darted from Will to Marcus, backing up to the opposite end. "You're lying."

Will hadn't expected to kill Raphael today, so getting Jake was worth the trade. He took slow steps forward, his hands upraised. "I swear to you. I only want Jake. You're free to go."

Jake studied Will with wary eyes.

Raphael stopped, obviously considering Will's offer. "Okay." Raphael put his hands on Jake's shoulders and took a step backward.

Dropping to one knee, Will reached out to Jake. "It's okay. Your mom is here and she's desperate to see you."

Jake took two hesitant steps.

Will watched in horror as Marcus shot rain toward Raphael and Jake, piercing their chests and legs. Blood saturated their shirts before the building collapsed, separating them from Will and Marcus.

***

The building collapsed and Raphael pulled Jake again, but Jake ran willingly this time, his stomach a tight ball of fear. Jake looked down, shocked at the blood soaking the front of his shirt from three holes. What had happened?

He glanced up at Raphael. Raphael's shirt was splattered with more bloody marks than he could count, and his mouth gaped. Staggering on his feet, Raphael leaned his shoulder into a building to hold himself up as guttural sounds came from his throat.

Jake watched in silence. Was Raphael dying?

"Don't just stand there, you stupid boy. Do something!" Raphael spat. He wrapped an arm around his stomach. "Goddamnit!" His head leaned back and rain splashed off his face.

The amount of blood on Raphael's shirt scared Jake, although as he watched the dark spots grow he wondered why he was shocked. How many people had he seen covered in blood?

"Come here." Raphael's words were muffled by his clenched jaw.

Jake stayed where he was, afraid to move. He looked down at his own chest. The blood had stopped seeping into his shirt.

"Get over here now or I'll do to your mother what Aiden did to your nanny."

Anger burned icy cold in Jake's mark. "You won't hurt my mother."

A grin formed on Raphael's mouth and his eyes filled with evil. "I'll take great delight making her scream with pain while you and Will watch."

A magical current filled the air around them.

"I said get over here! I need your power."

Jake crossed his arms. "No. I hope you die."

Raphael laughed, but it sounded like a grunt. "If I die, then you're at Will's mercy. Who do you think just hurt us? It was Will."

Jake's mouth dropped open.

Raphael's body shivered and his head rolled to the side, his eyebrows raising. "You didn't realize that did you? Who did you think did it?"

Shaking his head, Jake's rage grew. "No. Will would never hurt me. He wants to help me."

"You are so stupid. You stupid, stupid boy. Of course he wants to hurt you. If he kills you, then he has your mommy all to himself."

"No." Jake whispered. The possibility that Raphael's words were right made him lightheaded.

Raphael winked. "Oh, yes."

"But… He…"

"He stabbed us with water, you fool. He took the very rain your storm produced and used it as a weapon against you. Grow up and face the facts. Will would rather see you dead then take you to your mother."

"No!" Jake shouted. Thunder rumbled overhead and multiple streaks of lightning struck the ground around them.

"I can help you, Jake." Raphael reached out his hand. "Just take my hand and help heal me. Then we'll defeat Will together."

Jake's rage billowed out of control. Curtains in the windows of the building next to him burst into flames.

Shadows danced on the wall behind Raphael's body.

"Let me help you, Jake." Raphael's hand began to shake. His face was pale.

With a smile, Jake took a step toward him. "We can help you."

Confusion clouded Raphael's eyes. "We?"

"The shadows will help."

Raphael's eyes widened in terror and he stumbled backward, falling onto his bottom. "The shadows?"

"You let Aiden kill Antonia."

The shadows covered Raphael's body and he screamed.

"You hurt my mommy."

Raphael's clothes caught fire and he rolled to his stomach, his screams growing in volume.

The ground gave a violent shake, then shuddered with gentle ripples. Jake stood with his feet apart waiting for the shaking to settle down.

"You're screaming now, Raphael. Not Mommy. You'll never hurt her again."

"I won't hurt her! I swear!" His body was covered in a haze of dark gray. "Jake! Stop!"

He wouldn't stop. Not until Raphael was dead. Jake focused on his hatred, pulling energy from his mark, then pushing it toward Raphael. Raphael's entire body erupted into flames, while the shadows clung to him. Finally, he stopped moving but Jake's body still burned with energy, the heat scorching the walls around them, turning them pitch black, but Jake felt nothing but triumph.

The shadows slid off Raphael and made a circle on the now-blackened concrete next to him. The shadow figure rose up to face Jake.

"You have done well. You are now the keeper of Raphael's power. Do you accept?"

Jake scowled. He might only be five but he wasn't stupid, despite what Raphael said. "What's the catch? I had to agree to destroy the person who killed Alex. I'm not going to kill myself."

The shadow's cloaked head shook. "That was a gift. This is freely earned. There is no condition."

Then what was the problem? The more power he had, the easier it would be to save Mommy. "Yes."

A bright white light flashed from the figure and into Jake's chest. He felt alive, more alive than he'd ever felt before. His entire body tingled. He fell to his knees, expecting pain from his scrapes, but the wounds on his body were healed.

"I can kill Aiden."

The shadow figure reached a finger toward Jake.

Jake froze, holding his breath in anticipation.

The gray haze touched his chest. "It is not time for his end."

Jake's jaw clenched. "I want to kill him."

"In due time, but for now you must go with him."

"When? When can I kill him?"

"Tomorrow night. Aiden has decreed the end."

"And then I can kill him?"

"You must fulfill your promise first."

Jake shrugged. He could accept that.

"Now go. Aiden is coming, and he must not know that you killed Raphael."

The shadow disappeared, and Jake ran to the street, unsure which way to go. The building behind him emitted a long groan, then collapsed, obliterating the alley and covering Raphael and Jake's evidence. Aiden rounded the corner, confusion on his face. His eyes widened when he saw the blood on Jake's shirt.

"Are you injured?"

Jake lifted his chin. "Not anymore."

"Why are you alone? Where's Raphael?"

"He's dead. Will stabbed us with water and Raphael didn't have enough power to fix himself." A smug satisfaction filled him. It was all true. He didn't lie to cover his tracks.

"Where is his body?"

Jake pointed to the debris-filled alley.

Aiden looked worried. "Do you know if Will was the one to kill him?"

"He was the one to stab him."

Jake stared in fascination. Aiden, the man that was always so sure, was definitely worried.

"Come, Jake. We must prepare."

Jake hesitated. "Did you see my mommy?"

Aiden's mouth twisted, as though he was unsure what to say. "No. I couldn't find her. She wasn't here. It was only Will."

Will left Mommy behind instead of bringing her to find Jake. Mommy would never have stayed away from him. Will must have made her. And Will tried to kill him.

Will was going to pay.

CHAPTER TWENTY-SIX

GROWLING with anger, Will shoved Marcus into a pile of rubble. "You fucking lying son of a bitch! You told me you weren't going to kill Jake."

Marcus tried to get up, but Will slammed his fist into Marcus's jaw. His hand throbbed and he shook it at his side. "Get up, you fucking piece of shit."

Rising to his feet, Marcus rubbed his jaw.

Will had never hated anyone so much in his entire life. "We're done here. You can consider this the official end of our partnership."

Marcus moved in front of Will, anger glowing in his eyes. "Stop and think like a soldier, not a lovesick puppy."

"What the fuck does that mean?"

"I told you that you can't think with your *heart*. You need to think with your *head*. You need to find a way to emotionally distance yourself from this situation and look at it rationally. You are placing the life of a child over your own survival."

"Are you fucking insane? You swore to Emma you wouldn't hurt him. *You liar!*" Will wanted to kill him.

Marcus's eyes narrowed. "Do you expect me to agree to die so one of them can live? Don't think me to be so altruistic. Let there be no mistake, Will. My goal is for you and me to survive. I've already told you this. This is my gift to you."

Will shook his head, his breath catching in his chest. "Keep your fucking gift. I don't want it."

Marcus's face softened. "Will, listen to me. Emma isn't strong enough to survive this. You and I both know it, and I refuse to allow you to sacrifice yourself to save her. It's survival of the fittest. It's not her fault, but there's the truth nonetheless."

"You think I'm going to kill her? *Have you fucking lost your mind?*" Rage overtook his senses, and he fought to keep control.

"No. I would never expect that of you. In fact, I suspect it's impossible given your bond. I doubt you can physically hurt one another. I'll do it."

"*The fuck you will.*" A wall of water appeared out of nowhere, slamming Marcus into the debris.

The water splashed to the ground, and Marcus rose, anger narrowing his eyes. "I've been as patient with you as possible, Will, but the end is near and you need to accept the facts."

"There's something wrong with your carefully orchestrated scheme, Marcus. Won't killing Emma kill me?"

"No, I'm counting on my belief that killing her will give her power to you."

"So that's why you wanted me to be The Chosen One? You planned all along for her to die so I could get her power."

"I'm your father, Will. Can you blame me for wanting to protect you and give you every advantage I can?"

"Then why didn't you just kill her last night when you had the chance and be done with it? You could have told me that Alex did it and I'd be none the wiser."

"Because I can't kill her. It's part of the pact Aiden and I made. We can't kill each other's children. I could have let Alex kill her, but I know how much you love her, and I didn't want to destroy you. I was worried you'd be too grief-stricken to fight."

Will took a backward step toward the street. "Well, guess what? I refuse to fight. I never asked to be part of this fuckfest. I'm done."

Marcus advanced a step. "If you don't show up to fight, you will die. Opting out is not an option. To forfeit is to die."

"Then maybe I'll take a nap and die in my sleep, because there is no way in hell I'm going to agree to let you kill Emma. Besides, I thought you weren't able to kill her, your fucking rules and all."

"The rules are null and void at the battle." Marcus's eyes softened. "I know this is a lot to take in—"

Will grunted in disgust. "Don't you *even* try to use that bullshit on me."

"Will."

"No. I'm done."

Will took off at a sprint, leaving Marcus behind in the rubble. He had to find Emma. He had no idea where Jake was, but he hoped the boy had healed himself.

Emma, where are you? He tried to keep his terror from his voice. Marcus admitted he couldn't kill Emma until the final battle, but he wasn't going to take any chances.

I'm trying to find our meeting location, but with all the damage I can't find it.

Just stay where you are, and I'll find you.

Jake? Did you get Jake? Her tone told her she knew he hadn't.

No, we got separated. I'm going to get you, and we'll search for him together.

No! Go find him! You can find me later!

Emma, you're not safe. We can't trust Marcus.

She didn't respond as he climbed over pieces of concrete and debris, and headed toward the parking garage. It took him several minutes until he saw her standing in the middle of the street, her face and clothes covered in water-streaked soot.

He pulled her into his arms and buried his face in her hair, the smell of smoke and gasoline assaulting his nose. His love for her consumed him, filling him with fear. How could he protect her?

Breaking his embrace, he looked over his shoulder. "Jake might still be up that way. The last time I saw him, he was headed west. This is the edge of the destruction. Let's circle around and then head south and see if we can intercept him before Aiden finds him."

She nodded and started walking.

"Emma."

She looked up at him.

"If you see Marcus, shoot to kill. Got it?"

Her eyes widened. "What?"

"He can't kill you until the final battle, but as far as I know, there's nothing to keep you from killing him. Do it and you'll get his power. And save yourself in the process."

She shook her head. "What are you talking about? I killed Alex, and I didn't get his power."

Will sighed in disappointment. "You're right. Marcus must have lied about that too."

"I don't think so. Aiden wanted to know if it was you or Marcus who killed Alex. When I asked why it mattered, he said the one to kill him got his power."

"Maybe you got it and didn't realize it."

"I'd like to think it would have made a difference if I had. We both know it didn't."

"Power aside, kill Marcus anyway. He confessed that he intends to kill you at the final battle."

She resumed walking. "The final battle is tomorrow night. That was what this was all about. We have to be in Grant Park in Chicago tomorrow night at ten." She spread her hands wide. "This is our engraved initiation." She stepped around a pair of legs sticking out from underneath a collapsed building.

Aiden was one sick bastard. Will vowed to make sure he was dead before Will met his end.

"Can you feel Jake?" She bit her lip and cast a worried glance toward him. "I know that you can feel Raphael's power."

Will took her hand in his. "No. I didn't feel him, even when he was about thirty feet away."

Disappointment turned down her mouth.

"If he's here, we'll find him."

She stopped and swiped strands of wet hair out of her face. "No. He's gone. Aiden came to issue his invitation, offered his impromptu proposition, then got pissed that I refused and left."

"I'm afraid to ask what his proposition was."

"He offered to give me Jake. And to teach me how to use my power more effectively."

"What was the catch?"

"I had to leave with him. I had to leave you."

Will sucked in a breath in surprise. "Why didn't you accept?"

"He said that I had to leave you. I couldn't do that."

He stopped, searching her face. "You chose me over Jake?"

"No, I choose you both. You and I both know I wouldn't really have Jake if I went with Aiden. For all I know, he would have kept us separated. And how can I trust the man to really help me with my power? I don't. He could have trained me wrong just to get me killed. If I want to save Jake, I need to stick with you to make that happen. I trust you, Will. If I've learned nothing else in this disaster, it's to trust you."

He pulled her into his arms, overwhelmed with his love for her, and crushed his mouth onto hers. He'd prove himself worthy of her trust.

Even if it meant he had to die to prove it.

First they had to get to Chicago.

Will gave her one last kiss and pulled back. "Let's head back to the hotel, get our stuff and figure out how to get to Chicago."

"How are we going to get there since our car is in St. Louis?"

"With any luck at all, Marcus's rental car is where we left it. He wants me to survive and I have to be in Chicago to do it. He's not going to put obstacles in my path, and he has more resources than I do to get there."

"But what about me? He doesn't want me to survive this thing."

"I don't want you anywhere near the inside of the hotel when I get our stuff. You'll drop me off, then come back to pick me up."

He was glad when his theory proved correct. The rental car was parked by the curb, several blocks away. Peering in the window, he released a sigh of relief. "The keys are in the ignition but the door's locked." He paused and glanced back as he stood up. "The locking system is electrical."

"You think I can get the lock open?"

"It's worth a shot."

She put her hand on the car door, closing her eyes.

"Just a light touch. Too much could short out the car."

The locks popped. "It worked."

Will opened the door and motioned for her to get behind the wheel. "You sound surprised. You've done much bigger stuff than this."

"Yeah, bigger stuff. But even then it's flaky."

He walked around to the other side of the car. Marcus agreed with her and there was truth in her statement. Will had about thirty hours to figure how to make her strong enough to survive.

"I want you to drop me off at the hotel and I'll tell you when to come back and get me. If you see Marcus, shoot to kill. I mean it, Emma. No guilt. The man plans on murdering you tomorrow night. If I thought I could have killed him this afternoon, I would have done it."

"I expect Marcus is long gone. If he can't do anything to me now, he's not going to waste his time trying."

Will hoped she was right.

***

She dropped Will off at the front door of the hotel and drove away, trying not to think about the fact that tomorrow night this would all be over. Everyone involved in this thing knew that she was the weakest of them all. She was walking into almost certain death. Had she made the wrong choice not going with Aiden? Should she have spent the last day of her life with Jake instead of Will?

No. Will was her life insurance policy. He was her provision for Jake after her death. She would tell him all the things she wanted Jake to know and remember about her. She'd make sure he knew Jake's favorite foods and how he liked to be read to before he went to sleep. She had no doubt Will would be a wonderful father to Jake. She only wished she could see it.

She swallowed the lump in her throat. If she had to die, at least she'd had the chance to have real love. She'd never put much stock in it before, considering it a fairy tale until Will showed up and shook up her already chaotic life. She tried to imagine what their lives would be like if by some twist of fate they all survived, but try as she might, she couldn't see it. Maybe that was because it was never meant to be. Will's love was an incredible gift she'd take with her to the hereafter. If there was one. Maybe she'd fade into the shadow world.

I'm ready. Be on the lookout for Marcus.

While she was watchful, she didn't expect to see him. Why waste his time when he could easily do away with her tomorrow night? She pulled up to the hotel and found Will waiting at the curb, bags in hand. He tossed them into the back and climbed into the passenger seat.

"Where to?"

"North. Up 71 Highway to Texarkana to Little Rock."

"This is going to be a long drive, isn't it?"

"Not as long as you think. We're going to rent a plane in Little Rock and fly to Chicago. We'll get there tonight and be able to get a good night's sleep."

"Isn't that expensive? Do we have enough money?"

"We do now. I picked the lock to Marcus's room and borrowed some of his. He's all about me getting my inheritance. I might as well get some of it early. I already called the airport, and they're holding a plane for us."

Will looked up Grant Park on the laptop, trying to determine where the battle might occur. "I want to check it out tomorrow morning, then lay low until tomorrow night."

"Okay." She thought she'd be more nervous, but it seemed surreal.

In less than thirty hours, she'd be dead.

***

Emma was exhausted by the time they landed in Chicago. She and Will hadn't talked much on the trip. She'd tried to bring up the subject of Jake's fate after her death, but he'd cut her off every time, refusing to discuss it.

Will rented a car and they checked into a hotel downtown, about a mile from the park. Emma stood at the window, looking out onto Lake Michigan. That was good. Will would be next to a large body of water. He'd have plenty of energy to draw from. She could use the electricity from the city.

Will came out of the bathroom and stood behind her, bringing her firmly against him and wrapping his arms around her stomach.

He patted her tummy. "How are you feeling?"

"Fine. I was only sick this morning, so that's good." She watched the lights of a boat out on the lake. "When I was pregnant with Jake, I was sick all the time. It was horrible and near impossible to go to class. But I managed."

"And I'm sure you *managed* with straight As. The word impossible isn't part of your vocabulary."

She knew where he was headed. "Will..." She paused and rested her arms on top of his. "I think you know, better than anyone else, I'm never going to give up. Especially when it involves Jake. But we have to face the facts, Will. My odds aren't the best."

He tried to pull away, but she turned around and looped her hands around his neck. "*Please,* Will. I need you to hear this."

Anger flashed in his eyes. "No. You say you're not giving up, but even talking about it is giving up."

"No, Will. Talking about it is being practical. People buy house or car insurance and hope to God they never have to use it. But they're prepared if they do. How is this any different?"

Closing his eyes, he shook his head. "I can't... I just can't think about the possibility."

"Will. Please. I need to do this. I'm begging you." Her voice broke. "I need to know that if something happens to me, you'll take care of Jake."

His eyes opened, full of love and pain. "You know I would. How can you even doubt that?"

"I don't. You told me in Colorado that you'd find him for me if I'd died from the infection, but I need to hear it again. I need to know that you'll love Jake and raise him and not let him forget about me."

"Emma." He kissed her forehead, his lips lingering a moment before he moved to meet her gaze. "I will raise Jake, with or without you. I will love him as though he'd been mine since birth. I will always talk about you with him, whether you're in the next room or you're...not."

Biting her lower lip, she fought her tears. "Thank you."

"You have to promise me that you won't give up. No matter what, you have to fight as hard as you can, and we'll pray for a miracle that will allow all three of us to survive. I need you, Emma. I need you more than anything I've ever needed in my entire life. You're my reason for living. Life without you is pointless."

"No. You'll have Jake."

Tears filled his eyes. "Emma, he's not you."

"I know. But you promised me."

His mouth lifted into a small smile. "I did, but it doesn't mean I'll be happy if I have to live without you. You can't expect that from me. I swear to you that I'll love Jake and give my life to protect him, but you can't expect me to be happy if you're dead."

"I don't expect you to be happy. Not at first, but you'll learn to live without me."

"Emma." Will's voice broke. "How does someone live with only half a heart?"

She stood on her tiptoes and pressed her lips against his. His arm tightened around her back, pulling her body flush against him.

This would be the last night she ever touched him. Staring into his warm and loving eyes, she told herself she had to be grateful for this. Her love with Will was more than most people got in a lifetime.

She pushed him backward and down on the bed. He brought her with him, twisting her so they lay face to face on their sides. "I love you, Will. Do you know how much I love you?" She brushed his cheek with her thumb.

His mouth found hers, and she didn't need their connection to feel his fear and devastation. They were always so desperate for one another. Was that a good thing or bad? They'd both spent their lives hoping to find someone to fill the empty spot in their hearts. It didn't seem fair that they had so little time, but there was one thing life had taught Emma and taught her well.

Nothing in life was fair.

***

Will held Emma in his arms after they made love. She'd fallen asleep, but he lay awake, watching her sleep in the soft glow of the city lights outside the hotel window.

He couldn't accept that she might die. He'd give his own life first, but what if they both died in the process? Jake would end up with Aiden or Marcus and neither was an acceptable parent. Anxiety clawed at his skin. He needed to get up and move around to dispel his excess energy, but to do so meant losing precious time with Emma.

He needed a plan. But he had no idea what to plan for. Ideally, he hoped to eliminate Aiden before the competition began, but that seemed unlikely. Especially if Marcus was correct and Aiden had received Alex's power.

The best-case scenario was if Will could get Raphael in as the fourth. He was sure that Jake and Emma could destroy Raphael together. Will would let Raphael kill him first. It was the best plan he could come up with before he finally drifted off to sleep.

The next morning, Will woke up to Emma nibbling his neck.

"Good morning," she sighed into his ear.

"Good morning to you too."

They spent several hours in bed, ordering room service for breakfast. Emma refused to talk about what would happen later that night.

"Just a few more hours, Will. Please. Just let me have two hours where I can pretend tonight won't happen."

He agreed only because he wasn't sure what he could do that was more productive than spending time with her. But foreboding hung in the air, tainting what little happiness he felt.

Her two hours were up close to eleven, and Will pulled her off the bed. "Let's get lunch and check out the park."

She gave him a soft smile, realizing what he was asking. "Sounds like a romantic date to me."

Their hotel was close enough that they decided to walk. The sky was overcast, lowering the temperature from the sweltering heat they'd dealt with for the past several days. They walked along the edge of Lake Michigan, and Emma smiled as she looked out into the water.

"I know you're the one with the inclination for water, so is it strange I've always been drawn to it?"

He gave her his cocky smile. "Maybe it's because you've been waiting for me."

She laughed. "Is that the best you got, player? I don't fall for your cheesy lines."

"Oh yeah, what do you fall for?"

She answered him with a kiss. "How could I pass up a man who kept saving my life?"

Her words sobered them both and they continued on to the park.

Will glanced around at the crowd. "Grant Park is pretty big. Did Aiden happen to mention where we'd meet?"

"Buckingham Fountain."

They found the fountain, then investigated nearby parking lots, electrical lines and anything else they imagined that they might need to know.

Will rubbed his forehead in frustration. "I can't think of anything else."

"I think we've covered it all."

They were fighting for their lives and to prepare, they'd walked around a park. It felt so inadequate.

Emma put her hand on his arm and leaned into him. "There's nothing else to do, Will."

He refused to accept that. "We can work on your power source. You can try to learn to use something other than anger."

She leaned over the railing, watching the water shoot up from the fountain. "This late in the game? Do you think it would help or hurt? You made me work for a week in the desert so my actions would come naturally, and I still struggle with it. What's going to happen tonight when I panic? I might end up with nothing at all."

He rested his arms on the rail beside her. "But it might not hurt to try."

"And what am I going to use as a source? What do *you* use?"

He shrugged. "I don't know. It's just there."

"Lucky *you*."

"Marcus said my power is pure because I'm his first child. He said that you've been reincarnated so many times, your power is diluted."

"Lucky *me*."

"That doesn't mean we should believe him. We can't believe a fucking word that comes out of his mouth. He knows that you struggle with your power and he might have said that to psych you out. He told me that it was in his best interest to keep Jake alive. Until it wasn't."

She stood up. "What do you mean?"

"Marcus tried to kill Jake and Raphael in Shreveport."

"What? You're just now telling me this?"

"He didn't succeed. I stopped him. That's how I lost Jake. That and a building collapsing between us."

Her eyes were wide with terror. "But—"

"He's fine, Emma. I promise you."

"But how do you know that Marcus didn't follow him?"

He put a hand on her arm. "Because Aiden had already left you, and you know that he went straight to Jake. Marcus isn't going to engage Aiden until tonight. And I'm sure he's going to hope one of us kills Aiden first. Otherwise, why didn't he try it years ago?"

Lowering her gaze from his face, she sighed. "Maybe."

"I want you to practice using another source of power."

She glanced at the crowd near them. "With all these people around? Are you crazy?"

"No not here. We'll find somewhere else."

"Do we have time for this?"

"We have to try something."

He suspected that she agreed to appease him. He didn't care why she did it, just that she did. They walked back to the hotel and got the car and drove north, finding a secluded park.

She sat on top of a wooden picnic table covered with peeling paint. Leaning forward, she gripped the edge, determination on her face. Her eyes closed and she looked strained as she concentrated.

Will watched her, tempering his rising frustration. "You're trying too hard. It's just there for me."

"It's never been just there for me, Will. You know this better than anyone."

"Maybe if you relax."

She opened her eyes with a sigh. "I've tried it relaxed. I've tried it tense. I've tried is just about every way possible." She pointed to his hand. "At least you still have your ring. Maybe it gives you more power than you know."

He grabbed the ring on his finger and began to frantically tug.

She sat up. "What are you doing?"

"Testing your theory."

Getting the ring over his knuckle, he pulled it free and handed it to Emma. He stepped away from her and called to the water in the ground. He could feel it, but not as well as he could with the ring. Releasing an exhale of frustration, he shook his head. She was right. Now what the fuck was he going to do about it?

He grabbed the ring from her palm and shoved it onto her left ring finger.

Her eyebrows rose with a smirk. "Is this a proposal? It's all so sudden."

"Very funny."

"This is *your* ring, Will. It's yours for a reason."

"Indulge me anyway."

Sighing, she stood, grabbing the ring with her other hand. She closed her eyes again. "Am I supposed to feel something?"

"Please take this seriously."

Her shoulders dropped. "I'm sorry. I just don't expect anything to happen."

"Try it anyway."

She stood still, her face calm. It was the most relaxed he'd seen her in days, and his hope grew until she opened her eyes and shook her head. "Nothing."

He knew it had to be too good to be true, but he still wasn't ready to give up hope. "Where was the last place you saw your pendant?"

"In Montana, when James handed it over to Scott Kramer."

"James." Will dug his cell phone out of his pocket.

"He didn't have it, Will. Kramer did. Besides, you don't even know if he's…"

"Alive?" Will looked up from his phone. "I'm about to find out." Will was surprised when the phone actually rang. James answered on the second ring.

"So you made it out of the parking garage."

James scoffed. "As if there was any question. You screw me and don't call me the next day? A guy could get hurt."

"I could say the same thing."

"So what do you want now?"

Will felt like an ass. James was right. The only time he called was when needed something. He vowed to change that starting tomorrow. When this whole mess was over. "I have a question for you."

"No."

"You don't even know what I'm going to ask."

"It doesn't matter. The answer is no."

"Don't be a dickhead."

"What can I say? It comes naturally."

"My question is about Emma's pendant."

The line went silent.

Will took that as a positive sign. "Emma says the last time she saw it was when Kramer took it from you in Montana. Did you ever see it after that?"

"So you two are still playing Bonnie and Clyde?"

"Did you ever see the pendant after that?"

James sighed loud and long. "Yeah, I saw it in South Dakota when they held you and they wanted me to get information from you about Emma. Kramer had it in his office."

"Do you think it's still there?"

"Oh, fuck no."

"Is that a fuck no it's not there?"

"It's a fuck no, I'm not getting involved again."

"You owe me."

"I owe you? How the hell do you see that? *You* fucking owe *me*, leaving me in that parking garage to reenact the shootout at the O.K. Corral."

"You deserved that and more. You were going to hand Emma over to them. I won't even get into you turning her over in Montana, and you lying to me, and—"

"All right. We both know I've never been a Boy Scout."

"You've also never liked any girl I've brought home to meet you, Mom."

"Not true. I liked that one girl."

"Which one?"

"Oh wait. That wasn't you."

Will smirked. "You do this for me and we'll call it even. In fact, if I can survive the night, this whole deal is over and we can try to live a normal life. Maybe I'll be a fishing guide with you."

"You suck at fishing."

"Screw you."

"What do you want?"

"I need the pendant."

"Want me to grab you a couple of gold bars from Fort Knox while I'm at it?"

"Sure, why not? Gold bullion never goes out of style."

"When do you want it? A couple of days? Where the fuck are you?"

"We're in Chicago and I need it tonight." Will pulled the phone from his ear as James released a long string of curses.

"Have you lost your fucking mind? That's impossible."

"Nothing is impossible for you."

James released some guttural sounds then grunted. "I love that you have such confidence in my abilities. Lucky for you I swiped the damn thing when I saw it. Where do I bring it?"

"Buckingham Fountain, in Grant Park."

"In Chicago? Please tell me you don't expect this by dinner time."

"No. I need it by ten."

"Well, that's relief." His words dripped with sarcasm. "You realize it's an eight-hour drive. And that's ten hours from now?"

"So you'll do it?"

"Call me a sucker for damsel in distress." He paused. "You, not Emma."

"I owe you."

"No shit, Sherlock." James hung up and Will grinned, feeling more hope than he'd felt in a long time.

Emma had watched him during the conversation, her face guarded. "He knows where it is?"

"He saw it at the Vinco Potentia compound."

"There is no way he can go to South Dakota, break in and get it, then get to Chicago in eight hours."

"If anyone could do it, James could. But he doesn't have to. He says he already stole it from them."

Her mouth twisted as though she held back a retort.

"Do you want to practice more?"

She shook her head. "No. I'm not going to find a magical new source of power. I think that our best hope is the pendant. I say we go back to the hotel."

To stop practicing felt like giving up, but she was right. They'd worked with her power and its source for weeks. It was highly doubtful she'd suddenly find a new one in an hour or two.

After they got back to the hotel room, Emma sat at the desk with the notepad and pen she found on the desk. She told Will that she wanted to write down her thoughts. As he walked behind her, he noticed it was a letter to Jake. He almost protested, but understood her need to write it.

He only hoped Jake never had to read it.

CHAPTER TWENTY-SEVEN

EMMA was amazed that she could sleep, as anxious as she was. But between writing the emotional letter to Jake and the hormones raging through her body, she couldn't fight her drowsiness. When she woke a couple of hours later, Will lay next to her, watching her.

She gave him a lazy smile. "I think that's officially the sign of a creepy stalker. Watching a girl while she sleeps."

He laughed. "I'll keep that in mind."

"Sorry I fell asleep."

He gave her a light kiss. "No, I'm glad you rested."

"Any word from James?"

His mouth pinched tight before he swallowed. "No."

She hadn't given much hope to James showing up, but a small sliver of it was there all the same. "Aren't you tired of being cooped up in here all afternoon?"

"No, I got to spend the afternoon with you. There's no place I'd rather be."

She grabbed his hand and looped her fingers through his. "I had the most wonderful dream."

"You did?" He smiled, happiness radiating from his face. She'd seen too little of this side of him. She added it to her list of regrets.

"Yeah, I dreamed we were normal. No running. No powers. We lived in a house with Jake and the baby. And we had a dog."

Will's voice lowered. "I bet Jake was thrilled with that."

"Yeah." She smiled. "I have no idea what you did for a job, but you came home every night."

"Princess, there's no way I'd take a job traveling without you with me."

"Good." Sadness permeated every part of her, her bones aching with it. "Thank you. You've given me more than I could have ever asked for. More than I ever dreamed of having."

"Emma, don't do this."

She put a finger over his lips. "No. I need to say this. I think people don't say these things enough and then they're sorry when it's too late."

He grabbed her hand and held it to his chest. Tears threatened to spill down his cheeks and he swallowed, giving her a nod.

"I'd prepared myself to live the rest of my life alone. But then you showed up…" She laughed as her eyes stung. "You were such an ass."

He choked on a laugh. "You really know how to flatter a guy."

Her finger wiped a tear that fell from the corner of his eye. "But then you let your guard down with Jake, and I could see the man you really are, not the man you wanted the world to see. And I wondered, if maybe, just maybe…"

She couldn't stop her tears from falling, and she brushed them away. "Then you saved us, saved me, time and time again." She shook her head, grief burning in her throat. "I thought you were crazy when you told me you loved me. You hardly knew me. But I get it now. When you know you love someone, you know. You were worth the risk, Will. I'm just sorry it took me so long to figure it out."

He shook his head. "You make it sound like it's an amazing thing to love you. It's not. You saved me, can't you see that?"

"And you saved more than just my life. You gave me hope. Your love filled the empty places in my heart. As dark and cold as my heart was, that itself is magic, more powerful than any trick you can do with water. You made me whole."

She kissed him gently, and he wrapped an arm around her back, pulling her close.

He lowered his mouth to her ear. "We need to eat something. We have to leave in less than an hour."

"I'm not hungry. My stomach is in knots."

"Try anyway."

Will ordered room service, and they sat at the desk, eating in silence. Emma glanced around the room. "You packed up while I slept."

Will stabbed a vegetable off his plate, refusing to look at her. "I figured we'd want leave town as soon as this thing is over tonight."

Her stomach clenched. This was real. This was really happening. The fork in her hand shook. *Get it together, Emma*, she told herself. *You can't afford to lose it now.* "I have to go to the bathroom." She walked across the room, Will watching her with worried eyes. She hated that the most. That he worried so much yet there was nothing he could do.

She shut the door and sat on the side of the tub, twisting her fingers in her lap. If only she was stronger. If she'd tried harder. Or if she'd trusted Will sooner. Or admitted she loved him before it was too late. Would any of those things have made a difference? Did it really matter now? All she had was this moment. She needed to make the best of it.

Will knocked at the door. "Emma? Are you okay?"

She needed to be strong for him. And for Jake. If she fell to pieces, it would be harder for the both of them. This was the next to last gift she could give them.

She opened the door and gave Will a tight smile. "I'm fine. I just needed a moment."

His hand rested on her arm, his eyes full of concern. "It's time. Are you ready?"

Ready to face her certain death? She needed the old Emma for this. The part of her that was hard and bitter. "Let's go kick some ass."

Will brought their bags to the car, and they drove in silence to the park. He pulled out his cell phone but hung up without talking to anyone. She knew who he was calling and knew it was a wasted call. They were really on their own.

Will grabbed her hand, and she almost pulled away. Feeling close to Will weakened her. She lost the bitterness she needed to be strong. But she had a choice. Choose Will or choose the animosity that had drenched most of her life. Then she remembered her words to Aiden. "If given the choice, I'll always choose Will." If she ever needed to choose him, it was now.

Will parked in a lot filled with cars. "There are too many people here. They're going to get killed tonight." They got out of the car. Will reached into the bag in the backseat and grabbed his gun, checking the clip before handing it to her. "When all else fails, shoot them in the head."

"Good advice. Right up there with wearing clean underwear in case you're in an accident." She stuffed the gun in the back of her jeans. "So what's our plan? Tell me what to do."

He looked up at her with raised eyebrows.

"Why do you look so surprised? You're the expert on this. I told you back in Oregon that I trusted you to come with the plan."

"Not knowing all of the rules puts us at a huge disadvantage." His mouth pursed. "Two people have to be eliminated before this thing even begins, if the final battle really consists of four." He started toward the fountain and Emma fell into step beside him. "The easy choice of who to eliminate would be Raphael. I suspect he's the weakest."

"No, I'm the weakest. I'm going to be the first target."

"Not necessarily. I don't think we should focus on taking out the weakest. We should take out the strongest, so we have a better chance in the final four."

She tilted her head. "You think we should take out Marcus and Aiden."

"If we can, yes."

She walked in silence, processing his information.

"It will work if we use the element of surprise. They won't be prepared."

"I don't…" She took a deep breath. "So this is going to be one big free-for-all?"

"Yeah, I suspect so."

"Do we stand in a field? Are we around the fountain?"

"I have no idea. I wish I did. We could strategize better. I know for a fact that Marcus is thinking with a military mind. He's got a plan, even if I'm not privy to it. I think he's going to think like I am—eliminate the harder competition first. That means Aiden." He paused. "And Jake."

She sucked in a breath. Eliminating the competition—that's what this was about. Killing people. She needed to keep her head and think objectively. A difficult task when discussing the possible annihilation of your own son. She nodded. "Okay, so we know who Marcus will go after. What about Aiden and Raphael?"

"Aiden will go after me. And I suspect Marcus. As for Raphael's plan? Who knows if he's thinking logically."

"If it's revenge, he'll go after you and me. If it's logic, Marcus and Aiden."

"Agreed. But then there are other variables to consider. What about Jake? He might be forced to attack us."

Emma's heart seized. She hadn't considered that. "No. Jake would never hurt us."

Will nodded. "Marcus thinks killing you will give me your power. He might do it right away if he thinks it will be to my advantage."

"Will." Her tongue dried out and tripped on his name. She swallowed. "And if the three of us make it to the final four? Then what?"

He stopped and pulled her to his chest, and looked into her eyes. "I told you I'd defend you to the death and I meant it, Emma. Once I know you and Jake are safe and it's just the three of us, one of you has to kill me."

"You know I can't, even if I wanted to. That means Jake will have to do it."

"We might be able to…hurt one another in the final battle."

"No, no, no! I'll never agree to that!" She tried to pull out of his grasp but he held tight.

He brushed the hair off her cheek. "Emma, don't you see? It's been my fate since the beginning. I'm The Chosen One, the one destined to protect you. Mark or no mark, Emma, the job is burned into my soul."

Should she tell him Marcus's theory about the prophecy? Or that she suspected he was right? "But I'm the weakest one. I'm the one of the three of us who deserves to die."

"None of us deserve to die."

Anger burned in her chest. "I've done terrible things since this all began. I've become more and more like them."

He smiled but his eyes were sad. "Emma, I've done far worse things than you have these last few weeks. I'd confess them to you now to ease your guilt, but I can't bear the thought of you looking at me in horror before I die." He kissed her long and slow. "The mark is gone, but my need to protect you is stronger than it ever was. It's now branded in love. I don't deserve the love I've found in you, but I've accepted it, thanking God for giving it to me."

"There is no God."

"I hope more than anything that you're wrong and he'll show us some mercy tonight."

Tears fell down her cheeks. "Will, I can't let you do this. Please."

"This is the penance for what I've done, Emma, don't you see? Giving my life for you and Jake is my redemption."

He wanted to die for her and Jake. How could she accept this? "You've planned this all along! You planned to die!" She tried to pull away again, but he refused to let her go.

"No, Emma. I hoped we all could figure out a way to make it through, but yes, this was my backup plan."

"I can't let you do this, Will. No!"

He held onto her arms, his fingers pinching deep. "Do you think I would willingly agree to let you die? We both know Jake isn't an option."

Her fight left her and she sagged against his chest. "So it's you or me."

"Yes. I think it's always been you or me. Aiden and Marcus planned it this way."

"What are we going to do? I won't agree, and neither will you."

"For once, just once, please just accept my decision."

She shook her head against his chest. "How do you expect me to live with myself if I let you die? How will I look myself in the mirror?"

He leaned her head back and looked into her eyes. "You'll do it because Jake needs you, we both know that. *You know that*. He needs you more than he needs me."

"But you can protect him."

"Emma." His voice floated on the night air. "After tonight, Jake won't need protection."

The pain in her heart screamed for release, but she would not allow herself to break into sobs. She lifted her chin, glaring at him. She was the one who was supposed to die. "I refuse to discuss this."

"Burying your head in the sand won't change things. Don't hide from this."

"What do you expect me to do, Will? Do you expect me to just say 'Okay, Will. No problem. I'll kill you.' Are you insane?"

"You don't have to say any of that. You only have to say one word. Just say okay."

She shook her head. "I can't. You can't ask me that."

He kissed her again, his love seeping through their connection. *Just say it, Princess.*

Her heart was breaking, and she couldn't afford to be broken right now. Could she kill him, even if she promised?

Emma, please.

She loved him with every part of her, and she'd give him anything he wanted. Even this.

Okay. What had she done?

"Thank you." He kissed her again. "Now let's go."

She took small consolation that she wouldn't have to kill him, certain she'd be killed first.

She wasn't sure which one to hope for.

***

Aiden's car drove next to a big body of water.

"Is that the ocean?" Jake asked. After seeing Mommy visit an ocean in a vision years ago, he'd always wanted to see it.

Aiden stared out the window, and looked startled by Jake's question. "What? No. That's Lake Michigan."

That was the most he'd heard Aiden say since yesterday. He'd been distracted and looked worried after he'd found out Raphael was dead.

Aiden rubbed his chin. "Did you see Will after he killed Raphael? Did he emit a glow or look different afterward?"

"No."

"Well, what did he look like?"

Jake looked at him, wide-eyed and amazed. Aiden was afraid. "I didn't see him. After Will shot us, Raphael made the building fall down.

"Why didn't Raphael heal himself? Was he hurt that badly?"

Aiden had already asked this yesterday. And today. "He had holes all over his chest. There was lots of blood."

Shaking his head, Aiden turned back to the window. "It doesn't make sense."

Jake didn't answer. Part of him was surprised Aiden didn't suspect him, but then again, why would he? Jake hadn't fought back to save Antonia. Aiden probably thought Jake was too scared to kill Raphael.

The shadow figure told Jake that he could kill Aiden tonight at the battle. He'd spent all afternoon daydreaming about what he was going to do. He decided Aiden had to die the way Antonia did. Burning and screaming.

Aiden sat up and cleared his throat as though he'd just woken up after accidently falling asleep. "We need to talk about what's going to happen tonight."

I know what's going to happen. You're going to die.

Aiden's eyes flickered as though he read Jake's thoughts, but was unsure.

Jake tried to keep from smiling. He'd only partially hidden that thought.

"Marcus and Will are going to try to do away with you right away. They might not wait until the battle begins, so be prepared."

The shadow figure had told him that he had to kill the person who killed Alex. Jake was prepared. "Won't they try to kill you?"

"They can try." Aiden flashed a grin but it looked fake. "Since Alex and Raphael are gone, the final four determination is easy. You and your mother against Will and Marcus."

"And what about you?"

He smiled again, but it looked uneasy. "I watch."

"But the shadows in my dream said everyone had to fight."

Aiden's eyes widened and he didn't hide his fear. "What dream?"

"The dream in the desert. With the circles."

Aiden's hand shook as he rubbed his chin. "Dreams are meaningless."

"It said only two can live. Only two."

Aiden shook his head and forced a smile. "Nonsense. Besides, it doesn't matter. We'll kill Marcus. And it will still be us in the final four. Trust me."

Jake didn't trust Aiden, but he was sure of one thing.

Aiden would be dead before it was over.

CHAPTER TWENTY-EIGHT

MARCUS was waiting by the south end of the fountain when Will and Emma walked up. Will's muscles tensed into knots, and he made her walk behind him. He was thankful that she didn't argue. He'd considered leaving her by the nearby trees for more cover, but Aiden and Raphael were nowhere to be seen. Will didn't want to leave her unprotected, so he'd keep her with him.

He could feel her anxiety peak, then she shut their connection down.

Don't do that, Emma. You have to let me in.

Her anxiety returned but in a lesser degree.

Will's pulse sped up at the sight of Marcus, who leaned against the railing, watching them approach.

"Will. Emma. You made it." His arms were crossed and he tilted his head, trying to get a better glimpse of Emma.

"Where's Aiden?"

Marcus smirked. "With any luck at all he got held up in traffic and will miss the big show. Then we'll just have to figure out which two of us are the winners."

Marcus had already chosen his final two, and Will didn't agree.

Will shifted his feet, assuming a casual stance as he surveyed the area. It was almost ten o'clock, but there were still too many damn people here. "So how does this work?"

"I have no idea."

"You're the one who said opting out wasn't an option. How did you know if you don't know how this works?"

"The end had to come for Aiden's game. Once I joined in this version, all of us became involved."

Will glanced around. "Even though Aiden made the rules?"

"Aiden has deluded himself. It's out of his control now."

"Whose control is it in?"

"There are forces larger than all of us, Will. Laws of nature."

"You mean like laws of physics?"

"Yes. But Aiden has decreed something unnatural. There are meant to be four elements. He's announced that only two will remain."

"How can there only be two elements?"

"That's just it. There must be four. It's unnatural to have otherwise. The world will be thrown into chaos at the unbalance. Have you noticed the unusual amount of earthquakes today?"

"No, I've been a bit preoccupied to watch the news."

"It makes me think that Raphael is dead."

Will's eyes widened. "What? How?"

"When I attacked him yesterday, I might have killed him."

"Did you gain his power?"

"No."

Will snorted. "Well. There goes your theory."

Marcus watched Emma, a slow smile forming on his lips.

Rage exploded in Will's head. "I'm warning you now, Marcus. If you kill her, I will kill you even if you and I are the last two survivors. Then there will only be one element and the world will be fucked."

"Will…"

A voice called behind them. "No killing each other yet."

Emma gasped.

Aiden approached with Jake by his side, sauntering toward them as if he were out for a stroll. He stopped about twenty feet away and gave Jake a slight push. "Go ahead. Go tell your mother hello."

Jake bolted toward her and Emma fell to her knees, opening her arms to him.

"Jake." Her words were muffled as she buried her face into his hair and held him tight.

"Mommy!" He sobbed into her shoulder.

Will surveyed the area. "Where's Raphael?"

Aiden shifted his weight, as though he were annoyed. "Raphael is no longer with us, which I'm sure you're quite aware of, Will."

"What the hell are you talking about?"

With a smirk, Aiden studied Emma and Jake's reunion. "Don't play innocent with me. Jake told me that you're the one who killed him."

Will glanced down at Jake, confused. "What are you—
"

Marcus pushed away from the railing. "What's wrong, Aiden? Lose your lackey?"

"What about Alex?" Aiden asked, his voice hard. "Did you kill Alex too, Will?"

"Yes." Marcus took another step forward. "He killed them both."

Marcus's lie took Will by surprise. He must want Aiden to think Will had killed both of them so he'd think Will was stronger. His plan worked. Aiden looked frightened now.

Aiden shifted his focus from Will, apparently taking a different tack. "Get a good look at your son, Emmanuella. Get a good look at what you gave up. What you're forfeiting by choosing Will."

Jake broke away from his mother's embrace and glared at Will.

Emma grabbed Jake's arms. "It's not true, Jake. I didn't give you up. I'm not choosing Will over you. Aiden stole you from me and forced this whole thing on us."

Jake wore a pout. "You joined with him. Now I can't talk to you in my head anymore."

"I didn't know that would happen when I joined with Will. I swear."

"You picked Will."

"No, Jake. I picked you both."

"Enough nonsense," Aiden called, but he still remained a good distance away. That fact made Will nervous.

"Emma," Will said in a low voice.

She looked up at him with worried eyes.

His gaze shifted to Aiden and she stood, taking Jake's hand in hers. Will reached for her and she moved toward him, Jake in tow.

"It's time to begin," Aiden said.

Will pushed Emma and Jake behind him. Marcus said there was no opting out, but he didn't trust the man. "Now that we have Jake, I think we'll be going." Will backed up, Emma following his lead.

Aiden laughed. "That won't work." He closed his eyes and raised his hands. A glow surrounded him.

A bright light blazed the sky, and spread out and then down around the fountain and surrounding gardens.

The people still in the park began to scream and run in all directions.

Emma grabbed Will's arm. *What just happened?*

I think it's begun.

***

Emma's heart slammed against her ribcage. They were trapped in an enclosed area with two powerful, insane men. And countless innocent people.

Emma, run!

Not without you.

Goddammit, Emma. Will you do what I ask for once? GO!

With Jake's hand still in hers, she ran toward the opposite end of the fountain, away from the three men. She couldn't shake the feeling that she was abandoning Will.

People rushed toward the exit from the fountain area, ignoring the white, semi-transparent dome that encased them. A man and a woman ran into it and burst into flames.

Oh, God.

Jake watched the panicked crowd, then looked up at her in amazement but no fear. What had he seen that this didn't scare him?

A grove of trees lay up ahead. They offered little coverage, but they were better than nothing. It was night, but streetlamps lined sidewalk, shining pools of light into the trees. Focusing on her anger, Emma felt her power grow and she aimed it for the streetlights. Glass shattered as the lamps burst, plunging the area into darkness. The screams around them intensified.

She ran toward the cover of the trees and turned to see if Marcus or Aiden had followed them. Instead she saw bright flashes of light on the other side of the fountain. Aiden. If Will and Marcus were using water, she couldn't tell. The sound of the fountain drowned out everything else. She concentrated on her connection to Will and felt a hum of power, but no surge. That had to be a good thing.

Jake looked up at her with expectant eyes. "We need to fight."

Her anger simmered in her chest. "No, we do not. You are five years old. You will not fight for your life."

"I promised."

Her eyes widened. "Who? Aiden? You don't have to keep any promises to the megalomaniac."

"No, not Aiden."

Dread crept up her spine. Please let it be Raphael. "Then who?"

"The shadows."

She sank to her knees as the blood rushed from her head. Marcus was right.

***

Aiden took a step closer to Will as they watched Emma run away with Jake. "You do realize they've only gained a temporary reprieve?"

Will didn't answer, trying to determine his best source of attack. He wished to God that Aiden had done this two hours later after the park had closed, but he supposed Aiden got off on the panic.

Don't analyze your move. Marcus spoke into his head. *Just trust your power.*

Will didn't trust Marcus, but it was the same advice he gave to Emma.

Aiden had created the dome. If he destroyed Aiden, did it destroy the enclosure?

Trust his power. It lived in his chest, always present since he'd first become aware of it, but when he needed it, it coursed through his veins like ice water, pulsing with unimaginable energy. It was so different than what Emma experienced that he was sure his was wrong. But it turned out he was stronger. Her source was anger. His just existed. How had he lived with it for thirty-four years and never noticed?

Aiden stood across from him with a smug expression. A ball of energy shot toward Will and a wall of water shot from the fountain to block it, leaving sparkling water droplets suspended in the sky like stars. Will cast a glace to Marcus, who wore a look of concentration.

Aiden smirked. "Aren't you supposed to be attacking Emmanuella, Marcus? Now that you can?"

"I've decided to concentrate my efforts somewhere else."

"I never planned to be part of the final four."

Marcus laughed. "You pompous ass. I'll never know how you figured that. You're trapped in here like the rest of us. That dome's not going anywhere until there's only two of us left."

Emma. Where are you and Jake?

Hiding in some trees at the opposite end of the dome. This is wrong, Will. I need to help you.

You'll help me more if you stay out of the way. Maybe the three men could kill each other and Jake and Emma would be saved by default.

A stream of water flew from the fountain into Marcus's hand, forming a spear, and Marcus advanced toward Aiden. He pulled back his hand and threw the spear. It headed for Aiden's chest until a wall of red energy formed, shooting sparks when the spear collided with it. The water lost its form and fell to the ground with a splash.

Another water spear quickly followed, hitting with the same accuracy but crashing into Aiden's wall of energy.

A bolt of lightning shot toward Will and he ducked to avoid contact.

"Did you know that Aristotle named the elements?" Aiden asked with a grin. "Then Plato took the concept further. Do you know which element he decreed the most powerful?"

Another lightning bolt shot toward Will, and he dodged it again. "Let me guess. Fire?"

Aiden laughed. "Yes, fire. Believe it or not, the game was in progress then. I gave Plato a little help. I showed him that elements have power over one another, but that one was the ruler of them all."

Two lightning bolts shot from the sky, converging together to strike.

"I've ruled for thousands and thousands of years. I'm not about to let some newborn take that from me."

Water droplets filled the air in the fountain behind him, and he shot them toward Aiden, like tiny knives. Aiden blocked most, but a few penetrated his shield, striking him in the shoulder and the cheek.

Aiden growled, emitting a reddish glow. "Enough playing."

Fire erupted in the sky, raining down in tiny flames. Marcus created a blanket of water over their heads. The flames hit the cover, hissing as they died out. An arrow of fire pierced Marcus's side, sinking in until it was completely absorbed. Marcus fell to his knees, but the cover continued to hold over their heads.

But the fire rained over the entire area, landing on the innocent pedestrians. Their screams of fright and pain bounced off the dome walls, echoing in Will's head. Emma and Jake were in here somewhere.

Emma, get into the fountain.

He returned his attention to Aiden, who had focused his energy on a weakened Marcus.

I'm not throwing my life away so you can waste it, Marcus said. *You have to survive.*

What did Marcus mean?

Regroup and attack Aiden with Jake. Jake has more power than you can even imagine. I taught him where to find it. He gave Will a cockeyed smile that looked achingly familiar.

Will's breath stuck in his chest. *You planned it this way all along. You planned to die.* He sent a barrage of water pellets toward Aiden, but his wall of energy held.

Agony contorted Marcus's face and the water cover over their heads shimmered as it weakened. *Emma needs it to fulfill her role. She knows what she needs to do.*

What?

Go! Marcus got to his feet, clutching his side, Aiden's arrow of fire still buried deep within him. "What do you say, Aiden? Just us two old-timers fighting it out. This is the way it's supposed to be anyway. It's time for us to turn it over to a new generation, hopefully one that will show more respect for their positions."

"You've suddenly become all high and mighty." Aiden laughed. "You hardly seem to be in a position to negotiate. Are you trying to save yourself? "

"No, I'm trying to save the world." *Go! I'm sorry I can't help you save them both.*

Will took off running as Marcus was engulfed in flames.

CHAPTER TWENTY-NINE

EMMA and Jake ran to the fountain, dodging fireballs falling from the sky. Jake blew them away with gusts of wind as they hopped the short railing and trudged through the shallow water. They stood under a stream of rushing water in the middle of the pool, huddled together.

Jake's eyes glowed. "I need to be out there."

"No, you need to stay with me."

Emma! Where are you?

Will was close, closer than where she's left him.

In the fountain.

Others in the crowd had seen what she and Jake had done and followed suit, shouting and screaming as they piled into the fountain. They shoved one another, trying to get under the sprays of water, some climbing the concrete structure. Others lay down in the shallow pool but the panicked crowd trampled them. Emma and Jake were caught in the chaos as people fought to get to relative safety.

Will came into view, running next to the circular edge of the fountain. He jumped over the railing and ran toward them. Panic filled his eyes as the sky brightened over their heads.

"What happened?" Her breath caught in her throat.

"Marcus is dead."

"We're the final four."

His jaw clenched and he looked down at Jake. "Yes."

Emma grabbed Jake's arm, pulling him closer. "Why are you looking at him like that?"

Will ignored her, keeping his attention on Jake. "Marcus said you had more power than any of us. Is this true?"

Jake glared. "Yes."

Emma gasped. "No! No, he doesn't! He's just a little boy!"

"You were the one who killed Raphael. You got his power."

"Yes." Jake grinned. "I got Alex's power too. The shadows came to me and said Alex gave it to me as a gift. There was one rule, but I accepted." Hatred darkened his eyes.

This was all a bad dream, a horrific nightmare. It couldn't be true. "The shadows?"

Jake looked up at her with a grin, but his eyes were cold. "Marcus told me to talk to them. They're my friends. They gave me their mark." He pulled down his t-shirt and two black outlined joined circles were embedded on his chest over his heart.

"Oh, God." She looked at Will. "What does it mean?" But she knew. Marcus told her. She just refused to believe it.

"I don't know."

"*Why would Marcus encourage this?* How did he plan to use this?"

"He planned for a fresh start. He planned to die for me, Emma. His last words were to save Jake. He was sorry he couldn't figure out how to save you both."

"But why? Why lie and tell you he meant to kill us?"

"I don't know. So I wouldn't feel loyalty to him? He planned to die all along."

This was all too much. She shook her head. "So now what? The dome is still overhead."

"We have to kill Aiden."

"And then it will go away?"

He didn't answer.

"Will!"

"I don't know." He swallowed. "I don't think so."

"When will it go away?" She knew the answer but hoped he proved her wrong.

"When there are two of us left."

***

Jake watched Will in fascination, ready to strike at any moment. Will didn't act like he was going to kill him, but Jake still didn't trust him.

Will turned his gaze back to Jake. "Marcus says Jake is the strongest, and Jake just said he killed Raphael and that Alex gave Jake his power. And then there's his mark." He pointed to Jake's chest. "Emma, I need him."

"No! He's five years old."

"And I suspect he's stronger than you'll ever be. This is the only way."

"No! He didn't know what he was doing. He killed Raphael to defend himself."

Will's gaze narrowed. "Why did you kill Raphael?"

Jake squared his shoulders, his anger simmering. "I needed his power."

"Why?"

"So I could kill you."

"No!" Mommy screamed, jerking Jake to face her. "No. Jake! Stop this nonsense right now!"

Will pulled Mommy up and gave her a tiny smile. "Emma, stop. This is our answer. This is a good thing."

She wrenched her arm from his hold. "In what twisted reality can this be a good thing?"

"It's time." Aiden's voice boomed all around them. "The sooner we begin the sooner it all ends."

Mommy's breath came in short bursts, and her eyes looked wild. Will touched her cheek, giving her an intense look, and she calmed down.

But the people all around them were far from calm, still screaming and splashing water. Irritation crawled across Jake's skin.

Aiden's voice cut across the air again. "The three of you have two minutes to start this thing or I'm going to start killing everyone in here."

Will leaned into Mommy's face. "We will concentrate on taking out Aiden, then we let Jake do his thing."

Biting her lip, her chin shook, but she nodded.

Will grabbed her and kissed her. "I'll always love you, Emma. It doesn't matter where I am."

"I can't do this, Will."

"Yes. You can." Will looked down at Jake. "You'll do it for him."

Jake was confused. What was Will talking about? But he didn't like that Mommy was hugging and kissing Will and not him. "Get away from my mommy!"

Emma's eyes flashed in anger. "Jacob!"

"No. This is good. This will make it easier for him." Will released his hold on her. "Are you ready?"

"No."

"We have to do it anyway. You know this is the best plan. But I suspect Jake won't listen to me. You'll have to coach him."

"*To kill you?*"

"No, to kill Aiden first. That has to happen first."

Jake didn't like that Will was trying to tell him what to do, even if it was going to come through his mother. "The shadows already told me I could kill Aiden, but I have to do something else first."

"What?" Mommy's voice squeaked.

"It's a surprise."

"We have to go." Will took her hand. "Are you ready?"

Mommy nodded and reached for Jake with her other hand. The water had soaked through Jake's jeans, making his legs so heavy that he struggled to keep up with her. They climbed over the railing, Mommy helping him over as Will watched him with a strange look on his face. Holding hands, the three of them walked toward Aiden, who stood at the opposite end of the dome, glowing.

Aiden thought he was so strong and powerful, but Jake was going to show him how wrong he was. After he killed Will to pay for the gift from the shadows.

Will confused him. Will wasn't acting like he wanted to kill Jake. He acted like he wanted to help Jake, but it had to be a trick. Mommy had chosen Will over Jake before because Will made her. He didn't care about Jake. Will would try to make her choose the same way now.

Jake wondered why he wasn't nervous. There were four of them and two would die. Maybe it was because he was sure which two would die and which two would live. He squeezed Mommy's hand. She was with him again. That was what mattered.

"What a sweet little family." Aiden laughed as they neared.

Family? Is that what they were? He and Mommy had always been a family, but Will?

"Let's get this over with, Aiden." Will let go of Mommy's hand, but he stepped in front of her, blocking her from Aiden. "What are we supposed to do?"

"The only rule is that this goes on until two of us remain. Only then are we allowed to leave."

"How can you be sure of that? You thought you didn't have to participate and look at you now."

"For all I know I didn't. But when I killed Marcus, that left only four. I'm participating by default."

The shadows began to move. They had hung at the edges of the sidewalk, and the fountain, and the trees, waiting for their chance. But now they crept closer, giving Jake confidence. They were going to keep their word. But he had to fulfill his promise first.

The shadows danced around his feet and Jake was amazed that no one had noticed them yet. They tickled his ear. "Are you ready?"

Jake glared at Will with all the hate he could muster. Will might be nice now, but he'd tried to kill Jake in Shreveport. Will had to pay.

In Mommy's hand, Jake's twitched, and then began to burn. Snatching his hand from her, he looked down at the scorch marks, then up at her in surprise. Why would Mommy burn him?

She looked at him with equal confusion. "What did you do, Jake?"

"Nothing."

He took a step back as the shadows swirled, forming a thick black cloud that made a big circle around the four of them.

Will and Aiden glanced around in confusion.

"What's going on, Aiden?" Will growled.

"I don't know." Aiden sounded worried.

Jake smiled. He knew.

Emma's face paled. "You know don't you, Jake? This is your surprise. What's happening?"

"The shadows are here to help me."

"The shadows?" Aiden tried to look irritated, but his eyes told Jake he was afraid. "They're a fairy tale, Jacob."

"Tell that to the swirling black cloud." Will grunted, then turned to Jake. "What do the shadows do?"

"They do nothing." Aiden spat. "They were cast into their realm and have lived there for millenniums."

Jake took a step toward Aiden. "They are here to help me kill you. But I must do something for them first."

"What do you have to do first, Jake?" Mommy's voice shook.

Jake stood straight, squaring his shoulders as he stared at Will. "I have to kill the person who killed Alex. It was his rule for me to get the gift."

Mommy stumbled backward as Will ran toward her. Jake created a wind to blow Will away from her. "I'm going to kill you, Will. You stole my mommy and you tried to kill me."

"No, Jake! Stop this!" Mommy screamed. "Will has spent all this time trying to find you and save you! Aiden is lying!"

Jake's anger billowed like storm clouds inside him, filling him with hate. "No! Will killed Alex! I only got Alex's power if I agreed to destroy the person who killed him."

Mommy's eyes were wide, and her hands trembled. *"How could you, Jake?* How could you agree to such an evil thing?"

She sounded so angry. And hurt. Some of his confidence faltered. "I did it to save you. I needed more power to save you."

She fell to her knees as Will rushed toward her again, pulling her up into his arms. "Give it up, Jake." Will shouted. "Give up his power! You don't need it."

Jake's power grew with his rage. "You're only saying that because you want me weaker so you can kill me before I kill you."

"No, Jake! I'm begging you to give it up before you do something you regret."

"You aren't the boss of me! Besides I can't give it up! It's done!"

Will growled like an angry wild animal. Water flew around the circle. Droplets sprayed in all directions, stinging and drawing blood when they hit Jake's skin.

"Will! Stop!" Mommy's voice rose over the roar of the water, and the droplets rushed together and moved in a wave back into the fountain. She hugged Will, leaning into his chest. "It's okay. Just a change of plans."

Aiden began to laugh.

Jake's anger grew. "Why are you laughing?"

Aiden shook his head. "You haven't figured it out yet?"

"What?" Fear clawed at Jake's chest. What did they all know that he didn't?

Aiden continued to laugh.

"*What?*" A storm appeared overhead, the clouds tumbling and churning.

"It appears you're wrong about who killed Alex." Aiden twisted his lips into a smirk. "It appears we *both* were."

Jake held his breath then released it in a whoosh. "Will didn't kill Alex."

Aiden winked. "It appears not."

"Who?" But Jake knew.

Mommy.

What had he done?

***

Panic flooded through Emma's head and she struggled to sort through which emotions were hers and which were Will's.

What has he done? Will's hold on her tightened.

Jake's face turned from anger to horror.

He'll never be able to live with himself if he does this, Will. We can't let him do it.

I don't think we can't stop him. I don't think he can stop it. He won't have to kill me if I'm already dead.

No. That isn't the plan.

When has anything gone as planned?

The pain on Jake's face broke her heart. He hadn't realized what he'd done. He was just a little boy and he needed to know that his Mommy loved him no matter what he'd done. Emma took a step away from Will. "It's okay, Jake, You didn't know. You thought you were doing a good thing. You wanted to save me."

Tears glazed his eyes. "The shadows said I have to kill you."

If two of us are dead, then that leaves you and Jake.

Emma, what are you going to do? Terror filled Will's words.

She felt amazingly calm. Her death was imminent yet she knew she was dying for the best reasons—to save the two people who mattered more to her than anything in the world. "Jake, do you think I would ever hurt you?"

He cast his gaze to the ground. "No."

"I want to give you a hug. Please."

He nodded.

Will, I have to tell Jake goodbye.

I'll watch Aiden.

She knelt in front of Jake and pulled him into a hug, burying her face into his ear. "It's okay. You don't have to kill me," she whispered.

"But the shadows said—"

"Shhh…" She stroked the back of his head, the other hand running circles over his back. "I'm going to fight Aiden, but you can only watch."

"He's strong. Stronger than you." His body stiffened. "I won't let him kill you too."

"Jake, your deal with the shadows was that you had to kill me first. Before you could kill Aiden. You won't be able to interfere."

"But if you… who will take care of me?"

"Will. He'll take care of you."

Jake jerked backward. "No! He tried to kill me!"

Her voice was soft as she tried to soothe him with her touch. "No. That was Marcus. Will stopped him from hurting you any more."

"But Will took me away from you."

"No. Will has spent all this time trying to find you."

Jake's mouth twisted in indecision.

"Promise me that you'll try to love Will. He needs you. I promise that he'll love you too."

Tears fell down his cheeks. "But I want *you*."

"Will's the next best thing. I need you to promise to give Will a chance."

Jake nodded.

She kissed his cheek and climbed to her feet.

Will, I'm ready.

Before he could stop her, she found her anger, burning bright and white-hot. She walked between Jake and Will to face Aiden. "I won't let you destroy the lives of the people I love, Aiden."

"It's a fight to the end, Emmanuella. May the better man win."

"That's what I'm counting on." Emma thrust her energy toward Aiden, and Will sent several spears of water toward him.

Don't kill him, Will. Not yet. He has to kill me first.

Aiden deflected their attacks, sending electrical charges along the ground toward both of them.

It's electricity, Emma told herself. She felt the jolt and absorbed the power, but Will felt it too, stumbling after the contact. She had no intention of lying down and letting Aiden just kill her. He was going to have to work for it. She sent burst after burst of energy toward him, without any result.

Will had recovered and renewed his attack. *I'm going to weaken him. Maybe if you kill him, you can get his power.*

And I'll be harder to kill. Let Aiden and I kill each other.

She sent volley after volley toward her father as Will pelleted him with water spears. Aiden was weakening, and Emma was only slightly injured.

Aiden grew more desperate. "Time to end this, Jacob!" He sent a ball of fire toward Jake, who managed to narrowly dodge it. "Fight me, Jake!"

"No!" Emma screamed. Goaded, Jake forgot his deal with the shadows and sent a wind toward Aiden. It turned around and hit Emma with full force, slamming her into the shadow barricade.

Aiden sent another round of fire toward Jake, and Jake continued to defend himself—but the wind and fire he threw at Aiden was redirected and struck Emma. She felt her power weaken as she slid down the shadow barrier. The shadows crawled across her body, climbing toward her ear. "You can best him," they hissed. "You have the power."

"But I still have to die." Maybe she had it wrong. Maybe there was a loophole.

"Yessss…"

She accepted their confirmation. "But if I kill Aiden first, then Will or Jake will have to kill me. I can't make them do that."

"Trusssst ussss."

What did she have to lose by trusting them? They were the only ones offering help at this point. "Where is my power? How do I find it?"

"It's within you."

Will had stepped in front of her to take on Aiden's advances.

She shook her head in frustration. No, she'd searched for weeks for another source for her power. It wasn't there. And now Will was going to die too.

Will's power flooded her, giving her strength and healing her injuries. She clamped down on their connection. "Stop! You can't save me. You need the power for yourself."

"I have to defend you, Emma. I can't stop it."

"You agreed."

"No, you don't understand. It's our bond. It's doing this on its own."

She had to end this before Will became too weak. Climbing to her feet, she found her anger and let it grow.

The shadows slid up her body, covering her with an icy coldness. "Find your other source," they hissed.

"There is no other source!"

Will and Aiden stared at her in surprise.

"It's in you. It's been there all along. You only have to use it."

She wanted to sob in frustration, but she couldn't afford to expend the energy. What was in her that had been there all along?

Her vision faded and the memory of Will in the South Dakota field when she was learning how to use her power came to her in a flash.

"Maybe you can use something other than anger."

"Like what?"

"Like love."

The image changed. She was with Will in the hotel the day before, and she was telling him how she was different than Aiden.

"Maybe the thing that will save us is what we're fighting for. They fight for control and greed. We fight to save the ones we love. Which is more powerful in the end?"

Love. The answer was love. She'd wasted so much time on anger and hate and love had been the key the entire time.

She focused on her love for Jake and Will and how she'd do anything to protect them from Aiden.

Her power began to bloom.

Aiden watched in surprise, then shot a bolt toward her. She didn't deflect it. She needed to be close to death to do this.

Emma! Will's panic filled her head, but she blocked it out. She thought about the love she felt in his arms, basking in the knowledge that he loved her more than she deserved.

Aiden hit her again and she staggered. Not enough power. Not yet. She thought of Jake and how her heart had swelled with love and belonging the moment he was placed in her arms. She'd vowed to protect him with her life. And she would.

Power pulsed within her, white hot and pure, but somehow she knew it wasn't enough. She pulled energy from the electrical lines and power sources and still it wasn't enough.

Aiden hit her again, glee in his eyes.

Jake. She could use his power and Will's too.

"Jake! Attack Aiden!"

Jake sent a wave of air toward Aiden and Emma pulled the energy from it, adding it to her own. The wave disappeared.

Aiden sent another attack, but Emma pulled his energy too.

Aiden's mouth dropped and terror filled his eyes.

Emma, what are you doing?

Taking their power.

To finish Aiden off, she'd need to give everything within her until there was nothing left at all.

She walked toward Aiden.

Emma! Will took a step closer.

Will, stay back.

She paused in front of Aiden, her arms spread open. "Go ahead, Aiden, I'm right here. Kill me."

Aiden's eyes narrowed and a fiery glow surrounded him. Emma reached to steal the power from him, bringing it within herself and combining it with the writhing, unstoppable power in her chest, finally releasing everything in a fierce burst. Four pillars of fire twisted and burned, swirling in a circle around her and Aiden.

"Mommy!" Jake sobbed in wail.

Emma! Will screamed in her head. A wall of water washed over her, but she held onto the columns of fire until they converged into one, engulfing her and Aiden.

Aiden's screams reached her ears and she knew the fire would burn her flesh as well as his, but the shadows clung to her with their icy coolness.

I love you, Will. I'll always love you.

Darkness surrounded her and when Aiden's screams stopped, and she was sure he was gone, she gave one last shove of every bit of energy within her and faded into the nothingness.

CHAPTER THIRTY

"MOMMY!"

Jake's screaming brought Will out of his shock.

"*Momm-mmmy!*"

Emma lay on the ground in a charred circle, smoke rising around her.

Stars sparkled in the sky above them, the dome now gone.

She'd done it.

Jake ran to her, screaming her name over and over, falling to his knees next to where she lay.

Will shook his head. His breath came in short bursts as he tried to get control and recover his senses.

She'd done it.

The full weight of her sacrifice slammed into him, and he stumbled in his grief.

The streetlights had been blown out, but the moonlight provided enough illumination to see Jake laying over her. He grabbed her black sooty shirt and tried to pull her off the ground. "Mommy! Get up! *Mommy!*"

Will snapped out of his shock. Emma had just died in a raging inferno and Jake was now looking at her dead body. He'd seen enough burnt bodies in Iraq to know that Jake didn't need to remember his mother that way.

"Jake!" Will rushed to him, reaching over to pull Jake away from her, terrified of what he'd find. But while her clothes were blacked from smoke, Emma was unburned.

With a quick glance, Will confirmed that Aiden was a different story.

Jake looked back at Will, his face splotchy and wet with tears. "She won't get up! Why won't she get up?"

She looked peaceful, lying on her back with her eyes closed. *Please God. Please. I'm begging you.* Daring to hope, Will pressed his fingertips against her neck, finding no pulse.

His rage exploded. "No, goddamm it. You do *not* get to die on me!" He pushed Jake away from her, gathered her up in his arms and carried her to the grass. Tilting her head back, he opened her airway and blew, then started chest compressions.

Jake sobbed behind him. "Mommy!"

"One, two, three, four, five." Will pressed then blew into her mouth again, beginning the next round.

Most of the people caught in the dome had fled screaming once it disappeared, but a few remained and formed a small circle around them. Sirens grew closer and flashing lights approached. A searing pain filled Will's chest, and he gasped in surprise and panic. His bond to Emma had changed. What did that mean?

A hand touched Will's shoulder and he jerked.

"Will, you have to get out of here." James knelt behind him, his voice heavy with emotion.

"Where the fuck have you been?" Will choked out, trying to hold back his tears as he continued administering chest compressions. He couldn't afford to fall apart.

"I got here just as that giant dome closed in around you." James stood and pulled on Will's arm. "Will, you can't stay here. The place is going to be swarming with cops."

Will shook his head. "I'm not leaving her."

"I'm not asking you to. Bring her with you. But you have to get Jake out of here. When the police figure out that his mom is dead, they're gonna put him in foster care. Are you really going to do that to him after all of this?"

"She's not dead!"

Jake frantically tugged on Emma's arm. "Mommy! Get up! Mommy, *please!*"

Will struggled to think, his thoughts drowning in anguish. *Emma!* he screamed into her head.

"Will! Now!" James's voice rose with urgency.

Will paused his resuscitation and stared down at her, startled by the paleness of her face. CPR wasn't working. What was he going to do?

James's voice softened. "Will, I'm not asking you to leave her. I'm asking you to bring her with us so we can all get out of here. But we have to go *now.*"

Will nodded. That seemed to make sense. "Yeah. Okay." He scooped Emma into his arms and got to his feet while James picked up a sobbing Jake.

Several police cars pulled up to the curb a hundred feet way, the officers getting out of their cruisers. James glanced around and pushed through the crowd. "This way."

James sprinted down the path, Will on his heels as he held Emma close to his chest. Stopping at a van parked on the street, James opened the back doors, still holding Jake. "It's the airport cargo van, so you can lay her down in the back."

Will climbed in and gently settled Emma onto the floor of the van, worried that her body felt so cool. James shut the door and put Jake in the front seat. Jake leaned over the back, his body shaking with his cries as he watched Will resume CPR. James drove in silence, while Will concentrated on Emma's lifeless body.

He was vaguely aware that the van had stopped and the back doors had opened. James put a hand on Will's arm. "Will, she's gone."

"No." Will shook his head. His tears blurred Emma's face, and his arms ached, but he couldn't stop. He couldn't accept what it meant.

"Will. You've been doing this for twenty minutes. She's gone."

"*No.*"

"Mommy." Jake crawled between the seats and kneeled next to her, pulling her hand to his chest. "Mommy. Please."

Will sat back on his heels, tilting his head as he released a cry of anguish. "No!" He hadn't tried hard enough. He leaned forward to resume again, but James yanked him out of the van.

"Will, I'm sorry."

Pain exploded everywhere. No. He couldn't lose her, not after everything they had gone through. Didn't she know he couldn't live without her? He tried to tear himself away from James, but James's fingers dug into Will's arms.

"No, Will. She's gone."

Collapsing against the van, Will sobbed. "I failed her."

"No. You got Jake. You saved him. That's all she ever wanted. That's all she ever asked for. You didn't fail her."

"But I lost her." Will's knees buckled as he sobbed and James held him up.

"I know. I'm sorry."

Inside the van, Jake lay over Emma's chest. Gut-wrenching cries shook his small body.

Will sucked in a deep breath. He had to get himself together for Jake. Will had just lost his soul mate, but Jake lost his mother, the center of his universe. "Jake. Come here." Will grabbed Jake's shoulders, pulling him away from Emma's body and out of the van. He sat on the asphalt with Jake on his lap.

"She left me. She promised she'd never leave me." Jake lay limp against Will's chest, hyperventilating from his sobs.

Fresh grief stabbed Will's heart. She'd left him too. "She didn't want to. She loved you more than anything." Will clung to the assurance that she'd loved them both.

"I want my mommy," Jake's hoarse voice wailed.

Will released a fresh sob. He wanted her too, and he considered trying to join her, but he'd made a promise to Emma, a promise he intended to keep. God help the person who tried to hurt this child again. He cradled Jake's head to his chest. "I'm here, Jake. I'll take care of you."

Will took in their surroundings, realizing they were on an airport tarmac.

James looked down into his questioning eyes. "I wasn't going to make it in time driving, so I rented a plane. It's waiting to take off whenever you're ready. Where do you want to go?"

Will's heart splintered, and he struggled to keep himself together for Jake. He needed a plan—but where the hell did he go from here? The only person he'd ever truly loved was laying in the van behind him. "I don't know."

James knelt beside him. "Is there anyone still after you?"

His jaw trembled as he tried to catch his breath. "I don't know... maybe Warren. We killed Alex, but no one knows for sure it was us."

"What about Aiden or Raphael?"

"They're dead. So is Marcus."

"Who's Marcus?"

"Water. My biological father." It all seemed so fucking ridiculous now.

James paused a moment, then stood. "My friend has a lake cabin in Missouri we can use. I say we lay low there for a few days and wait for any fallout."

Glancing down at Jake, Will let James's words sink into his addled brain. Hiding seemed like a good idea. They needed to figure out if anyone was still after Jake. "Yeah. Okay."

"What do you want to do with..." James swung his gaze toward the van.

A fierce protectiveness flooded Will's senses, agony following in its wake. The thought of leaving her lifeless body for anyone to find lacerated his soul. Who would find her here? What would they do with her? Maybe it was their bond or maybe his love for her, but he couldn't walk away. He'd protected her in life. He'd protect her in death too. "I can't leave her here."

James didn't seem surprised. "Okay, we'll take her with us."

Will nodded, a lump burning his throat.

"We need to get going in case anyone followed us here." Bending down, James gently lifted Jake from Will's lap. "Come here, buddy. We're going to go on a plane ride."

Jake tensed then kicked as he reached over James's shoulder. "No! Will!"

"He's coming with us. He's getting your mommy."

James carried Jake to the plane while Will lifted Emma into his arms, the coldness of her body cementing what he already knew but still couldn't accept. She was really dead.

Where the hell did he go from here?

CHAPTER THIRTY-ONE

EMMA sat in a short, dark tunnel, disoriented and propped against a stone wall. Where was she? She knew she should be afraid, but instead she was suffused with an overwhelming sadness. Why?

Memories flooded her head. She was dead.

Echoes of sobs reverberated through the space, and she swore she heard someone call out her name. Cocking her head, she closed her eyes to concentrate on the sound. After several seconds, she gave up, disappointed. She was imagining things.

Unsure what to do, she turned a corner and found a gate blocking her path. A padlock bolted it shut on the other side. When she shook the gate, the metal groaned in protest, but the lock held tight.

Where the hell was she?

Emma spun in a circle, realizing she was trapped. The only place she could go was back into the short tunnel behind her. So this was it? This was her eternity? She slumped to the ground too heartbroken to care. The damp sank into her body, chilling her bones.

"I didn't think you'd give up so easily."

Emma's head jerked up and she noticed that beyond the gate was a circular, stone room. More gated openings lined the walls, all empty except for one. A hooded figure stood in the gate directly opposite Emma's.

"Who are you?"

The figure laughed. "The question is, who are *you?*"

Shaking her head, Emma leaned her forehead against the bars. "I'm not doing this. I've played enough games to last a fucking lifetime." The irony of her words hit her and she snorted.

"Who are you, Emma Thompson?" a woman's voice asked.

Grabbing the metal bars, Emma pulled herself up, irritation burning her chest. "If you know my name, then why the hell are you asking me who I am?"

"Emmanuella Thompson is your name, but you've fought that name your entire life. Who *are* you? Without the name?"

Who was she? The last six years had redefined her. "A mother."

"Yes, what else?"

If Jake defined her, so did Will. How could she describe what she was to him—and he was to her? Her other half. "A soul mate."

"And what is the commonality in those two roles?"

Emma shook her head. She'd learned this too late. What good did it do her now? "Love. Undying love."

"Do you want to stay here, Emma Thompson, mother and soul mate? Possessor of undying love?"

"Do I really have a choice?"

"Yes."

The word echoed and bounced off the stone walls before settling on Emma's ears. She shook the bars. "Then I want to leave! I want to go back." She stopped. The figure had asked if she wanted to stay *here*. She'd been through enough of Aiden's mind games to realize that somewhere *not here* could be much, much worse. "Where can I go?"

"Back to Will and Jake."

Emma's breath caught in her throat and she eased it out carefully. "What's the catch?"

A chuckle floated across the space. "You've learned your lessons well."

"I've learned that everything has a price. What's this one?"

"You have to help me."

Emma studied the figure, trying not to get her hopes up. "How do I do that?"

"You have to let me free."

With a derisive laugh, Emma glanced around at her cell. "How am I going to do that when I can't even get out myself?"

"But you can. You have the power."

It had to be a trick. "So I get out, and then I let you out and I go back to Jake and Will. Will I still be dead? Will I just be a ghost?"

"No, you'll be very much alive. You and the baby."

Emma instinctively reached for her stomach. "You're going to tell me how to go back?"

"Yes."

Emma remained wary. She'd learned that you didn't strike a deal with these creatures and then go about your merry way. There was always a catch.

But what if she could go back to Jake and Will? And save the baby? How could she refuse? She cast a glance at the figure. Who hid under the cloak? Emma couldn't decide until she knew. "Who are you? Do I know you?"

"You know me better than you think. I'm the one person who has an inkling of what you've been through."

Emma's voice escaped in whisper. "Who are you?"

But she knew, even as a slender hand reached up from the robes and lowered the hood. She knew before the woman's chin lifted so Emma could look into her own face—a younger, softer version.

"Emmanuella."

A gentle smile lifted the corners of her mouth, but sadness haunted her eyes. "Will you let me help you?"

"If I agree to help you?"

"We're not so different, you and I. We want to be with the ones we love."

Emma sucked in her breath. "Raphael."

Emmanuella's eyes glistened with unshed tears. "Yes."

Raphael didn't seem worthy of anyone's love, but who was she to judge? James didn't think she was worthy of Will's. "Okay, I agree. What happens now?"

"It depends."

"On what?"

"Will and Jake."

"What about Will and Jake?" Had she failed them after all? Did she have to wait for them to join her, and then they could all share the same cell? No, Emmanuella had told her she could return to them.

"They have the power to help bring you back, but only during a short window of time. You've spent too much time here already."

"But how does it work? What do I do?"

"The three of you must work together. You and Will using your bond, and Jake with his mark from the shadows. He can use their power to open the gate."

Emma's mouth dropped open. "How will they know what to do?"

"They only have to ask."

How would they know to ask?

"Will might be able to hear you, but your bond has already begun to change."

"I thought we were bound forever. Even in death. How do you know it's changed?"

Emmanuella raised her hand and pointed to Emma. "Your glow. Your aura contained equal amounts of both your color and Will's when you first showed up, but Will's blue is fading and your red is growing stronger. You'll always be bound together, but the bond is weakening. It's necessary for Will to survive without you."

She'd never noticed an aura before, but she'd never looked for one. Glancing down, she noticed a reddish glow emanating from her body, interwoven with streaks of blue. "What do I do?"

"Talk to him. Tell him to get Jake to open the gate."

Fear crashed through Emma in roaring waves. It couldn't be that easy. There had to be a catch. What if she unleashed a terrible calamity on the earth? The old man in Kansas City had declared her the destruction of the world. What if this decision meant destruction?

"Emma!"

Two choices. It seemed so easy. "What if it doesn't work? What if my connection to Will is too weak?"

"You'll never know if you don't try."

Selfish or not, she had to try. She would regret it for eternity if she didn't. *Will!* Emma listened to the silence, then tried again. *Will! I'm here! Can you hear me?*

"You're running out of time! Will's light is continuing to fade. It's happening faster than I expected."

"No." She had to reach him. *Will, I'm here. I can come back, but I need you to help me!*

Nothing.

There had to be something that would reach him. Something stronger than the both of them.

Their bond was the key. What better way to try to reach him than to say the joining words? She closed her eyes and recited the oath that bound them together.

***

Will was almost to the plane when he heard Emma's voice in his head.

To the last ray of light from the stars at the end
I join my heart with yours

The joining words. His grief was making him hallucinate.

But the words reminded him that they were bonded. In life and in death. They were joined for eternity.

He stopped, reciting the words in his head.

Onto an endless path that winds through infinity
And sears our souls and power into an unbreakable bond.

Their joining was the key.

Through life and death and all that lies in between
I vow to be yours, forever.

"I think I can bring her back! I hear her in my head."

James stuck his head out of the small plane. "Will, don't do this to yourself. You've already tried, man. She's gone."

"No. No, I tried CPR. I need to use our bond. It joins us in life *and* death. Maybe I can reach her. Maybe I can bring her back."

Jake scrambled over the plane seat past James, jumping out of reach as James grabbed for him.

James climbed down and lowered his voice. "Will, don't do this to Jake. Don't get his hopes up, or yours."

"No, I heard her in my head."

"You only *think* you did."

"I want to try to save Mommy." Jake's eyes narrowed and he looked remarkably like Emma when she'd made up her mind to do something.

James shook his head. "What do you want to do?"

"I don't know." It all sounded great in theory, but how would Will actually make it happen? "Do you have her pendant?"

"Yeah." James dug it out of his pocket.

"Help me put it on her." Will lifted her head and James fastened the clasp. Will laid her down again, the pendant at the base of her throat.

"Now what?"

Will grabbed her hand, frustrated. "I don't know. Maybe if I say the joining words out loud." He tried to ignore the fact that he and Emma recited them using telepathy when they joined.

"Okay."

"With echoes from the beginning of time
To the last ray of light from the stars at the end."

Emma's pendant glowed.

"It's working," Jake whispered.

"Not yet." Will shook his head. "It's not enough." He ignited his power, his body glowing a bright white. Water bubbled from the earth, and several geysers shot into the sky.

James fell back on his ass. "Holy shit."

***

"It's working," Emmanuella said, her words whispered like a prayer.

Emma kept her eyes closed, afraid to open them and lose contact. "It's not enough."

"You need Jake to open the lock. But Will's connection to you is getting weaker. You're running out of time."

***

Although her pendant was glowing, he didn't feel her at all. He only heard faint snatches of her voice, and he wondered if that was his imagination. Panic threatened to overwhelm him, and he struggled to reason out what to do next. "It's still not enough." He looked up into Jake's hopeful eyes. "Jake. Can you help?"

"Shadows! Come to me!" Jake shouted. The shadows crept toward him, dancing as they approached. "I need your power." His mark glowed under his shirt, the outline of his intertwined circles a bright white. Jake took Emma's other hand.

"Through life and death, and all that lies between
I vow to be yours, forever."

White light burst from her pendant, shooting into the sky.

Emma, please. Come back to me. I need you. Will sent one last surge of power into her.

***

"It's working!" Emmanuella shouted.

Emma's body was on fire. She opened her eyes and saw a vivid reddish light shining around her. Then a bright white light shot from the base of her throat toward the padlock on the gate.

Reaching up, her hand brushed the pendant. How did she get the pendant?

She shook the gate, but she was still trapped, even though the white beam shone on the padlock. "It's not open!"

"You have to get Jake to open the lock!"

Emma closed her eyes, focusing all her love and power on Will. *We're so close, Will. But we're almost out of time. Tell Jake to open the lock.*

Emma?

Tears burned her eyes. He heard her. *Jake has to open the lock. Tell Jake to open the gate!*

She felt his confusion, and she was certain he didn't understand.

"Will's light is fading, Emma! They have to hurry!"

Will!

There was nothing. She couldn't hear him.

The white light faded.

"No!" Emmanuella cried out. "You're too late."

***

The light faded, and Will's eyes grew wide. "Jake, we need more."

Jake's heart felt like it was going to explode. He could hardly see through his tears as he shook his head. There was no more, but he knew where to get it. Climbing to his knees, Jake shouted into the air. "Shadows! You promised to help me save my mom! *You promised!*"

A spot of light on the asphalt grew brighter until it became blinding. A black shadow spot moved toward them.

Will sucked in his breath. "Jake…"

Jake glared at the shadow figure, angry at its betrayal. "He can help."

The dark spot stopped in front of Jake and the figure rose from the ground.

Will gasped and reached to pull Jake back, but Jake shrugged him off. "No. He can help." Turning his attention to the creature, Jake's eyes narrowed. "You tricked me."

"The gift was freely accepted. You knew the conditions."

"You said you'd help me save my mom, but you didn't. You're a liar. You're just like Aiden."

Will stiffened, his fingers digging into Jake's arm, but the shadow figure remained silent.

"I need you to bring back my mom."

The shape nodded slowly. "It comes with a price."

"What is it?" Jake wasn't going to be tricked again.

"The original elements are now gone, and you must take their place. You are Air. Will is Water. If you save your mother, she will be Fire. The baby, she will be Earth. Someone will need to stand in for her until she is born." The figure lifted a single finger toward Jake. "The price is simple, but steep. The time of immortal elements is over. If you bring your mother back, you will give up all claims to immortality. You will live like humans. Your only power will be your element, a power you must pass on to someone else before you die." Jake glanced over his shoulder at Will.

Will leaned closer, worry on his face. "He's telling you that you won't live forever. None of us will. Aiden could live forever until your mother killed him, but you will get old and die like you normally would have before…before all this. That is the price you pay to save your mother."

"Then I'll do it."

Will's mouth twisted, and he looked torn, but he also looked desperate. "I want you to do this, but I'm not sure if I should let you. It's a big decision. It means you'll die someday."

"But Mommy will still be dead if I don't."

Will swallowed, and his voice was scratchy. "Yes."

Jake's anger ignited. "He asked *me*. Not you. You don't get to decide." Jake turned back to the shadow. "I agree to the price. What do I have to do?"

The figure nodded and Jake thought he saw the hint of a smile, even though if he looked closely he couldn't see a mouth. "Put your hand on your mother's pendant and think about opening the lock."

"What lock?"

"The lock keeping your mother from you."

Jake nodded. "Okay."

"Will must help too."

Will put his hand over Jake's.

"Let's begin."

***

She slumped against the cold bars. "I failed them again."

Emmanuella released an anguished cry from her cell.

She'd failed her too.

As she began to slide down the wall, a beam of light burst from her pendant, burning the skin at the base of her throat. "It's working," she whispered.

The blinding beam illuminated the room, and Emma's gate swung open with a creaky groan. She stumbled into the circular stone floor, shielding her eyes, but unsure what to do. Gates blocked all the openings to the tunnels. Where was she supposed to go now?

"Emma!" Emmanuella stood at the gate, clinging to the bars. "You have to free me."

She'd agreed to get Emmanuella out, but she didn't know how to make that happen.

"Emma, please!"

The bright light exploded from her neck again. The lock on Emmanuella's gate fell to the floor with a metallic clang. Smoke billowed into the room and an unsettled feeling washed over Emma. Something wasn't right.

Pushing the gate open, Emmanuella rushed out, her face lighting up with delight. "You did it!" She spun around in a circle, her robes swinging around her legs. Stopping abruptly, she pulled Emma into a tight embrace. "Thank you!"

Emma was about to tell her she hadn't done anything, when Emmanuella gripped her shoulders and pulled her away, staring into Emma's face. A smile lifted the corners of her mouth, but her eyes held an ominous glint. "Just remember, everything isn't always what it seems to be."

And then everything faded to black.

***

The bright light faded but Emma still lay limp and unresponsive on the asphalt. They'd been so close. Had it not been enough to save her? The shadow creature faded away.

Will grabbed her hand and squeezed. "Please, Emma. Come back to me."

Her body twitched then jerked. Emma gasped, drawing a deep breath.

"Mommy!"

"Holy shit," James mumbled, scooting away a couple of feet.

Emma's eyes opened, and she gave Will a weak smile. "You did it. It worked."

Will pulled her up into his arms, burying his face into her shoulder. "Don't you ever scare the shit out of me like that again."

"I'll try not to die again anytime soon." She wrapped an arm around Jake and pulled him into their hug.

"Good to see you back, Emma."

She turned, her eyes widening in surprise. "James. You made it." Her hand reached around Jake, touching her pendant. "Thanks for bringing this."

"Just call me *errand boy*." He grinned. "We were about to give up on you."

Will raised an eyebrow. "We?"

James gave a half shrug. "We really need to get out of here."

"In a minute." Will refused to let go of her yet.

Emma's arm around him tightened. "How did you save me?"

"James had the pendant, and Jake and I used our powers, but it was the shadows that did it. Jake convinced them to help." He brushed a strand of hair from her cheek. "What was it like...where you were?"

"Cold and scary. I was in something like a jail cell. A light came from my pendant and opened the lock."

"Thank God."

"There was someone else there."

Will was afraid to ask. "Who?"

She looked up into his face. "Emmanuella. She was the one who told me to reach out to you. She told me that you two could save me." With a grin, she kissed the top of Jake's head. The grin faded when she looked at Will again. "She offered to help me if I helped free her. She said she wanted to be with the one she loved."

"Raphael?"

Emma nodded. "After my lock broke, hers did too." She paused. "Emmanuella was happy and gave me a hug, but then she got the strangest look on her face. She said, 'Everything isn't what it seems to be.' And then I was back here."

"What do you suppose she meant?"

"I have no idea."

James scratched at his back, letting out a grunt. He craned to look over his shoulder. "Holy shit."

Will's chest tightened in anxiety. "What?"

"There's a mark on me! It looks like a tree."

Will laughed in disbelief. "Looks like you're the temporary guardian of earth. Until the baby's born." He turned to Emma. "I know what we're having. Do you want to know if it's a boy or a girl or do you want it to be a surprise? Although I should warn you that both of these two know, so I'm not sure how long they'll last before telling you."

James swiped at his shoulder blade. "Temporary guardian? I do not accept!"

Emma smiled. "Tell me."

"I hope you like pink."

She wrapped her arm around his neck and pulled his mouth to hers. "I feel sorry for any boys she brings home."

Will laughed.

James continued brushing at his shoulder. "No, Will. This isn't funny. You asked me to get a damn necklace. I did not agree to become the element earth!"

Will stood and pulled Emma up with him. "None of us asked for this, James. It was forced on us. Welcome to the club."

"I don't want to be a member!"

Emma helped Jake into the plane. "Too late, James."

"Don't I get a say in anything?"

Will shook his head. "Get in the plane and fly, James."

James swore under his breath as he climbed into the cockpit.

Jake sat in the seat next to Emma, his head on her lap. Her fingers played with his curly hair. She looked up at Will, love shining in her eyes.

"What happens now, Will? What do we do now?"

"Now we start the rest of our lives."

She pulled his mouth to hers. "I like the sound of that."

ABOUT THE MANDORLA

WHEN it became apparent that there would be four books in The Chosen series instead of three, I quickly realized I needed a new mark.

I went through multiple ideas, researching a lot of ancient runes. My original thought was to have two interconnected triangles. I'd studied Plato's philosophy on the elements when I came up with the qualities of the elements. Plato assigned symbols to the elements: Fire is an upside down triangle. Water is an upright one. Since Will and Emma were joined, it made sense to use the connection of the triangles as the symbol.

But I dug deeper and came across the mandorla, which means "almond" in Italian. While it's most associated with Christianity, it has deeper, more ancient roots.

The two circles represent opposites and the almond is the interconnection of the two, also called the *remain*. The almond typically represents the intersection of heaven and earth, life and death, but can also represent spiritual and self, masculine and feminine, the known and the unknown.

Shadow and light.

Jake joined the two worlds to save Emma. The question remains—was this a good thing or a bad thing?

ACKNOWLEDGEMENTS

WHEN I started this book, I was terrified I would screw it up. This was the last book of an awesome series and I didn't want to disappoint my readers. Thankfully, I had people behind me who believed in me more than I did. Many thanks to my critique partner, Trisha Leigh, who never questioned that I could write *Redemption* and do it justice. Also thanks to my developmental editor, Alison Dasho, who read the first draft and didn't fire me as a client. She spotted the problem areas and gave me awesome ideas to make *Redemption* even better. Alison provided support and hilarious YouTube videos to encourage me as I spent three crazy weeks in August rewriting one fourth of the book as well as adding fifteen thousand more words.

Redemption wouldn't have the current ending without the feedback of my beta readers. They liked the first ending but thought it lacked something. Thank you to Brandy Underwood, Anne Childon, Rhonda Cowsert, Wendy Webb and Janelle Alexander for being honest with your feedback.

Many thanks to Branli Caidryn who is still my friend after I pestered him mercilessly, asking "how do you say this in Spanish?"

I also need to thank my children who sometimes have to put up with a cranky, stressed-out mommy but love me anyway. I tell them that it was pure coincidence that I wrote

Redemption and tortured poor Jake without mercy while they were home for the summer driving me crazy. That's what I tell them…

Thank you to my copy editor, Jim Thomsen. This is our seventh book together and he always takes my words and makes me look so much better.

To my proof readers Christine Wilmsen and Kristen Yard—thank you for making me look good.

And finally, thank you to my readers, who liked this series enough to stay with me to the end. What a ride.

ABOUT THE AUTHOR

DENISE GROVER SWANK lives in Lee's Summit, Missouri. She writes urban fantasies without vampires and werewolves. She also writes romantic comedy mysteries set in the South. She has six children, three dogs, and an overactive imagination. She can be found dancing in her kitchen with her children, reading, or writing her next book. You will rarely find her cleaning.

You can find out more about Denise and her other books at www.denisegroverswank.com or email her at denisegroverswank@gmail.com

Friend her on Facebook: www.facebook.com/deniseswank
Follow her on Twitter: www.Twitter.com/DeniseMSwank

20987440R00257

Made in the USA
Middletown, DE
15 June 2015